WINNER

Advance Praise for *Just a Couple of Days*

"I'd go so far as to say that this novel read by anyone who still values th selves. Real writing speaks for its

—Kris Saknussem

"Like a technologically savvy modern-day Rabelais, Vigorito gives humanity a swift, playful, and long overdue slap on the ass."

—Chris Genoa, author of *Foop!*

"Tony Vigorito's brilliant novel is a *Dr. Strangelove* for the biotech century, a witty and wise end-of-the-world romp that manages to be optimistic—even joyous—yet cynically dystopian at the same time. *Just a Couple of Days* is savvy, wickedly funny, and profoundly disturbing. An absorbing, thought-provoking read."

—Richard Heinberg, author of *The Party's Over* and *Powerdown*

A Harvest Book
Harcourt, Inc.
Orlando
Austin
New York
San Diego
Toronto
London

just a couple of days

TONY VIGORITO

www.HarcourtBooks.com

Excerpt from *Nine Kinds of Naked* copyright © 2007 by Tony Vigorito

First U.S. edition published by Bast Books, 2001.

Library of Congress Cataloging-in-Publication Data
Vigorito, Tony.
Just a couple of days/Tony Vigorito.—1st Harvest ed.
p. cm.
1. Biological weapons—Fiction. I. Title.
PS3622.I48J87 2007
813'.6—dc22 2006027199
ISBN 978-0-15-603122-6

Text set in Minion
Designed by Lauren Rille

Printed in the United States of America
First Harvest edition 2007
K J I H G F E D C B A

For Jessica.
Three words never seemed enough.

Life is paradise, and we are all in paradise, but we refuse to see it. If we would, we should have heaven on earth the very next day.

—Fyodor Dostoevsky

prologue:
Logos Libido

Why aren't apples called reds? What a dumb question, I used to think, before a five-year-old named Dandelion taught me otherwise.

Why aren't apples called reds? One could just as easily ask, Why aren't bananas called yellows, or why are oranges called oranges? These are essentially the same question, no matter the outfit in which we dress her.

Why aren't apples called reds? All questions are female. All answers are male. If you're wondering why this might be the case, you are thinking with your feminine sensibilities. If you're considering why this *is* the case, you are thinking with your masculine senses. Questions are creative, intimidating, and periodically irritating. We may think them docile, we may try to ignore or suppress them, but their destabilizing power persists, pushing us toward our proper destiny. Answers are protective, giving us some ground, however shaky, on which to stand. Answers are cool, logical, but they can also become stubborn know-it-alls, resisting the emergence of new questions and answers and deteriorating into conservative old farts. Truth is a precarious balance between poignancy and peace. Truth lies within the perpetual prance of yin and yang.

Why aren't apples called reds? Look at her. She blushes exactly like an apple in the harvest sunshine every time she's pronounced. She is an honest question, unassuming and not at all arrogant. She is demure, to be sure, but her diffidence is her only defense to the endless parade of listless shrugs and wise-assed banalities that have been answering her every utterance since shortly after the dawn of time.

Why aren't apples called reds? She's an old question, one of the oldest, in fact, and a bachelorette until Dandelion introduced her to her long-lost answer. The oldest question, that is to say, the first question borne on the vibrations of a monkey's larynx, is of course *Why are we here?* After all, if we are to believe those rumors about Adam and Eve, this question surely occurred to them while they were still munching their apples of knowledge. It could not have been very long, perhaps while they were abashedly affixing fig leaf pasties over their genitalia, before one of them wondered why that stupid fruit was called an apple (or a pomegranate or whatever) in the first place.

Why aren't apples called reds? She does not mind these repetitious pronouncements of her essence. She used to fumble and fret, but now she pays her continued vocalizations only courteous heed. She found her answer, though most of us never received the wedding announcement. It was a wild party, some say the wildest the linguistic universe had ever seen. But the Logos, the realm of all questions and answers and the ultimate source of all knowledge, knows this to be an exaggeration. There is another question, the oldest question, whose impending union promises to be the highest time of all.

Why are we here? Come on people now, let's introduce them already. We know her answer. We're just afraid to admit it.

part one:

Gliding with the Glow

1 No event, no matter how preposterous, will fail to find itself indispensable to some future happenstance. Hence, as I sit here sipping instant coffee in my makeshift prison cell, I am led to wonder when the daily accidents of my existence began whispering among themselves and conspiring to place me, and perhaps humanity, in such a dire and peculiar predicament.

This is nuts, really. This is some previously undiscovered variety of craziness. This is a singularity, something else entirely, and I just don't get it. Everyone in town is laughing and dancing like there's no tomorrow (and that cliché may well be a literality), and I'm left counting my fingers like some bewildered bumpkin. Consequently, it would be premature of me to assert what exactly *this* is, and so, borrowing an irritating habit from a very good friend of mine, I must leave *this* temporarily undefined.

Here's the thing. I could theoretically retrace the path of occurrences leading to *this* from the beginning of time (and perhaps I well should), but I cannot risk courting such infinite regress. It's a long story, as they say, but not that long, and so instead I shall retreat to a much safer point of departure from which to commence my telling: the weather. Yes, let's talk about the weather. Let us linger for a nostalgic moment in the safety of the humdrum, the shelter of the mundane, where the commonplace is common and not some misty reminiscence.

The weather was awful. It was hot—sticky, stinky hot, hot like a smoggy sauna with an overdue litterbox stewing in the corner, and it stayed that way all summer. The season had been pranked by the El Niño weather devil in the Pacific Ocean. Dr. Blip Korterly, my best friend, says El Niño is Spanish for "global warming." He's joking. El Niño means "the child" (or more precisely, "the boy"), and indeed, the candy-brat climate was pegged on sugar and unable to simmer down. It was in this hyperactive atmosphere that Blip went mad. I hasten to add that he was not what you might term psychotic. Rather, he lost himself somewhere on the harmless side of lunacy, slightly south of innocuous but definitely north of demented.

It is at least possible that the disagreeable climate had something to do with the blossoming of Blip's eccentricity. He certainly wasn't the only person in our big Ohio town acting suddenly screwy. Last summer it seemed as if everyone was rocking their chairs frightfully close to the tip of their arcs. But lest I scapegoat the prevailing meteorological milieu, the sweaty weather cannot be held solely responsible for toppling Blip off his rocker. He had, after all, recently lost his job, and before then he was already tempting the point of no return. Never much of a cheerleader for cognitive conformity in the first place, he charged instead through the brambles and brush on the margins of consensus reality in search of berries most people wouldn't touch even if they could reach them. This past summer, however, Blip ate the wrong berry and lost sight of the beaten path altogether, and however hazy the line between innovation and insanity may be, he was unmistakably sipping iced tea with the hatters and the hares.

Perhaps it was appropriate, then, when he became the accidental and anonymous ringleader of what his wife once referred to as "mass meshugas." As far as I can tell, or as far as I'm willing to see, events began their inexorable dance toward *this* with a mania-inspired misdemeanor committed by Blip, unemployed and unesteemed professor of sociology and nouveau graffiti artist. He found a canvas for his artistic expression on an overpass near campus, a bridge under which most of the city's commuters had to pass every afternoon. After covering all the FUCKS and I LOVE YOU TRACYs on the bridge's side with black paint early one morning, he replaced them with a simple, unexplained expression, written in dripless white: UH-OH. Then he called at 4:00 A.M. to tell me about it, justifying his vandalism as "freedom of landscape" and refusing to explain what it was supposed to mean. He made me promise not to tell anyone, not even his wife, but it matters not who knows any of these trespassings and transgressions now.

For a few weeks, countless drivers on their way home from work could not help but read Blip's tag along with the dozens of billboards for a dazzling variety of consumer crap. As it happened, it piqued their collective curiosity and gave the urban workforce pause to think. Drive-time disc jockeys quickly assumed the role of moderator as commuters called in from their cellular phones to argue about the significance of the graffiti.

Untold speculation abounded as the dreary, air-conditioned masses projected their own anxieties onto the bridge, and it very quickly became the favorite topic of idle chatter as coworkers gabbed about the vandalism during their cigarette and coffee breaks like it was last night's popular sitcom. Blip's graffiti gave people something in common, however bizarre, and an esprit de corps never before known settled over the city like an intoxicating cloud of good cheer.

Then it happened, inevitably and yet wholly unexpectedly. Some bold soul responded, and an entire city was surprised and a little embarrassed that they had not thought of doing the same. It was simple. One day the bridge was broadcasting UH-OH, and the next day the graffiti had been replaced with an equally confounding message painted in a distinctly different style: WHEN? Blip nearly choked on his delight at this turn of events, and called me every hour to talk about it so he wouldn't burst and tell someone else.

"I'll let it be for a while," he resolved. "But I'm gonna have to respond."

"What will you say?"

"How should I know? I don't even know what we're talking about."

This was not the case with everyone else, who now debated their personal takes on the graffiti exchange at every opportunity. Local religious zealots claimed it was an omen from on high or thereabouts, while employers pointed out that the number of sick days taken by their employees had plummeted since the enigmatic declarations had appeared. One local columnist offered his own wry observations, claiming to be surrounded by morons and casting himself above such desperate ridiculosity.

He was relieved of his column following a torrent of angry letters from readers. Wise guy.

And so it developed. Public enthusiasm for what came to be called "Graffiti Bridge" was overwhelming. Mayor Punchinello originally decried the graffiti as a blatant show of disrespect for the law and a scar upon the landscape, and vowed to put whomever was responsible behind bars. He toned down his rhetoric immediately, however, after a public outcry ensued when someone leaked to the press that he had ordered the bridge sandblasted. The mayor's spokespersons immediately denied the rumor, what with an election in November, and the graffiti stayed.

Then came Blip's response, despite increased patrols around the bridge. Surprising everyone, he broke with the initial one-word pattern and wrote an entire phrase, taking the time to paint: JUST A COUPLE OF DAYS. He resisted phoning me until the next evening to see what I thought.

"It works," I said, not wanting to encourage him.

"My ass it works. That phrase has never worked a day in its life. It dances, man, it dances across the side of that bridge."

Working or dancing, the city was in a mild uproar for the next two days, eager to see what would happen. Strangers shared amiable smirks of solidarity with one another on the street, bars and coffeehouses made record business, and the traffic jams under the bridge took on a festive atmosphere no authority could or would suppress. Vendors set up tents and tables on the median, and picnics and Frisbees soon followed.

Local ad guys were surely incensed. Some sloppy graffiti on a highway overpass was gaining the coveted attention they never received for their flashy billboards. To add insult to injury, a monkey-wrenching truck driver demolished a billboard near the bridge with a few pounds of dynamite. He was arrested and questioned about the bridge as well, but his travel log, stamped at truck stops around the country, provided a reasonable alibi. In the end, he received a nine-month jail sentence, but SALE EXTRAVAGANZA! had still been reduced to ZA!

But two days passed, then three, then four, and nothing at all happened. Nevertheless, it was generally agreed that the meaning of COUPLE was not to be taken literally, for if it was, the mysterious scribe would have written TWO DAYS instead. COUPLE was taken to mean a few, or several, or however long it took for something to happen or for another reply to appear. Granted, the traffic snarls around the bridge were no longer so lighthearted (or frequent, for that matter), but the local population enjoyed the saga too much to let semantics get in the way. Blip was thus granted poetic license. He had been worried when the initial excitement dissipated, fearing he had foolishly ruined all of the fun.

"All right," Blip breathed a sigh of relief one day in late September, after it was apparent that Graffiti Bridge had not waned in popularity. "It's his turn. But God help him. This dialogue has outgrown us already, and there's no telling where we're headed now."

2 "What if this happened?" Blip halted our heretofore silent stroll across Tynee University, which despite its name was the largest campus in the country. I stopped reluctantly, sensing a stark-raving delusion on the swell. My intuition was confirmed when I turned around and found Blip standing motionless, staring into his Styrofoam cup of cranberry echinacea tea and muttering under his breath. "They're putting," he began aloud, "they're putting poison in the teas. Small amounts of a mild toxin, so that anyone who drinks herbal tea for health will only get sicker, see?" He slapped my arm with the back of his hand.

"What?" I looked past him at a small crowd of people gathering nearby in an attempt to hide my irritation at his increasingly fantastic paranoid fantasies.

"Poison!" he emphasized. "Don't you see? Any healing properties are canceled out then!"

"Blip . . . ," I began.

"Who's gonna drink tea that makes you feel sick, eh?" He heaved the tea out of his cup. The broken mass of liquid flew several feet to his side and splotched onto a squirrel, flattening its tail and making it look more like a rat as it raced madly up the nearest tree.

"Christ, Blip! No one's poisoning your tea!"

"You heard it here first," he persisted. "They're poisoning the teas." He shook his head in sorrow, and so did I. Blip was a professor of sociology, but his department was being combined with the Anthropology, Political Science, Psychology, History, English, and Philosophy departments. It was part of Tynee University's downsizing and restructuring plan, combining all these departments into a single Humanities Department, which itself would be smaller than any one of the previous departments. Consequently, a good many Ph.D.s were going to lose their jobs. Blip was one of them, and he was not taking it well. He began spouting bizarre conspiracy theories the morning after the decision was finalized late last spring, calling to tell me that Tynee Industries was disposing of its low-level radioactive waste by selling it off in minute quantities as staples through its office supplies branch. I, Dr. Flake Fountain, was unaffected by the restructuring. I was a molecular biologist then. Now I'm a threat to national security as well.

"Here's something interesting." Blip snapped out of his herbal tea despondency and stooped to pluck a mushroom growing in a patch near the walkway. "Do you realize that this mushroom is bigger than the entire Green?"

"You haven't been eating those mushrooms, have you?"

"These are Haymaker's mushrooms. They're only mildly psychotropic, but very poisonous," he responded matter-of-factly, beginning to tap his foot, as was his way whenever he became excited. "But see, this isn't a separate organism. What's in my hand is only a single part of a much larger whole. Look around, man. You'll notice these little brown bells all over the Green, whenever it's drizzled a lot." He walked me along the sidewalk, pointing out the peppering of small mushrooms that were scattered everywhere. "See, the mushrooms are just the fruiting bodies of a much larger organism that exists underground. Mushroom roots are called mycelium, and the mycelium is actually a huge network of fibers that are entwined and interconnected beneath our feet. It's just like an aspen grove. It looks like a bunch of different trees, but they grow rhizomatically, and are actually only a single tree. Did you know that?"

"Since when are you a botanist?"

"Mycologist," he corrected. "And you should know the difference, a biologist like yourself. Mushrooms aren't plants. They don't have any chlorophyll."

"I'm a *molecular* biologist," I began to explain, then waved him off. Blip already understood the distinction. He was only hassling me for what he claimed was my excessive knowledge of the minutiae of life and my relative ignorance of the bigger picture. I amended my question. "Since when are you a *mycologist*?"

"I overheard a student talking about a class she was taking. She said there's probably a single mycelial network beneath the entire Green. One organism. Pretty cool, huh?" Before I could nod, he continued, quickening the tap of his foot. "And you know what else? There are more connections in this mycelial network than there are in a human's neural network. That means it's *aware*."

"She said she learned that in her class?"

"Well not the last part. I added that on. But it makes sense, don't you think?" He hopped in front of me. "You think for one minute this humongous fungus under our feet isn't observing us right now? Think about it. There must be more than a hundred billion connections underground here. This thing is humming with awareness. You can even feel it if you pay attention." He closed his eyes and made a show of feeling the ostensible hum of the mushroom. After a moment he popped them wide open in theatrical excitement. "Man," he gushed. "People don't even realize they're being scanned by an extraterrestrial as they amble across the Green." He nodded his head and looked around the ground. "Yeah, it's got us all figured out."

This last embellishment marked a new direction for Blip's eccentricities. Heretofore, his delusions had been confined to the surface of the planet. "What's this now?" I asked.

"This giant mushroom is an extraterrestrial probe, man. It's called a von Neumann probe, a self-replicating machine. That's what the space cadets at NASA and SETI theorize would be the logical first step in space exploration. The way it works is you send a few off into space in different directions, and whenever one of them detects a planet with favorable conditions, it lands and collects materials to build a duplicate of itself. The duplicate then takes off to another planet, and the original stays behind to search for life and collect and transmit data. For efficiency, the probes would have to be small, no bigger than a hockey puck, according to the astrophysicists. With a gizmo like that, they say the entire galaxy could be explored for signs of life in no time, relatively speaking of course.

"But here's their mistake: They're right on with the theory, but they're wrong about the size. What they missed was right in front of their faces. The best example of a self-replicating machine is life. An advanced civilization, as a *molecular* biologist like yourself would no doubt agree, would have mastered the appropriate use of biotechnology by the time they engaged in interstellar exploration. So why would they build it out of metal or plastic? And guess what else? Mushroom spores are so small and light they can drift right off the planet. And their shells are so hard they can survive outer space until they meander across another planet. The beautiful part of it is that they'll only self-replicate—reproduce, that is—if there's life on the planet. That's what fungi do. They're really more like animals in that they live off the energy and nutrients of other life-forms. So, the spores won't germinate until and unless there's life on the planet. If there is life on the planet, it germinates and fruits." He held up his mushroom. "And don't you think the mushroom cap looks suspiciously like some sort of antenna or transmitting device?"

I shook my head more in amusement than necessary disagreement, although his reasoning was certainly absurd. "It's an interesting theory."

"It's very interesting," Blip nodded gravely, scrutinizing the mushroom in his hand. "But it's not a theory."

I marveled at the internal validity of his figments, and that all of it was inspired by a few stray remarks of some college student. "So do you always eavesdrop on other people's conversations?"

"Of course!" He tossed the mushroom aside. "There's nothing better than walking around catching little snippets of the conversations of others. You wouldn't believe how many different things are being talked about out there, and all at the same time. Hell, I hope someone else heard what I was saying and spreads the word." He paused, waiting for an approaching student to draw near. "Little snippets of conversation," Blip spoke to me as the student passed. Blip broke into a smile so broad the corners of his mouth were patting him on the back. "Little snippets of conversation," he said to me again as an uptight-looking woman walked by. She put on her headphones.

"Come on," I said, growing irritated with my best friend–cum-lunatic. "Let's see what's going on over there." I pointed to the crowd, which had grown to be quite large and raucous.

Blip eyed the crowd warily. "Yes, let's do that." He led the way immediately, as determined as Don Quixote embarking on yet another fool quest. True to form, he stumbled as he strode off the sidewalk onto the grass, then yet again over an exposed root of the tree the squirrel had darted up earlier. The squirrel, sitting on a branch above him fluffing its tail, seemed to laugh at Blip's lack of grace before leaping and skipping along ever smaller boughs and twigs until it was in the limbs of another tree. There it stopped and turned around, just in time to see me, captivated by this rodent's gymnastic ability, stumble over the very same root.

3 "Hearken unto the Lo-ord, all ye fornicating heathens! Jeyzus is coming!" A preacher, wearing a T-shirt with READ THE BIBLE printed on the front and DRUID HILLS BAPTIST CHURCH on the back, stood in the middle of the crowd, hollering about hell and gesticulating like an inept stage magician all the while. "Jeyzus hates this copulating campus, all you whoremongers and masturbators!" His ranting canting delivery was constantly interrupted by heckles from the mass of students gathered, but he was nonetheless thoroughly enjoying himself. This was very clear. I had seen him on the Green before, and he seemed to thrive off the ricochets of his damnations and denunciations like any sadist grinning at the blood spattering off his whip.

"Jesus said, Judge not lest you be judged yourself,"[1] a female student bleated, attempting to argue with the preacher.

"He was not referring to those of us without *sin*!" the preacher boomed back. "*I*, Brother Zebediah, am without sin, ladies and gentlemen. *I* have entered the Kingdom of Heaven, and *I* am here to tell everyone in this infected flock that you are heading straight for the lake of . . ." He rotated his arm as if playing an air guitar. "*Fi-yurrrrr!*"

"All right, Brother Zygote! You tell 'em!" A large male student jeered and cheered. The congregation followed his lead.

"You're like a bunch of copulating rabbits! Just spill your seed anywhere you feel like it, governed by your penises!" The crowd burst into laughter. "Worshipping your penises! Letting your *penises* rule your lives!"

"You just like to say *penis*!" the heckler yelled back, much to the amusement of all assembled. "Say hey, where's the little woman today?"

"At home, of course," Brother Zebediah snorted.

"She pregnant?" someone else called out.

"Not yet, but the factory's still open. Sister Sally and I are going to repopulate the Earth with people who think like us."

"*Seig Heil!*" Heckler clicked his heels together and saluted him with an outstretched fist.

"Sir, you're being rude!" Brother Zebediah thundered at him. "I'm trying to preach a message!"

"Sir, you're going to hell! How's that for rude?" Heckler responded. Other members of the herd contributed less belligerent protests. "Tell us again about the time you did acid!" Heckler's voice boomed above the rest.

"It's true," Brother Zebediah admitted. "I lost half my brain to LSD in the sinful sixties. But that just makes things fair, children, otherwise I'd be so far above you kids that we couldn't communicate! So listen carefully and *be not deceived*!" Brother Zebediah picked up a bright orange laminated poster board and began to recite what was on it. "Masturbators, Feminists, Adulterers, Whores, Homosexuals, Lesbians, Hippies, Buddhaheads, Evolutionists, Blasphemers, Drunkards, Pro-choicers, Pagans, Potheads, Mormons, ~~Jews~~, Muslims, Hare Krishnas, and especially *Fornicators* are going to *hell*!"[2] He hurled the poster of the damned aside and roared in self-congratulatory fury, "Jeyzus is coming! Jeyzus is *coming*!"

"Jesus is coming?" Heckler retorted. "Is that some kind of dirty joke?"

"Let's take a little survey." Brother Zebediah ignored the laughter and began anew. "How many *masturbators* do we have here?"

Heckler raised his hand, followed by others. "Wait, does it count if I masturbate by myself?"

"Masturbators! Be not deceived! You're going straight to *hell*!"

"Do you masturbate?" Heckler called back.

"No, I do not masturbate, you pervert!" Brother Zebediah pointed at him, flinging righteous lightning from his fingertip. "You sinner! You covet my godliness! You're jealous 'cause you're running around jackin' off! You could lay one of these cheap campus whores every night and still go home and smack your monkey!" Uproarious laughter prevented Heckler from responding immediately, and Brother Zebediah quickly continued. "And how many *pot* smokers do we have here?"

Heckler and his buddies cheered enthusiastically.

"Well I got bad news, children. You fail. Go directly to hell! Do not pass Go, do not collect two hundred dollars. Smoke that pot, you're gonna rot! Drink that booze, you're gonna lose! *Fornicate*, and you're not gonna see that pearly gate!"

"But God made marijuana!" one of Heckler's comrades yelled.

"God made poison ivy, too, that doesn't mean you should roll around in it!"

"Well, what if you eat it?"

Brother Zebediah furrowed his brow a moment, considering the question, then replied, quite seriously, "Well, you're still ingesting it, so yes, you qualify for hell."

Heckler's comrade, not terribly swift, crossed his arms and shook his head, shifting awkwardly from foot to foot. Brother Zebediah took advantage of his upper hand and immediately resumed his evangelical survey.

"And how many *feminazis* do we have here?"

"What if I like women to dress up like Hitler and crap on me?" Heckler came back strong, and I laughed out loud with everyone else. I glanced at Blip, perhaps to share a smile, but he seemed oblivious of everything but a cup of tea resting near Brother Zebediah's feet.

Before the laughter dissipated, a female student, wearing combat boots, lots of leather, and a buzz cut, pushed out from the crowd and sauntered into the middle of the circle. "You think you're some prophet and we're the jeering heathens, don't you? But you're not; you're just the village idiot, do you understand that? You don't know anything about spirituality, brother. You're not preaching love. What you're preaching is *hate.*"

"'Woe unto them that call evil good, and good evil; that put darkness for light, and light for darkness!'"[3] Brother Zebediah quoted his Bible to the woman and the crowd. "Love is the fulfillment of the *laws*! See what sin, what feminism, will do to you girls?" He pointed at the woman. "It'll turn you into a whorish butch bull dyke feminazi witch! God'll pick her up and skip 'er across the lake of fire like a flat smooth stone!"

The woman paused a moment, then, to everyone's astonishment, slugged Brother Zebediah square in the jaw, knocking him flat. Scarcely had the collective "Oooooooo . . ." escaped the lips of everyone when three large men, apparently plainclothes security guards, tackled the woman. Instantaneously, three of her similarly clad friends jumped into the struggle. The crowd, including Blip and myself, stood dumbfounded. A fourth security guard entered the clearing, eyed the coed wrestling brawl (which was still anybody's match), and yelled into his radio, "We need backup on the Green!" Then he grabbed ahold of Brother Zebediah, who was dazed and getting up slowly from the ground. "Are you okay, sir?"

Brother Zebediah nodded, looking slightly stunned, and reached for his cup of tea on the ground.

"Come with me then," the guard said. "I'm afraid I'm going to have to place you under arrest."

Brother Zebediah nodded, wiped his brow, and took a sip of tea. It was at that moment that Blip cracked, as suddenly and dramatically as an ice cube fracturing in a hot beverage.

"No!" he screamed, racing toward Brother Zebediah. "It's poisoned!" He slapped the cup out of the preacher's hand and into the face of the security guard, who then grabbed Blip seconds before the crowd rushed inward like a collapsing star, and pandemonium was born.

I was jostled backward, and eventually stumbled out of the melee. I ran to a bench and stood on it to try and find Blip. I needn't have bothered. A great wind suddenly descended, radiating everyone's hair out from the center and startling the throngs back into individuality. A stealth helicopter, an inexplicable presence, hovered directly overhead.

"DISPERSE IMMEDIATELY," came a disembodied, steely command from the bullhorns mounted underneath. "DISPERSE IMMEDIATELY OR YOU WILL BE GASSED."

Everyone more or less dispersed, as much as was possible under the circumstances, and pandemonium became panic. I located Blip, still in the center, struggling against the wind and the grip of a security guard who had him in a bear hug. Shortly thereafter, the helicopter began moving in larger circles around the area, and the wind died down. The other security guards had lost the women they were originally combating, and instead arrested Brother Zebediah and Blip with a vengeance. Blip spotted me and hollered, "Flake! Call my wife!" just before being dragged off with the preacher to a nearby patrol van.

Brother Zebediah, also struggling against the guards, screamed rabidly at the fleeing students. "I am your spiritual alarm clock! Don't hit that snooze button! I'm your wake-up call! I hope you all run home and are tortured by nightmares of *hell*!"

4

The average ocular distance, that is, the space between a set of human eyes, pupil to pupil, is 6.5 centimeters. Tibor Tynee, the president and CEO of Tynee University (so renamed at his financial insistence), has an ocular distance no greater than 4 centimeters. A lifetime of narrowing his eyes and tightening his lips has left his face decidedly pinched. The expansive facial features of Blip's wife, Dr. Sophia Carthorse, are precisely the opposite. This was apparent even over the telephone as I called her and relayed the news about Blip. She did not seem surprised, and asked only that I meet her at the police station in an hour. I agreed, allowing that I'd be a little late due to a 1:30 meeting that had been scheduled for me with President Tynee.

Tibor Tynee is a short man. He has short hair, a short body, and a short temper. Small but powerful, he is a dinky Lilliputian who nevertheless manages to manipulate everyone around him into following his orders. Disrespected by all who are yet humble in his presence (Tiny Tynee, the students, and sometimes the faculty, call him), he is nonetheless comfortable wielding his power. He enforces his will on others and enjoys doing so, rattling sabers like a teenage boy jingling his car keys for all to hear. New rumors emerge and circulate monthly concerning every aspect of his character, from doubtful assertions that he wears a hairpiece to plausible claims that his carnal habits tend toward masochism. In particular, it has been alleged that he has a self-flagellation fetish, and is known to slap himself during intercourse.

At the risk of further coloring your assessment of him, Tynee is just thrilled with who he thinks he is. What he does not realize, however, is that he is actually a whoopee-cushion windbag, and that everything he says sounds like so much blustering flatulence. Possessed by a gluttonous pride, the voracious cravings of his ego demand the admiration of others for their vile nourishment. Approval is not nearly enough. He has to convince others that he is special, unique, and, most of all, superior. His breathless gasconades not only have to be accepted, but applauded. With such a covetous appetite, it was inevitable that he would become rather fatheaded, and he is, yet his hunger has never slowed. It is as if he nurses a tapeworm at the core of his soul that leaves him in perpetual need of more attention. It is a conceit borne of a Brobdingnagian insecurity, constantly seeping through the ersatz netting of his vanity and launching horrific hernias of introspection that threaten to burst the entire supercilious membrane sustaining his delusional self-concept. He dares not let this happen, for the decrepit web of his narcissism holds back nothing but a depraved and vainglorious mass of wormrot.

The effort required to expel such a soul-sucking leech is less than the effort required to maintain its decaying rind. However, this necessitates facing the nauseating prospect of pulling the parasite out of his own being and thus witnessing what truly motivates him. And Tynee's motivation is disgusting, make no mistake. I do not like him, that should be clear enough, but it is difficult for me to believe that anyone would care for the company of such a gusty, muckety-muck schmuck. There is nothing appealing or attractive about compulsive public masturbation, jerking off in a haughty display of self-gratification. I once made the mistake of paying him an admittedly obsequious compliment and was utterly disgusted when I saw that my congratulation had been perverted into so many sickening strokes of his already engorged ego. His cocksure arrogance increased a degree, bathing his consciousness with self-lust and pushing him one step closer to a climax where all memory of kindness and consideration will vanish, ultimately collapsing him into a solipsistic orgasm of megalomania.

5 Tibor Tynee moves very fast, a high metabolism fueling his slight frame. He wastes no time whatsoever. In fact, he steals time from those around him. He's known for starting his meetings fifteen minutes ahead of time, so that someone arriving five minutes early is actually ten minutes late. Owing to the fracas on the Green, I was twenty minutes late in Tynee time. His secretary was just about to call his 2:00 meeting when I arrived at his office. It was 1:35.

“Flake Fountain!” He announced my presence in his office as if I’d just entered a debutante ball. He stood up in his hot tub, exposing an unwelcome portion of his gaunt and pasty frame to me as he toweled off.

“Sorry . . .” was all I could manage before a bellow ridiculously out of proportion with his flimsy build cut me off.

“Save it!” he roared, stepping out of the tub and disappearing behind a partial wall.

Tynee’s office was also an enormous studio apartment. He lived and worked in a single room converted from an entire floor of classrooms. I wandered aimlessly around as he dressed, mildly impressed by the arsenal of military antiquities that decorated two of his walls. They were displayed with an air of imperial majesty, framed by a trellis overgrown with the same wall-crawling ivy that covered the outside of the building. Masses of simple, deep green leaves dangled around and between the various swords, axes, daggers, and maces, perhaps, I thought, intended to emphasize the age of the weapons.

“Better wash your hands.” Tynee spoke from behind me.

“Sorry?”

“Leaves of three, let them be, Doctor. That’s poison ivy.” I looked at him incredulously. “Don’t worry,” he continued. “If you wash off the oil within an hour you won’t have any reaction.”

I did so immediately, even though I couldn’t remember whether I had touched any of the leaves. Angrily, I asked him why he had poison ivy growing in his office.

“To keep people from touching the steel.” He spoke as if it were perfectly self-evident. “This,” he carelessly reached past some leaves and picked up a small amber bottle near the base of a crossbow. “This is pure urushiol, the toxin in poison ivy. I had a severe case of it when I was five, all over my body, in my eyes, ears, nose, mouth, everywhere. It itched like a son of a bitch, for over a month, no matter how much calamine lotion my mother slathered on me. She cut my fingernails short to prevent me from scratching my skin off, and the only way I could get any relief was to smack or scald the skin where it itched. It itched down to my bones and out the other side, completely took over my body." He stood a little more erect, apparently proud of his ordeal. "But I survived, and I've never had it since."

"So you grow it all around you?"

He nodded and continued without explanation. "It covers the outside of this building, too. I had it planted when I first accepted this position years back. Had to pay the landscapers time and a half, too. Haven't you seen the signs posted?"

"But why?"

"There was a student demonstration and some monkey hippie climbed up the exterior wall and started pounding on the windows. I had *them* replaced with high-density, double-thick glass."

"You're not afraid of getting poison ivy again?"

"I'm immune," he said, plucking a leaf triumphantly. "I have been ever since the first time. No doctor has been able to explain it to me. I don't even react to mosquito bites." He paused a moment, and chewed the stem of the leaf pensively. "When I was a child, though, and my little sister would get mosquito bites, I used to scratch them when she wasn't thinking about them just to make them itch again." He tossed the bottle into the air and caught it. "But poison ivy is an entirely different type of itch. Did you know it's one of the most potent toxins on Earth?" He shook the jar ponderously, speculating on his unholy botanical alliance, and his voice took on a tone resembling that of a necrophiliac singing the praises of rigor mortis. "What's in this bottle, one ounce, is enough to give every human on this planet a rash they'd *never* forget. Can you imagine that?" He chuckled and appeared to be lost in reverie, no doubt carried away by his fantasy of a global orgy of orgasmic itching, and perhaps slapping. After a few moments his faraway grin fell slack, and he abruptly changed his demeanor. "Anyway," he hissed, "I have an assignment for you." He led me to the far side of his poison palace in silence, to the Ping-Pong table. He tossed a paddle at me, apparently expecting me to play.

"Genetics," he began, serving the ball with a vicious spin on it. I succeeded only in swinging my paddle clumsily through the air after the ball sailed past me and across the room. "I have a client who is interested in genetics," he continued as I chased after the tiny plastic orb.

"What about genetics?" I grunted as I reached under the pool table to get the ball.

"I'm getting to that," he growled. "My client is interested in viruses and their utility for altering biological processes, specifically brain chemistry."

I tossed the ball to him. He gave me the same serve again. This time the ball bounced across the refinished hardwood floors and landed in the Jacuzzi.

"Before I got into administration," he continued, "I studied neuropsychology. It's a fair statement to say that the mind, thinking, perception, everything that goes on in your brain can be reduced to electrochemical reactions. Electrochemical reactions, Doctor, are occurring in my head right now as I explain this to you, and in your head as you understand what I'm saying. We call these electrochemical reactions thinking, or dreaming, or whatever else. The point is that such electrochemical activity produces the consciousness you experience. Psychotropic drugs like antidepressants, for example, alter the electrochemical environment and consequently change your perception of the world. Now, there are also viruses and bacteria that alter the electrochemical activity in your brain. Syphilis, if left untreated, can leave you insane. A simple fever can make you hallucinate. Our client is engineering a virus, a truly remarkable virus, to work as a sort of gene therapy."

I retrieved the bobbing ball from the swirling whirlpool, wetting my sleeve in the process, and tossed it back to him after drying it off. He caught it and served immediately, before I even got to my side of the table. The ball bounced away toward the door. I paused, not wanting to chase it, and hoping he would just continue with his exposition. Tynee looked at me with incredulous hostility. "Get the goddamn ball already! The score is three–zero. Play to five."

I retrieved the ball once again, feeling more like a dog playing fetch than an opponent. This time it lay nestled on a velvet cushion on his antique sofa as if it were a Fabergé egg. Tynee continued with his explanation of my assignment, which, in spite of everything, was beginning to intrigue me. "Our client has been attempting to create viruses that elicit predictable psychological effects."

"Who's the client? And what are the effects of this virus?" I waited until I reached my side of the table to toss the ball to him this time.

He caught the ball and paused, frowning. "Everything you need to know is contained in the memo you will receive. Rest assured that this research is proceeding according to established protocols. As a matter of fact, one of your colleagues in the former Philosophy Department is currently developing a paper exploring the ethics involved in such research. Feel free to contact her. I can't recall her name, but she's the philosopher we retained for the new Humanities Department."

"Dr. Carthorse?" He was talking about Blip's wife, Sophia.

"That's the one. I always get her and the historian confused. She's a woman, too." Without warning he served the ball, this time giving it a backspin. It curved crazily after it bounced and I managed to catch it to avoid having to give chase once again.

"What the hell was that, Fountain?" He barked at me like a high school gym teacher.

"Sorry." I tossed it back to him and ignored his abrasive manners.

"You know," he snapped the ball out of the air after it bounced. "I've always had a knack for this game." He fondled the ball as he vaunted on about his Ping-Pong heroics. "It's like an inborn ability with me. My body is somehow congenitally outstanding at table tennis." He paused his thrasonical throes, waiting for my response, but my intellect was preoccupied. When it became apparent that no kudos were forthcoming, he tossed the ball back to me. "Score's four–zip, Fountain. Game point. That means it's your serve."

My serve was clumsy, but it made it over the net. Sneering, Tynee spun it back to me with a broad stroke of his arm. My mind, however, was not on the game, but rather was rapt with curiosity, turning over the possibilities of the assignment. Consequently, I reacted to his volley with no conscious effort, returning the ball in a neat bounce off the corner of the table on his side. I was momentarily stunned, as was Tynee, only I was surprised at my own sudden unpracticed skill, and he was vexed that I had denied him a sweep and easy victory.

"Well." He abruptly checked his watch. "I've another meeting. The details of your assignment are in the purple envelope by the door. Beware of academic espionage. I expect a reply by Friday." He placed his paddle on the table. "We'll just say I won."

6

The institution of the university was transformed long ago from a center of learning into a center of earning. The pursuits of wisdom, truth, knowledge, and freedom are as antiquated as the masonry monuments that bear such academic platitudes, having given way, respectively, to the corrosive pursuits of profit, efficiency, technical expertise, and employment. Ivy-covered buildings shelter the bespectacled neurons of technocratic consciousness, department after department attracting grant money to generate research to create new industries and professions to make more money. Status competition keeps us racing to publish, and if we fail in that regard, punishment is swift and severe: teaching. Dr. Blip Korterly taught full-time, though his employment was considered part-time. I, on the other hand, have not taught a class in over five years. I, Dr. Flake Fountain, molecular geneticist, have been a willing and well-paid servant, a slave butler who gets to wear fancy clothes and sleep in the mansion, but a slave nonetheless, and subject to beatings if I don't cower with a bow.

My department attracts millions of dollars to the university, and only the football program generates more revenue. Many of my colleagues believe, with the peculiar pride of a master's pet slave, that we will overtake the TU Turkeys within a few years. They are probably correct. Only four years ago, we seceded from the Biology Department and formed the Department of Molecular Genetics. There had been considerable hostility between the ecologists, drawn to biology via the essays of Emerson, Thoreau, and Muir, and the molecular geneticists, drawn to biology via the promise of research stipends the size of sequoias. Our new department, though in its infancy, is already well larded by a smeary smattering of government agencies, private foundations, and corporate sponsors. Piggish and raised on the blubber of bureaucracy, we show no signs of shedding our baby fat.

My specialization is recombinant genetics. I have found my tasks challenging, and have gotten a thrill from attracting grant money to the department. Just last year, I received the largest grant yet. The windfall came from a venture capitalist who was financing the formation of a start-up biotechnology corporation. He wanted me to break the thirteen-mile-per-hour barrier in tomato harvesting. The problem was that when corporate agriculturists harvested their still-green tomatoes, they could not shoot them into the truck any faster than thirteen miles per hour without the skins splitting. This constraint incurred significant product loss, not to mention costs in time and ultimate profitability. If we could develop genetically modified tomatoes with more resilient skins and his company could own the patent, he could dominate the market for tomato seeds sold to large-scale agribusiness. We succeeded wildly, pushing tomato skins to withstand sixteen-mile-per-hour collisions, and new strains showed promise of even greater durability.

Blip scoffed at this project, and accused me of contributing to inappropriate technology. If genetic engineering is only explored for the purpose of making money, he argued, we'll end up with bigger, longer-lasting, tougher, and less nutritious fruits and vegetables. He's right, of course. Nutritional content is not a primary profit concern. Size, shelf life, cosmetic appearance, and herbicide tolerance are. I was not unaware of these things, nor was I unaware that the pursuit of knowledge had become more twisted than a double helix. Much to the chagrin of Blip, however, I could not be persuaded to care.

7 Such were the hallowed hallways of academia I slithered through daily. On this particular day, I left my meeting with Tynee and drove around half the circumference of the university to the city jail. It was located directly behind the Physical Facilities Department, in a new building. The site had been chosen because little NIMBY resistance was expected from campus-area residents. Indeed, if students knew about it at all, they did not care, since they would be gone in four or five years anyway. The university asked only that the building match the local architecture, and so it looked like any other dormitory but for the exceptionally narrow windows.

Upon entering, however, all architectural pretensions ceased and were replaced by an unsoothing din of dingy irritability. Owing to the unexpected brevity of my meeting with Tynee, Sophia was nowhere to be seen, so I approached the desk sergeant barricaded behind the fenced-in reception counter. A roundish police officer, wearing a nametag that read WILT, glowered out at me.

"Excuse me," I cleared my throat. "I'm looking for a Dr. Blip Korterly. He was arrested earlier today."

After staring at me for a few seconds, Sergeant Wilt took a deep breath and shoved himself on his wheeled office chair across the room to a computer. "Can you spell his last name?" he hollered at me over his shoulder as if he were saying, "Can you stop putting that blade of grass in my ear?"

"K-O-R-T-E-R-L-Y," I called back to him loudly.

After a few moments, he coasted back to the reception desk and said, without looking at me, "I can't release any information on that arrest."

"Is there a reason?" I asked, once it became apparent that he wasn't going to volunteer one. He stopped tapping the stack of papers on his desk and held them in midair for a few seconds before responding.

"I can't release any information because there isn't any information to release." He tossed the stack onto his desk, sending the papers back into disarray.

"I'm sorry, I don't know how this kind of thing works, but it seems to me that I should at least be able to talk to him."

"Are you his lawyer?"

"I'm his friend."

"Well, *friend,* I can't release any information on that arrest."

"Could you if I was his lawyer?"

"No."

"No?"

"Buddy, there isn't any information to be released. That's all I can tell you."

"Look, this is asinine," I said at last. "Can I at least speak to the warden?"

Sergeant Wilt grinned arrogantly at me. "The warden?"

"Yes."

"There's no warden here. This is a jail, not a prison."

"Oh." He had succeeded in making me feel foolish. "Well, who's in charge?"

"We have a captain."

"Can I speak to your captain then?"

"Captain'll tell you the same thing I've told you."

"But you haven't told me anything."

Sergeant Wilt shrugged. "What can I say when there's nothing to say?"

"Can I please just speak with your captain?" I glanced around for Sophia, hoping she would show up and tag me out of this squabble.

Wilt picked up the phone with a tired look on his face. "What's your name?"

"Flake Fountain. *Dr.* Flake Fountain." I made a witless attempt to pull some rank.

"Captain," Sergeant Wilt spoke into the phone. "There's a *Dr.* Flake Fountain here that wants to see you." After a pause he continued, "I don't know, his friend was arrested earlier today or something." He nodded into the phone and hung up, then said to me, "Well, *Doctor,* the captain will see you now."

8

Captain Porton Down is a doll of a man. His natural expression is a suntanned, clean-shaven, gaudy grin, and his blond hair falls leisurely to one side. Relentlessly self-assured, he could sneeze with a mouthful of toothpaste lather and make it look charming. He's a real-life Ken doll, and I reckon his wife drives a pink Corvette.

I explained Blip's situation, that he was a professor, and that Sergeant Wilt had refused to release any information about his arrest status. Captain Down's rosy smile was softened by an expression of frivolous concern.

"Well, Dr. Fountain, I sympathize with your friend's situation, I truly do. But the fact of the matter is that my hands are tied." He showed me his hands, invisible rope holding them fast.

"Is this standard policy, not to release information?"

"Oh no no!" He laughed heartily. "Goodness no."

"What's the problem then?"

"Without going into much detail, Doctor, all I can say is that the mayor has declared a city crisis. We simply cannot risk releasing a potential criminal."

"Potential criminal? Crisis?" I didn't know where to start. "He's a professor, for chrissakes, and since when is there a crisis?"

"As of this morning. Mayor Punchinello declared a crisis in response to all the flap over the new graffiti on the bridge. In a crisis situation, there can be no exceptions." He slammed his palm down on the desk, swatting and missing a fly, and for the instant he attempted the kill, the nearly intransigent smile on his face contorted into a hideous visage of anger and aggression. Then, almost as quick as a housefly's reflexes, his smile snapped back into place.

"I didn't know there was a new message," I said. Although the dialogue had been taking place on the side of the bridge heading out of town, I was nonetheless surprised that Blip apparently had not yet heard about this new graffiti either. He surely would have mentioned it to me if he had. "What does it say?"

Captain Down shrugged. "I don't commute, and I could care less about the scribblings of vandals."

"Right," I hastily agreed, feeling like I was lying. "I don't know anything about this crisis, but there must be something that can be done for Dr. Korterly. What about his wife or his lawyer? Could they intercede on his behalf?"

"There can be *no* exceptions, Dr. Fountain."

"I can't believe this. Declaring a city crisis and suspending civil liberties over some graffiti?" Exasperated, I got up to leave. The purple envelope Tynee had given me caught on the arm of the chair and fell from my jacket's side pocket. I snatched it off the floor angrily. "You can bet you'll be hearing from Dr. Korterly's attorney," I threatened, pointing the purple envelope at him.

Captain Down's smile dropped once again, though not so severely this time. "That's an interesting envelope, Dr. Fountain. Might I ask where you acquired it?"

I looked at the purple envelope and, remembering Tynee's warning, tucked it into my inside breast pocket. "I'm not sure why you're curious, but, without going into much detail, it's from President Tynee."

Captain Down grinned with all of his teeth and pulled open the top left drawer of his desk, out of which he pulled an identical envelope. "Well, well, Dr. Fountain." He waved his own purple envelope enticingly from side to side. "Perhaps we can do something about your friend after all."

The Book o' Billets-doux

rosehips: Who are you, anyway?

sweetlick: Who am I? Who the hell are you? I'll say this: One thing I am certain of is that I don't know who the hell you are. I know who the hell I think you are, but I don't know who the hell you think you are.

rosehips: Are you the hell talking to me?

sweetlick: Listen. You're a diamond, but I can only see one facet on your side. What is more, when I look closely, I only see myself reflected back at me. I see what I project, vice versa, et cetera.

rosehips: Yes, yes. But my question is who the hell are you?

sweetlick: I don't know! How the hell am I supposed to know who the hell I think I am? I only know what the hell I want to know.

rosehips: So what the hell do you want to know?

sweetlick: What the hell do you think I want to know?

rosehips: I think you know I love you, whoever the hell you think you are.

sweetlick: Fair enough. I think you know I love you too, whoever the hell you think you are.

9 Sophia had arrived during my meeting with Captain Down, and I found her entangled in the same brainless argument with Officer Wilt that I had been in earlier. She looked weary, but her smile was nonetheless genuine when she spotted me. This set a swagger to my gait as I guiltlessly imagined that she was my wife. (I've had the silliest crush on her since the first time we met some ten years ago. It is a harmless infatuation, and not at all a covetous lust.) I informed her that Captain Down was straightening things out.

"We're terribly sorry about the trouble we've put you through, Mrs. Korterly." Captain Down shook her hand gently, wearing a face of strained compassion that would rival the best politician touring a disaster area.

"My name is Dr. Carthorse," she politely corrected him.

"Of course," he replied. "Officer Wilt," his tone turned commanding, "prepare the paperwork for Dr. Korterly's release immediately. And have him escorted up here straightaway!" He turned to me, smiling and cool once again, a swashbuckling sugarshit. "I'm certain we'll be in touch, Dr. Fountain." He winked and gave a conspiratorial salute with his purple envelope before returning to his office.

"How did you get him released?" Sophia asked me, relieved. "I've been arguing with this guy for ten minutes." Wilt pretended not to hear us, engrossed once again in his paperwork.

"I'm not really sure." I led Sophia to the wire chairs, which looked to be recycled from old prison fencing. "I think it was this envelope. He had one just like it. This one contains a special assignment Tynee gave me about an hour ago. I didn't know what was going on, but I just played along."

"That's strange." She looked at me quizzically. "What's the assignment?"

"Haven't had time to look it over yet." I put it back in my breast pocket. "Besides, I'm not supposed to talk about it to anyone."

She rolled her eyes. "Well, I sympathize with you. He gave me my first 'special assignment' last month. Good luck."

"Right, Tynee mentioned that. He said you're writing a paper exploring the ethics of genetic research. You never told me about that."

Sophia laughed in my face. "You already know how I feel. We shouldn't be tinkering with the process of life until we understand the purpose, and that's a long way off in this society. Nothing personal, but without a spiritual conception of nature, biotechnology is just one more iteration of foolishness. My mind was made up as soon as you told me about the genetically modified corn whose insecticidal traits were spreading to milkweed and killing monarch butterflies."

"I told you that was a fluke," I interrupted her. "It hasn't been replicated."

"It doesn't matter. I don't trust anything that *might* hurt a butterfly. Simple as that. Philosophy and ethics don't enter into it. And as far as that paper is concerned, it's perfect garbage, my worst work ever, filled with assumptions and fallacies. I only began writing it because it's what he wanted, and I didn't want to lose my job, too."

"What did you write?"

"In defense of sacrificing values for self-interest," she spoke cryptically, shaking her head and scolding herself, "while doing the same. Any rationalization implies that the action doesn't flow from your values. It's like kicking your faith in the teeth and still expecting it to comfort you." She sighed. "It doesn't matter anyway. I burned it and deleted it. I'm not about to cry over spilled ideals."

Thinking that I might change the subject from something that was obviously distressing, I tried to ask how other things were. Sophia shrugged. "We're fine, but Blip thinks creditors are plotting to lay siege to our castle."

"Oh. Are you two okay financially?"

"We're really fine. We barely have any debt, but that doesn't seem to matter to Blip. He can't use a condom without whining about what it costs." She spoke with characteristic frankness and fell silent.

The image took me by surprise, and I cleared my throat, feeling suddenly guilty. "Umm, I think I read in *The Torch* that they distribute free condoms at the student union . . ." My voice trailed off into awkwardness. Sophia did not appear to be listening anyway.

"I am worried," she abruptly confided, despair tightening her voice like a broken wing oppressing a bird's song. "Normally, we keep up with each other. But he's been getting pretty far out lately." She locked eyes with me for an instant, and in that moment revealed to me the depths of her despair. Her lower lip trembled, and my heart nearly broke.

"He'll be fine." I tried to comfort her, but I found that I could not meet her gaze. Our conversation was interrupted by a commotion in the corridor anyway.

Blip entered the room momentarily, handcuffed, with a

guard on each side of him. Upon seeing us he yelled, "Why the hell am I being released? No one's supposed to be released! I need to stay here! I need to stay in prison!"

10 My sincerest apologies, but I must interrupt the forward flow of events at this point. Fear not, I will come back around to the purple envelopes and reveal their tale of secret weapons and corrupt conspiracies in due time. But for now, please forgive me. It is only right that I digress and provide a short history of these people who quite possibly have forever changed the world. It is their daughter, after all, who answered the question *Why aren't apples called reds?* Hence, what follows is a tangent. It will not be the only one, I am certain. My current confinement makes it difficult for me not to dream of happier times.

I have known Blip and Sophia for all of a decade, ever since Blip strode into my office one gray December morning and introduced himself. Grinning like he had just gotten off a roller coaster, he said he had a few questions related to genetics that needed immediate answers, and which, although they were elementary, I could not immediately answer. But I liked him at once. He had a sagacity and a wit to match, a rarity in the straight and narrow hallways of academia. And besides, I had about as many friends as used Scotch tape, and so I clung to anyone who showed me the least bit of attention. Blip and Sophia found me and my work fascinating, and thus very quickly became my closest friends. And though they were the ones always asking questions, I have lately come to recognize that they were also my greatest teachers.

When Blip blew into my office ten years ago, he was interested in the idea that genetic traits recede and disappear if they are maladaptive. If a trait threatens survival, it recedes and is succeeded by more adaptive traits in the long run. For example, a polar bear with black fur is less likely to hunt successfully. The uncamouflaged polar bear thus will not survive to pass on his maladaptive trait. I suggested to Blip that he might be better served by a biological anthropologist, as I studied molecular, and not population, genetics. If he heard me, he made no indication, but only continued more furiously, tapping his foot all the while.

"But is a parallel between society and genetics appropriate? Because if it is, then all this shit," Blip stood, gesturing broadly, "is just a flush in the toilet, a temporary turd in the whirlpool of the double helix. We will evolve, because greed is not adaptive. Am I right?"

At the time, I only nodded stupidly. Like most academicians, I was pusillanimous and proud, and timid of looking for big-picture connections. I had my head stuck either in the ground or up my ass, or more often, kissing someone else's.

The very next day Blip called on me again, this time to discuss the concept of *genetic drift.* Genetic drift describes how random genetic traits, such as eye color, meander through a population almost purely by chance, eventually differentiating that population from others. He likened this to mannerisms and slang, explaining that he was beginning to see more and more people in town tap their feet when they argue. "But the thing is, I never see it when I travel. And," he pointed to his tapping foot, "*I've* been tapping my feet when I'm making a point for years, and I picked it up from Sophia."

"Who's Sophia?" I asked.

Blip ceased his tapping, and, smiling with simple-hearted sexuality, he answered without hesitation. "She's my lover."

11 Sophia embodies everything wonderful about wildflowers and hillsides and waterfalls and sunshine. Slender and curvy is her form, and her hair, harvest brown with a few strands of silver she refuses to pluck, tumbles with abandon around the spurs of her emphatic cheekbones, flows freely down her neck, and sunders at her shoulders to scatter into locks, chasing one another down past the small of her back, past the parabola of her waist, tickling the backs of her knees like goose down in the springtime. Her limbs are lithe and strong, and her breasts are eclipsed only by her emerald eyes in their generosity and freedom.

She knows her body like a bird knows its wings. Space moves swiftly and smoothly around her aerodynamic form, and her clothing is more colorful than a lepidopterist's field guide. It's no wonder Blip sometimes walks like he has shoe boxes on his feet. The poor chap has gotten his wish, and can do nothing but fall all over himself in her presence.

Sophia has her flaws, certainly. For instance, her frequent laughter is brightly colored by a tendency to snort if she laughs too hard. But she does so unabashedly and repeatedly, for how could such a silly thing as embarrassment muzzle her glee? Besides, it only makes others laugh all the harder. Also, she confesses to an unhealthy love of sugar, and never hesitates to reach for a plate of cookies.

If I gush, forgive me once again. As I have already admitted, I developed a powerful crush at once, though I have never communicated it to anyone until now. Such secret longings are now no longer noteworthy. Perhaps they are even impossible. In any case, Blip and Sophia are the proverbially perfect couple, and as such, they are both thrilling and incomprehensible to me. There is no envy on my part, only vicarious delight. If they have any failings as a pair, I simply choose not to notice. I idealize them like any workaholic romanticizing his childhood. Childhood isn't perfect, nor are Sophia and Blip. Nevertheless, they represent an easiness and a playfulness far too absent from my own life. You may think me sappy, but as far as I am concerned, Blip and Sophia are meant to go together like strawberries and bananas, and I consider myself lucky to be permitted to enjoy the delicious treat of their company.

12 Sophia greeted me at the door the first time I was invited to their geodesic dome home for a dinner party. She wore an oversized T-shirt with the words ARGUE NAKED silk-screened across the front of it. After introducing myself, I found I had nothing to say and nowhere to look for fear that I would make transparent my immediate and inappropriate lust for her by attempting to instigate a disagreement. Blip, meanwhile, was busy crashing around the kitchen like a rhinoceros working on a deadline. Despite all his noise, I could hardly bear the silence and was desperate to break it.

"You have long hair." I stated the obvious, establishing myself as a creep for certain. But she smiled, her eyes as bright as her hair was long.

"It won't grow any longer," she stated matter-of-factly, ponderously pluming the hair that fell across her shoulders.

"How do you suppose it works? What limits the length of hair?" She began tapping her foot, and Blip became suddenly quiet in the kitchen. "Is it the length or the life of the follicle? Does my hair have a predetermined length, such that when it reaches that point it ceases to grow? Or is it the rate at which you lose your hair that determines its ultimate length? Because we're losing hair all the time, but we're also growing new hair all the time."

I nodded, then shrugged prosaically, not really sure what sort of a response was expected.

"Homeostasis." Blip strode into the room, drying his hands on a dish towel and nodding a greeting in my direction. "It's the average life span of your hair. The maximum length of your hair reflects the perfect balance between life and death. An equinox of locks."

Sophia nodded taplessly, the point having been made. "Of course."

13

I had arrived before any of the other guests, so I joined Blip and Sophia in the kitchen and watched them dodge and duck around each other as they dashed about preparing the meal. Eventually I could stand it no longer and I asked what "Argue naked" was supposed to mean.

"Exactly what it says," Blip responded. "Argue naked. We've printed up T-shirts and bumper stickers to sell at music festivals next summer."

"Argue naked?"

"We argue naked," Sophia explained.

"Oh."

"It works very well," Blip elaborated. "It's hard to be naked and take yourself too seriously. Think about Adam and Eve. As the story goes, they were naked in the Garden of Eden. There was no bickering in paradise."

"You think everyone should argue naked?"

They nodded, grinning like naughty teenagers.

"Even politicians?"

"Especially politicians," Sophia proclaimed with a slinky lick of her lips. "C-SPAN in the buff. Of course, Congress would never agree to it."

"They certainly wouldn't," Blip added. "And besides, the way men are these days, can you imagine how hostile a naked Congress would be? A room full of naked men is only likely to increase insecurity and aggression, like a locker room. We'd have senators snapping towels at each other, making rude jokes. No, that would never work."

Sophia nodded. "But only because our leaders are interested in victory and defeat, rather than reconciliation and compromise." She shrugged. "Arguing naked is only possible among friends and lovers."

14

As it happened, I was the hit of the dinner party that evening, owing to Blip and Sophia's unbridled fascination with what I was able to explain about genetics. Their questions turned cartwheels around the table, and everyone soon caught the enthusiasm. Such exuberant conversation, I discovered, was not at all uncommon at their gatherings. Indeed, Blip's favorite toast and blessing over the meal was "To excellence in human communication."

I should mention that I wasn't particularly interested in what I was talking about that night. The topic of genetics only arose out of academic small talk about current research projects, and I would have been perfectly content to let it die a dullish death. Sophia and Blip, however, were determined not only to keep it alive, but also to convince it that life was all wind chimes and butterflies. They pumped me with questions as if they were the Heimlich cousins, and before I knew it I was spitting pabulum all over the table and coughing every boring detail across the room.

Sophia asked me if it was true that humans share 99 percent of their DNA with chimpanzees. I replied that it was actually 98.4 percent.

"Fascinating. So what percentage do we share with dogs?"

"I don't know offhand," I said. "But I do more than just compare genotypes. For instance, I'm currently working on mapping the genetic sequence that causes velvet worms to grow appendages."

"Velvet worms?"

"They're little worms that walk around the forest floor. Worms with legs."

"Worms with legs. Wow," Blip remarked sincerely. "So what are you finding?"

"Well, I don't want to bore everyone. It's just boring, technical . . ."

"Not at all." Sophia dismissed my attempt to pass the fat and continued to gaze at me with uninhibited curiosity. "Come on, tell us more about these velvet worms."

She was joined in her request by everyone else present, and I acquiesced. "There's a gene which organizes the cells of the velvet worm into legs. If that gene were to be switched off, so to speak, the velvet worm wouldn't grow legs."

"Switched off?" Sophia immediately asked. "Why on Earth would you want to switch it off?"

"Well, it's interesting because a nearly identical gene is found in vertebrates, including humans. It's even more interesting because our legs are completely different from invertebrate legs, but the growth of both seems to be stimulated by the same gene. In fact, every animal that's been examined has an almost identical genetic sequence stimulating limbed growth." I paused. "It indicates that we have a common ancestor."

Blip nodded. "I've suspected as much."

"It's the same story with eyes. The genetic sequences that produce eyes are all but the same across flies, humans, squid, velvet worms, you name it. In fact, it's pretty much a given in my field that all life shares a common ancestor."

Sophia sighed like a sunset and asked, "So what percentage of our DNA do we share with velvet worms?"

"Again, I don't know offhand, and I don't really know if anyone's actually sat down to figure that out."

"Just estimate. Please. I beseech you."

I had never been beseeched before, so I obliged her as best I could. "All I can say is that we're genetically more similar than we are different. We're made out of the same patterns. That's what the biotech industry is built upon. You can successfully transfer genes between bacteria and mammals, and the genes remain functional."

"All is one," Blip suggested, an exaggerated mystical resonance coloring his voice.

"All is driven by genes."

"But what exactly are genes?" another guest asked. She was a suburban dropout turned kabbalist theologian. She called herself Rabbi Rainbow. I think Blip and Sophia were trying to set us up, but neither of us took to the other.

"Some say the genetic level is the authentic level of reality, what's actually occurring, and we're just half-conscious vehicles for its expression and reproduction. Our life is driven by selfish genes."

"But what drives the genes?" Sophia asked, like a child demanding a further why from every explanation.

"Nothing." I shrugged. "They drive themselves. In an infinite amount of time, a molecule with the characteristic to copy itself only had to happen once, and reproduction as a characteristic of matter began, ultimately leading to life as we know it."

"Hooey!" Sophia dismissed my explanation with an ireful scoff. It took me by surprise; up until that point she had been mercilessly chirpy, as prone to irritation as a bird is to singing off-key. "You give yourself too much credit. Just because you can reduce the causal sequence down to the actual material occurrences, it doesn't necessarily follow that that's *all* that's occurring. That's just how things are manifest in this particular plane of reality. You can trace a person's depression down to an imbalance of electrochemicals in her brain, but that doesn't mean you've found the cause. That's only the process. An antidepressant only treats the symptoms of depression. More often than not, people get depressed for reasons larger than the chemicals in their heads. That's like saying a headache is caused by a constriction of blood vessels in your brain. Headaches are caused by too much work or stress or fatigue or caffeine, not an aspirin deficiency. You've only explained the process of life, not the cause."

I shrugged again and recited the motto of science. "You have to base knowledge on what you can reliably observe."

Sophia shrugged back, smiling. "Maybe you're not observing the right things."

I had no immediate reply, and after a silent pause Blip redirected the discussion. "Tell me more about the similarities of genes."

Grateful for his tact, I obliged. "Basically, we know that humans, chickens, fish, all look nearly the same at the embryonic stage of development. Insects are like cousins, primates are our siblings. Chimpanzees even have a rudimentary culture. The major difference between humans and apes is the extent of our linguistic capacity."

"So what does that make humans to each other?" Either Blip or Sophia asked this; it's impossible to say for certain which.

Regardless, the other had the answer, and spoke it with flagon of wine raised. "We're the same person! *L'Chayim!* To life!"

And we drank.

15 In fact, I felt compelled to point out that night, humans are not the same person, although we are very close. Identical twins aside, any two people differ in about one DNA letter per thousand. It may not sound like much, but humans have over three billion DNA letters. This means there are three million places on the DNA double helix that differ from person to person. Additionally, new variation is constantly being introduced in the form of mutations, making our genetic structure a realm of infinite possibility. Thus, although we are variations on the same motif, any given individual is different from everyone else who has ever lived or will ever live.

"We're like snowflakes," Sophia chimed. "Each of us is unique, but it's still pretty hard to tell us apart."

16

There was great excitement later that evening as Sophia and Blip were serving some of their freshly baked bread, topped with cold-pressed extra-virgin olive oil. I asked for mine to be toasted, and Sophia obliged me by cutting the large slice diagonally and placing each half in its own slot in the toaster.

"Fantastic!" Blip commented upon seeing her do this. "How did you come up with that?"

"I saw you do it this morning," Sophia replied, somewhat confused.

Blip was dumbfounded. "You must have seen the toast cut diagonally *after* it came out of the toaster!" Blip turned to those assembled around the kitchen island and explained, his foot tapping away. "See, our homemade loaves come out taller than the grocery store bread the toaster is designed for. If we want to toast a slice of homemade bread, the top of it sticks out and doesn't get toasted. But here, the solution is so simple. Cutting each slice of bread diagonally before putting it in the toaster results in a more perfect toasting, because only the narrow corner of the slice sticks out the top. An elegant solution, to be sure, but not mine. What my lover saw this morning was the toast cut in half, but she incorrectly assumed that it had been cut in half *before* it went into the toaster, which it wasn't. Had she looked more closely, she might have noticed that it was not evenly toasted. But she didn't do this, leading her to 'imitate' me."

"Only it wasn't imitation at all." Sophia enthusiastically picked up on where Blip was headed and joined him in tapping. "I was still sleepy, and my incorrect assessment of reality revealed a solution, which I myself did not come up with. I thought I was only copying."

"Right." Blip nodded and turned to his guests. "Now, my question to you is," he gravely pointed his wooden spoon at each of us, "where did that idea come from?"

17 Later, while drying the dishes with Blip, my unhandy hands flung a plate to the floor with a crash. I began to apologize but Blip instantly grabbed another plate off the counter and tossed it into the air, managing to say "No worries!" before it shattered on the tiles as well. "See," said Blip, holding two more plates before me. "None of our plates match anyway. Sophia's parents got us a complete twelve-place dinner setting, but we sold it back and hunted through thrift stores, yard sales, and antique shops for single pieces, most of which cost around twenty-five cents. Now we have a couple dozen beautiful dishes, and as many bowls and goblets. And we still treasure hunt, so the variety is in constant flux." He kicked a shard that was in front of him. "I like to think that we rescue random molds of mass-produced suburban uniformity and turn them into a motley hodgepodge of proud and individual works of art."

"But you just threw one on the floor."

"So did you."

"So what kind of a rescue is that?"

"It was a blaze of glory!" He gestured to the floor. "Look at it. What an explosion! All that potential energy contained in the plate, held in the molecular structure of the ceramic, escaping in one smashing instant. The plate was only the shell for a spirit, a spirit who stepped apart from the rest and reveled in its individual beauty. It's escaped, see? Ultimate release only comes to those who achieve their potential. It was ready." He stepped on a shard and ground it into further smithereens. "It was a good death."

"But you just killed it."

"Flake," he smirked, drying a goblet. "What are you talking about? It was just a plate."

18 "Which do you like better?" Sophia once asked me as she sat in her rocking chair knitting with the joy of a kitten playing with a ball of yarn. "The tingling, needles-and-pins sensation when your foot falls asleep, or the dizzy, seeing-stars feeling when you get up too fast?"

"I don't much care for either, actually," I responded. "Besides, they're really both the same thing. Your foot tingles because it's not getting enough oxygen, and you get dizzy because your head's not getting enough oxygen."

"Good." She gave her chair an emphatic rock. "Now I don't have to choose between them."

19 The union of Blip and Sophia is far greater than the sum of its parts. Singly, they are mere sounds, notes with no purpose. Together, they harmonize like a chord never before struck, dancing to a tune only they can hear, living in a world only they can see. They are a providential pair, a dyad reunited, and the happiest couple I've ever met. Strangers are forever commenting that they look like twins, a dually flattering pronouncement, for each is tremendously delighted at being likened to the other.

Sophia and Blip had already been dancing together for five years when I first met them ten years ago, but they got married (or *merried,* as they insisted) only eight years ago. They made certain, however, that their wedding guests understood that they were not about to start counting their anniversaries all over again.

It wasn't a legal ceremony anyway. In fact, they promoted it as an outlaw wedding. And indeed, it was a blatant disregard for normalcy. No one presided over the ritual but themselves, and it was held deep inside a gorge at a state park where such activities were not permitted. They took great delight in this fact and played with it from the start, sending out parchment invitations sealed inside bottles, daring their guests to attend this bandito matrimonial, to applaud them as they sought treasure in one another. Flamboyant costumes were required.

When the day of the wedding arrived, and they had dressed those who hadn't taken them seriously about costumes (myself included), they divided their guests into five groups of six. They gave each group a separate treasure map, five different paths leading to the same secret rendezvous. Then they disappeared, by which I mean they somehow ducked out of the picnic area while everyone else stood around looking ridiculous and trying to meet up with the others in their group. There was some grumbling but much amiability, for Blip and Sophia had succeeded in turning us into an unlikely gaggle of gypsies and jesters and monks and pirates. Since even the grumblers weren't about to skip out on a wedding, there was nothing to do but follow our directions.

I was an elf. Blip gave me some green tights and a tunic, then popped elfin tips on my ears and painted my face, "emphasizing your laugh lines," he said. "You don't laugh enough. I'll bet you get cramps in your cheeks when you laugh too hard. That means that you're not laughing enough. Your face should cramp up when you frown, not when you smile. When you smile, the corners of your mouth point the way to heaven." He stepped back and admired his work. "Did you know that all of your laugh lines ultimately emanate from a single point on your face?" He touched his green eyeliner pencil to a central point on my forehead. "That point is your third eye."

20 Blip, of Italian and Irish ancestry, likes to call himself a Hindu, though he practices almost nothing of the religion, condemns the caste system as a justification for inequality, and chides karma as a charming but silly concept. He is, however, very enthusiastic about imbibing bhang to celebrate Shiva's birthday. He claims that this prevents the quick-tempered deity (who really only symbolizes an aspect of our own collective consciousness, he never neglects to add) from growing irritated and destroying the entire world with his third eye. When is Shiva's birthday? I do not know, but I am quite certain that it is not as frequent as Blip seems to celebrate it. As for Sophia, she's half Huichol Indian and half Russian Jewish, with a touch of Romany buried somewhere. She practices as much Judaism as Blip does Hinduism. On some Saturdays, she studies the tarot deck with Rabbi Rainbow.

When they had a child a couple of years after the wedding, I couldn't help but ask what religion that made their daughter, since descent is matrilineal in Judaism and patrilineal in Hinduism.

They only shrugged the question off, as if it were as obvious as the purpose of existence itself. "She's a Hinjew," they spoke in unison.

21 Blip and Sophia are not averse to their Catholic and Native American spiritual influences either. Along with Christmas and Hanukkah, which they celebrate on winter solstice with some local pagans they've befriended, they fast on High Holy Days and were never hesitant to engage in peyote and other such ceremonies in their youth.

Mostly they practice good cheer, which, they maintain, is the obvious purpose of existence.

22 Blip and Sophia imitate the innocence of their daughter, whom they adore. They named her Dandelion, though her eternally astonished eyes are more like black-eyed Susans caught in the headlights of heaven. Her nickname is Dandy, and she is the benevolent and undisputed head of their household. If ever she has a question, all else ceases until it is answered to her satisfaction, at which point she does a little dance halfway between a skip and a jumping jack and scampers into the next room.

When she was very young, she would sometimes wander over and join any company Blip and Sophia might have been entertaining. She would listen intently to the talking, and after a while attempt to participate. Thus our conversation was often reduced to "yabble wuzzel fossy kline," or some such piffle, no matter how serious the issue at hand. At first this was quite innocent, but after a while it seemed to take on something of a mocking tone. She would dance around us, imitating the motion of our flapjaws with her hands, prattling and chanting nonsense. Or perhaps I project my own insecurities.

Dandy never uttered an intelligible word except for *gardyloo* until her third birthday, at which point she commenced speaking with nearly perfect pronunciation and syntax, singing "Happy Birthday to You" along with everyone. Prior to that, Blip and Sophia thought their daughter might have aphasia, a psychological disorder in which the affected person cannot use speech, cannot connect words and ideas. They were not particularly concerned about this possibility, reasoning that it would keep them honest, since you cannot lie to someone who doesn't understand language. "She perceives your actual emotional presence, not what you claim it to be," they cautioned. "So no b.s."

When she finally did speak, it was a considerable relief to the rest of the adults who interacted with her, though not because anyone was concerned about her cognitive development. She was clearly advanced in that regard. Rather, we were relieved that she simultaneously relaxed her somewhat unsettling habit of listening attentively to whatever an adult might be saying, and then invariably answering "Gardyloo!" while pointing and giggling. She had a disarming ability to make one feel utterly foolish with this pronouncement.

Sophia explained that she was partially to blame for this, as she was the one who taught her the word. It was, as I've said, Dandy's first "real" word, and the only one she used until she was three. Gardyloo, Sophia explained, was an expression common in some towns of medieval Europe. It was hollered out one's window just before heaving one's pail of piss or bucket of shit into the street below, for that was the extent of indoor plumbing in those days.

"That was Dandy's first word?" I asked.

"She learned it when she was being potty-trained. I always said it when we flushed the toilet."

"But we think she extended the meaning to when she thinks we're full of crap," Blip added, lifting Dandy onto his shoulders.

"Hardly complimentary."

Sophia shrugged. "That plumbing detail is often missed in historians' accounts of the plagues that swept through Europe in the Middle Ages. They were wading through their own sewage, and blaming their sickness on witchcraft. Anyone who tried to reason otherwise was burned at the stake for heresy."

"You say that like they were a bunch of shitwits and we're so much more advanced," Blip challenged her. "We have toilets that flush now. So what? We still eat, drink, and breathe our own pollution and wonder why we get cancer."

"Actually," I couldn't resist debating, "some of the most current research is suggesting that genetics plays a large role in causing cancer. It's often very difficult to demonstrate environmental influences."

"What does it matter if there are genetic factors?" Sophia dismissed my comment. "Those are only predispositions that would decrease as the environment became more pristine. And what's the point of that line of research anyway? Are we trying to alter our genes so we'll be able to live in our own shit without getting sick?"

I fell silent, Blip laughed, and Dandy answered for everyone. "Gardyloo."

23 While I am on the topic of excrement, it's worth mentioning that Blip and Sophia were quite fond of their own. They went so far as to save it, compost it, and fertilize their organic garden with the fruits of their rectums. Their commode was a composting toilet. I, however, was forbidden from contributing to their fecal fund. They had a second toilet connected to a septic tank for guests such as me.

"It's an *organic* garden," Blip explained gently to me one afternoon in their kitchen. "And I've seen the food you eat. We only eat pure, organic foods. Humans are at the top of the food chain, and the toxins we dump in our rivers and spray on our plants and inject into our animals eventually work their way back to us in the food we eat. That's why our fertilizer has to be organic. Otherwise we'd be cycling the toxins through ourselves. I hate to tell you, but human shit is the most toxic shit of any species in the world."

"Our poop doesn't stink," Sophia quipped. "Which is not to say that we think we're something special."

"We're not hot shit," Blip added.

"And we're not full of shit either," Sophia continued. "You can take that figuratively or literally. I poop three times a day. Gardyloo hooray!"

"Me too," said Blip. "And it's easy, clean, and has a pungent, earthy fragrance. If your shit stinks to high heaven, something's wrong, and Glade isn't the answer."

Sophia chuckled. "It's like body odor."

"Right!" Blip interrupted. "Have you heard about that? I saw this commercial the other day, trying to sell something called *deodorant.* Deodorant. Have you heard about this shit?"

Before I could answer his sarcasm, Sophia pursued the point. "An advertiser would have you believe that humans couldn't stand the smell of each other until deodorants and antiperspirants were developed in the 1800s. Tell me, Mr. Geneticist, how would that be conducive to the survival of the species? Body odor is most unattractive, and so how could such a trait be expected to survive the gauntlet of natural selection? If we stink, it's because our bodies are excreting poisons. Poisoned people are not healthy, and thus do not make very attractive mates. Consequently, we hide behind petrochemical perfumes."

Blip nodded, tapping away. "And did you know the toxins we 'throw away' from us reach their highest concentrations in our own bodies? There was a public health alert in California in the sixties that advised against breast-feeding. Toxins reach higher and higher levels of concentration at each level of the food chain. Because we're at the top of the food chain, human breast milk had dangerously high concentrations of DDT, absorbed from the food the mothers ate."

"That reminds me," Sophia asked with an abrupt air of sensuality. "Would you like some cheddar cheese, Flake? I made it from the milk of my own breasts. One hundred percent organic, free-range. Aged three years."

I was astounded, horrified, and embarrassed. I was on the verge of either screaming or laughing out loud. "No thanks."

"Are you sure?" She got up from the table and walked over to their solar-powered refrigerator. "Weren't you breast-fed?"

"Don't be ridiculous. I was also weaned."

"No you weren't," she teased. "I've seen you drink cow's milk. *That's* ridiculous. You'd rather drink milk that comes from the teat of a cow than from a woman."

24 Once, when she was about four, Dandy tumbled into the dining room when Sophia and Blip had guests over. "Why do power flowers stink?" she asked directly, wrinkling her nose.

"Power flowers?" Sophia responded. "You mean flower power, Dandy, and flower power doesn't stink at all. Flower power is wonderful." Have I mentioned? Sophia is what some crusty clerk at a gas station off the interstate in the middle of nowhere might mutteringly refer to as a "damn hippie." She did not, after all, shave her legs.

"I know what flower power is, Mommy." Dandy giggled. "*Power* flower."

"You're the power flower," Blip teased her. "You don't stink."

"No." Dandy was adamant and becoming frustrated. "The *power* flower."

"Power flower?" Blip and Sophia asked each other, puzzled.

"It stinks," Dandy added.

"It stinks?" they repeated.

"Yuck," she nodded hopefully.

"Where is the power flower?" Blip attempted.

Dandy fell to the floor amiably. "I don't know." She sat up suddenly. "The *power* flower, remember?"

"Where did you smell it?" Sophia inquired.

"In the car."

"How did it smell?"

"Real bad."

Everyone fell silent, stumped at this four-year-old's riddle. "Ideas, anyone?" Blip opened the floor to all present at the table, but we may as well have been spinning around blindfolded trying to pin the tail on the donkey at a piñata party.

"What does it look like?" I tried, and for a moment I was the hero of the house. But the congratulatory backslapping ended abruptly when we looked to Dandy for an answer. She only giggled at our evident idiocy.

"I don't know." She collapsed backward onto the floor once again. "I couldn't *see* it."

We looked witlessly at one another, until Blip seized upon a partial solution. "She saw it in the car, right?"

Sophia finished his thought. "And she's not tall enough to see out the window." Blip snapped his fingers in agreement.

Dandy looked at them, perplexed. "*Power* flower."

"When did you see this power flower?" Morty Drecker attempted. He was a sociologist in Blip's department who earlier that evening had lost his temper while debating with Sophia that rationality was superior to emotionality. Blip called him "Mr. Bad Vibes," gave him a peppermint candy, and told him to chase it with a glass of dandelion root iced tea (which he claimed aided relaxation) to chill out. Now, Morty's question was immediately chased off the table with barks of "She couldn't see out the window!" from every other adult present. He wasn't invited back.

"When did you *smell* the power flower?" Blip recommenced with Twenty Questions.

This question bewildered Dandy, who, it appeared, had never before considered the notion that there was any other moment but the present. She pointed behind herself and turned around, baffled, and finally satisfied herself with this answer: "Then."

"Did you see anything else then?"

"Pumpkins."

"The Roundtown Pumpkin Jamboree!" Morty leaped at the opportunity to redeem himself, but the answer was obvious to everyone. The Roundtown Pumpkin Jamboree is a heavily publicized autumn festival forty-five minutes south of town. Every year, to celebrate the harvest, the people of the nearby rural borough of Roundtown throw a pumpkin festival to coincide with Halloween. It's the biggest event in Roundtown, whose next biggest attraction is a merry-go-round in the middle of the town circle. Everyone nodded courteously at Morty's observation, but he mistook it for encouragement, and continued cerebrally. "So the power flower is somewhere between here and Roundtown."

All fell silent, while Dandy amused herself by turning and looking behind her own back, first one side, then the other.

"Power plant." Sophia announced the solution simply and eloquently.

"Right! The power *plant* south of town," echoed Morty.

"You smelled the power *plant*, Dandy?" asked Sophia. Dandy nodded innocently. "It's a power plant," Sophia explained. "Not a power flower."

Dandy smiled compassionately at her mother. "Flowers are plants, Mommy."

"But not all plants are flowers," Blip explained.

Dandy was as thunderstruck as the time she discovered that her parents had names other than Mommy and Daddy. "Then what's power?"

"You tell me." Blip waved his spoon at her. "You smelled it."

Dandy wrinkled her nose again. "I don't like power."

"What do you like?"

She giggled like a ticklish faerie and galloped out of the room. A few moments later, having had time to consider, she called back to us in a voice that would give a hailstorm second thoughts. "I like flowers!"

25 Having a daughter allowed Sophia and Blip to circumvent the circumcision decision, although Sophia, despite her Hebraic heritage, made no secret of what the decision would have been had the chromosomes fallen differently.

"Why fix it if it isn't broke?" she explained one summer afternoon at a picnic they hosted in the organic garden behind the 50 percent self-sufficient geodesic dome home they had built atop a hill twelve miles outside the center of town. "It doesn't matter what the Bible says. Do you really think Mother Nature would create and evolve (for these are hardly mutually exclusive, she forever reminds me) sexual organs, *reproductive* organs, that are any less than perfect?" I shook my head no, feeling suddenly awkward with the discussion. I was trained to think about such matters in terms of nucleotides and DNA, or chromosomes at the worst. Larger processes made me uneasy.

"And besides," Blip interjected, handing me a glass of his homemade dandelion wine. "Did you know that the loss of your foreskin decreases your enjoyment *and* your stamina?"

I could only shake my head again. My Anglo-Aryan background made me want to flee from these ethnics and their indefatigable frankness.

"It's true," he continued. "The natural foreskin slips over

the head, where all the nerve endings are, every time you withdraw." He used his hands to illustrate. "This breaks up the stimulation, and consequently you last longer. See?"

Sophia nodded in hot-blooded agreement.

26

Falling water, spent by a summer's worth of sunshine, trickled groggily into a shallow pool, yawning and stretching and preparing to hibernate for the winter. Draped only in billows of chiffon with modestly placed samite accents and wreaths of the autumn forest's most exquisite finery, Blip and Sophia met barefoot at the center of an ankle-deep lagoon, a few feet in front of the waterfall, and promised to be merrymates for as long as they both should live.

The acoustics of the gorge allowed them to project their voices easily over the sound of the waterfall as they vowed in front of their costumed family and friends and the rest of Creation not only to spend their lives together expressing love for one another, but also to search relentlessly for a word, a word whose existence was whispered breathlessly to them by a whirling dervish in Turkey, a word which expresses that which the overuse of the word *love* fails to express. As they took turns proclaiming this tale to their guests, a shower of rose petals fluttered upon us from an unseen source, causing me to sneeze and wheeze, as I was prone to do around such beauty.

Their dithyramb continued as they promised never to go to sleep angry with each other and to immediately disrobe whenever the circumstances of human communication pushed them into an argument. "Quarrels are best had naked," they pronounced in turns, "stark, bare-assed naked; where a cantankerous mood is difficult to maintain; where pride dissolves like the salt of our tears into the Sea of Love, lapping against the shores of Eden; where communication becomes true, honest, open, telepathic. We will reclaim the Garden our ancestors lost, experience the world and each other with no thought of ourselves. We will not fail you. Like Weeble-Wobbles, we may wobble but we won't fall down. We will keep the hope of humanity alive between us. For if love is not enough, if two people can't get along and make it work out, what hope remains for our world?

"And so may we be like two halves of an eternal sandwich. May we stick together and nourish those around us. May we never get moldy. May we never get soggy." Pausing for a moment after this rhapsody, they vowed, "till death makes our union complete." Proceeding to place rare autumn dandelions behind one another's ears, they looked expectantly at all of their guests and asked, "The rings? Who has the rings?" This caused a general murmur and shifting of hooves until a voice thundered from above, "Rope!" followed by, indeed, a rope plummeting and landing just next to the rows of seats. All heads immediately turned skyward, where a silhouette of a figure, hidden by the glare of the sun, was preparing to rappel down the rope into our midst. As he descended, an accordion strapped to his back, he belted out a dirty limerick in an accent thick with the verdant hillsides of Ireland.

I once met a magical faerie
Who pranced with raiments a-nary.
On her bosom she wore
Two rings of gold ore,
And gave them to me with her cherry.

Upon landing, he unclipped himself swiftly and fairly danced to the water's edge, proclaiming his possession of the needed rings. "I've the rings, kind folk, but I cannot enter the pool of your union!" At that, he unstrapped an accordion-like contraption from his thigh and hung the rings on the end of it. When he pressed the handles together like a bellows, it extended out to Blip and Sophia, who took the rings and nodded graciously.

As Brad the Red, as the airborne accordionist was called, bowed out of the picture, Blip and Sophia faced one another, and we could only witness them enter the universe they shared behind one another's eyes. Lips trembling but limbs moving with the grace of a dancer's dreamscape, they simultaneously placed the rings on each other's fingers and spoke their final vow in unison.

"Tickle tickle hee haw, whenever we get bored."

At that, they turned and waded a few feet back toward the waterfall. Pausing briefly, they ventured beneath the trickle, and as the water leaped licentiously off their bodies and the currents of the swirling mist shifted around them, a circular rainbow burst forth and embraced them like only Mother Nature can. So near was the rainbow that I could see each individual droplet of mist drifting through the spectrum, shimmering and humming blessings like a choir of kittens purring in a sunbeam, as Sophia and Blip, wet but unruffled, kissed, and a glad-hearted geyser of spontaneous applause erupted, for we saw that it was good.

27

After the Pomp and Circumstance, as the ceremony was called, the Prance and Dance followed at a nearby inn. Brad the

Red and his accordion circulated among the guests, cracking jokes punctuated with his squeeze-box. Every few minutes, "just to keep everyone sharp," he explained to me later, he bellowed a "mystical limerick" from his considerable repertoire:

There once was a planet called Earth
Who screamed with the pains of childbirth.
On her surface befell
A monkey-made hell,
Till she whelped out the spirit of mirth.

And,

The monkeys who call themselves human
Are still embryos in albumin.
In their heart there does dwell
A seed in its shell
Which will grow till their soul does illumine.

I thought the man a raving moron. In between his sets of Celtic good cheer, I asked him what else he did besides play accordion.

"What I can, good man." He clicked his heels and sounded his instrument.

"What *don't* you do then?" I asked.

"I huff and I puff," his accordion bellowed along, "but I don't do enough."

"A jack-of-all-trades, master of none, eh?"

Faster than an auctioneer's stenographer and grinning like only a redhead can, he replied, just before launching into another set of Celtic delight, "My good man, 'tis better than a jackass of one trade and bored as all hell."

28 Speaking of jackasses of one trade other than my former self (for it now appears that I tinker with words as well as nucleotides—though the two are more similar than I ever imagined), let's not forget about Officer Wilt, the desk sergeant at the jail. He would release Blip into my custody only, since it was me, and not Sophia, who had talked to Captain Down. Blip insisted on riding with me anyway, which understandably hurt Sophia's feelings.

"Flake, you're not going to believe what I'm about to tell you." Blip broke his sulking silence as we pulled into the campus parking lot to get his car.

"You're probably right. Where are you parked?"

"Up front there, under that big tree."

I spotted his car, up on the grass and under the shade of an enormous sycamore. I pulled into a nearby space, not bothering to ask why he didn't use the lot.

"Aren't you going to ask why I didn't use the parking lot?" Blip asked, smiling triumphantly.

"Why didn't you use the parking lot?" I monotoned.

"Because I'll *never* pay the tickets they keep giving me. They're university parking tickets, and I won't be working here no more!" His voice rose a few decibels. "I can park anywhere I damn well please!"

"They could tow you. Haven't you thought about that? Look, Blip—"

"Flake, listen," he interrupted. "There's something strange going on in that prison."

"Jail," I corrected.

"In the jail. They're doing some kind of experiments."

"Blip, I really don't have time for this. You need to start thinking about others."

"Flake, this is serious." He put his palms up in surrender. "I'll admit I may have been wrong about the poisoned tea and radioactive staples, but you have to believe me on this."

"What about the extraterrestrial mushrooms?"

"I'm not budging on that one." Blip shook his head. "But listen, I'll buy you a coffee . . . no, an herbal tea! Just promise me you'll listen."

I hesitated, and in that moment I recalled the way Sophia had looked when I was talking with her at the jail only a few minutes prior. A frightened despondency quenched the light in her eyes, her lower lip trembling like a weeping rose petal. What was happening here? Blip and Sophia are my rock, my reassurance that life is funny and beautiful. How can such perfect playmates be unhappy? Blip's madness and Sophia's sadness were shattering my precious illusions. Witnessing my two best friends, my two only friends, have difficulty with their relationship caused me great uneasiness. Perhaps I had a crush on their union and not just Sophia. A comfortable constant, a reassuring given, a taken-for-granted pillar of stability was beginning to shudder and come asunder. An island was drowning in the raging sea. A pool of water was evaporating in the blazing desert. There was no question. Of course I agreed to listen to what Blip had to say.

"Great! I know a good place. I'll get my car!" Blip leaped out of my car and ran over to get his. I followed hesitantly, feeling suddenly confused, as if I had just agreed that stepping on my reading glasses was a fine idea. "What the hell?" he whined when he got to his car. "Would you look at all this birdshit? Why is it all in one place? What the hell were they doing, having target practice?"

I looked at his car, and sure enough, there was a small pile of whitish excrement on his front hood, just before his windshield. Three fluorescent orange parking tickets under the wiper were flecked and peppered here and there with the shrapnel of exploded bird droppings. Looking up, I saw a nest directly above the car. Blip, however, did not make this connection.

"Imagine that," he said, surveying the damage. "Those birds, when they get bored of just flying, they try some fancy stuff. Probably taking turns, flying low, dropping their payload, whistling all the way. Nothing better to do than play all day, making fun of us busy humans, shitting on our shiny cars, letting us know who's really alive." He chuckled, and I decided not to cue him in on the actual cause. "Must be nice," he murmured. "Must be nice."

The Book o' Billets-doux

sweetlick: Do you believe everything happens for a reason?

rosehips: Of course! Every result has its antecedents.

sweetlick: Pardon me. What I meant to say was, do you believe everything happens for a larger purpose?

rosehips: No. But I believe everything happens.

sweetlick: But if there's no larger purpose, what meaning is there in existence?

rosehips: To assume that everything happens for some larger purpose is to justify tragedy. Don't mistake the result for the purpose.

sweetlick: Well-spoken. Nevertheless, it is a comforting way to think.

rosehips: Only as comfortable as hiding your head under the covers and refusing to accept the double dare of free will. You'll suffocate eventually.

sweetlick: But I'm warm.

rosehips: True enough. Yank those covers back and it will be mighty chilly, no doubt about it, but *Brr!* and *Mmm!* and *Ohh!* and *Oop!* Drop your chains and fly the coop. *Ow!* and *Ha!* and *Oof!* and *Wow!* Find your path to peace somehow.

29 Reluctant to climb into the passenger seat with Blip on the slippery brink of mania, and bewildered as to how that had come to be a possibility in the first place, I offered to drive.

"No can do," he shook his head. "You should be careful even saying that. You'll disrupt the natural flow of events. What if you drove and a truck sideswiped us and I was killed in the passenger seat? You'd never forgive yourself, obsessing over what would have happened if you'd been there instead. Don't fuck around with fate, man. Think about the people who walk away from seventy-mile-an-hour crashes just because of the way they happened to be sitting or the angle of the collision, or any infinite combination of variables. Life is a high-stakes poker game, and cheaters aren't treated kindly. The dealer can't disrupt the natural order of the cards once the shuffling is done. Predetermined elements of the game are sitting right there in the pile, waiting to be brought to bear. Someone loses a game after a misdeal? Look out."

"So now you believe in fate?"

"Dependent on current circumstances, of course. But yeah, your destiny, our destiny, humankind's destiny, it follows necessarily given present premises. Conclusions must agree with their premises. Seems pretty simple to me."

"Who's to say that me driving isn't the natural flow of events?"

"Clearly, it isn't. I naturally walked to the driver's side, and you naturally walked to the passenger's side, without even thinking about it. Probably this conversation is disrupting the dance of chance. Things take care of themselves as long as you trust and don't try to control too much. Things will happen.

Things tend to occur. Why resist what's inevitable? That's like swimming against the current, salmon notwithstanding. Go with the flow, you know? Glide with the glow, man. It's easier."

I went with the flow, or glided with the glow, or whatever, and hence what I am about to relate happened as it should have happened.

30

"The word in the joint," Blip began as he started his car, "is that they're shipping us to the big house."

"The big house?"

"State pen, you know."

"Right." I had hardly spoken when Blip floored the gas pedal, turfing the lawn he was parked on and leaping the curb back into the parking lot. He flicked his wipers on and brushed the three tickets off his windshield.

"I hate these things!" he yelled over the noise of his struts clanking in protest as we crashed over three consecutive speed bumps, leading me to once again question the wisdom of letting him drive. "So," he continued as he pulled onto the road, "Manny Malarkey says it's because they're screening us for these experiments."

"Manny Malarkey?"

"Yeah, a guy I met in the slammer. Turns out we're kindred spirits. He's the trucker who got nine months for blowing up that billboard."

"You met the guy who blew up the billboard?"

"He's done hundreds of them, actually. It's his hobby when he's driving rigs across the country. But these experiments, see, I think I heard them. Manny tells me there's a subbasement under the jailhouse that's used as an isolation tank. Anyway, I swear I heard noises coming through some of the air ducts."

"Did he hear them too?"

"No, but he's half deaf from when his last billboard job exploded before he was clear. That's how they caught him. He was knocked unconscious by the blast. Stupid cops think it was an isolated incident though." Blip laughed. "They don't even know he's done it all over the country."

"So what were the noises?"

"No idea. That's what was strange. I couldn't tell if it was horrified screaming or hilarious laughter. What I think is that they're torturing prisoners down there, Flake. That's what the screaming is. And the guards are laughing at them; they think it's funny."

"Then why did you want to stay there?" I tried to speak to his sense of self-preservation. "What if you were tortured?"

"I want to find out what's going on." Blip scratched his chin thoughtfully. "But that would really piss me off, though."

"What's that?"

"Getting tortured. Getting tortured would really piss me off."

I nodded at the truism. Getting tortured would really piss me off, too.

31

"So what about Sophia?" I ventured out of nowhere after we'd driven in silence through a couple of blocks in the high-end residential zone near campus where most of the university administrators lived. He was quiet for a time after I said this, gazing out the window, and I was vain enough to think I might have actually gotten through to him. We slowed to a stop at

Gentry Avenue, a steady stream of fast-moving cars leaving me nervous that Blip would pull out in front of one at any moment. Eventually a man in a primered El Camino slowed to a stop and motioned us in front of him. Blip turned right and gave the man a genial wave.

"See that, Flake? That's a beautiful human." My question was apparently forgotten, and I decided not to press the issue. "You'll run into them every so often, you know? He knows that there are real people inside these cars. He sympathizes with a stranger's aggravation. A Good Samaritan."

Blip accelerated as a traffic light up ahead turned yellow. It turned red while he was under it. "Oh no!" Blip glanced in his rearview mirror. "He got caught at the light. He would have made it through if he didn't let me in. He gave up his destiny, his spot at the light, for a complete stranger. That's the kind of person who would give his life for another if the situation demanded it."

"So he interfered with the dance of chance, as you call it?" I interrupted his discourse on saintly drivers to point out his apparent contradiction. "He shouldn't have broken the flow of traffic. He missed the light, but he might also avoid an accident, or get into an accident that he would not have otherwise." Blip fell silent again and furrowed his brow. As the next light turned yellow, he slowed to a stop.

"Whoa!" Blip slapped my knee while looking joyfully in the rearview mirror. "There he is, Flake! Our boy made it through in the long run! See? He let me in and didn't lose any time anyway. He knew he wouldn't get where he's going any faster. Destiny comes around despite our efforts. That's a beautiful human. Beautiful! Wow! We could use more of them on this planet."

I turned around in my seat to have another look at this roadway angel. There he was, Blip's karmic bookie, the frontiersman of fate, sitting idly in his car and picking his nose.

32

Blip's unbridled glee with the nose-picking hero of the highways tapped out its enthusiasm all over the steering wheel. My mind occupied with matters presumably more important than the existence of free will in human destiny, I pursued the debate no further.

"Did you know poison ivy is one of the most potent toxins on Earth?" The events in Tynee's office earlier that day were still tickling my curiosity. "One ounce of the extracted toxin could give everyone on Earth a rash."

"Poison ivy is an evil plant," Blip replied. "Mephistophelian. Sophia doesn't agree with me. She claims that since humans are the only animals that are allergic to poison ivy, and since it doesn't grow in the deep forest, only along roadsides and in clearings and suburban backyards and such, that it's Mother Nature's way of discouraging us from areas that need to recover from the ravages of our oafishness. I say poison ivy is like shopping. If you scratch it, oh man does it feel good, it's immensely satisfying, but as soon as you stop you want to scratch it again more than ever. Same with buying things. You can never satisfy it. Poison ivy is pure greed, lust, covetousness. Sophia acquiesced a bit when we had Dandy. It took me years to clear all the poison ivy from the areas we tend. Demonic plant. Scratching it is better than sex. Nothing should be better than sex."

"How does Sophia feel about you getting arrested?" I awkwardly tried to introduce the topic once again. Blip, however, continued his speculations unencumbered.

"One ounce? That's it? Wow. That's weird . . ." His voice trailed off, and his eyes grew wide then instantly squinted. I had been watching him, and when I followed his eyes it was immediately apparent why he was so astounded. I hadn't noticed entering the freeway, but there we were in a steady flow of thirty-mile-per-hour after-work traffic, rolling toward Graffiti Bridge. So much had happened that I'd completely forgotten to tell him that JUST A COUPLE OF DAYS had received a reply. The message was simple. It read: NOW!

For a few moments it seemed that Blip's already excited state was about to erupt into a full-blown manic attack. But instead of screaming and raving, as I expected, he released the enormity of his elation with a simple snicker, like the muffled hiccup of a massive earthquake.

"No time but the present, old friend," he pronounced as we passed underneath, gently tapping the gas pedal. "That's the writing on the wall. Time is now." He gave the horn a couple of happy honks. "Now or never."

33

Surprisingly, traffic was not particularly snarled around and under the bridge, as was typically the case. A short way beyond it, however, we slowed into a traffic jam.

"Why can't everyone just go the same speed?" Blip whined. "Didn't they just see the bridge? Now! Live in the now, the perpetual present. Dig the day. Can you imagine? If we could just get in sync, get in tune, man, if we could harmonize, hear the same rhythm, there'd be peace on Earth, and no traffic jams."

"Where are we going?" I asked, again mystified as to how I happened to agree to come along in the first place. I'm now certain it was a decision made by an imp who took possession of my will at the crucial moment of judgment.

"Look at that." Blip ignored me and pointed to a bumper sticker on the car in front of us. It read: CAUTION! THIS CAR MAY BE SUDDENLY EMPTY WHEN RAPTURE COMES! "Pride is one of the deadly sins!" Blip called through his windshield to the person in front of him. "Look at her, sucking down that Coke, waiting for rapture."

"Blip, where are we going?"

"The freeway."

"We're already on the freeway."

"Yes, the freeway is a big place, one of the closest conceptions of eternity we have, don't you think?" He flashed a vast grin at me as we passed the accident scene that was the source of the backup. "Don't look!" he commanded, grabbing my knee to pull my attention away. "That's the whole problem, don't you see? All it takes is one coward afraid of his own mortality to throw everyone off balance. You have to live in the now."

Just past the accident, traffic loosened and quickened almost immediately, and Blip responded by veering into the left lane and opening up the engine all the way. Within seconds, the speedometer was pushing past eighty miles per hour.

"Going a little fast, aren't you?"

"Yes," he agreed, yelling over the increasing wind and engine noise. "Of course, the stars offer a better example of eternity, but we don't see too much of them anymore, what with city lights and TV and all."

"Blip! Slow down!" The needle looked peculiar so far to the right on the speedometer.

"What would you rather do, spend eternity gazing at the stars or driving on the freeway?"

I bellowed a scream as we flew past a semi, the drag of the eighteen-wheeler making our car feel airborne.

"All right, all right." He removed his foot from the accelerator and friction quickly brought us back below 100. "Take it easy. You don't have to scream, for God's sake. I'll set the cruise control. Imagine being a truck driver though. *That's* an eternity on the freeway." He locked the speed at 90, which felt slow compared to the 110 we'd been doing only moments before.

"What's going on, Blip?"

"Relax. Haven't you always wanted to go this fast?"

"Just slow it down to eighty, how about that?"

"Where are all the cops when you need 'em, eh?"

"What?"

"You may as well get comfortable, because I'm not stopping until I see some sirens."

"What are you talking about?"

"Prison, Flake." He looked at me, his expression humorless. "One way or another I'm getting back in there."

I did not think to mention again that it was actually a jail.

34

The paranoid, hyperaware, self-conscious reaction that typically accompanies the presence of a police cruiser on the highway was noticeably absent as we sighted one ahead. "Ah! There's one!" Blip shouted and immediately floored the accelerator.

Soon we were doing well over 100 again. I glimpsed the officer's startled face as we roared past and must confess a feeling of roguish delight. I chuckled involuntarily, and Blip looked at me in fraternal approval.

I often lived vicariously through Blip's antics. Regardless of anything else, I had begun to enjoy myself, gliding with the glow, as it were. I felt like a couple of ex-cons on the lam. "Fuckin' cops," Blip muttered facetiously as the siren wailed behind us. He reduced his speed as the officer gave chase. By the time we were doing fifty we were moving intolerably slowly.

"What do you want me to tell Sophia?" I asked, sighing in resignation. Blip was silent again as he pulled onto the berm.

"Well," he began, after we had come to a stop. "Tell her I said to remember the hounds of hell, and how everything turned out all right in the end. Tell her I promise that everything will turn out all right, and that I know what I'm doing."

"The hounds of hell?"

"She'll know what I mean. And don't try to get me released again, at least for a few days."

"What are you doing anyway?"

"I'm being a conscious tool of the universe, of course."

"Because some delinquent had the gumption to reply to you on the bridge?"

"You've never understood such things, Flake." He sniffed at the air. "Do you smell that?"

I sniffed. "I smell nothing."

"It's change." He inhaled deeply, elaborating with his right hand. "You can definitely smell it. Change is in the wind, my friend, like the fart of a flower child."

"What?"

He waved me off. "Never mind."

"What about your car?"

"Who cares? Do what you want with this heap. I think I blew the engine." Blip looked behind him and saw the police officer approaching. He pulled a twenty-dollar bill out of his wallet. "But I'll bet you a twenty I can talk my way out of this."

35

Blip rolled down his window and smiled pleasantly at the officer, whose nametag read APPLEBEE. "Good afternoon," he said as he extended his license and registration toward her.

"Can I see your license and registration please?"

"It's right here." He gestured his hand toward her again.

"Oh." She was taken off guard by Blip's preparedness.

"You're welcome," Blip replied cordially, without being prompted by rote gratitude. "The reason I was going so fast," he continued, again not giving her a chance to ask, "is that I've recently been fired from my job. I have an interview for another job, and I didn't want to be late."

"I'm sorry to hear that." Officer Applebee held up a yellow card he had handed her along with his papers. "What's this?"

"It's a Get Out of Jail Free Card," Blip grinned and explained the obvious. "You know, from Monopoly. Community Chest." He succeeded in amusing her.

"Well, you're not going to jail, but speed limits are for safety, and you were *way* over the speed limit."

"How fast was I going?"

"My radar wasn't on when you passed me, but I was going seventy, and you flew by me out of nowhere. Given that, I'm estimating at least eighty-five."

"I'm real sorry, Officer, it's just that I heard Warden Hoosegow is a real stickler about punctuality."

"You have an interview with Hoosegow?" she asked with sudden camaraderie.

"Yeah. I lost my job at the university. I did some homework, and it turns out corrections is a growth industry. We already imprison more of our citizens per capita than any other country in the world, and that's going to double in the next decade. So, there's high demand and job security, not to mention a decent salary, and they kick in for dental."

"What're you going to do there?"

"Consulting criminologist. Mostly it entails maintaining the internal structural organization of the facility. They want the successful applicant to maximize the number of prisoners they can hold while minimizing the possibility of any disturbances."

"Sounds interesting."

"Yeah, it is. And if I get the job, I'll get a hefty commission for each additional prisoner I can add, since they get a tax credit for each head."

"Wow."

"Yeah," Blip nodded affably and let the conversation pause. "So, do you think we can wrap this up quickly? I'd hate to lose this opportunity."

"Oh," she smiled, handing him back his license and registration but keeping the Get Out of Jail Free Card. "I'll tell you what, let me give you an escort there. If you get the job, put in a good word for me. I could use some part-time work."

"Great, I will. What's your first name?"

"Anne. Anne Applebee. Just follow me, okay?"

"Thanks, Anne." After she left to go back to her cruiser, Blip turned to me with his palm out.

"I don't understand," I said, slapping a twenty in his hand. "I thought you wanted to go back to jail."

Blip pocketed the money, smiling. "I do." At that, he got out of the car. "Hey Anne!" he hollered to Officer Applebee, who had not yet gotten back to her cruiser. "Everything I just told you was a ranking pile of birdshit, and it's just like a moron pig cop like yourself to fall for it!"

36

Blip was arrested. According to Officer Applebee, the charge was reckless driving and verbal assault on a police officer. She instructed me to "take your wiseass friend's car the hell off my road before I have it impounded." I obeyed smirkingly, and after parking his car back in the campus lot (not under the sycamore) and cleaning the droppings off his hood, I finally arrived home as dusk was just beginning to stretch its shadows before fading off to sleep. I poked around my kitchen for a while, postponing the inevitable call to Sophia. It wasn't long, however, before she rang me.

She was scared and angry, wistful and distraught. She cried on the other end of the line, and the most I could do to comfort her was swing the phone cord from side to side and echo Blip's words, "Everything will turn out all right." I told her that he had mentioned something about "the hounds of hell," and that elicited a chuckle. She must have sensed my curiosity, and she related the story behind it. I was grateful. It gave me goose bumps.

On the first anniversary of the day they met, Blip surprised Sophia by taking her to a luxury cabin for the weekend. On the way there, they picked up a hitchhiker who, after learning that it was their anniversary, presented them with a bag of magic mushrooms as they dropped him off. Thrilled, they thanked him and went to explore a nearby gorge, where they consumed their gift. They decided to leave, however, when they saw a father smack his son for jumping into the creek with his shoes on.

By the time they returned to their car, the effects of the mushrooms were beginning to manifest, and they thought they'd better hurry to their cabin while they could still drive. Along the way, however, the two of them were so awestruck by a grassy hillside that they pulled over and decided to run to the top of it.

As it happened, a nearby resident was in the habit of leaving his Doberman unleashed. When they were a good distance away from their car, barefoot and defenseless, the dog came trotting along beside them. It did nothing as long as they kept moving away from his territory, and their car, but as soon as they would stop or try to make their way back, it would bare its teeth and growl. Tripping madly by this time, they wound up having to go to a stranger's house and ask with trembling voices if the alcoholic woman who answered the door could please call her neighbor and have him bring his guard dog in. After this ordeal of the surreal, Blip and Sophia made straight for their luxury cabin to try and salvage what was left of their trip, their anniversary, and their sanity. Blip kept repeating, "Fucking Dobermans and 'shrooms do *not* mix, fucking Dobermans and 'shrooms do *not* mix," until they got to their country cabin, where the couch pillows were embroidered with a picture of a big black dog on a grassy hillside.

After turning over all the pillows and leaving speculation about such a formidable coincidence until later, they discovered that they had their own grassy hillside. It was even better than the one they had seen earlier, there was no Doberman guarding it, and they'd paid for their right to be there undisturbed. So that's where they stayed all day, running around the gentle slope, marveling at the dandelions that had been flung about the entire hill, finding cherubic shapes in the clouds, and making love under the dome of the sky. Toward evening they watched the sun set and the stars come on from their hilltop perch, then retreated back to the cabin with its full kitchen and a hot tub on the porch. Sophia described it as the best day of their lives, when no matter what tumultuous events were going on in the world or just down the road, they were alive and at peace. They decided that day that if they ever had a little girl, they would name her Dandelion.

"And do you know what he said to me just before I went to sleep that night?" Sophia said, her voice filled with affection at the close of the story. "He said, 'At the gates of heaven lie the hounds of hell.'"

37 It was an appropriate anniversary of their auspicious beginning, and it was the beginning, their first moment of pure and innocent delight in each other, that they forever strove to keep in their hearts. This was apparent to any visitor to their home. A tattered placard from which their union commenced was elegantly framed and hung in their front room, and they relished any opportunity to tell and retell the story of their meeting.

Of what am I speaking? Pardon my verse, but I speak now with honor of tale well-worn, a love story born, a mythic event that came to pass at a festival of forgotten origin. It was outside, that is certain, for Blip tells of an irritating glare blinding him as he ambled, flashes of refracted sunshine glancing at him from ahead. The source was a sign, a shiny white poster held by a joyous young sylph. She was dancing and prancing and sparkling all over, a woman whose legs were purportedly hidden by a gauzy sarong of mandalas and rainbows. But all is revealed in the pure light of day, and so were her limbs seen barefoot and blissful, skipping and stepping, tapping and hopping, foxing and trotting.

She presented her sign to all passersby. Some people frowned and hurried away, but most of them smiled and embraced her with glee. His attention thus distracted, his libido so attracted, he wandered to where he might read the inscription on the poster she picketed with such glad-hearted pith. His mind and his body conspired to drench him with curiosity both sensual and intellectual, pushing him, prodding him, shoving him toward the zing-zippety zaftig. As he approached the proscenium of her performance, her placard pitched left, ducking the sun and revealing its message to the kind, sexy man strolling her way: FREE HUGS!

The connection made, the communication given, the poster bounced on its corners like a card on the run, flirting and bidding him beckon her call. The letters held fast, together they carried the words of their hostess, two words that she uttered and breathed into life: "Free hugs!" Sophia gushed with the lilt of honest joy, and meant them as much for Blip as for anyone else.

He smiled at the sign, and the fingers that held it, and looked up to see the eyes that propelled it. Their eyes locked tight and squinted with grins, swollen pupils stretched forward to soak up more sight. It was but a moment, an invisible instant, no simpering stares or protracted eye goggles, only a glimpse and a blink with recognition complete. He glanced toward her sign and smirked to himself, the smirk of a fool, blind to the inevitable but brave nonetheless. "Who," he scratched his head like a gorilla, then asked her the question that leaped from his mouth. "Who is Hugs?"

38

Thus was their relationship born on the swift kiss of a pun. Neither suspected what the other would become to each of them. Like phrases running wild in the Logos, they knew neither who nor by what mechanism nor for what reason they were whistled for (if they understood that they were whistled for at all). They were simply compelled to come together. Sophia was the question, and Blip was the answer. And vice versa.

It happened like this: *Free Hugs*, confident with his identity as a gallant suggestion, suddenly slammed into *Who is Hugs?*, some smart-assed interrogative who turned him into an emotional imperative by her very presence. What a ridiculous rendezvous! Christ, the two utterances really didn't have anything to do with each other, drawn together by some clever misunderstanding, some sly twist of fate. But sense or nonsense, that which motivates the plane of language cannot be resisted any more than that which motivates the plane of life. The soul knows this, of course, as does its equivalent in the communicative cosmos. It keeps its head in the heavens, and has but one toe in the untamed tides of this world, just enough to animate the mind, which fails to see what is perfectly apparent.

Another question, *Why aren't apples called reds?*, who longed for her answer but bragged of her independence nonetheless, once heard rumors of such fantastic foolishness, such confident meaninglessness, and she scoffed.

39 In my own time and space, I retired to the front porch with my dog, Meeko, a good-natured mutt, surely the furthest a canine could be from a hound of hell. I sat stroking his ears, watching night settle onto my isolated residential street, trying to fathom the events of the day. After a bit, I remembered Tynee's enigmatic purple envelope, whose contents I had not yet found a chance to read. I didn't know it then, but the boastful introduction would turn out to be no hyperbole. This is what the letter said:

> Congratulations, Dr. Fountain!
>
> Due to your extraordinary expertise in the area of molecular biology, you have been selected to participate in research of monumental historical importance.
>
> We represent a top-secret committee of military and industry representatives that has been long disturbed by the nature of warfare. Mind you, we are not so foolish as to believe that war can be done away with; indeed, we recognize the utter inevitability of it in human nature. However, the Committee for Peaceful Conflict (CPC) was founded upon a sincere belief in the possibility of *humane weaponry and warfare.* Briefly, the concept of humane weaponry and warfare is to incapacitate, rather than terminate, an enemy. Traditional warfare decimates entire population centers. This renders natural resource reserves virtually worthless by destroying vital transportation routes and causing billions of dollars in prop-

erty damage. The toll in human suffering need hardly be mentioned.

The CPC has been actively promoting and sponsoring a shift away from these foibles of the past for some time now. Humane weaponry and warfare *is* possible, and recent research in genetics puts humanity on the threshold of an era when the economic and human devastation wrought by war will be nothing more than a memory.

Our research program has proceeded in three stages. Stage one, Operation Moneybags, was dedicated to the identification of the most efficient incapacitating agents. To that end, a massive survey of chemicals was undertaken, without success. Chemistry is the technology of the past, as you must surely realize, and genetics is the technology of the future. With that realization, the program was scrapped and begun anew.

Let us remind you before we go any further that our goal is *humane weaponry and warfare,* not germ warfare. We are not searching for or looking to create a new plague upon humankind. Rather, we seek to remove the plagues of economic devastation and human suffering from the annals of warfare. War cannot be helped, but it *can* be peaceful.

All disclaimers aside, once a suitable carrier virus was identified, it was brought into the laboratory for genetic mapping. This has been accomplished. Stage two, Operation Recount, involved the manipulation of the genome. We believe we have engineered a highly unique virus with specialized symptoms that, were it introduced into a population center, would almost immediately incapacitate it without a single building being destroyed and with a minimum of human suffering.

> Stage three, Operation Small Change, involves you, Dr. Fountain. In short, we need your expertise. Humanity needs your expertise. A viral incapacitating agent such as we have been describing is useless without a cure or a vaccine. We possess neither of these. Although President Tynee has assured us that you would be glad to provide your services, we prefer to allow you to decide. At the time of a decision in the affirmative, you will be fully debriefed and allowed access to our records and laboratories, as well as provided with luxurious and sequestered accommodations. Let us know of your decision via President Tynee.
>
> This letter is necessarily vague. It is not, however, news to any intelligence organization in the world. Suffice it to say that we are not the only nation developing such weapons. For your protection and reassurance, a team of agents has been watching your every move.
>
> The choice is yours, Dr. Fountain. Humanity anxiously awaits.

The memo was signed with the letters CPC, and carried a postscript a few lines down. It read: "P.S. Better living through genetics."

40 The letter left me both intrigued and apprehensive. I had a team of agents protecting me? Was I in danger? I strained my eyes into the darkness off my porch but could see no one lurking about. I attempted to reassure myself by noting that Meeko seemed relaxed, and surely he would sense another's presence nearby. But it was fast becoming impossible for me to think of anything but torrents of frightful scenarios fed by a lifetime of espionage movies. The state of mind that emerged within me was utterly unexpected and terrifying. I have since harbored nonfalsifiable suspicions that it was not entirely without psychotropic influence, given the activities of the CPC and their objectives concerning me. But this is conspiratorial conjecture.

As I recall, I began to panic when Meeko stirred and I imagined that he heard something across the street. I glanced around wildly, scanning the charcoal shadows, then thought better of it and inspected my body for the point of a laser sight. I was clean, it appeared, but then I realized that the point was probably on my head. I felt naked and wide open, and a nightmarish dread was crawling over me like all the roaches in hell, smothering my rational faculties. I tried to calm myself, and succeeded in forcing a smile onto my face when I mused that perhaps Blip's irrationality was contagious. I patted Meeko's side, and he thumped his tail appreciatively. Good dog, protecting your paranoid proprietor.

"You'll let me know if you smell anything, won't you, boy?" I said to him, loud and lightsome, but only succeeded in unnerving myself further by the agitated sound of my own quaking voice, greeted as it was by an antagonistic silence that stomped on my already tenuous grip on reality.

My imagination then suddenly threw an embarrassing temper tantrum, and I sat in a frightful paralysis, immobilized by panic, for the subjective hour or so that it took a single leaf, a pioneer of the coming autumn, to drift to the ground. At last, the hum of a distant car began to fill in the shrieking void. This gave me some brief comfort, but I soon realized that the car was getting louder, much, much louder, and coming closer. Presently, I saw its high-beam headlights glare into view as it turned the corner a couple of blocks away. It was on my street and would be passing my house any moment.

I had an impulse to race inside and hide under the covers, but acting on one's fears only makes things worse. So I stayed put, filled with horrific apprehension, tied with the terror that bound me to my chair, refusing to let the floodwaters of fright rising in my soul chase me to higher ground. It was an enormous effort, like holding on to a scalding plate until you get it to a table, but I was determined not to move until that car passed. Nothing less than my sanity seemed to be at stake. Afterward, in a few seconds, I would surely relax again and laugh at myself.

Meeko, irritated at the sound of the vehicle's broken exhaust system, lifted his head and growled as the car crossed the intersection onto my block. Human and canine, we shared a few moments of consciousness that night. The approaching car filled our perception. Its high beams lit up the entire street and the unmuffled combustion of the engine was like cinematic machine-gun fire over speakers with blown woofers. Meeko sat up as the car's noise increased. My heart was pounding and my stomach hurt, but then, glory be, the car was past my house.

Boom! A deafening blast knocked the wind out of the sigh of relief I was breathing. Meeko and I scrambled to our feet simultaneously. Our two brains, still operating at the same primal level, struggled savagely to make sense out of the noise that had confronted them. Meeko began barking madly, more ferociously than I'd ever seen him. Our few moments of shared consciousness were soon over, as I very quickly realized that the noise was just the car backfiring. This knowledge did nothing to quiet my pounding heart. Thinking I was the more rational species of the two of us, I took charge and calmed Meeko down, then went inside and telephoned Tynee at his office-apartment.

"President Tynee," I was still breathless, and my voice was trembling. "I want to be sequestered tonight. I've read the letter." Meeko began barking violently again, snarling at the door, giving rise to my own survival instincts once more. "Quiet!" I roared at Meeko, into the receiver.

"Take it easy," Tynee said calmly. "What's going on?"

"I think the team of agents might have lost me. I want to be sequestered tonight. I don't like this one bit, goddamnit!" Either I was losing my mind or I saw a movement outside the window.

"I'll make the arrangements. Hold on."

I held on. No, I thrashed and struggled furiously against the deranged quicksand of delusion sucking me into a pit of dread. I watched Meeko in horror as he sniffed and whined frantically at the door. I felt I was facing certain death. Violent death. Any moment my head could explode from a sniper's bullet, I kept thinking. What were my last words? Was it "goddamnit"? That can't be a good note to end on.

"Peace on Earth," I stammered aloud, just in case.

"What?" came Tynee's voice on the other end.

"Nothing. What's going on?"

"Someone will knock on your door any minute. Trust them. They will bring you in safely." Tynee was remarkably cordial, even hospitable, in his tone. In retrospect, it strikes me as suspicious that he was not the least bit irritated or alarmed at my desperate state.

"Okay," I said tentatively, like a child promising to stop crying if given a lollipop. "Is that it?"

"That's it."

"Is there a code word or anything?"

"No, that's it. I'll talk to you again in the morning."

"All right." I hung up the phone, somewhat disappointed that I wasn't to be privy to a secret knock.

The Book o' Billets-doux

rosehips: I have a riddle for you. What does everyone have in common that they can never share?

sweetlick: That's easy. The recognition that we really have nothing in common. But wait, have we stumbled across a paradox?

rosehips: You speak nonsense, my lovely! We have much in common. Our genes are all but identical, remember? It is only our sense of self that we think is unique, and that notion is impossible to verify. Upon reflection, however, I suppose you are close.

sweetlick: Nonsense? Certainly. As a linguistic representation, how could it be otherwise?

rosehips: Have you the answer to the riddle?

sweetlick: See, a paradox is only a contradiction of the conditions. Change the conditions and you'll exorcise the paradox.

rosehips: You can't expect to change the subject in written communication. We must focus here. The answer may be a clue in our quest.

sweetlick: Subjects change themselves, I'm afraid. They can only be controlled by an enormous effort of will. Conversing is best an experience rather than an activity. The answer will turn up.

rosehips: No it won't. You at least have to look for something before you can declare that it will turn up.

sweetlick: Specious monkeybusiness! You bring a smile to my face, sweet babe-a-la-pook-a-la-co-co-pow, but enough of this. Come now, I give up. What's the answer?

rosehips: You can't give up! That's like committing suicide to discover the purpose of life. The purpose is the process. A riddle demands attention and mindfulness. Ponder your paradox. Answers will come when the time is right.

sweetlick: Of course you're correct. The meaning of life is revealed at death. Oop! There it is, it turned up, just as I said. Death is what we have in common that cannot be shared. Your riddle is good, but the paradox will remain until conditions are changed, or until death becomes irrelevant, or as we discover, one by one, that death is shared after all.

41

The next thing I remember is waking up like some luxurious lush, naked and hungover, nestled between silk sheets that did nothing to soothe my vomitous headache. I was in an enormous room decorated in an exaggerated Southwestern desert style. Though I did not appear to be anywhere near a desert, an assortment of cacti filled every corner of the room and occupied the surfaces of the nightstand, desk, and dresser. A tumbleweed bouquet graced the center of the table, set in a vase that matched the angular, zigzag artwork of the Navajo blanket on my bed. The table itself sat under a wagon wheel chandelier, and a variety of American Indian and Western ghost town bric-a-brac decorated the walls. Meeko was sitting on a deck outside, dutifully sniffing at the deciduous forest beyond, and a clamorous chorus of songbirds and insects drifted in along a glaring sunbeam that stretched across the foot of my king-size bed. I sat up and retched.

I located my clothes from the day before, freshly washed, pressed, and folded neatly on a chair across the room. Seeing I was awake, Meeko trotted inside and trailed me happily about the room as I inspected my new accommodations. The bathroom was equipped with a combination whirlpool/shower, a deep-bowl, splatter-proof toilet, a sink I could have taken a bath in, and a dressing room mirror framed by incandescent bulbs. As I flicked the light switch, soft strains of rhythmless music assaulted my throbbing head. I flipped the switch off and on again experimentally, noting that the music followed suit, and feeling a bit like an ape gruntingly examining some new causal connection.

A curiously familiar rap sounded at the door to the suite. "Yes?" I croaked, then cleared my throat and called out again.

"Good morning, Doctor," came a woman's aggressive voice, also familiar. "May I enter?"

"Um," I faltered, extraordinarily confused. "Who are you?"

"Agent Mella Orange, Doctor. Your personal bodyguard. We met last night."

Anxious to make sense of my lavishly fake surroundings, as well as the apparent bender and resulting blackout I'd had last night, I opened the door. Before me stood a woman of about six feet in height, with dark, shrewd eyes, deep brown skin, and long hair, tightly braided into a rough-and-tumble heap of medusan locks. She was dressed completely in black, and carried a pistol on her hip. She was the most potent woman I had ever laid eyes upon, both physically erotic and maternally intimidating, and could doubtless have fought off a circle of attackers while nursing an infant.

"President Tynee has asked me to inform you that he would like you to join him for breakfast soon." She was perfectly motionless but for her serpentine eyes, scanning the room warily, and finally coming to rest on me. "He told me to tell you that the kitchen has made your favorite, Italian toast."

"Italian toast? How did they know that was my favorite?"

"Your account at the Faculty Club was analyzed to identify your preference patterns."

"Oh." I crossed my arms in defensive privacy, feeling like she had just jerked my shirt off.

"We've also arranged for a new wardrobe to be delivered by tomorrow based on purchases made to catalogs found in your home."

I stood dumbfounded a moment, my pants just having been yanked off as well. "I can't recall anything after phoning Tynee last night."

"I'm surprised you can recall that. You were exhibiting symptoms of anxiety when I arrived, so I gave you a sedative. It results in short-term memory loss, as well as general malaise the following day."

"Jesus. Did you happen to mention that to me last night?"

"No, Doctor. For security purposes, it was necessary to eradicate your recollection of this sanctuary's location."

"What?" I asked calmly, though I felt sure I should be angry.

"It is my job to guarantee your security, Doctor. I use every device available toward that end. The sedation was mandatory, as was the body cavity search." Agent Mella Orange spoke with martial precision. "I have never lost a client."

"Body cavity search?"

"Yes, Doctor." She gazed down at me in supreme authority, completing her degradation ceremony by giving me a swift wedgie with her words. "You'll be happy to hear that you were not carrying any tracers."

42

I sat at the end of a gargantuan table, alone, waiting for a man who tolerated tardiness about as much as an infant tolerates hunger. I picked at my gourmet Italian toast, which was in truth French toast. There is, so far as I know, no generally acknowledged toast called Italian toast. My father, however, who was one-eighth Sicilian on his mother's side but acted as if he were Mario Lanza, taught me from an early age that French toast was called Italian toast. It was not until I spent the night at a friend's house when I was nine that I discovered, upon politely asking for another piece of Italian toast, that the rest of the country called my favorite breakfast French toast. My request was greeted with laughter, which succeeded in shaming me into adopting the culturally accepted label for bread sopped in eggs and milk and fried.

Much to my chagrin, however, my father's designation was

deeply imprinted, and unless I make a conscious point, I often slip and ask for Italian toast. When this happens I merely relate the story behind my confusion to the waitperson or whomever and usually get a courteous laugh. I can order Italian toast with impunity at the Faculty Club, as all the waiters and waitresses are familiar with the anecdote.

Whatever it's called, I wasn't enjoying it. I sat there joylessly, trying to imagine the chain of communication that led to Agent Mella Orange informing me that Italian toast was being served for breakfast. It appeared as though someone had not only examined my account to discern my likes and dislikes, but also must have interviewed the employees concerning my quirks and idiosyncrasies. The strangest thing was not necessarily the suffocating pampering I was being subjected to, or even the gross invasions of privacy. It was that it was actually somebody's job to build a culinary dossier on me. Someone had interviewed the waitstaff, asking if I always finished my coffee or if there was anything else they could recall, and then noting as significant and important the fact that I sometimes forget what French toast is correctly called.

In any case, there is one dining room detail that person somehow overlooked. Raised in the suburban cul-de-sacs of consumerism and suckled on the vapid teet of television, the buxom blather of the boob tube, I have always detested pure maple syrup.

43

At last Tynee entered the dining room, accompanied by a formally dressed waiter whose steroidal size more properly matched the immensity of the table. "Dr. Fountain!" Tynee greeted me as he traversed the length of the table, requiring twice as many strides as his muscly maître d'. "Glad to see you've recovered from your ordeal last night." Upon completion of the trek, Tynee extended his hand to shake mine. Reluctantly, I stood up and he shook my hand like we were old classmates at a reunion just about to say the hell with it and give each other a backslapping hug. Thankfully, embraces were not forthcoming.

"Enjoying your *Italian* toast, I hope?" He snapped his fingers at the waiter, who placed two covered platters on the table, one in front of Tynee and the other off to the side. At Tynee's nod he removed the lids with as much flair as his muscle-bound physique would allow, revealing a plate of French toast for Tynee and an inexplicable cucumber and celery stalk on the other.

"*Italian* toast all around, eh, Doctor?" Tynee laughed and lifted his plate slightly. He glanced at my plate of cold, soggy, but gourmet French toast. "Is everything okay with your *Italian* toast?"

"To tell you the truth," I said, deciding to take full advantage of my coddling situation, "I don't really care for pure maple syrup. I prefer regular grocery store syrup, you know, high-fructose corn syrup and preservatives, with artificial maple flavoring."

"Not a problem." He looked up at the waiter. "Volt, do you have anything like that in the kitchen?"

The mesomorphic tower of muscular obsession spoke with a jarring French accent. "I am afraid not, sir. My keetchen *eez* a gourmet keetchen. I use only zee finest ingredients."

"Well, find a way to get some!" Tynee reverted to his usual commanding tone.

"Of course." Volt the Waiter and Chef bowed and strode quickly out the door.

Tynee beamed obsequiously at me once again and poured some pure maple syrup on his French toast. "So where were we, Doctor?"

I looked at him blankly, for we had not yet discussed anything more substantial than French toast and syrup. "Well, I'm concerned about a few things."

He waved me off and seized the vegetables off the second tray, clutching the cucumber in one hand and the celery in the other. "You and I have a lot in common, Doctor," he said, holding the vegetables before him ponderously, as if perhaps we were both salad tossings.

"How's that?"

"We thought we'd humor you this morning with Italian toast, but in all honesty, I have the same problem, only with me it's cucumbers and celery." He placed them back on the tray, sporting a sneery grin as if he'd just told a dirty joke.

"I'm not sure I understand."

"I can't get it straight either. I'll be talking about this," he pointed to the cucumber, "and I'll call it celery. And vice versa."

"How about that."

Tynee nodded, pausing to take a bite of his French toast. "I suppose it doesn't really matter. After all, words are just arbitrary designations, right? As long as at least two people agree on what's called what, words work just fine." He took another bite. "Mmm, I'll tell you what though." He slapped me on the shoulder, now that we were comrades in confusion, I suppose. "This is the finest I-talian toast I've ever had."

44 I should mention at this point that I had not yet decided whether I would actually take the assignment. I only agreed to be sequestered at the sanctuary for my peace of mind. I'm a scientist, after all, and we aren't generally known for our courage.

I finally managed to express my reservations and grievances toward the end of breakfast, or rather, when Tynee was finishing his, for although I'd gotten my Aunt Jemima and a fresh order of French toast, I had the appetite of a crapulent mortician. In between gurgles of bald nausea, I complained that the cloak-and-dagger escapades were a little unusual for an academic project. I didn't like being followed, or knowing that I might be in danger, and I especially didn't like being drugged. I also told him, in so many words, that I felt like I had pushed the concept of a hangover to a heretofore unsuspected level of misery.

Ignoring everything but my last sentiment, Tynee smiled his dirty-joke smirk again. "Right. I heard all about you last night."

"What?"

"Agent Orange debriefed us. I must say, I had no idea a professor like you could be so, how shall I say, licentious."

"What are you talking about?" I demanded, feeling anger at last. "I can't remember a damn thing about last night."

Tynee forced the smile from his face. "I'm sorry, Doctor, but the sedative was necessary. This is a top-secret project we're involved in."

"Top secret? Does that mean I have no privacy? Come on, the kitchen knows all the details of my eating habits?"

"Of course it means you have no privacy," Tynee interjected. "And anyway, I'm surprised you don't recognize Volt. He's been working at the Faculty Club for the past few weeks, keeping an eye on you ever since you were identified as a candidate for this project."

"What?" I said, flustered and shirtless once again. "What about ordering me a new wardrobe? What's that all about?"

"Agent Orange gathered that information last night, although she had a difficult time of it with you all over her." Tynee flashed his locker room grin once again.

"I suppose strip-searching me was necessary as well?"

"The body cavity search," Tynee made a point to clarify, "was necessary only during your initial entry. Henceforth, you'll always have an escort in and out, and no more sedatives either. I guarantee."

"Wait a minute," I challenged, fumbling as I pulled out my purple envelope. "It says here that a team of agents was watching my every move."

"Yes?"

I leaned forward. "I was in the passenger seat of a car yesterday driven by a maniac at over 100 miles an hour. How was whoever the hell supposedly watching me then?"

Tynee looked at me, expressionless. "You're going to have to elaborate your point."

"I'm saying I think this is bullshit!" I began to raise my voice. "I'm in no danger, and no one has been watching me. Jesus!" I threw up my hands, befuddled and belligerent. "How do I know I haven't been slipped other drugs? How do I know this isn't all a setup to make me paranoid to get me to agree to come here and work on this project?"

Tynee smiled as if I was suddenly the butt of his raunchy ha-has. "Remember that riot you witnessed on the Green yesterday?" He creased his brow derisively, the furrow forming a wishbone above his nose. I wished he would shut up.

"How did you know I was there?"

"Do you think I have stealth helicopters patrolling campus preachers, Fountain? The CPC was watching you then, and they were watching you when you were on the freeway."

I slumped back in my chair, beaten into submission, save for one last punch-drunken swing. "What if I refuse to work on this project . . . on ethical grounds?"

Tynee's face darkened, as if he had just belted back a shot of some mad scientist's Jekyll and Hyde cocktail. His lickspittle grin became a hurlspittle sneer. "You'll be released," he growled. "Not only from this sanctuary, but from any employment opportunities at any educational institution in this hemisphere. I'll see to it that the only job you'll be able to get will be teaching high school biology to a bunch of oily-faced teenagers who'll shoot spitballs and small firearms at your head when your back is turned." Tynee pulled another purple envelope out of his jacket and handed it to me. "On the other hand," he relaxed and regained his diplomatic composure, "if you do accept, the CPC will provide you with room and board here at Valhalla Acres, and remunerate you generously for your services."

The envelope contained a cashier's check written in the amount of ten million dollars. My research stipend, Tynee called it.

I agreed to work on Operation Small Change wholeheartedly that morning, and despite any hang-ups or hangover, I was smiling like a Cheshire cat on laughing gas.

45

After breakfast, Tynee escorted me back to my suite, where we waited on the patio with Meeko to meet with the head of the CPC. He was part Italian too, Tynee told me, although he referred to his French toast by the traditional moniker.

As we were talking, the door to the suite opened and a spotted but husky old man marched in. He was General Veechy Kiljoy, the chairman of the CPC. His face was hard enough to deflect a cannonball, and his stride could have sprained the hamstrings of a kangaroo.

"General, come in!" Tynee said with an outstretched arm. Meeko scrambled toward the door to greet the new person. This consisted of frantically sniffing General Kiljoy, and thrusting his nose between the overstarched trouser legs of the general's military uniform.

"Hey there, fella!" General Kiljoy bellowed like artillery fire. "You don't need to be checking if *I* have balls! See these stars?"

"Meeko!" I commanded. "Kapow!" Meeko sat obediently, and I explained that I had been in the habit of watching old *Batman* reruns when I'd adopted him, and so had trained him using the onomatopoeias that covered the screen whenever a punch or kick was thrown.

"Is that right?" General Kiljoy marveled, looking at Meeko in amazement. "Whammo!" he yelled, punching the air in front of him. Meeko cocked his head in canine confusion.

"He doesn't know that word."

"He doesn't, huh?" General Kiljoy put his hands in his pockets and idly began playing with his privates, a practice that turned out to be a nearly constant habit of his. "What words does he know?"

"Try B-I-F-F," I offered. "That's how you get him to shake."

"B-I-F-F?" he repeated, as if we were spelling out C-A-N-D-Y in front of a four-year-old. He looked down at Meeko, who was still sitting obediently, and swung an uppercut, yelling, "Biff!" Meeko pawed at the air, and General Kiljoy shook hands with my dog.

"That's very interesting how you trained your dog, Doctor." Tynee stepped forward. "But I'm sure General Kiljoy is anxious to get our meeting started."

"I'm anxious for you to keep your pink panties on, Tibor." General Kiljoy motioned Tynee back, then looked at me again. "Can he play dead?" he asked hopefully. "Does he know how to play dead?"

"Just say B-A-N-G."

General Kiljoy smiled, then made a gun with his hand and pointed the index finger barrel at Meeko. "Bang!" he hollered. "Bang! Bang!"

46

Tynee and I returned to the patio to wait for General Kiljoy, who was having a grand time pretending to shoot my dog. Meeko, for his part, yelped and threw himself down again and again, wagging his tail like he had just hijacked the gravy train. If only all animals could be so joyous when they're shot at.

The two of them joined us after a bit, both panting heavily. "Whooee, Doctor. You got yourself a fine hound." Meeko sat next to him, gazing up in hopeless devotion. Anyone who paid any attention at all to Meeko won his friendship immediately, even when they made believe they were killing him.

"He is something." Tynee leaned forward and patted Meeko

on the back. "But Dr. Fountain here, well, he can do more than a few clever tricks." He patted me on the back, too.

General Kiljoy studied me as if I were a teenager taking his only daughter out on a date. I smirked pubescently and shifted in my seat. "You come highly recommended, Doctor. I hope you consider our offer seriously."

"Not to worry, General," Tynee gleefully interrupted. "Dr. Fountain agreed to work on Operation Small Change at breakfast this morning."

My smirk broadened into an all-out goofy grin, shamelessly excessive. I still had a buzz from the check I'd received.

"Well, well." General Kiljoy looked at me in genuine astonishment. "Congratulations! Welcome to the millionaires' club!" He extended his hand to shake mine, but tightened his grasp prematurely, thus catching only my fingers in his bruising grip. He let go immediately, homophobic disgust coloring his bellicose features. "I'll be damned, though," he said, wiping his hand on his jacket. "I thought you'd be a harder nut to crack."

"No . . ." was all I could think to say.

47

"Let's get down to business then." General Kiljoy slapped his knees. "What we have created is the ideal incapacitating agent, just as you read in the letter."

"An incapacitating, nonterminating agent," Tynee echoed.

"This sort of research," General Kiljoy talked over him, "you may or may not know, has been going on since World War II. As we said, it originally focused on chemical incapacitants, but these always presented problems. It was impossible to guarantee dosage, so they were very unreliable in their effects and duration. The biggest issue, however, was that they required the dropping of a bomb, or at least spraying by planes, and hence were not terribly covert. Contaminating the water supply had its problems as well, since the presence of chlorine, fertilizer, and other water pollutants often reacted with the incapacitating compound. Our viral incapacitant has none of these problems."

"How does it work?" I asked, truly curious.

"You're gonna love this," Tynee bubbled.

"What are we doing right now?" General Kiljoy asked, squinting his eyes mysteriously.

I looked at him, then at Tynee, who was wearing a smile that would mortify a clown. "Sitting on a porch in the woods?"

"Yes," he nodded, "but what else? What are you taking for granted?"

"Breathing?"

"No, well yes, but that's not what I have in mind."

I paused, thinking, but Tynee could no longer keep the answer from kicking its way out of his mouth. "Talking!" he bawled. "We're talking!"

"Goddamnit!" General Kiljoy barked. "Would you keep your trap shut?" Meeko, sensing his new friend was angry, growled at Tynee, who slumped back in his chair with an affected scowl over a satisfied smirk.

"Talking," General Kiljoy continued, looking at me. "What our virus, we've called it the Pied Piper," he chuckled, "what the Pied Piper virus does is take away a person's ability to talk. It's not like laryngitis, where a person can still write and understand what others say. When a person is infected with the Pied Piper virus, their entire *symbolic capacity* is eliminated on the cognitive level. They lose the ability to use and understand symbols, language, words, so that what we are doing right now," he gestured around the three of us, "becomes absolutely impossible."

"Isn't that ingenious?" Tynee squealed. I later learned that it was Tynee's innovation to attack the problem from a genetic rather than chemical standpoint.

"Symbolic capacity?"

"We're referring specifically to *shared* symbols, any designation that at least two people agree upon," Tynee explained. "Like *Italian* toast, for instance. Any word, sign, gesture, or color that we agree means something. The Pied Piper virus removes the ability to share symbols. Society isn't made out of bricks and mortar, it's made out of shared symbols. Without communication, an enemy nation would, in a very real sense, disappear."

General Kiljoy continued, smiling with irrepressible pride. "Now, if we were at war with another nation, and if we were to destroy every individual's symbolic capacity, that society would immediately cease to exist. If one person can't communicate with another, they can't coordinate their actions. The ultimate infrastructure of their society is obliterated, without a single building, bridge, or railroad being destroyed."

"Or a single person being hurt," I added.

"Naturally." General Kiljoy was quite excited, and was rubbing Meeko's belly in such a way as to cause him to kick one of his rear legs spasmodically. "What we like to say is," he leaned forward and did his best impression of a Grand Inquisitor, "we have ways of making you *not* talk."

48 "The Pied Piper virus has been created?" I asked. My prosperity buzz was fast reverting to nausea as I realized the implications of what General Kiljoy was saying.

"Affirmative." General Kiljoy crossed his thick arms.

I glanced over at Tynee, who was sitting on his hands in what seemed like an effort to keep his mouth shut. "You've been using human subjects?" I asked, loath to look directly at General Kiljoy.

"Prisoners, actually," General Kiljoy responded, making no effort to conceal the truth from me. "Primarily death row inmates. Naturally, it would have been impossible to develop the Pied Piper virus without observing the symptoms in humans, not to mention enhancing its infectiousness." He eyed me evenly. "The only reason I'm being so frank with you is because of the role you must play in Operation Small Change."

"How do you mean?"

"Come now, Doctor. Do you think that every one of the tens of thousands of people who have contributed to this project over the years was privileged to what I've just told you? This project is much bigger than any individual. People have known only what was relevant to their task. You're receiving these details because of the nature of your task, which, incidentally, you share with a few others. As new research and findings emerge, details are shared between relevant researchers. No one knows any more than they have to, and no one knows who else is involved. Unfortunately, this system of secrecy has its drawbacks. Because so many people have contributed to the development of the Pied Piper virus without knowing what they were doing or what our ultimate goal was, we've created something that no one individual fully understands. Until it is understood, we will be unable to develop a cure. That's why we're providing access to all available data and history concerning the Pied Piper virus to a few select scientists."

"What happened to the prisoners who were infected?" I asked, unable to hide my concern.

"They're being kept underground in supermaximum security. They're at varying stages of the disease." He sensed my next question and continued. "It is just as we assured you, Doctor. The Pied Piper virus is not a terminating agent. The illness doesn't directly result in death. At this point, however, it does permanently alter a person's neurochemistry, and that's why we need you. That's why your country needs you."

"You want me to find the cure for this disease you've created?"

"Or at least a vaccine. And by the way, Doctor, don't think of it as a disease. A disease, it seems to me, ultimately consumes its host or is eliminated or kept under control by the immune system. The Pied Piper virus permanently alters the genetic structure and function of the neurons of very specific regions of the brain. Think of it as gene therapy."

"Gene therapy? Therapy for what?"

"For warfare," he replied. I rolled my eyes involuntarily, overcome with impatience at his ludicrous reasoning. He narrowed his eyebrows and continued. "I realize how tempting it is to get hung up on the ethics of this project, Doctor, but I need you to make your best effort to see the big picture, the potential for good. So try to understand the strategic necessity of what I'm about to tell you." General Kiljoy stood up, hands in his pockets, frolicking to and fro. "You may not agree with the methods we've employed, but we need to be certain that you're with us 100 percent." He pulled a notepad from his inside breast pocket. "I've been informed that a close friend of yours is in custody. The owner of the speeding car you were in yesterday, Blip Korterly?"

"What about him?"

"For your motivational purposes, understand, we're having him conscripted into the human subjects pool."

49

After incapacitating *my* linguistic capacity with his flaunting display of malevolence, General Kiljoy wished me a nice day (without shaking my hand). Tynee walked him to the door, where they spoke in hushed tones for a few moments. General Kiljoy appeared angry at Tynee. At one point, he poked his trigger finger into Tynee's breastbone. Tynee returned, massaging his chest.

"You brought that on yourself, Fountain," Tynee reprimanded. "'What happened to the prisoners who were infected?'" he mocked my hesitance.

"How could you get me involved in this?" I demanded.

"What the hell is that?" Tynee scoffed at me in dismissal. "Are you trying to assert yourself or something?"

"These are human subjects. Don't you realize how unethical this is?"

Tynee faced me, odium fleering from his nostrils. "Ethics? These are prisoners, death row inmates, burdens to society. They owe a debt to society, a debt which may be forgiven through their participation. Consider it debt reduction."

"What?" I asked incredulously.

"Listen." Tynee's nostrils flared again, slinging slugs of spite my way. "Military ethics are pragmatic by necessity. The Manhattan Project ended World War II and saved thousands of American lives. People are counting on you. And besides, you've already agreed to participate. The CPC," he gestured toward the door, "is paying you a hell of a lot of money. Ethics depends on context, and in this context there are over a hundred men, soon to include a friend of yours, imprisoned underground with an incurable disease, no, an incurable gene therapy . . . condition. Regardless of how they got it, you can help them." He passed General Kiljoy's poke my way by jabbing me in the chest. "If you don't, *you're* the unethical one."

"An ethical means to an unethical end?"

"I don't think you understand, Fountain. Unless you cooperate, you're now a breach of national security. That means you can be shot. Or better yet, just to make sure you don't talk about this to anyone, they could throw you into the tank with the rest of the guinea pigs." Tynee paused a moment. "Just do your job. If you're so concerned about ethics, where's your work ethic?"

50

Any rationalization implies that the action doesn't flow from your values. Sophia's statement of yesterday recollected itself as the realization of my own greed emerged from the shadows, put its thumbs in its ears, and wagged its fingers and tongue at me. In defense of sacrificing commonsense ethics for self-interest, I've since tried to explain to Sophia in countless make-believe conversations that I would do good with the money. "I'll be a benefactor," I protested, "a philanthropist. Look at all the wealthy people who don't do good with their money."

"Why do you think that is?" Sophia smiled patiently, persistent in her quixotic notions. "They don't get that money by doing right, by being nice. That's the nature of money. You can only collect it by hoarding it."

"But who am I to say what others will do with my research?"

"First of all, it's *their* research. You're just a tool, an intellectual extension of their selfish intent. At what point are you prostituting yourself?" She executed a less-than-perfect pirouette, delightful nonetheless for its honesty of expression, like the raspy, cannabis-strained voice of a blues musician who can't quite hit all the notes but reaches for them with supreme confidence of spirit anyway. "Besides," she balanced herself, "you already know what it's for."

"But if I don't do it someone else will."

"Most likely," she granted, bowing graciously. "But at least it won't be you. You only have responsibility for your actions, for your decisions. Only you live inside your head. Only you have to confront your self-image."

"Okay. So what if someone took something you wrote and used it to a negative end?"

"That sort of thing happens all the time," she said with sad exasperation. Her smile faded like a flower closing in the face of the night, weary, guarded, but ready to smile once again at the slightest hint of sunshine, never failing to trust that the Earth will turn, as is its way. "Look at the Crusades, or the Inquisition. The Bible didn't cause that. The message was twisted to serve selfish interests. And besides, I have to be confident that my intentions are good. Are yours, or are they selfish? Are you just looking for a license to be greedy?" I frowned, and she continued maternally. "Don't think this is some unique circumstance. This same situation plays itself out again and again every time an idealistic youth replaces their hope and their values with practicality, and an obsolete society convinces another generation that everything's working just fine."

I rolled my eyes at her histrionics. "How am I responsible for the situation of the world? I'm just trying to do the best I can."

"For the world or for yourself?" she replied, unoffended and compassionate. "Forgive me for sharing the hardships of ethical action with you. I know it would be easier to just do your job, watch TV, and not consider such things." She reached forward and gave my forehead a gentle shove. "What was your first impulse in this situation?"

"Not to do it."

"Well, there you are. That's Truth. Don't lie to yourself. Who do you think you're kidding, anyway? You don't respect people you lie to, and you don't respect people who lie to you. Look where you leave yourself. No matter which way you turn it, you'll have no self-respect. Of course you can make yourself cozy with creature comforts, but what kind of creature will you be?"

"Aha!" I exclaimed in my sixth or seventh rehearsal of this confabulation. "If I were to follow my instincts, I would have kissed you the moment I met you." I congratulated myself on this reply, imaginary though it was. Sophia, however, wasn't the least bit flustered, or if she was, she immediately pretended not to be, quite like a feline in this regard.

"Perhaps you should have," she said, "or at least let me know that you would have liked to. At least then the interaction could have proceeded honestly and openly." She winked at me. "I thought you were acting weird when we met. You only made yourself awkward by trying to suppress the truth."

"So I should have kissed you?"

"Not at all," she snickered. "There are other less intimate ways to express admiration and affection. A warm smile, a bow. To have actually kissed me would have only made me uncomfortable. So we have a qualification: Trust your instincts to the extent that you don't disturb others. Your example doesn't change what I'm saying." Sophia leaned forward and kissed the top of my head as if tucking me in to bed. "Make the right decisions," she counseled, a smile unfurling on her face like a frond after the final frost. With this straightforward wisdom, she disappeared from my imagination, but not before slipping me a dandelion for luck and sweet dreams.

51 Ethical conduct is like parachuting. It's easier to daydream about it than to do it. Imagining it even gives me a thrill, a windblown rush of vicarious morality, a self-righteous confidence that I could do it if I really had to. However, in this situation, I had no parachute, nor even a plane, though I had no idea that an entire squadron was just beyond the horizon and heading my way. But having no real choice now, my conscience had no objections to pursuing my assignment. I was comfortable with the trusty conditional that I *would* have made the right decision, if only I could have.

After convincing myself thus and neutralizing any moral willies, I decided to learn what I could about the Pied Piper virus. My colleagues and family, none of whom I was particularly close to, had been informed that I had taken a research sabbatical. I was thereby free to spend the next week reviewing volumes of existing data and research on the virus. I found myself an eager, if not drooling, pupil once I got started. It was far too captivating to stop, and any moments of guilt were immediately overwhelmed by the allure of seeing more. This was forbidden information, after all, and I felt like I was peeping through a keyhole while voluptuous secrets unveiled themselves, engorging me with uninhibited curiosity.

This is what I learned. The Pied Piper virus was so named because of its origin. A fossilized specimen of a previously unknown virus was extracted from corpses found in an anthropological dig covertly sponsored by the CPC in Hamelin, Germany (the alleged location of the Pied Piper's legendary parade in 1284). This provided the raw genetic material from which the Pied Piper virus was eventually engineered.

Finding the DNA fossil was not mere good fortune. Rather, it was precisely the goal of the excavation. Medical historians have argued that the Pied Piper myth has some basis in fact and may reflect an outbreak of an enigmatic medieval malady known as the Dancing Plague, or Saint Vitus' Dance. Apparently, the Dancing Plague swept through human populations in epidemic proportions with some regularity from the eleventh through the sixteenth centuries, especially in Germany. Its symptoms were widespread mania, furious dancing and raving, convulsive chorea, and irresistible hilarity. Hallucinations were also common, and in some cases dancers claimed to have seen the Virgin Mary or, less frequently, God. If this was the case, neither vision was particularly puritanical, as hordes of tranced-out dancers often overtook entire cities, sometimes engaging in orgiastic revelry of bacchanalian proportions. Indeed, in Cologne in 1374, more than one thousand women reportedly became pregnant as a result of the Dancing Plague.

These hysterical processions of elemental humanity frequently continued for days, lasting until the afflicted finally collapsed in stark exhaustion or died as a result of their unrestrained recklessness. In one instance in Utrecht in 1278, over two hundred people perished when a mob of dancers tapped, twisted, hopped, and stomped on a bridge until it collapsed under the sheer force of their collective energy. When people survived these plagues of dance and debauchery, however, they awoke from their footsore slumber perfectly normal. Although doctors and priests of the day argued that the Dancing Plague was a form of demonic possession resulting from invalid baptisms performed by corrupt clergy, many survivors nevertheless claimed catharsis, and that they were healed of other ailments.

This healing aspect introduces some confusion between Saint Vitus' Dance and Saint John's Dance. Saint John's Dance was a healing dance performed on each solstice, with origins in European paganism. The Church designated Saint John's Day to coincide with the solstice as an effective method of assimilating the nature worshippers' beliefs into the pantheon of Christian saints. The mass insanity associated with the Dancing Plague was mistaken for epilepsy, and Saint John the Baptist was thus dubbed the protector of epileptics. This was all very fascinating to me, but the most astounding aspect was that the Saint John's Dance processions were led by (and I shudder to utter such a coincidence) a piper.

The two events I mentioned above, in Utrecht and Cologne, occurred around Saint John's Day. This has led some religious scholars to suggest that the dance was actually a manifestation of reactionary paganism in a time of oppressive Christianity. In other words, newly immoral pagan rites could only exist legitimately under the guise of disease. There were, however, cases of the Dancing Plague that did not coincide with the solstice. In Zabera in 1418, a swarm of the dancing helpless were supposedly cured when they rushed into a chapel and fell down before an image of Saint Vitus sitting in a cauldron (it is rumored that he survived being boiled in molten lead). Thus did protection from the Dancing Plague become Saint Vitus' responsibility. In addition to this considerable task, good Saint Vitus is also the patron saint of Bohemia, as well as of actors and dancers, and is invoked to protect from dog attacks, snakebites, and oversleeping.

By whomever's appellation the saintly prance goes by, the purported causes were all incomplete. In addition to the already-mentioned explanations, the Dancing Plague is sometimes attributed to mass hysteria. This is tautological nonsense, and is akin to saying darkness causes night. A more intriguing explanation is that it was a reaction of the collective unconscious against the miserable realities of pestilence, crop failures, and famines, as well as the horror of the Black Death, a contemporary of the Dancing Plague known to have killed half the population of Europe and Asia. In such grim circumstances, as the theory goes, spontaneous outbursts of wild celebration would take hold of the population and sweep across the countryside as a sort of emotional release. This sounds plausible, and was probably involved at some level for some people, but there was also an organic cause.

Since the symptoms of the Dancing Plague seemed promising for incapacitation purposes, potential organic causes were exhaustively researched by the CPC. In Italy and Arabia, where the phenomenon was called tarantism (after the town of Taranto in southern Italy), it was attributed to the bite of the Lycosa tarantula, which was thriving due to the deforestation of the Apulian region of Italy and its consequent hot and dry climate. This explanation, however, does not account for the massive scale the Dancing Plague sometimes achieved. Other theories argued that the widespread mental illness was due to ergot poisoning. Ergot is a fungus that grows on some grains, prevalent when the spring is especially wet. When consumed, it causes hallucinations and bizarre muscle spasms, induces abortions, and in those who are vitamin A deficient, makes their fingers and toes turn gangrenous and fall off. The ergot theory has also been invoked to explain the Salem witch trials. Both theories have some intrinsic validity. Compounds have been derived both from spider venom and a variety of fungi that can elicit muscle spasms and extreme mental confusion. As already mentioned, however, all of these compounds were eventually dismissed in the search for the ideal incapacitant.

The ideal incapacitant, of course, is the Pied Piper virus. As it turns out, the spider-bite theory was probably partially correct, insofar as the spider was the vector that introduced the virus into the human population. In any case, the virus that caused the Dancing Plague has undergone extensive renovation since the Middle Ages. In its unaltered form, it was not terribly infectious or chronic, and transmission was most likely blood borne. Hence, assuming an individual was exposed via a spider bite, the virus still required a further vector to reach epidemic dimensions. This most likely occurred through the local food or water supply. Consequently, dancing plagues in the Middle Ages tended to have a limited range, sweeping across villages rather than across nations or continents. The largest estimate of those afflicted at one time was eleven hundred. Thus, while impressive in its incapacitating capabilities, from a military standpoint its contagion was inadequate.

Enter influenza, a virus whose virulence scoffs at all attempts to shield oneself. In terms of its sheer speed of transmission and the spine-sapping power of its grip, it is the superlative pestilential presence on our planet. Contagious by breath-borne droplets and via animals such as birds, the tiny influenza myxovirus is behind one of our planet's most horrific and awe-inspiring phenomena. Influenza epidemics trot the globe annually, and a few times a century a pandemic emerges that infects most, if not all, of the world's population at once. These blitzkriegs are possible because of the virus's characteristic genetic instability. Proteins on its shell undergo slow but constant genetic change, rendering any acquired immunity obsolete. Essentially, it becomes unrecognizable by our immune systems as soon as it puts on a new outfit, or even changes a single accessory.

Influenza was named by eighteenth-century Italians who blamed it on the *influence* of heavenly bodies. And indeed, there is a curious correlation between influenza pandemics and sunspot activity. Possibly, increased solar radiation from solar flares triggers mutations that rapidly transform the surface of the virus into something our immune systems haven't experienced. Thus, we get the flu again and again, immunological virgins every time.

Influenza is not to be trusted. By changing its face, it seduces its way past our defenses, a vengeful Svengali with an infectious charisma. In 1918–1919, the virus swept the globe in three successive waves, killing millions, many of them young adults. It asserted itself with such a presence that World War I was nearly canceled due to the difficulty of waging war with everyone sick. In the United States alone, flu casualties outnumbered battle casualties by ten to one. The most modest estimates state that it killed 21.6 million people worldwide, more than twice as many as were killed in all of World War I. Coincidentally or not, the disease faded soon after the signing of the armistice that ended the war.

Influenza and the Dancing Plague, linking and merging, intertwining and recombining. The sum of this union came to be known as the Pied Piper virus, and it was something altogether different from either of its ancestors. It was "a humane weapon capable of contagious incapacitation," or so said the mission statement. It was a hybrid pattern spliced and tweaked to be chronic, more infectious, and more maddening than either of its predecessors. Its acute symptoms, relapses of gut-yanking hilarity and a mild pulmonary edema, serve to launch billions of copies of the virus into the local atmosphere. What is more, the virus could last up to two days outside of an organism before disintegrating, an impressive achievement given that most viruses dehydrate and break down within hours.

Genetically speaking, the Pied Piper virus was a work of art, though more in the sense of a Jackson Pollock than a Rembrandt. That is, the artist did not want anyone figuring out what it was, though he certainly wanted to leave one hell of an impression. Designed to fool the immune system, it is a Trojan horse virus, hidden within the shifting disguises of influenza. Indeed, the shell of the Pied Piper virus is just as mutative as the influenza virus, virtually guaranteeing it a perpetual presence after an outbreak and rendering any sort of vaccine all but impossible.

Once in the body, it is nothing more than a very mild chest cold, except in the brain, where it binds with proteins specific to the cell membranes of the neocortex, and in particular Broca's area, the region devoted to the control of symbol and language processing. Via this treacherous manipulation of endocytosis, the Pied Piper virus shoves its way inside and takes over, reproducing itself and rewriting the neurochemical functions of its host cell. Within hours, affected individuals demonstrate a marked linguistic confusion, ultimately resulting in a complete loss of language-processing skills. Acute symptoms persist with decreasing frequency for up to a year or longer, but the electrochemical activities of the neocortex remain permanently altered.

Thus we have the Pied Piper virus, a smart-assed scamp with the wit and the wherewithal to yank communication out from under a society, and yet a pattern of ribonucleic acid so puny that fifty million of its clones could slam-dance on the head of a single pin.

52 While I spent my days swimming invigorating laps in the balmy ether of cerebral abstraction, another part of me grew increasingly impatient with my eggheaded shenanigans and highbrow justifications. It was not an unfamiliar facet of my self, a surly-churly, no-bullshit, hands-on worker who stops in to belittle my intellect from time to time. It was a necessary balance, it seems, between mind and body, for while my mind was free to roam, my body was thoroughly discontent with its imprisonment, cozy though it may have been. As for my soul, well, it barely ever says a word, taking over only when the body and the mind can't work things out for themselves. Mostly it lets them get their kicks while they can.

While my mind was getting off on the venereal delights of its task, a stubborn guilt kept creeping around me, a wounded cretin whose trail of blood, sweat, and tears made for an increasingly slick foundation on which to stand. In retrospect, this must not have gone unnoticed by my soul. Guilt, especially when suppressed, is a destructive presence in one's consciousness, leading very quickly to despair and self-hate.

For a time, however, life was halcyon. There were inconveniences and irritations, to be sure, but they were mild, even amusing. For example, a few days after being incarcerated in the country mansion, I met Miss Sophia Loren. She was a forty-something tobacco heiress and a major benefactor of the CPC. Her given name, she told me, was Mary, but her adoptive parents had it legally changed. Her adoptive father, it seemed, was an avid admirer of the popular Hollywood actress, so he renamed his new daughter after her. Although she wished to be called Miss Sophia, in this narrative I shall refer to her only by her given name, Miss Mary Loren, or Miss Mary, in order to avoid any confusion between her and Blip's wife, as well as the Hollywood actress.

Miss Mary had an evil little dog, whom she called "Tippy," but whom I called "Ratdog" when Miss Mary wasn't around. Since I have already taken liberties with Miss Mary's appellation, henceforth I shall refer to her dog as "Ratdog" rather than "Tippy." Ratdog was a miniature pinscher, a diminutive breed that nevertheless acts as if they are full-sized Dobermans. Ratdog reminded me of Tynee. My dog Meeko, by the way, was inexplicably fond of Ratdog.

Once, while walking Meeko along the grounds of the estate, Ratdog came zipping toward us from around a curve in the path, yipping viciously. Meeko scrambled to meet her, and they set upon sniffing each other immediately.

"Tippy!" Miss Mary's raspy, upper Manhattan, nicotine voice sounded from up ahead. She had just rounded the bend and was greeted by the sight of Meeko gracelessly attempting to mount her hoity-toity pinscher, a hilarious sight given their relative sizes. Be that as it may, both parties seemed agreeable to the situation. Miss Mary, however, was mortified.

"Tippy!" Miss Mary screeched again, then addressed me in haughty disdain. "Don't just stand there! Take your mutt off my Tippy!"

Despite the fact that I didn't approve of my dog's taste in bitches, I found the carnality entertaining. I thus failed to react immediately, and so Miss Mary took it upon herself to separate the copulating canines by hurling her handbag at them. It was ineffective. A falling tree could not have captured their attention. I finally stepped forward, grabbed Meeko's collar, and pulled him off Ratdog. Miss Mary rushed forward and frantically snatched her up. Both dogs were panting heavily.

"How could you let this happen?" Miss Mary wailed. "Dear God, what if she has puppies, what then? Oh my lord, how uncivilized!" She started back along the path, but paused to scold me some more. "You should be ashamed of yourself, Doctor. Ashamed!" She turned to go once again. "I've never seen anything so *horribly* unnatural."

53 On my twenty-eighth day at Valhalla Acres, I was awakened at 5:00 A.M. by Agent Orange, who was leaning over my bed like a malevolent mother, telling me to get dressed immediately. It had been arranged, I was informed, for me to observe the CPC's human subjects. While I was dressing, Tynee poked his head in and asked me if I would mind if he walked Meeko this morning. I agreed groggily. I suspected Tynee just wanted to have an excuse to hang around Miss Mary, so I neglected to tell him that she did not approve of my dog.

My ride to the observation site, along with everyone else at Valhalla Acres, was a forty-foot soundproof security limousine. It was rated for presidential protection, which meant that it could withstand the blast of a grenade. Volt the Waiter and Chef was also Volt the Chauffeur, but whereas before he spoke with a thick French accent, he now greeted me with a southern Italian accent. I questioned General Kiljoy about this as the two of us sat in individual recliners in the far back of the limo, waiting for the others.

"Volt? He's training for a field mission. He'll be working at some of Europe's finest restaurants, where elites are known to frequent."

"Oh." I looked out the window, which really wasn't a window at all, but an opaque piece of black, high-density, bulletproof polycarbonate. From the outside, it looked like a dark-tinted window. But when the wall to the front seat was up, the interior of the vehicle was hermetically sealed from any exterior light or sound.

This being the case, I gave a start when one of the front

doors suddenly opened and the bright morning light poured in, along with the flirtatious noises of Ratdog and Meeko, not to mention Tynee and Miss Mary, who were engaged in a mating ritual of their own.

"Allow me, Miss Mary." Tynee took the squirming Ratdog from her arms as she stepped into the limousine.

"Thank you, Tibor," she gushed like an oil spill. "You're such a gentleman." Her seat was at the front, about thirty feet away from General Kiljoy and myself. Tynee followed her with Ratdog, who was kicking at him, and of course Meeko followed Ratdog.

"Are we all settled then?" General Kiljoy asked our assembled group.

Tynee gave a thumbs-up, and Miss Mary, who was fumbling with the plush leather cushions on her recliner, squawked, "I suppose we'll have to be."

General Kiljoy pointed a remote control toward the front end of the cabin. At the push of a button, the soundproof and lightproof screen separating us from the driver's seat slid open, revealing Volt the Chauffeur, with Agent Orange riding shotgun.

General Kiljoy gave the command for us to be on our way, then hit the button again and the wall slid shut, leaving us ostensibly important people once again in womblike comfort. Within minutes we were humming along at a steady pace, strains of unidentifiable classical music filling the cabin from unseen speakers. The motion was barely perceptible in our ergonomically designed orthopedic leather recliners, save for a gentle vibration that eventually lulled the lot of us to sleep like infants in car seats.

Voluntarily lying down and succumbing to a loss of waking

consciousness has always unsettled me. Despite the inevitability of slumber, I often find myself lying in bed resisting it, kicking awake again and again as soon as I begin to drift off. To sleep, or more to the point, to dream, suspends the control of our ego and whisks whatever portion of us still loitering about to a realm without surety or stability, a realm of shameless fantasy and stupendous absurdity. Dreams may grant us tranquillity, or they may teach us terror. They ridicule the notion of cause and effect, and explore peculiar ramifications of preposterous events with a nonchalance appropriate to sipping weak tea. Indeed, nothing, no matter how devoid of reason, seems to surprise what remains of our faculties in this state. Nothing, that is, except the sudden realization that you are dreaming, the unwelcome intrusion of that conceited know-it-all, the ego. Whatever entity existed to experience the dream state is shoved back into more predictable circumstances, and oddly, we are grateful, relieved by the illusion of control.

For this reason (which is probably best understood as a prideful fear of death itself), I was the last to surrender to a siesta. I shilly-shallied on the cusp for quite some time, flirting with blurry moments of rushing weightlessness before jolting awake again and again. At last I lost all memory of wakefulness, or its significance thereof, and entered into a state of such vivid intensity that I remain as yet unconvinced of its unreality. Call me a heretic, but this could not have been a mere dream, in which recollections are as slippery and elusive as a wet watermelon seed. No, these images have stayed with me in all their visceral fury as if they happened only a moment ago. This dream was a vision of myself, rapturous and disturbing, an epiphany that demanded my heretofore slack attention. Thus, although I am not without hesitation to strip my subconscious naked, I must record what was both the most fantastic and terrifying dream I have ever had.

It is difficult to say where it began, since it just seemed to be what was already occurring. Hence, the best I can say is that I was already an eagle. Though I was soaring through the atmosphere hundreds of feet high, and perceiving the passing scenery in supernatural detail, it was not at all remarkable at the time. Ecstasy is recognized as such only in retrospect. As I said, it was what was occurring; it was a given. Myopia was utterly forgotten and replaced by a keenness of sight both fantastic and fierce. The outline of every leaf on each passing tree was blazingly apparent, as were the patterns of the veins on their richly textured surfaces. All was green, a verdant spectrum of untold hues—emerald, jade, holly, ivy, kelly, chartreuse, aquamarine, olive, and pea—every conceivable ratio of blue and yellow had been mixed and flecked across the landscape below. Splendid indeed, but this was much more than a celebration of chlorophyll. Shadows cast by the ceaselessly shifting leaves sent darker green channels racing and scattering through the treetops, whispering the wind's intentions to me as I sailed along the air currents. I processed all of this information with less effort than traveling on a freeway, and despite our highways' misdesignation, with considerably more freedom.

Eventually, I spied a narrow river below, meandering its way through the thick forest like a child scurrying through a crowd. I followed its course, studying the synchronous silver streaks dancing in the sparkling stream. They were fish, and if it had suited my fancy, I could have had my choice. But the sun was setting, and at my altitude I could sense the true nature of the movement in the turning of the Earth. Realizing this, I flew ever west toward the rapidly sinking sun, trying to stay in the light of day and out of the darkness of night. But the shadow behind me was encroaching much faster than I was flying, and soon I could feel the cold winds of darkness tugging at my tail feathers. Within seconds I was yanked from the sight of light and overwhelmed by the night. This aroused substantial panic in me, but before I lost complete control in the tempestuous wind, I arched my back hard and rocketed skyward, aiming to escape through the top of the planet's penumbra. Shuddering, my hollow skeletal structure pulled taut against the buffeting walls of vicious gales. At the breaking point between my being and my environment, I burst at last into the swiftly moving sunset once again, my velocity nearly tripling as I rocketed exultantly into the gently drifting dance of the beatific atmosphere.

My elation, however, was short-lived. Once again, I was soon losing ground to the ever-approaching night. I strained my avian body to its limit, taking advantage of any breeze my feathers could catch. Then came salvation. An updraft swept through the trees along the river, and telltale shadows flowing through the leaf patterns told me where to expect it. I caught the gust, but before I could rejoice a brutal projectile from below tore me from the heavens. It maimed my right wing and I screamed in rage at the immensity of my vain efforts. Defeated and destroyed by a heartless beast that knew nothing of my struggle, I surrendered into the torrential winds of the night. I tumbled madly, yet I could distinguish every blackened blade of grass as the banks of the river spun toward me.

It was upon impact that I jerked awake. The night was replaced by the dimly lit interior of the limousine. General Kiljoy was leaning over me, jabbing me in the arm with his remote control. His face was contorted into a dutiful scowl, a grimace of curious disgust, as if he were poking a dead animal with the tip of his rifle.

The Book o' Billets-doux

Rosehips: What do you mean when you say, "until death becomes irrelevant"? Explain yourself. Do you really think death is irrelevant, or do you dismiss it as such because you fear it? I hope this is not the case. If you are afraid of dying, you are afraid of living. A life of fear is a living death, devoid of any lasting happiness. Truly now, are you afraid to be alive? Life is either lived or left behind, I should think.

sweetlick: Life, live it or leave it? Your words are certainly true, though irrelevant as well. But irrelevance is not insignificance, and the irrelevant is certainly nothing to be afraid of. Irrelevance is a panacea for predictability, but I drift considerably askew. What I meant to say is that a fear of death is irrelevant, and, as you have pointed out, contradictory to the moment-to-moment experience of life. It is only a convenience of language that makes the words *living* and *dying* sound like opposites.

Rosehips: A convenience or a corruption? Any soul who pauses to think for five minutes should realize that life depends upon itself for sustenance. Death is a necessary stage in the spiral of evolution. I shudder to think that humans might never evolve further than this.

sweetlick: I agree. We're not really disagreeing here, my maenadic wonderwhipsy. Life is short in the long run, but we humans, for better or for worse, are rather absentminded when it comes to our mortality.

Rosehips: Perhaps this is that which afflicts our civilization so horribly. What injustice, avarice, laziness, or bad mood is conceivable if death is kept in mind? We haven't been paying attention to our expiration dates for centuries, and the land of milk and honey has gone sour.

sweetlick: A tragic statement, though beautifully put. But I have to add, death must not only be kept in mind, but laughed at as well. Why represent death with the grim reaper and wring our hands over the inevitable? Why not the glad reaper? *Joie de mourir!* Death is a hop, skip, and a jump away from birth, and the whole sh'bang is a happy hootenanny. When I die, scatter my ashes upon the ground and dance them into the Earth. Shed only tears of joy, oh lipsa-la-doodle-do-wee-bang-bang, for I love life, and I suppose that is why I must die someday.

54 "Wake up!" General Kiljoy ordered me. He pointed the remote control at the glossy opaque window to my immediate left and it hushed open, unleashing the light and noise of the street to overwhelm my stupefied senses. My pupils shrieked, blinded and disoriented, as if I had just stepped out of a matinee on a sunny day. The others were so far away that their respective feature presentations went on uninterrupted. As my eyes adjusted, I could see that we were in the business district across from Tynee University, stopped in the morning traffic jam along the bustling street.

A panhandler stood on the edge of the sidewalk, rhyming to passersby. He wore a dirty white T-shirt too small for him, and his belly peered unabashedly out the bottom. The words HELP IS ON THE WAY had been silk-screened onto the shirt, and they stretched across his chest like some exaggerated SALE EXTRAVAGANZA! pitch. Despite his appearance, his rhythmic and confident delivery drew smiles and coins from the students and professionals passing by.

My friends, my friends, it might sound strange,
But can you spare just a little change?
It's just a drop,
But it helps a hell of a lot,
And help is on the way, my friends.
Help is on the way.
A penny'll help out,
A nickel or a dime,
But if you give me a buck,

It just might change my luck!
'Cause help is on the way, my friends.
Help is on the way

Now if you give me a dime,
Why that'd be just fine,
But if you give me a dollar,
That'd really make me holler!
Help is on the way, my friends.
Help is on the way.

The limo glided forward a few feet as the traffic crept along, and the panhandler, having noticed me observing him, followed us along the sidewalk, never pausing in his delivery.

I don't wanna rob you,
And I sure don't wanna steal,
But I'm not a monk,
And I might get drunk,
'Cause help is on the way, my friends.
Help is on the way.

I live on the street,
And I might get beat,
But have no fear,
'Cause tonight we're drinkin' beer!
And help is on the way, my friends.
Help is on the way.

God loves us all,
The big and the small,
So please don't you doubt it,
Make no mistake about it,
That help is on the way, my friends.
My friends, help is definitely on the way.

55

General Kiljoy closed the window before I could find some change, sealing us once more in silence. "Hey Fountain." He poked me again with his remote control. Leering deviously, he pointed at Miss Mary, Tynee, and the dogs, all of whom were still sleeping at the far side of the limo. "Wanna have some laughs?"

"Excuse me?" I asked, looking across the cabin. Tynee had rolled onto his side, and was somehow lying atop both of his arms, drooling. Miss Mary's skirt was hiked up such that I could see the tops of her knee-highs, and she was snoring like a didgeridoo. As for Meeko and Ratdog, they were at last free to sleep together, side by side in tranquil repose.

"Here." General Kiljoy handed me the remote control. "Press the big red button."

"Why?"

"Just press it."

"What does it do?"

"Come on." He leaned forward, his eyes evil and excited. "I *dare* you."

"But what does it do?" I demanded.

He sighed impatiently. "This transport is equipped to carry

dogs trained to kill at the sound of an ultrasonic whistle. Pressing that button causes the speakers to blare that whistle at top volume. We wouldn't hear a thing, but the attack dogs would be out the door and lunging for throats before I could take my finger off the button." He pointed at Meeko and Ratdog. "Those dogs there ain't killers, but it'll sure make 'em jump and howl, probably right onto Tynee or Miss Mary's laps if we're lucky." He smiled at his image, then added, "I've set it so the doors won't open."

"I'd really rather not." I handed the remote control back to him.

"Chicken?" he said, and I almost expected him to start clucking. "I can tell you're no soldier. You've got cotton puffs for balls." Reminded thus, I suppose, he leaned back and reached into his pocket to adjust himself. "Do you dare *me* to do it? Because I'll do it."

I looked at this obnoxious lump of military madness sitting across from me. His face shared the menacing scowl of every playground and barroom bully that constantly dares others to look at him wrong, and I decided to play along. After all, what did I care? He would shut up, the dogs would get over it, and it would be a sight to see. I might even get some laughs.

"I dare you," I said. General Kiljoy was caught off guard, his eyes going briefly agog with astonishment before they narrowed, and he leaned forward, licked his lips, and pressed the big red button.

56

It was just as General Kiljoy had envisioned it. Meeko and Ratdog yelped awake and, after wrestling over each other for a moment, began racing around frantically, barking savagely at the walls, and leaping on and off Miss Mary and Tynee as if their laps were trampolines. Both of them screamed, General Kiljoy roared with laughter, and I couldn't resist a snicker myself. After he had control of himself, General Kiljoy pressed the button again. The dogs, their tongues foaming with frothy excitement, instantly ceased their rabid behavior and began whining, whimpering, and deliriously licking Miss Mary and Tynee.

"Get the . . ." Tynee threw Ratdog off him and cringed as Miss Mary screamed again. "What the hell's going on!" he bellowed, starting to get up but abruptly pausing to inspect his left arm, which was dangling lifelessly by his side, still asleep. Miss Mary screamed again as Ratdog joined Meeko on her lap. "Goddamnit!" Tynee yelled, shaking his inanimate arm with his working hand. "What's happened?!"

General Kiljoy stooped across the cabin to assist them. "Take it easy." He moved the dogs off Miss Mary's lap. "Something must have spooked the dogs is all. Nothing to get all worked up about." Miss Mary burst into tears at the suggestion, and Tynee did his best to comfort her with his right hand while gesticulating madly with his left arm, still trying to shake some circulation back into it.

"Don't just sit there," Tynee hollered over to me, where I was, as charged, just sitting there, stunned and rather elated by the sequence of events I had set into motion. "Get control of your goddamn mutt!"

"Crash!" I commanded, and Meeko obediently trotted across the cabin to me. He sat by my side panting and wagging his tail, apparently having thoroughly enjoyed the experience.

"You might apologize for your dog's behavior, Fountain," General Kiljoy reprimanded me with a sadistic wink.

"What?" I asked, flustered, and Miss Mary wailed louder still. I was, however, spared from the dilemma by Volt the Chauffeur's pleasantly Sicilian voice over the intercom, sounding oblivious to all the fuss and fur behind him. He informed us that we would be arriving shortly.

This news seemed to cheer everyone, and an air of anticipation settled over us, as if we were on our way to an amusement park. Even Miss Mary regained her sniffy composure within a few minutes. Not having had a cigarette for an hour or so, she was visibly irritated at General Kiljoy idly tossing his remote control back and forth in his hands. She asked him if she could see it.

"Sure," he extended it toward her. "But whatever you do, don't touch that big red button."

"Why?" she inquired, examining it. "My remote control doesn't have this button. What does it do?"

"That's classified, Miss Mary," he said, glancing my way in simpering villainy. "Just pretend that you're Eve and the big red button is a big red apple on the Tree of Knowledge. Don't touch."

Miss Mary smiled at the image, and General Kiljoy did, too. He had good reason, for if Miss Mary was Eve, then the one giving her such instructions was God.

57

The limousine at last came to a nearly imperceptible stop, and a knock sounded on the side door nearest me. General Kiljoy told Miss Mary what button to press, which she did, and the door next to me swung open. Instead of sunlight pouring in, as one might reasonably expect, a buzzing flood of shadowless fluorescent light greeted me like some sallow, jaundiced host poking me in the eyes and insisting I partake of a headache.

Outside my door, Agent Orange stood at attention. General Kiljoy joined me after instructing Miss Mary how to open the door closest to her, where Volt the Chauffeur waited. We were in an expansive garage with only one other car, a modest sedan of some sort. There were no windows, and the extreme silence, combined with a peculiar heaviness in the atmosphere, led me to surmise that we were considerably underground. Meeko and Ratdog, finding nothing interesting to smell, trotted gloomily about, tails as still as tombstones.

After retrieving the remote from Miss Mary, General Kiljoy barked some incomprehensible orders into it and led us toward what looked like a bank vault door built into the wall of the garage. He pressed a series of buttons on the remote's keypad, causing the door to give an unsettling clank as it began to open. Like some gigantic bottle of beer being cracked open, a gust of air burst from the chamber beyond. This, however, was nasty beer, and some joker had shaken it. Moreover, a drunken genie resided therein, and it was belching a cacophonous chorus of sounds best left unheard. Both dogs began to snarl, and I felt an impulse to join them as the hair on the back of my neck stood at combative attention.

It was a horrifying noise, yet it made everyone smirk. Many of the howls sounded like uncontrolled eruptions of ferocious laughter. It was the laughter of the Furies, the hilarity of hell, the roaring guffaw of pure terror. It sounded like a high school gymnasium full of people *literally* dying of laughter, shrieking and convulsing and reverberating. Though distant and somewhat muffled, it was surely the soundscape of the lake of fire, the annunciation of damnation.

Since the dogs were rattled beyond recovery, General Kiljoy instructed Agent Orange and Volt the Chauffeur to await our return and tend to the dogs, an order they responded to with snappy salutes appropriate to a top-secret mission. After they'd tugged the growling dogs away, General Kiljoy led us into the safe with no explanation.

"That noise?" I inquired at last.

"Those are the boys." It was Miss Mary who spoke, a perversely maternal gleam in her eyes.

"Those, Doctor," General Kiljoy began, hitting a button on the remote that caused the vault door to boom shut. "Those are the subjects you're here to observe."

58

General Kiljoy led us down a stark concrete passage reminiscent of the back service hallways in shopping malls. Every surface was coated with a glassy polymer of astounding smoothness. When I attempted to inquire about it, the sound of my voice made me cower at once, for I was shouting in my own ears. My vocalization reflected off the walls and was amplified back at me with such immediacy that I could not speak a word without having the disquieting sensation of yelling at myself. This was the case for everyone and, barring our thunderous footsteps and the fading reverberations of the subjects, we walked in fanatical silence. Later, in more congenial acoustics, I learned that the resin coating the walls made the compound virtually seamless and therefore ideal for testing biological agents.

In any case, we soon came to a modified golf cart sporting a plastic bubble enclosure. We packed ourselves into it like circus clowns, exceptionally asinine though not at all silly. Initially, Tynee had made a move to get in the driver's seat, but General Kiljoy jostled him out of the way. Miss Mary already occupied the passenger's seat, so Tynee was obliged to crawl in the back with me. All of this occurred without a word, though with considerable scowls and frowns. Once everyone was inside and the doors were closed, we would have been able to talk with a more comfortable degree of resonance, but I didn't discover this until my next ride. For now, a sulking silence prevailed in our party.

After I was thoroughly lost in the maze of passages, General Kiljoy turned the cart into a dead end where an identical cart was parked, across from an ornate door that looked like it had been stolen off a Victorian mansion. Seeing the door was like coming across an antique reading chair illuminated by a Tiffany lamp under a highway overpass. Its presence there was as incongruous as a singles resort in a Third World nation, yet it was appealing. After doing our best to exit the vehicle without grunting at ourselves at top volume, we entered a spacious room with hardwood paneling, which softened the acoustics and the mood nicely. A library occupied one side, opposite an elaborately decorated living room, complete with houseplants, a bar, a bearskin rug, and an elk's head mounted on the wall. All of the furniture faced a curtained wall. The lighting was especially attractive, compared to the fluorescent labyrinth from which we'd come, and my eyes could not help but voice their gratitude.

"Sunlight, Doctor," General Kiljoy informed me. "We get it piped down through fifty feet of optical fiber."

"It's wonderful for the plants," Miss Mary croaked as she took out a cigarette.

"Members of the CPC were down here quite a bit, observing, and we weren't getting enough sunlight," General Kiljoy continued. "That'll make you half crazy, you know." He paused to chuckle for no clear reason. "But it's not the lack of sunlight that's making our subjects crazy." He gestured to Miss Mary and Tynee. "Shall we initiate our neophyte then?"

Tynee rolled his eyes, still pouting. Miss Mary smiled a conspirator's smile from behind the flame of her lighter, then nearly coughed the cigarette out of her mouth. General Kiljoy rubbed his hands together and herded us to the sofas. When he was sure we were all comfortable, he pressed a button on his omnipotent remote control. The curtains parted swiftly and softly, revealing a wall of glass—a two-sided mirror, I was informed—which separated us from a barren room on the opposite side. The room was empty except for a toilet, a sink, and a small round table. The table was set for tea, complete with a Gothic silver teapot and matching teacups. Around this table sat a tremendous stranger, Brother Zebediah, and Dr. Blip Korterly, sipping tea and playing cards.

59

After watching me watch them gesture and move their mouths in silence for a few moments, General Kiljoy pressed another button on his remote control and we suddenly had audio for our movie. Full-blast stereo, actually. State-of-the-art fidelity, General Kiljoy boasted.

"Let me tell you something, Padre!" The stranger leaned toward Brother Zebediah, his baritone voice booming over the sound system. It was a mellow bellow, for although he was speaking in a conversational tone, it was amplified to an affable roar in our ears. "God ain't holdin' this country together. Trucks are. Infrastructure." A bar graph displaying the volume being lowered appeared on the window as General Kiljoy adjusted it.

The Herculean stranger turned out to be none other than Manny Malarkey, the half-deaf, serial billboard terrorist truck driver Blip had mentioned earlier. Manny wore a sweatshirt that looked too small on him, but a king-size toga would have looked too small on his enormous frame. He made the chair he sat in look as if it were made for a first grader. He was a thick man, a true brute, an authentic strongman.

Brother Zebediah wasn't afraid of him. "Blasphemy," he muttered as he tossed a card from the stack in front of him onto the table. "You're locking your soul out of heaven, I hope you realize. Nothing can hold Babylon together." He spoke with increasingly guttural thunder. "Babylon will be judged. Babylon will fall."

"Babble on, babble on," Manny mocked him.

"You're right about Babylon." Blip tossed one of his cards. "But the only thing holding this country together is an uncritical acceptance of the dominant, maladaptive, social paradigm."

"Don't listen to this academic." Brother Zebediah gestured toward Blip. "He'll poison your soul."

"I think you're both fulla shit, how 'bout that?" Manny tossed his card, cocky. "Besides, Brother, I'm already locked outta heaven, ain't that right? And since the perfessor here ain't talkin' so much shit about lockin' me out, I'm more likely to listen to him, though I still think he's fulla shit."

"Well, the both of you can wallow in your sins. I want no

part of it." Brother Zebediah angrily tossed his card. "More room for me in heaven!"

"Ain't you the hypocrite?" Manny challenged him. "You tellin' me you never sinned?"

"The few sins I've committed have been removed." Brother Zebediah straightened himself. "As far as the East is from the West, my sins have been washed away."

"What were your sins?" Blip asked, tossing his card.

"Right on, yeah. What were your sins?" Manny tossed his card.

"My sins?" Brother Zebediah frowned and bowed his head as he prepared to reveal his confession. "When I was young, I'm ashamed to say, I enjoyed looking at women in a sinful way."

"Shit," Manny laughed. "Ain't nothin' sinful 'bout lookin' at women, Brother. You ain't even seen heaven till you've sat in the cab of an eighteen-wheeler while a carload of them college sweethearts in their short shorts on their way to spring break passes right under you. Lord!" He tossed his card, then moved in close to Brother Zebediah. "You see, Brother, the angle is just right, probbly designed that way. It allows us haulers a convenient view of their Lord-have-mercy legs, you know what I'm sayin'." He patted Brother Zebediah on the back.

"I do *not* know what you're saying, pervert!" Brother Zebediah raised his voice and tossed his card. Blip smacked the table.

"Goddamn," said Manny. "How'd'ja get so good at Slapjack, Doc?"

"You just gotta be alert, my friend." Blip gathered his cards. "Just keep watching, keep watching, and when opportunity presents itself, dive into it with everything you've got, you know what I'm sayin'." Blip, it appeared, had taken to imitating some of Manny's expressions.

"Amen to that. That's why I'm cool with this experiment shit. Gonna get me an early release, be back out in no time." He looked at Brother Zebediah. "I got this apartment lined up in Jersey, with a front window that's just like I'm in the cab of a truck. It's on the corner, with a stop sign, and all the women drive their cars right under me. You'd love it."

"I would *not* love it," Brother Zebediah insisted.

"Yes you would, yes you would, I know you would, Brother Jeremiah. Yes sir, a little monk like you, you could be a happy hermit in that apartment. Ain't that right, Doc?"

"I don't know," said Blip, as he tossed his card and smacked the table again, winning another round. "New Jersey's a little crowded for anyone to be a hermit."

60

Manny threw the remainder of his cards on the table. "Man, I'm tired of this Slapjack shit." He reached into his shirt pocket and pulled out two dice. "Let's play some craps."

"I'll remind you again that Jeyzus hates cussing and gambling," Brother Zebediah spoke woefully.

"Jesus don't have to play," Manny said. "You game, Doc?"

"I'll play."

"Right on." Manny looked at Brother Zebediah. "Now, how 'bout since you got your way and picked the last game, I get to pick this one?"

"Jeyzus does not allow gambling, Lucifer."

"Who you callin' Lucifer, goddamnit? I already told you, Jesus don't have to play."

Brother Zebediah looked Manny up and down, then growled, "I'm the closest thing to Jeyzus you'll ever see."

Blip guffawed explosively, loud and derisive, with no attempt to hide his mocking amusement. "Give us a break, will ya? If you're gonna run around mouthing off about Jesus, at least know what he taught. He preached nothing but love, and all you keep saying is how he hates this and hates that."

"This is a holy hatred," Brother Zebediah replied gravely. " 'God hates all workers of iniquity.' "[4]

"Oh for crying out loud, man. I'm tired of this." Blip leaned back in his chair and began playing with his long hair, tapping his foot. "You know what your problem is? You went on a Christ trip in the sixties and never came down. Don't you understand anything, man? Don't you see? You're the bad guy here. Is that really the role you want in life? I'll tell you what. I'm gonna convert *you.* How do you like that? Can't you see it's hate and fear that's keeping us from heaven in the first place?"

"It may be keeping you from paradise, but nothing's keeping me." Brother Zebediah raised his voice. "God's already called me, but I said, no siree, not yet, I have to teach Your Word."

"You're not teaching anything, you're just condemning people."

" 'By thy words thou shalt be condemned.' "[5] Brother Zebediah raised his fist, threatening to unleash God's eternal fury on the beast seated before him.

"How can you spend your days just damning people? Man, where do you think we are right now? Not just right here, but here, alive on this planet? This is hell, Brother, look around. It doesn't have to be, but we make it so. I can even prove it. All life on this planet is carbon-based, right? Do you know what the atomic number of carbon is? Six. That means six electrons, six neutrons, and six protons, 666, the mark of the beast is the illusion of matter! Who was cast out of paradise? Lucifer, right? Well, guess who else was kicked out? We were, Adam and Eve, eating the forbidden fruit, the Tree of Knowledge, driven from the garden like varmints. We're the beast. DNA is the coil of the serpent. Duh. Hell is separation from the Source, man. Dig?"

"Right on," Manny spoke up. "I can dig that."

Brother Zebediah raised his hand toward Blip and uttered a curse. "May the deepest levels of the inferno consume your soul."

"We're already in the inferno, man! That's what life is." Blip turned to Manny. "Can I see your lighter?"

"Sure." Manny dug into his waist pocket and slid his Zippo across the table. Blip picked it up and flicked it alive with a flair off his pants leg.

"Check it out." Blip studied the motionless flame. "Fire is a process of oxidation, manifest here as a chemical reaction between butane and oxygen, catalyzed by a spark. No one would argue that this is fire, but we fail to see the flames when the oxidation process is slower." He took a deep, demonstrative breath. "Respiration is an oxidation process. So is metabolism. We eat food and *burn* calories. And it doesn't even stop there. Everywhere you look, things are oxidizing—decaying, rotting, rusting, metabolizing, burning, combusting, exploding. Everything is on fire, bro, we just don't realize it. We've been splashing around in the lake of fire since birth. Do you understand? We are in hell *right now.*"

"Shit," Manny said.

"Nah." Blip waved him off. "Don't worry about it. It's all good. Hell isn't permanent, and it certainly isn't as bad as Brother Zebediah here thinks." He snapped the Zippo shut. "Hell is part of the process. You know, yin and yang, and all that jazz. We'll get ourselves back to the Garden eventually."

"Beast! Beast! Beast!" Brother Zebediah pounded his fists on the table in zealous fury.

"Exactly! Now you're starting to get the picture, Brother. But listen," Blip smiled, "didn't Jesus say the kingdom of heaven is within you?"

"Oooo," Brother Zebediah mocked him. "Mr. Big Shot, think you can quote the Bible now, eh?"

Blip, not wanting to get into a Bible-quoting match, ignored him and continued to wax metaphysical. "I take that to mean that paradise is a matter of perception. We exist here and now only for a short time, yet we waste our existence on selfish endeavors, deluding ourselves into hell. The kingdom of heaven is right in front of our freaking faces, and we're blind to it, man. Wake up!"

"Heathen! You wake up!" Brother Zebediah turned to Manny, as if the argument he was having with Blip had become a contest for Manny's soul. "You see where he's going, don't you? That immoral idealist has a first-class ticket to *hell*!"

"Hell yes I'm an idealist," Blip interjected, imitating Brother Zebediah's pulpitine intonations. "Romantics of the world, rejoice! The return of the romantic reaction and triumph is at hand!" Ceasing his sarcasm, he continued: "Anyway, what's the alternative? Realism? No thanks. I'll take ideality over reality any time. If I were a realist I'd have to kill myself."

"Ain't you the hopeless romantic?" Manny jeered, slapping Blip good-naturedly on the arm.

"A hopeless romantic is a contradiction in terms, an oxymoron," Blip corrected him. "I'm a hopeful romantic."

"Either way, you're going to hell. Paradise isn't for you, Satan!" Brother Zebediah looked to Manny, who was rattling the dice in his hand. "Isn't that right?" he asked, as if here, down in a dungeon in the bowels of the Earth, these three men had just reached *the* moment of reckoning, judgment day, revelation, and now, the word of Manny Malarkey would decide the profound fate of the universe for eternity.

"Paradise?" said Manny, and he tossed the cubes upon the table. "Paradise is pair a' dice."

61

"Snake eyes!" Manny hooted. "How 'bout that?"

"They're snake eyes all right, the eyes of Satan!" Brother Zebediah picked up the dice and hurled them across the room toward the mirrored wall, causing the four of us to instinctively duck and shield our faces.

"Whoa!" General Kiljoy blurted as the dice bounced off the glass. "That looked real!"

"It *was* real," I said.

"Well, yeah, but you know what I mean," General Kiljoy laughed. "It's like TV."

"Shh!" Miss Mary and Tynee shushed him.

Back on screen, Manny was offering a cigarette to Brother Zebediah. "How 'bout a smoke, bro? You need to relax."

"Please remove that devilish drug from my presence. Only the vile and the wicked depend upon such things."

"Well, I was on the preacher's side till that," Miss Mary spoke up, exhaling defiantly. No one acknowledged her vomitous remark.

"How 'bout you, Doc?" Manny offered a cigarette to Blip.

"No thanks."

"You think it's devilish, too?"

"No." He shook his head. "I'm just allergic to poison."

"Allergic to poison, eh?" Manny eyed his cigarette suspiciously. "I guess I'm addicted to poison then, this poison anyway. Everybody's got a poison though. What's your poison, Doc?"

Blip smirked. "Me? I don't really have any poisons." He considered a moment, grinning to himself, then shrugged. "I do enjoy a little grass on occasion."

"Grass?" Manny laughed. "The perfessor likes the joy smoke."

"Devil smoke," Brother Zebediah corrected, then added, "Potheads are going to hell, you know."

"I can just see you tokin' up with your long white hair," Manny continued. "Pot-smoking perfessor, how 'bout that? We gotta get together after we're outta here."

"Sure thing."

"Smoke that pot, you're gonna rot!" Brother Zebediah reprimanded them both.

"Man, shut up." Manny turned to Brother Zebediah. "God made marijuana, didn't he?"

"God made poison ivy, too, that doesn't mean you should roll around in it!" Blip joined Brother Zebediah in reciting his standard reply to that line of reasoning. Tynee shifted in his seat at the mention of his cherished botanical.

"What's that s'posed to mean?" asked Manny. "Who's rollin' around in marijuana?"

Brother Zebediah spoke, slow and condescending. "Just because God made marijuana doesn't mean you should smoke it."

"You're crazy, Brother." Manny pointed at the Bible in Brother Zebediah's hand. "Who d'ya s'pose wrote that there Bible?"

"These . . ." Brother Zebediah lifted his Bible. "These are the inspired words of God himself."

"Well, just 'cause God wrote the Bible don't mean you should read it."

"Heretic!" Brother Zebediah yelled, his eyes wide in unfeigned horror.

"Hypocrite!" Manny returned the favor. "I know what your poison is, Padre. Religion. You make yourself feel good by puttin' others down. You like to inject your soul with that hellfire and damnation talk, pointin' out everyone else's flaws. Yeah, that's right, that Bible's your poison. Every time you point your finger at someone you're stickin' a needle in your arm, shootin' yourself fulla pride and self-righteousness. You think you know somethin' the rest of us don't? Bullshit. You don't know shit. No one knows shit. And anyone who thinks they know shit definitely don't."

Brother Zebediah was flabbergasted, so much so that he was, for a thick moment, at a loss for words. "My God, may God strike you down this instant!"

"There you go, you see what I'm sayin'? There ain't enough trucks in this country to haul the load of bullshit you're try'na sell." He looked at the fluorescent lights on the ceiling of their cell. "I don't see no lightning, Brother."

"It doesn't seem likely," Blip entered their argument, gazing pensively at the ceiling. "It doesn't seem likely that lightning could come into an enclosed room."

"Wouldn't matter if it could," Manny said. "I've already been struck by lightning."

This revelation brought a pause to the conversation, as both Blip and Brother Zebediah (as well as the assembled studio audience) studied Manny's face to ascertain whether or not he was serious.

"No lie. When I was fifteen I tried out for the football team at my high school. I was tacklin' on a weighted dummy when suddenly it kicked back. I guess it threw me about thirty feet. I had all my gear on, but it still felt like I'd just gotten my ass run over by an eighteen-wheeler."

"Jesus," said Blip. "You might have told me that when we met. That's like having a twin. You're not supposed to keep something like that a secret."

Manny smiled and shrugged. "Anyway, I couldn't sleep for a couple weeks after that. I wasn't even tired. I still only need a couple hours' sleep a night now. That's why I got into haulin', plus I wanted to see the country. I found out soon enough that would be difficult, what with a billboard every time I turned a bend tellin' me what I needed or what lay ahead, just like you, Brother Zachariah. I say fuck that. I know what I need and I'll see what's ahead when I get there. So, I use my spare time doin' billboard jobs."

"Cool," said Blip.

"You're abusing a blessing from God," Brother Zebediah informed Manny.

"A blessin' my ass. I couldn't make the team 'cause of that."

"Why not?" Blip asked.

"Ever since that day I ain't never shed a drop of sweat on the whole left side of my body."

"Come on . . . ," said Blip.

"No lie, Doc. I can't sweat on my left side. Look." Manny lifted his arms to display his armpits. Sure enough, the underarm of his shirt on the left side was a virtual antiperspirant commercial, as sure as the Statue of Liberty, while the fabric on the right was darkened with dampness.

"Now that's something, eh, Brother?"

"Remarkable," Brother Zebediah responded with uncharacteristic geniality, his mind preoccupied momentarily with something other than Biblical literalism.

"And the nice thing is," Manny peeled off his shirt, revealing a mountainous build. He pulled it back on inside out. "When the right side of the shirt gets all wet, I can turn it inside out and practically have a fresh shirt on."

62

The mad tea party continued along in much the same manner. At one point I turned to General Kiljoy to inquire what the itinerary for the day was, only to discover that he and the others were no longer sitting with me. So engrossed was I in the squabbles of the trio before me that I hadn't noticed the others had moved to the far side of the room, where they were now talking quietly at the bar. Stupid as General Kiljoy's earlier comment had been, it *was* like TV.

I stood up to join them, and they abruptly ceased their hushed conversation. Pretending not to notice, I raised the question of the day's activities.

"This is it," General Kiljoy responded, gesturing across the room with his palms.

"We're going to watch them all day?"

"It should get interesting shortly," Miss Mary assured me.

"It's been interesting," I said, "but I'd like to have a few words with Blip before we," I fumbled, "before you get down to business."

"Impossible," General Kiljoy said flatly. Tynee and Miss Mary chuckled as if watching the antics of a four-year-old.

"The least you could grant me is a meeting with him before you begin experimenting on him."

General Kiljoy shrugged his chin, considering. "It's not that I wouldn't grant you that," he said, emphasizing that it would indeed be a regal gesture. "But we've already begun the experiment." The three of them looked at me as if they'd just whooped "Surprise!" at a birthday party.

I turned and looked at Blip, Brother Zebediah, and Manny, who were still sitting around the table, talking, arguing, and drinking tea. Blip asked Manny if he was deaf on the same side he couldn't sweat on. He was.

"The tea, Doctor," Miss Mary informed me, smiling with the depravity of an executioner.

"What about the tea?" I asked, glancing at the incongruously opulent teapot, with which Brother Zebediah was pouring himself another cup.

"Your friend should love it." Tynee smiled. "It's an invigorating herbal blend."

"But it's sweetened," General Kiljoy continued, "with our very own secret ingredient."

"The Pied Piper virus!" Miss Mary exclaimed. Happy birthday!

Astounded beyond reaction, I slumped down onto a barstool, then immediately hopped up and walked around the bar to pour myself a drink. I grabbed the meanest bottle I could find, Wild Turkey. I wanted punishment. "How long before its effects manifest?" I asked, after belting back a shot and shuddering as the ethanol spirits possessed me.

"I donated the teapot," Miss Mary crowed.

"How long?" I repeated.

General Kiljoy glanced at his watch. "Typically takes about one-and-a-half, two hours. That gives them about a half hour to forty-five minutes, tops."

I took another slug of whiskey, and though I was salivating madly from the alcohol, began to feel a John Wayne edge coming on. "I want to talk with him," I said, swallowing the bile rising in my throat.

"That's not an option, Doctor," General Kiljoy responded evenly. He was more John Wayne than me.

I took another shot, swallowed my gag as a chaser, and regained my composure. "Work something out." I slammed the glass down on the bar. Tynee commandeered the bottle, but I would've rather bitten on a fork than toss back another nip of that demonswill. "I want to meet with him now," I continued, loud and surly, "or I'm off this project." I spoke my *j*'s as if pronouncing *Jacques.* "Release me, kill me, or throw me in there with them, do what you want, but you'll get no cooperation from me. I've only one request." I also pronounced my *qu*'s as in *Jacques.* "I want to talk to him while he can still talk back."

General Kiljoy looked at me, his eyes narrow. Miss Mary and Tynee retreated to the sofas. "You got balls after all, Fountain." He gazed at me, scanning my features, looking for signs of a bluff. But I held my cool. I was a wild turkey, after all, fast and furious, look out. He reached into his pocket and pulled out his remote control. Still looking at me, he hit a button, and the bookcase to the left of the observation window slid open. "I'll send him in in a minute. There'll be a glass wall separating you to protect you from exposure, naturally, but you'll be able to see and hear each other."

"Thanks," I managed, just before I threw up on the bar.

63

General Kiljoy swore at my alimentary upheaval, handed me a bottle of ginger ale, and ordered me into a small room behind the bookcase to await Blip. He warned me that he would be watching the meeting via closed-circuit camera. The room had the same interior designer as the room in which Blip, Manny, and Brother Zebediah were hanging out. It was, however, quite a bit smaller and it had a thick glass wall in the middle. It felt much more like a confessional than I would have preferred.

I sat there, dizzy, sipping my bottle of soda, trying to wash the acidic grittiness from my teeth, and drawing profound connections between alcohol and the French language. Was it so romantic to talk like you were plotched? And if so, why weren't women helplessly attracted to slurring alcoholic vagrants? What if an alcoholic vagrant were French? Aha! Context is crucial, of course. That stream of thought was dammed with the realization that women also like chubby, bald, drooling people when they happen to be infants, but not when they are adults.

I suppose now is as good a time as any to mention that I am, or was at the time I am writing about, one of those chubby, bald, drooling men that women are so disinclined to coo over. I trust I have not seriously violated the mental image readers may have constructed of me. After all, I was basically an evil scientist cooperating with the military-industrial complex in yet another dunderheaded scheme to tighten the Gordian knot of technocratic domination.

The Gordian knot, for the uninitiated, was a knot of mythical complexity that supposedly existed in the Asian city of Gordium in 333 B.C.E., when Alexander the Great and his army took up winter quarters there. While there, he heard about a legend surrounding the knot, which stated that whoever could untie it would become king of Asia. Clever Alex, quite the wild turkey himself, took one look at the knot, drew his sword, and cut it in half. Asia, of course, was destined to be his.

Today, the knot is of a different sort altogether. Whoever unties the military-industrial knot won't conquer the world, but free it.

64

The door on the opposite side of the glass opened, and Blip entered. His face leaped into a smile when he saw me.

"Flake!" he called out, his voice tinny through the intercom. "How are you?" I raised my bottle to him in greeting.

He shrugged exuberantly, clearly pleased with his predicament. "Chillin' like a villain. I'm right about the experiments, you know." He grinned, then cocked his head. "So what are you doing here? You're not bailing me out again, are you? I think I'm just about to figure out what's going on."

I shook my head. “I don’t know where to begin,” I said, thinking how much easier it is to confess a wrongdoing to some priest than to the person whom you’ve actually done wrong. “Strange events have transpired lately.” A maudlin lump formed in my throat, and I felt like bawling. A chubby, bald, drooling, bawling man. “I didn’t know what they had in mind. I didn’t have any choice.”

“What are you talking about?”

“I don’t know what to say.” I took a swig of ginger ale, then looked him in the eyes for the first time since he’d come in the room. “You were right. Absolutely right. They are doing experiments. I’m here to find a vaccine. I didn’t want to help them, but then they have you.”

“Whoa.” Blip ran his hands over his head, pulling his long white hair back. He sat confused and silent a few moments. “Who has me? Vaccine for what? What are you talking about, man? You’re starting to wig me out.”

I sighed impatiently, wishing I hadn’t demanded to meet with him. “The tea the three of you were drinking,” I explained, tired and resigned. “It contained a virus.” I paused, but Blip didn’t respond, only looked at me with wide eyes. To my comfort, they were filled with shock and not accusation. “It won’t kill you,” I continued. “It’ll barely even make you sick. But it will destroy your ability to use language, your symbolic capacity.”

“Symbolic capacity,” Blip murmured.

“They just told me you’ve got about a half hour before it becomes apparent.”

“Who’s they?”

I shrugged, pointing to the air around the room.

Blip leaned forward, his elbows on his knees, facedown and

hair every which way. “Symbolic capacity,” he repeated. He looked up, pursing his lower lip, deep in thought. His face relaxed into a realization. “That makes sense, I guess.” He looked through me, still thinking. “This is some kind of germ warfare, isn’t it?”

I shrugged again. “I can’t say.”

“Well, I can say that it’s brilliant,” he called out loudly.

“You think it’s brilliant?”

“Yeah, as a means to an end. It’s just a strange end. Destroy a nation by destroying the capacity of the individuals to communicate with each other, am I on the right track?” He shook his head. “Very clever. A weapon of mass anomie.”

“Anomie?”

“Comes from the Latin *nomos*. Roughly translates as the social universe, language, society, norms, the space we share in which we interact. Anomie is the disintegration and destruction of that universe.” He pursed his lower lip again, shaking his head and pausing long. “So society collapses, but what happens to individuals?”

“They say it’s not lethal.”

“But what’s the subjective experience like?”

“You tell me.”

“I will,” he said eagerly. “If a person doesn’t have a symbolic capacity, they have no self.”

“Why’s that?”

“Because the self is social.”

“What’s that supposed to mean?”

“It means that your sense of self emerges by interacting with others. It is born and raised in the process of human communication and interaction.” He gestured his hand back and forth between us. "In order to communicate, you must be able to evaluate what you are saying from another person's perspective, to be sure you're making sense. The imaginary reflection that your mind creates is your sense of self. In recognizing that you are an object in another person's perception, you become an object in your own. That's just the way it is.

"Of course, that doesn't mean that there isn't some deeper Self with a capital *S*. But that sense of self you are most acquainted with, the phantasm of your ego, that self is social. So, as far as your symbolic capacity goes, if this fundamentally human ability is undermined, then, ipso facto, your sense of self will dissolve as well." He sat nodding to himself in satisfaction for a few moments before continuing. "It works like this: You become self-aware, self-conscious, only after you imagine yourself from another's perspective. Think of Adam and Eve in the Garden of Eden. When they ate the fruit of the Tree of Knowledge, they became self-conscious, right? They felt embarrassed and covered themselves. Well, the *knowledge* that particular myth is referring to is our symbolic capacity, our ability to order, categorize, and name objects in our environment, including our selves. That's what differentiates us from all other animals. Now, why were Adam and Eve embarrassed?"

"Because they were naked?"

"Right. But what I'm trying to say is that they only realized they were naked because they became self-aware. They imagined themselves from each other's perspective, and became bashful. You're the most self-conscious when you're embarrassed, see? When you're painfully aware of how others see you. *That's* the basis of society, *imagining*, not knowing, each other's perspective. Human consciousness is a big game of make-believe. It's nothing more than mutually fanciful speculation, and the self, consequently, is nothing more than a ridiculous illusion at best and a destructive delusion at worst. We can't *know* each other's perspective, we only pretend we can. That's why people walk around so terrified of each other most of the time." He pointed to himself. "Do you see what I'm talking about? Right now I'm trying to evaluate whether or not I'm making sense by imagining how you perceive what I'm saying. Apparently, I won't be able to do that for much longer."

"So what's going to happen?"

"That's what I'm trying to tell you. If my symbolic capacity goes, so does my self-awareness."

"But what does that mean?"

"It probably means a total dissolution of the ego."

"But what will it feel like?"

Blip smirked and shrugged. "Who knows? Probably the same way death feels." He clapped his forehead in profound amazement. "Wow! That makes perfect sense. The entire path of human history has been a death wish. As a species, we have a death wish driving us toward self-destruction. It's in every last one of us, part of our collective unconscious. We're hell-bent on Armageddon, because with Armageddon supposedly comes revelation. Then we'll know for certain if there's any meaning at all to our existence." He tapped his head with his index finger. "That's the basic problem with being human. We're aware that we exist, but we're also aware that we'll die someday. That's too much to handle, so we force God's hand. If the ultimate ground of being, the spirit of the universe, Brahma, Allah, Yahweh, or whatever, won't let us in on why we're here, we'll just fucking try to destroy ourselves and see how It likes that. We figure It'll have to step in at the last minute and tell us the point of all this unhappy horseshit." Blip leaned back again in his chair, considering. "Or . . . !" The front legs of his chair slammed down as he sprung up. "We've had this death wish since we were cast out of Eden. See! The devil is only a drive in our mind, greed and selfishness driving us toward destruction and death. Why? Because at the end comes unity, oneness with Creation." He sat down, tapping both feet and drumming on his kneecaps with his palms. "I should tell Brother Zebediah that." He felt around the pockets of his clothing. "Do you have anything to write with?"

"I have a pen." I pulled it out of my pocket and held it up. "But I don't have any paper."

"Can you remember all that and write it down letter?" Blip asked, then looked confused. "Letter? Later, I meant to say. Can you write it down *later.*" He shook his head. "Do you suppose it's starting?"

"I'll write it down," I promised. After a moment's hesitation, I meekly added, "Do you understand the situation I'm in?"

"Don't worry." Blip waved me off. "I got myself into this."

"I appreciate that." I paused, feeling like crying again. "I guess the road to hell is paved with good intentions, huh?"

"I suppose. But then the road to heaven must be paved with bad intentions."

He could not have been more correct.

Part Two:

The Kaleidoscope Collapses

65 What responsibility awaits, fellow human, upon your deathbed! Consider: Out of all the phrases you have ever uttered, the one remark those close to you will remember with verbatim precision is your last words. Be prepared! Lest you get caught with nothing to say, or worse, with some knuckleheaded assertion echoing in your wake, have your words of wisdom or witticism at hand. Think it through. It is your final oration, your ultimate declaration. The Buddha, for instance, left his disciples with the following phrase to mull over: "That which causes life, causes also decay and death." Certainly a more impressive note to end on than that of Franklin Delano Roosevelt, whose dying insight was "I have a terrific headache."

On the other hand, perhaps all social obligation becomes incredibly dumb when death decides to tap you out of this marathon round of Duck Duck Goose. Indeed, the very notion of language may seem bizarre and old-fashioned at that point. For example, when Karl Marx's housekeeper pressed him for his last words, he reportedly muttered, just before expiring, "Last words are for fools who haven't said enough."

Dr. Blip Korterly did not feel he had said enough, although I do not wish to give the impression that he was therefore a fool. Blip was not dying, but having been recently informed that he was soon approaching the end of his ability to communicate, he was understandably anxious to say something meaningful, if not clever.

"Last words, man." Blip was pacing around his chair. "I have to come up with something good."

"What were you saying about the collective death wish?" I asked, trying to be helpful.

He stopped a moment, considering. "No, doesn't count. It's not my . . ." He paused, confused. "What? What's the word? It's right on the tip of my tongue." He licked his lips and turned to me. "What was I just saying?"

"You were talking about society," I lied, trying to redirect his thoughts in a more productive direction. "Something about a collective death wish."

"Right!" He clapped his palms together and sat down. "See, the thing is this. History has taught us that every society that has ever existed has failed in the end. Eventually, no matter how great the civilization, every one of them has crumbled. But we moderns think we're somehow different, that our slick technology will save us or that our knowledge base is too great to succumb to catastrophe. We forget that we live in a historical moment. Consequently, you hear all this talk about progress and building a global society. All that crap."

"I'm not sure I understand."

"Well, progress. Progress! Progress toward what? What's our

goal? When do we get to dust off our hands and say, 'Okay, done. That'll do for now. Let's kick back, pass a pipe, celebrate, and get down to living our lives the way they were intended to be lived?' What's progress if we can't define the goddamn goal? We aren't progressing toward paradise, that's for fucking certain. So what's the point then? The rat race is on a treadmill, and the axle's about to bust. Would you run a race if you didn't know how long it would be? Well, don't look now, bro, but that's what we're doing, and though we all want it to end we're too afraid of what would happen. Desperate, impatient lives make a desperate, impatient society, eager for the future and our own demise. Chasing eternity, man. We're like dogs who do nothing but chase their own tail, and we wonder why we're unhappy or why we feel sick, and we despair over all the things we're missing. Isn't it hilarious? No, it isn't. It sucks, and it makes me want to cry. We're making fools of ourselves. Let's admit it, let's all just get together and pause for one goddamn minute, everyone everywhere at the same time, and look around. We're doing something wrong here. We're missing the bigger picture while we fret about what to wear. Let's give it up already, you know? It's okay, man, it's nothing to worry or be embarrassed about. Every society fails eventually. No big deal. It's like worrying about death. Change is the only constant in the universe. It'll happen. Enjoy the ride in the meantime, be nice, and be prepared. When it does happen, rejoice! Something new. Excitement. Novelty. All societies fail, and we're attempting to create a worldwide society. We're setting ourselves up for ultimate disaster. The harder they are, the bigger they fall."

"You mean the bigger they are, the harder they fall?"

"What did I say?"

"You said, 'The harder they are, the bigger they fall.' "

"The harder they are, the bigger they fall?" He shook his head in animated amazement. "What on Earth can that possibly mean?"

I shrugged. "So finish what you were saying."

"Crisis, man! It's arrived. The lawn mower's here, see? Our anthill's being decapitated while we pretend everything's buttery. We're sewing ourselves into a corner, you know what I'm saying? Doom is on the loom, man, knock on wood." He rapped the side of his metal chair.

"Doom is on the loom?"

"Yes sir." Blip nodded emphatically. "Worlds without awareness soon end in all fairness."

66 Those were not, I should emphasize, the last words of Dr. Blip Korterly. Be that as it may, the introduction of the topic of last words places me in a precarious position vis-à-vis the reader, for where our respective moments meet, you the reader possess the awesome ability to divine what my last words will be, while I the writer am pathetically clueless in this regard.

Consider: As I record these thoughts and events, I know not where, nor how, it may end, if at all. You who are reading these lines, on the other hand, are an entirely different person than I, and you may, with or without my permission, casually flip to the end to sneak a peek at the last paragraph. For what it's worth, you do not have my consent, though this is surely an unenforceable request. Indeed, by writing this, it occurs to me, I may have done little else but draw your attention to something you may not have considered previously, like a chest that reads

DO NOT OPEN. But, in the terrible tradition of Pandora's box, this is a risk I have to take. For when Pandora (who bears a striking mythological resemblance to the Biblical Eve) opened her box (or ate her apple, as the case may be) and unleashed every affliction and imperfection upon humankind, hope drifted out along with them, to play either the cruelest joke ever perpetrated or to offer us a memory of our inevitable destiny, the faintest whiff of which will arouse an indefatigable desire to continue, to persevere in the journey, to keep the faith alive.

And so I hope that I may finish this manuscript, for what started as a favor to a friend has become the only point of my continued existence. I also hope that you, oh righteous reader, will honor my wishes and read in the order I have written. If you are reading this (itself an improbability given the manner in which my situation has developed), it is likely that I have finished it. However, as I write this, you must understand, I am living with the anxiety of not surviving (or perhaps not retaining the ability to craft such words) to see the completion of my work. Thus, I implore you to exist with me, here, in my temporal dimension, and resist the temptation to take liberties with your free will. Patience. Everything in time. Remember, after all, that taking liberties with free will is what got us kicked out of the Garden in the first place.

If I have created more curiosity than necessary here, it is only so that you may feel the pleasure of being trustworthy. To be worthy of the trust of a total stranger is a trait all too rare in the recent history of our species. And I am a stranger to you. Perhaps I am the asshole who, during the sour years of my life, blared my horn at you when you moved too slowly in traffic. Or, I could be someone you shared a smile with as we passed in the rain without umbrellas. I may be no more than a gravestone in a spooky cemetery you fearfully pedaled past on your way to school as a child, and now we interact across pages and lifetimes, and isn't it marvelous to think that I might be dead, and yet still you honor this silly request?

And doesn't it feel nice to be trustworthy?

67

Blip trusted me, as did Sophia, though I've no idea why. It has become clear to me in my present loneliness that I was on the pompous side of conceit when we met. Over time, my toplofty attitude softened to a cordial arrogance, but in all our years of friendship, I never abandoned a sense of my own self-importance and superiority around them. They were far too playful for me to take any of their ideas seriously. I found them amusing, like children, but as I sat across from Blip, divided by a wall of glass, I realized which one of us was the child. I was a surly fool whose presence they welcomed nonetheless, and they were as patient and persistent as the Earth's erosion, mellowing me out, bit by bit, like drops of water smoothing a jagged rock.

These are the thoughts that occurred to me as Blip stood pacing and panting, raving and ranting before me. "Society is like a fire, see? We sparked it from the friction of rubbing our minds together. It's what we all sit around, what we have in common. It brings us together in a circle. We gaze upon it. We chatter. It's endlessly useful. It comforts us, it assists us, it enables us to survive at all. It's an indispensable tool, but we must always remember that it is a powerful gift." He smiled. "It's a power tool." He laughed at his own weak joke. "The gift of

Prometheus can so easily get out of our control, choking us, consuming us, killing us. We must remain its master, or be ordered around by our own tool. Imagine that, becoming tools of tools, slaves to our selves, deluded fools allowing our own fire to destroy us. We must recognize what the fire is, learn how to channel it in appropriate directions. If we can dictate how the tool is used, rather than allowing the tool to dictate how we are used, then we can build the best of all possible worlds."

A masculine voice interrupted us over the intercom, commanding Blip to return to his fellow inmates. Though it sounded familiar, I did not recognize whose voice it was. "Inmate 104, return to the primary observation area, Inmate 104." Voice spoke with the pleasantly lifeless tone of a hospital page.

Inmate 104 was momentarily rattled by the order. "Tell Sophia," he said. "Um . . ."

"Inmate 104, please return to the primary observation area, Inmate 104." Voice's demeanor remained persistently vapid and professional.

"Tell my wife." Inmate 104 stood up, struggling with his thoughts and trying to maintain his composure despite the hyperactive spasms bouncing around his features. "How do you say it?"

"I'll tell her."

"Inmate 104, your presence is required in the primary observation area, Inmate 104."

"Please," Inmate 104 said, perhaps meaning thank you. He scratched his head in puzzlement and departed through the door on his side. As soon as his door shut, the door on my side opened.

"Fountain, get out here, on the double!" General Kiljoy barked at me. "Time to go to work. You're here to observe the subjects."

I obediently exited the confessional. My head, however, was not awash with spiritual catharsis, but throbbing with clanging pangs of guilt. Wincing, I joined Tynee and Miss Mary in the viewing area. They were too engrossed with what was occurring on the other side of the mirror to acknowledge my presence.

"*Paid in full!*" Brother Zebediah was standing in front of Manny Malarkey, preaching like a televangelist on fast-forward. Manny Malarkey was laughing hysterically; indeed, it seemed like he was on fast-forward as well. "Paid in full, Jeyzus thought in excitement as the last drop of love dripped down that old rugged cross at Calvary! 'For ye are bought with a price,'[6] heathen! Receive Him *today,* sinner!"

Blip wandered into the cell aimlessly and eventually took his chair at the table. "Receive who today?" he asked, as the door through which he had entered shut automatically.

"Doc!" Manny managed to suppress his belly laughter just long enough to squeeze out a question. "Where'd you come from?"

"Hell is where he came from and hell is where he's going!"

"You missed it." Manny caught his breath. "Zachariah here farted, and he's been hellfire ever since."

"He's a demon on the prowl!" Brother Zebediah continued working himself into a brimstone ecstasy, oblivious to everyone but himself.

Manny pointed to Brother Zebediah's chair. "Sat right there on that metal chair and farted like a highway rumble strip. Vibrated the whole goddamn table, too." He barely finished his sentence before wild chuckles once again overwhelmed him.

"Lucifer begone!" Brother Zebediah cried out.

"Who are you talking about?" Blip asked, an ample smile beginning to stretch the corners of his mouth.

"Good heavens!" Brother Zebediah roared. "Are you a simpleton *and* a heretic? I'm talking about you!" Manny pounded the table in maniacal mirth, laughing with his head resting in his other hand.

"Me?" Blip asked incredulously. "You want Manny to receive *me* today?"

Brother Zebediah, looking like a child who can't figure out that his pointing classmates are trying to tell him his fly is open, stumbled back a step, as if trying to avoid the whirling slingshot of confusion whistling dangerously close to his noggin. Manny's laughter fizzled out with an extended, high-pitched sigh. The three of them looked at one another in mutual bewilderment, goofy grins playing upon their lips and simpering smiles prancing around the crow's feet of their eyes, cavorting upon the muscle spasms in their foreheads. Before they had time to wonder why they were smiling like idiots, the grin-jaw rollicking all over their countenances frolicked into their mouths, declared their entire bodies a playground, and, with a salute and a somersault, let the three of them know who was now in charge.

68 Anthropologists have observed that laughter is humankind's most distinctive emotional expression. We share anger, fear, loyalty, grief, and myriad other states of mind with other creatures, but laughter is an emotional delicacy only humans can taste. Chimpanzees, our closest genetic relatives, will pant and puff if tickled, but that's as close as it comes. Other animals become overjoyed, certainly—witness a dog wagging its tail—but the expression of that affective state in laughter is ours alone. (And never mind hyenas, by the way. Hyenas do not laugh. That's just the sound they make.) Joyous vibrations barge in unannounced and bring nothing but breathless bellyaches and wailing convulsions to our sentimental potluck. If we're lucky, chuckles very quickly take over the entire affair, and paroxysms and conniptions seize hold of our musculature and shake us free of obligation like a dog shaking out of a leash. We hyperventilate until we're wailing like a madman in a marathon. We snort like swine at a trough of corn husks in honey. Tears run down cramped faces, we roll, we holler, we beg each other for mercy. It is brutal joy, as if a benevolent faerie has grabbed us by the heels and given us a few snaps, shaking dust off a doormat too many people have wiped their feet upon.

Sometimes, however, the merriment is interrupted by a faraway shriek, sounding asinine and absurd, and we realize the hideous sounds are our own. What must others be thinking? Good god, get control of yourself! Self-consciousness lashes out at the faerie, stinging her tickling fingers, forcing her to cast the rug aside in pity and love, and leaving a crumpled but exuberant heap of gladness behind.

Such was not the fate of Blip, Brother Zebediah, and Manny. From the moment they simultaneously erupted into roaring guffaws, swells of laughter gushed forth one on top of the next, a gleeful volcano of hilarity, dormant far too long. Brother Zebediah was particularly explosive. For the faerie, he was an especially dusty rug, perhaps owing to a lifetime of holding back nearly unbearable church pew snickers. The seismic stresses along the stern and rigid lines of his face (the San Anxiety Fault) were colossal, and when they broke, brand-new canals and topographical features were etched into his American Gothic physiognomy. Fresh, cocky skid marks strutted their stuff in front of the well-worn treads, the times they are a-changin'.

The three of them were, to be sure, laughing their asses off, and their amplified amusement showed no sign of letting up. The faerie wasn't letting go of these welcome mats. In the observation lounge, we spectators of this chorus of thunderous tantrums were not without our titters and tee-hees. Glass wall or not, laughter has an infectious quality that's difficult to resist. Compared to their jocularity, however, our gaiety had the canned quality of a studio audience.

"Fantastic, eh?" General Kiljoy slapped my knee, as if turning the APPLAUSE sign on. I was, for the moment, speechless. If I could have spoken, I might have remarked that if this was indeed the Pied Piper syndrome, then never was a disease so mercilessly kind to its host. Instead, I exhaled the best assessment I could manage.

"Heh."

69

General Kiljoy hit the mute button, abruptly ending the supernatural ruckus as if it were music in a game of musical chairs. Tynee was left without a seat, caught holding a comment, the bozo at the party who alone is shouting his conversation when the tunes are cut off. His assertion at the moment of silence, intended only for Miss Mary's ears, was "I'll bet the professor loses it first."

Tynee shrunk from his statement, drawing his head down and his shoulders up, becoming even smaller, a Tynee turtle. A snicker escaped Miss Mary's lips like a fart escaping the sphincter of a hot-dog salesman.

"Loses it?" I asked.

Tynee looked helplessly at General Kiljoy, who answered for him. "You'll see, Fountain. Why don't we go for a walk?" He looked back toward Tynee and Miss Mary. "Care to come along?"

"I'd rather stay and watch these subjects," Miss Mary said. "This is my favorite part." She pointed to the window, where Blip, Brother Zebediah, and Manny were now rolling around on the concrete floor, holding their stomachs, screaming in muted silence. They were either in agony or ecstasy; the two are often difficult to tell apart. I have even heard that fear and love, agony and ecstasy, are the same feeling, and that it's all a matter of perspective. This makes sense, of course, since everything is a matter of perspective.

"I'll stay too," Tynee piped in.

"Make a note of anything unusual," General Kiljoy ordered them as he walked toward the door. His words seemed odd to me, as I had never witnessed anything more unusual in my entire life. To Tynee and Miss Mary, however, who both nodded impatiently as if to say *of course*, this was apparently a typical display. "Shall we, Fountain?" He opened the door to the hallway, and I got up and followed reluctantly. General Kiljoy hit his mute button again and restored the sound as we exited. The sudden return of ferocious laughter chased me into the hallway.

"How long do they go on like that?" I asked, my voice resounding back at me off the concrete walls.

"Not too much longer, usually," General Kiljoy whispered as he piddled with his knickknacks. He led me into the short, dead-end passageway where the two customized golf carts were parked. We crawled into the glass-bubble cabin of one of them, and when the doors were shut, I found we were able to talk without the hellish reverberations of our voices.

"That crazy laughter," General Kiljoy continued, starting the golf cart, "is symptomatic of the initial onset. It usually lasts a half hour or so, then they're just a little dazed for a while." He drove the cart around a couple of corners and down some short passageways.

"What happens then?" I asked. We were humming down a very long passageway, going only a few miles per hour. The narrow hallway stretched farther than I could see in front of us, so that the lines created by the walls meeting the ceiling and floor appeared to intersect at the point of infinity, like a big *X* on a sheet of paper, connecting each corner to its opposite, and the center.

"All holy hell breaks loose."

"Holy hell?"

"*All* holy hell, Fountain. What Tibor was saying back there," he gestured over his head and behind him, "is that the subjects eventually go stark raving mad."

"Eventually?"

"Well, it comes and goes. But the subject always relapses, and each progressive stage is longer and more severe. After about a month their symbolic capacity is completely out of commission."

"Permanently?"

"That's what you're here to tell us."

"But it leaves them insane?"

"You'll see," he said paternally, as if I were a six-year-old named Billy on my way to a surprise ice-cream cone. He might have ruffled my hair, if I'd had any. "Anyway, we're almost there," he said. I looked ahead, and the passageway no longer went off into infinity. Instead, a bright yellow steel door was emerging and growing out of the center. Something was painted on the door, and as we drew nearer, it took the shape of a skull and crossbones.

"Here we are." General Kiljoy slowed to a stop, grinning like Long John Silver or some such buccaneer. "*X* marks the spot."

70 I expected no treasure behind the door. Perhaps I could say that it was the end result of the desire for treasure that lay behind that door, but then who am I? I'm a greedy man, remember. I sold my soul for ten million greenbacks. You shouldn't listen to a word I have to say.

Nevertheless, there we were at the gates of holy hell (a designation which seems like it should be better than hell, but somehow sounds more like *very* hell). General Kiljoy, still looking like Long John Silver, stretched his legs forward and adjusted his crotch.

"What you're about to witness," he began, "twelve other people have seen."

"The members of the CPC?" I asked.

"Affirmative." He paused, eyeing me scornfully. "Of course, there have been a few other scientists like yourself who have seen this, but unfortunately they ceased cooperating. We had to terminate their contract."

I kept my mouth shut, not wanting to take his bait, fancying myself the ancient, giant trout of which local legends are made, and General Kiljoy as just another drunk and overweight fisherman trying to snag me for a month's worth of barroom braggadocio.

"We couldn't just let them go," he continued, throwing the worm into the water as a freebie. "Originally we had a nice even set of one hundred subjects, all prisoners who had been sentenced to death. We've since added three scientists, plus your sociologist friend and his cellmates."

"Why did you include the minister and the truck driver?"

"They were a convenient opportunity. Use your brain, Fountain. One hundred death row inmates is not a very representative sample. The Pied Piper virus could conceivably have different effects on noncriminals, although so far their reaction has been standard, just like the scientists."

"Are there any women?"

"Negative," he said, fishing into his pocket to tinker with his rod and sinkers. "That wouldn't be very gentlemanly, now would it?"

I was about to mention that it might be biasing the sample as well, but I didn't want to give him any ideas. Besides, it's been common enough in medical and pharmaceutical research to only study men and generalize the results to women.

"All the prisoners are sealed behind unbreakable glass walls, just like in the observation lounge," General Kiljoy explained as he slapped on a pair of sunglasses. "As an additional measure, we're hermetically sealed inside this cart, behind the strongest and most resilient polymer yet developed. We'll pass through a disinfecting airlock before and after our tour. Any questions?"

"Just one," I replied. "Why do I need to see all of this?"

"Just some additional insurance."

"Insurance?"

"Doctor," he grinned roguishly and tossed me a pair of sunglasses. "We want you to see what awaits you if you fail in your task."

71

General Kiljoy entered a code on the keypad of his remote control, and the doors in front of us opened with a baleful boom, revealing a blazingly bright room and an identical pair of doors just beyond. After the cart pulled forward, the doors clanged shut again behind us. Dozens of arcs of electricity immediately stretched across the room, centering on our vehicle, writhing and slinking across the surface of the bubble.

"Primary disinfection," General Kiljoy explained. "The ultraviolet radiation destroys microbial genetic material. The high-voltage electromagnetic radiation disinfects as well. It also completely ozonizes the atmosphere, which finishes off any remaining organisms." After about a minute, the lightning ceased and a mist discharged from the eight corners of the cube we were then enclosed in. "That's cryogenic helium," he pointed to the mist on the outside of our bubble. "Near absolute zero. Failsafe security measure. In the event of unaccompanied intrusion, it will freeze all larger forms of life to death instantly. We've left nothing to chance. You wouldn't want to be on the outside of this bubble. At this moment, there is nothing else alive in this room but you and me. The goddamn Holy Ghost couldn't survive out in that."

I knocked on the glass tentatively, fascinated despite the larger situation, and feeling very much like a tourist riding through a concentration camp gas chamber in a golf cart.

"Don't knock too hard," General Kiljoy cautioned. "Our best polymers still become brittle at these temperatures." I sat on my hands, not relishing the thought of breaking the bubble that kept Jack Frost from nipping at my nose, or perhaps chipping off my nose. I gave an involuntary shiver. Shiver me timbers.

"Come on, come on." General Kiljoy drummed his fingers on the steering wheel as if we were in rush hour traffic. In fact, if I may point out the obvious, we were in an ice cube fifty feet below ground level.

The hissing stopped, and through the fog I saw the Jolly Roger flag in front of us bisect vertically as the doors opened. This caused an immense crackle as the atmosphere from the chamber beyond instantly vaporized the ultracold helium, like young hussy Spring chasing old man Winter out of town. He didn't stand a chance. In a downhill race between a tricycle and a sled, if the air's too warm for snow, the red trike will win every time. Spring always prevails.

Lest I mislead you with such a hasty analogy, I should note the ways in which this was not at all like the dawn of spring. For instance, the parting of the pirate flag brought with it not rainbows and lilac bracelets and pan flutes, but rather a very long row of glass cells lit by fluorescent tubes stretching ahead of us. There were no birds, there were no bees, there were no trees.

Even if there had been trees, there wouldn't have been any shadows. The boys were not out at play, but were confined to their bedrooms. Grounded. Undergrounded. And none of them wore shorts.

72

The ectoplasm of the metaphysical universe was frozen stiff. The goddamn Holy Ghost dared not tread the halls of holy hell.

"Holy shit," I muttered.

"Holy hell," General Kiljoy corrected as he pulled the cart forward. What we were both referring to was the spring thunderstorm of shrieks and bellows and howls that filled the aural cavity left by the rapid dissipation of the cryogenic helium. It sounded like a laughing gas party at a dentists' convention, with just as many root canal patients there, too, only they didn't sound like they'd been privy to the nitrous oxide.

We sat in the midst of this chaos, in our golf cart with its *Jetsons* bubble option, for a very long while. General Kiljoy never took his eyes off me, and I didn't quite know where to place mine. In the cell to my immediate right, two men were slapping out a rhythm on each other's faces while a third sat clapping frantically in front of them and yelling, "Tofu! Tofu!"

In the next cell, two men were sitting together, weeping with loud, anguished wails, beating their chests, pulling their hair, and sticking their fingers in their mouths. A third was spinning himself around and around and making airplane noises like a child wired on sugar-frosted espresso beans. He continued this for far longer than I would have thought possible, then suddenly flew off balance and toppled onto his lamenting cellmates. Although he kicked one of them in the face and bumped heads with the other, they took no notice of him and continued bawling, even when he began vomiting all over them with the force of a fire hose.

When my ears and eyes focused on the confusion to my left, I was greeted with the peculiar scene of a small, barefoot man wearing his shoes and socks on his hands and rubbing them together while his three much larger cellmates swung their hips in perfect unison, hula hoop fashion. All four were laughing profusely and sweating hysterically.

In the cell next to them, four men were each standing with their faces in one of the four corners, screaming, screaming, screaming, and screaming. Screeching bellows filled with ferocity, fear, or both tore from their throats, straining the ligaments of their vocal cords beyond repair, shredding the sinews until they were spinning and popping apart like a rope with far too much weight on it. Focusing my ears, I recognized that their shrieks and roars were actually extended howls of a single word.

That word was "MOM-MEEEEEEEE!"

73

Blip once told me about a fantasy he and Sophia had. If they were ever to come into considerable wealth, they'd buy a VW Vanagon and go on the road in search of good conversation. When they found it, they'd talk and talk, and if the person was honest and idealistic but capital poor, they would offer to pay for the start-up costs of their dream, but only on the verbal promise that if they succeeded, they'd do the same for others. Then they would disappear on down the road, no name, no thank-you. Until such time, they satisfied this urge by slipping anonymous notes of compliment and encouragement to deserving strangers. They believe such activities spread good cheer exponentially, and are worth the effort just to see the looks on people's faces.

General Kiljoy liked to see the looks on people's faces when he showed them holy hell, and it was equally priceless for him. The visage was identical from person to person, he told me, and I was no exception.

"It's fascinating," he said, muting the external noise. I hadn't been aware that he had that power, so I was somewhat awestruck when a wave of his hand caused such impossible pandemonium to cease, like God twitching a pinky to still an earthquake. "It's an expression I've never seen anywhere else."

"Do I still have the expression?" I asked, feeling the lines of my face as a blind person might, only I lacked such tactile talent.

"No, now you just look confused."

"How did I look before?"

"I don't know, Fountain, that's what I'm trying to tell you. There's confusion in it, but also surprise, panic, awe, pity, and amusement. It's an entirely new pattern of contracting and relaxing facial muscles. I've never seen it before." He studied my face inquisitively. "Did I tell you I'm a dilettante physiognomist? It's a hobby. I study people's faces for clues to their personality. It helps me professionally."

"Um." I became painfully self-conscious of my possible expression. Conversing with someone concerning your countenance is about as comfortable an interaction as discussing the dynamics of eye contact. Consequently, I had to turn away, only to be greeted by the sight of the two formerly weeping men now mercilessly beating the third, the dizzy one who'd fallen and vomited upon them. I turned back to General Kiljoy, but was only met with his physiognomic scrutiny once again. "What's happening?" I pointed to the brutal violence occurring to our right, attempting to change the focus of attention from my face. "Is that normal?"

"Happens all the time in cities all over the world," General Kiljoy talked through a yawn. "Seems normal enough."

"I mean, is that behavior symptomatic of the Pied Piper virus?"

"Hard to say for sure. That's why we're interested in some subjects without a history of violent behavior. Anyway, any behavior after infection has to be taken as an effect of the Pied Piper virus, since losing your linguistic capacity must certainly alter the entirety of your perceptions. With these prisoners, anyway, there's certainly been an increase in violence."

"Have there been any deaths?"

"I knew you were going to ask that, I could see it in your face. I suppose now you're going to accuse me of lying to you and start your self-righteous moralizing again. Well, save it for Tibor, I'm sick to shit of it. These men were condemned to death anyway, and besides, I didn't lie. The Pied Piper virus doesn't *directly* result in death, that's what I said."

"Why don't you just say your fingers were crossed?"

"If they were," General Kiljoy sneered, "it'd have to be good enough for you. Now drop it, Fountain, that's the end of it." He jabbed his beefy index finger in my chest. It hurt. "You're here to do a job," he continued, mellow but menacing, "and I expect you to do it. Are we clear?"

I nodded, rubbing my throbbing breastbone. I then asked in a professional tone, "I think it's relevant information for my research, however, to know how many have been indirectly killed."

"Forty-three, last I checked. Forty-four, if they keep it up on that bastard."

I looked to my right, just in time to see Dizzy's head crushed under the boot of one of his cellmates. His skull collapsed as if it had been a mere watermelon, and they continued kicking his now lifeless body. Inevitably, the aphorism "no sense kicking a dead horse" popped into my mind. Try as I might, however, I could find no wisdom in that adage, for there is even less sense in kicking a living horse.

74

"Yep," General Kiljoy said, droll and aloof. "Forty-four." Horrified and disgusted, I began to dry heave.

"Don't go hurling in here, Fountain," he reprimanded. "You saw what happened to that guy."

"What?" I asked between gags.

"You heard me, wonderbelly. You would've never made it in 'nam."

"Vietnam?" I said, swallowing a retch.

"Four years," he bragged, driving us farther down the corridor. "I've had my fair share of skull-crushing, I can say. Strange feeling, putting the heel of your boot through someone's brain. Both crunchy and squishy. Once, on routine patrol, our platoon was ambushed by some VC. They came at us from all sides, but I'll never forget, something came over me that day. I went absolutely berserk, pure combat, flawless form. I have thin memories of racing through the brush, hitting every gook I aimed at, completely . . ." He paused. ". . . aware. I couldn't fail, and I knew it, knew it like I had never known anything before." He became sickeningly passionate in his description. "I had this grace, this totality of perception. When it was over, only two men in our platoon sustained injuries, and twenty-seven Vietcong lay dead, fourteen or fifteen by me—we weren't sure who got one of them. I was awarded the Medal of Honor for that, and it got me to the position I'm in today." He paused wistfully. "I told Tony Temper about that once. He was in my platoon, got into that Buddhism crap after the war. He told me it was a Zen moment. I slugged him for that, joining an enemy religion, I mean."

"Hmm."

"The last person I killed that day was only wounded before I ran out of ammo, so I had to stomp his skull in. Tony Temper, he also told me he was psychic, like he could read minds, you know. He told me he knew what the last thing to go through that slope's Oriental brain was that day. You know what it was?"

"What?"

General Kiljoy grinned enormously. "My boot."

75

General Kiljoy encouraged me to continue observing the subjects as we slowly moved down the corridor. I declined and, reminding him that I was hungover, warned that I could offer no guarantees of digestive normalcy. His only response was to hit the brake suddenly, causing me to lurch forward. I somehow managed to keep myself from turning inside out, but I heaved so hard I blacked out momentarily.

"Sorry!" He slapped me on the back. "Couldn't resist."

I smiled weakly and asked to please return to the observation lounge.

"You're probably dying to know what's going on with your friend, eh?"

I nodded submissively. In turning the cart around, we were brought face to fundament with a single man in a cell, naked, pressing his buttocks up against the glass, mooning us. He stepped away from the glass for a moment, then threw his posterior up against the glass once again.

"Now that's a sick bastard," General Kiljoy commented. "He was at boot camp for the Marines, seemed a damn fine cadet, when he suddenly went ballistic and raped and murdered his drill sergeant, then threw a grenade into his bunkhouse. Killed more than a few good men. Since he's been in here, he's managed to do the same to his cellmates."

"How are the corpses removed?" I asked, suddenly curious as to this little housekeeping detail.

"It's all automated," he waved off my question. "This compound is equipped with state-of-the-art automation routines, to eliminate the possibility of human error. But listen, his little episode at the Marine barracks resulted in a top-secret court-martial. I was present." The Marine took another flying leap backward onto the glass. "You know what that asshole's only statement was?"

I shrugged.

"All he kept saying, over and over again, was '*Semper fi, semper fi, semper fi.*'"

76

In truth, boredom is a fine stimulus to creativity. If you stare at an empty wall long enough, your mind will begin to occupy itself with hallucinations. Sensory deprivation chambers operate on this principle. Take away all the noise, and what you're left with is far from nothing; indeed, nothingness can be something else entirely. Thus, while many assert that you can't get something for nothing, you can certainly get something *from* nothing. This is, after all, the nature of the universe. Creation *ex nihilo.*

I am hemming and hawing about so much nonsense here because I have nothing pertinent to say. I am avoiding the issue, it seems, but it can be avoided no longer. The story was pretty much unfolding on its own, until suddenly I found myself struggling to relate the ride back from holy hell to the observation lounge, during which time nothing at all happened. Certainly I could have said, *We returned uneventfully to the observation lounge,* but I could not satisfy myself, nor would I presume to ask you to be satisfied, with such a cheap segue.

But it is the fact of the matter. Nothing happened. An event is, by definition, anything that happens, but the ride was, as I said, uneventful. I suppose I breathed, as did General Kiljoy, and the wheels rolled, and we may have shifted in our seats, but these hardly qualify as events, do they? Holy hell was unmistakably happening, this entire story has been one significant occurrence after another, but the ride back to the observation lounge was without incident.

Stories are eventful, full of circumstances of importance and intrigue, but this is not at all an accurate reflection of life. Life, like this chapter, can be rather uneventful at times. Oftentimes you find yourself on the toilet, or in a traffic jam, or watching television commercials, or countless other instances that get edited out when someone asks what you did with your day.

Blip sometimes boasted of how little he did on some days.

As he argued it, the aphorism that you can't get something for nothing is dubious at best, and is probably a product of our culture's capitalist work ethic. Therefore, he said, he actively did nothing, especially when the money politics of the university aggravated him. He saw his behavior as subversive, akin to factory workers who deliberately slow down the pace of their work to reduce the owner's profits.

Blip told me of a time last spring when he continued doing nothing even when he was home from the university. All evening he sat in an easy chair in his living room, no book, no television, nothing. Every time Sophia wandered in and asked him what he was doing, he replied, "Nothing," and immediately fell silent again. After the third or fourth time, Sophia finally insisted that he must be doing *something,* even thinking, but Blip persisted in asserting his inactivity. Sophia could not accept this on a philosophical level, and attempted to engage her husband in a debate as to whether or not one can actively do nothing. This only made Blip irate. He told her she was interfering with his subversive act, and declared her a strikebreaker. Sophia responded that he shouldn't bring his work home with him. Blip conceded that she had a good point, and proceeded to occupy the rest of the evening unsuccessfully attempting to communicate the significance of the incident to me over the telephone.

I thought he was crazy when he related that story to me, but now I find myself taking his advice and actively doing nothing much of the time. It is not difficult, at least in more mundane states of consciousness. One need only recognize that most of the moments that pass us by do not carry events of any consequence. To give an example, if you watch a pot of water until it boils, the only moments that carry any meaningful events are those when bubbles of steam begin to form at the bottom of the pot to ultimately rise to the top. After staring at a pot of water for ten minutes, this can be profoundly momentous. It is a moment in which something actually *happens.*

Out of all the moments we perceive, those that actually carry events that command or attract our attention are relatively rare, and should be treasured. This does not mean, however, that we should lament the unending procession of naked moments, the peaceful pulsations flitting constantly past with every flap of a hummingbird's wings, offering us nothing but the incessant assurance that a tock will soon follow their tick. An uneventful moment gives us a grand opportunity to explore nothingness, which is really something else entirely. Boredom is the coward's reaction to staring at a wall.

Just before writing this chapter, in fact, I was sitting at the desk in the laboratory where General Kiljoy makes me work, actively doing nothing. I did not wish to do what I was being told to do, and as I said, I was altogether stumped as to how to proceed with this story. I had been sitting with my feet on the desk for perhaps twenty minutes, just looking at the various objects in the room, when very suddenly a book fell sideways on the shelf, startling me and causing me to jolt upright. That moment was *eventful.* The variables that caused that happenstance had been gradually gathering strength for an untold amount of time. Pages were settling, weight was shifting, the stress on the forces holding it upright was building, all at an imperceptibly slow pace, until WHAM! Wake up! A tree falls in the woods, and a moment has spoken. What does it say? It says nothing. It only smiles, and it is gone.

The Book o' Billets-doux

rosehips:	Guess what? I watched a tree fall on television last night, with the volume off. It didn't make a sound. A tree fell in the woods, someone was around to hear it, but it still didn't make a sound. Nothing, just silence. Television stumps the Buddha, eh?
sweetlick:	A vision on the television! If a tree falls in the woods, and no one's around to hear it, does it make a sound? Such words have been said to point toward paradise, but I'm dying to ask the Buddha what he was thinking about, for if no one is around to see them, then where are the woods?
rosehips:	On the other hand, what is the sound of one hand clapping?
sweetlick:	What other hand?

77 And so we returned uneventfully to the observation lounge. Upon entering, we were greeted with the sight of Tynee leaping across the sofa from Miss Mary. He moved with the speed and grace of a hobbledehoy adolescent nearly caught

stealing third base, and landed in a sitting position as awkward as a hypertensive attempting a yoga posture. His back, along with other parts of his anatomy, was erect, and he sat frozen with one hand on his knee and the other across his chest. He turned to us only after some seconds had passed, as if he had just then noticed our arrival.

"Hello!" He tried to imitate pleasant surprise as he stood up stiffly. Miss Mary still had not turned to acknowledge our presence. Instead, she was fumbling with her lighter, trying to light a cigarette.

General Kiljoy wagged his finger at Tynee, shaking his head in mock disapproval at their bumpery. "Hello indeed," he said, causing Tynee's ridiculous pretensions to evaporate as fast as the cryogenic helium from the golf cart, and leaving him with an expression more timorous than that of an ochlophobic who suddenly and inexplicably finds himself naked and on third base at the World Series opener with a hundred thousand drunken sports fans pointing at him and guffawing. "Your fly's open," General Kiljoy added mercilessly.

"Greetings, gentlemen." Miss Mary stood and casually exhaled a lungful of poison in our direction. "How was your tour, Doctor?" She exuded a supreme nicotine confidence.

"Good," I answered, not at all meaning it, and not at all sure why I said it. Tynee struggled with his zipper.

"Wonderful," Miss Mary continued with her preposterous pleasantries.

General Kiljoy sighed impatiently at the fatuity of the situation. "What's happening with the subjects?" He walked toward the observation window and turned on the audio, drawing our party's attention there as well. Blip, Brother Zebediah, and

Manny were sitting around the table, catching yawns from one another, and looking exhausted but slaphappy. Apparently, they had been laughing for the entire duration of our absence. The topic of their conversation had not changed.

"What?" Brother Zebediah asked. "What are you talking about?"

"When I came in you were saying 'receive him today, sinner,' to Manny, right?"

"'Receive him *today,* sinner!'" Manny imitated, giggling and smiling.

"Who?" Brother Zebediah asked, confused.

"Yes. Who do you want him to receive?"

"Him?" Brother Zebediah pointed to Manny. "Receive *him* today?"

"Aooww!" Manny said, massaging his cheeks. "Goddamn, man. I think I sprained my face."

"Is that what you meant?" Blip continued.

"When did I say this?"

"What are we talking about?" Manny, still trying to wipe the smirk off his face, entered the conversation. No one answered immediately, and an awkward silence ensued.

"Him?" Brother Zebediah pointed at Manny after a few moments.

"That's what I'm trying . . . ," Blip replied, looking exasperated. "What is this 'him' you keep referring to?"

"Never mind." Brother Zebediah attempted to swat the confusion away as if it were a cloud of no-see-ums. "Just never mind." They fell into silence once again, each appearing to be lost in their own thoughts. Brother Zebediah fidgeted uneasily, rubbing his nose, perhaps wishing he could duck out of sight for a quick pick. In an effort to maintain a lack of expression, his face bore a grimace that would frighten the horns off a demon. “It’s not my fart, you know,” he said abruptly, but neither Blip nor Manny paid him any heed. “Fault,” he immediately corrected himself. “It’s not my *fault.*” He brushed frantically at his ear, as if a mosquito had flown into it.

Blip and Manny were absorbed in other things. Manny was massaging the cramped muscles in his face, still grinning as if he were trying to see all his teeth in a mirror. Blip, meanwhile, was leaning back in his chair, hands behind his head, lower lip pursed, thinking. His eyes were unfocused, or rather, were focused inward, and periodically, as his thoughts bore fruit from some tree he’d been irrigating with his stream of consciousness, he raised his eyebrows and smiled. The fruit was sweet, but also tart, like a firm plum, and his smile was the smile of an aesthete. It was accompanied by a pucker playing a sassy bass line with his lips and a sunny squint twanging a cheerful banjo with the crow’s feet of his eyes, and his foot was a-tappin’.

78

People do not tap their feet. Feet are tapped. Passive voice. To say people tap their feet implies some sort of conscious activity. Foot tapping is not willed, or if it is, it isn’t in rhythm. You may try to will your feet to stop tapping, but this is never successful for long, and soon your feet are tapping away even more furiously than before. Thus, the foot of Blip was tapping. This was not terribly unusual for him. He was forever pulsing with some cadence or another. His grade school teachers undoubtedly tried to embarrass him into sitting still by asking him if he had ants in his pants, but they never had to tell him to shake a leg. When he got really stimulated by a discussion, he was liable to get up and tap-dance around your sombrero. What made this particular foot-tapping situation significant, however, is that the feet of Brother Zebediah and Manny were tapping as well. Moreover, they were in perfect time with Blip, although none of them seemed to be aware of it.

"I love when women wear makeup," Manny said dreamily. "How 'bout you, Zachariah?"

"I think Mr. Fancy-Pants Professor wears makeup." Brother Zebediah, beginning to perk up, leered at Blip. "Look at his hair. He looks like a girl."

"Girls are cool," said Blip. "Besides, Jesus had long hair."

"Jeyzus most certainly did not have long hair, you homo, and he definitely wasn't a vegetarian!"

"Vegetarian?" Blip looked at Manny, then back at Brother Zebediah. "What?"

"Do I have to spell it out for you, you ho-mo-sex-u-al?" Brother Zebediah's pious energy was fast returning. "Doesn't work, does it?" He gestured broadly with his arms, pointing his index fingers, apparently intended to represent erect penises, toward each other.

Manny suddenly sneezed three times in a row, only momentarily interrupting their synchronous foot tapping.

"A triple," General Kiljoy quipped, nudging Tynee.

"God bless you," said Blip.

"Oh no!" said Brother Zebediah. "God can't spare a blessing for someone who doesn't even know how to wear a hat." He pointed to Manny's cap, which was purposefully turned around. "Hey," he addressed Manny directly. "You got your hat on backwards, son, must mean your head's not on straight."

"Zachariah was a bullfrog," Manny sing-songed.

"The name is *Brother Zebediah.*"

"I think it's *Jeremiah* was a bullfrog," Blip added.

"Ribbet, ribbet," Manny taunted Brother Zebediah, flapping his elbows as if he were imitating a chicken.

Brother Zebediah ignored Manny's mockery and turned back to Blip. "You!" he said. "You said, 'God bless you!'"

Blip nodded affably. "I did."

"I love sneezing," said Manny.

"I didn't expect you to admit that you believe in God," Brother Zebediah said to Blip.

"I'm not talkin' 'bout weak wheezes," Manny continued, addressing no one at all.

"Maybe you shouldn't have any expectations," Blip replied to Brother Zebediah.

"I'm sayin' strong sneezes," Manny persisted with his soliloquy. "Now that's what pleases." All three tapped out a punch line.

"It pleases Jeyzus to know that you believe in Him."

"Please us Jesus?" Manny rhymed. "Sneeze us Jesus?"

"Whatever," Blip yawned. "All you've got to do is be honest and kind. How's it go? 'Blessed are the pure in heart, for they shall see God?'[7] I've always liked that sentiment."

"Read on, false prophet! On judgment day, Jeyzus will rebuke those who think they've served Him, saying, 'Depart from Me, ye that work iniquity.'[8] *That's* the conclusion of the semen on the mount."

"Semen on the mount?" Manny spoke loudly. "Semen on the mount? Did'ja hear that, Doc? Semen on the mount!" Blip nodded and chuckled in weary but unflagging amusement.

"Blasphemy!" Brother Zebediah stammered, mortified. "Your evil is unspeakable!"

"Don't try to blame me, Brother. You said it. You said 'semen on the mount.'"

"I said no such thing!" Brother Zebediah insisted, reddening from embarrassment or anger. "I said *sermon* on the mount."

"No, not quite. You said 'semen on the mount.' That's exactly what you said." Manny rocked back and forth in his chair, uncontainably delighted at Brother Zebediah's slip of the lip. "I can see where your mind is at. You *still* enjoy lookin' at women in a sinful way. Semen on the mount. Hoo-wee! Yeah! Right on! Semen on the mount. Semen on the mount. You're blushin', Brother. If your mouth was a semi, a runaway truck ramp on the interstate couldn't've slowed you down a few minutes ago. Now you've hit a roadblock. Semen on the mount."

Blip leaned forward and posed a riddle. "What do you call a rerun of the semen on the mount?"

"A rerun of the semen on the mount," Manny repeated. "What do you call it?"

Blip made the sign of the cross and grinned. "The second coming."

79

There was a tangible beat after Blip's heretical punch line, followed immediately by the uproarious laughter of everyone present, Brother Zebediah included. The studio audience chuckled as well, though our laughter was quick to fade. Blip, Brother Zebediah, and Manny, however, continued to laugh far past the point of lethargy. After several minutes, their fatigue finally subdued their hilarity, and they sat about in lassitude.

"Here's something interesting." Blip abruptly stood up after a few minutes had passed and began addressing the mirror. He was trying to look at us but was instead lecturing the bottle of Wild Turkey behind us on the bar. "Language is a piss-poor attempt at telepathy is what it is. We try to put our thoughts in each other's heads through language." He laughed and yawned, but continued talking through them both, making his voice high and strained. "But half the intended meaning gets lost in the transmission, and the other half is filtered through existing assumptions. Everything is a half truth!"

"He's mad," Brother Zebediah declared, looking woefully at Blip, whose feet were tapping like an insecticidal maniac on an anthill.

At that remark, Blip pivoted on his heels and pointed victoriously at him. "See!" He drew close to Brother Zebediah. "That's the whole problem! You can't understand me through the smog of your presumptions and prejudices. Multiply that six billion times and you'll begin to understand the desperation of our global situation."

80 Evening was falling, though it was as graceful and subtle as a wink from a figure skater. The fiber optic cable tips that had been piping in lumens and lumens of Indian summer sunshine all day were now fading considerably in their intensity. The room dimmed further when General Kiljoy caused the curtains in front of the observation window to hush together, and it became indisputable that the near side of twilight was upon us.

"That's the last you'll see of your friend until your work is finished, Fountain." General Kiljoy walked over to where I was leaning on the bar. I had moved from the sofa to the bar in order to stand in Blip's line of sight, so I wouldn't have to watch him lecture at a liquor bottle. I entertained a fleeting notion of kicking General Kiljoy in the shins as he stood before me juggling his jalopy, but did not follow through with it. In retrospect, that was probably fortunate, since it conceivably may have set into motion an entirely different sequence of events than the ones you are soon to read. As it turned out, he was wrong anyway. I would see Blip again just after the far side of twilight tonight, in less than an hour.

The cellular phone built into Tynee's remote control buzzed, and after taking the call, he strode over to the bar as well. "General, my presence as university president is required immediately upstairs."

"Required?" General Kiljoy turned to Tynee. "What's that supposed to mean?"

"Some students are trying to throw an illegal Halloween party tonight on the Green."

"Halloween party? Why should I give a jack-o'-lantern's shit about a Halloween party?"

"It's not me. The board of trustees has banned the party. I was only to be contacted to manage a crisis. I'm expected to be there. It's part of the role of university president."

"Oh fer cryin' out loud," General Kiljoy snorted. He paced to and fro, temperamentally twiddling his tiddlywinks. Abruptly, he paused, smirking wickedly. "Give me a minute. I need to use the john."

General Kiljoy returned within a minute, still groping about his groin. "Tynee, call Volt and have him meet us at your office. We'll all accompany you upstairs. We won't be returning here tonight." He glanced at me. "I think the Doctor has seen enough."

Tynee pulled his phone out again and called Volt, who, remember, was with Agent Orange, Meeko, and Ratdog. He instructed him to meet us at his office.

"I think Volt needs more training, General," Tynee said after he disconnected the call. "His accent sounded funny."

"I adore his Italian accent," Miss Mary spoke wistfully, and Tynee appeared to make a mental note of this romantic detail.

"Something wrong with his accent?" General Kiljoy asked shortly.

"No," Tynee said as he gingerly put his cellular phone back in his inside breast pocket, as if there was a mouse in his jacket and he was carefully setting a trap. There was no mouse in his jacket, but there might have been one in General Kiljoy's pants, and from the looks of things, it was cornered and getting pawed and batted about helplessly. "He was doing a southern Hindi, in fact."

"I don't care for that one," Miss Mary asserted.

"So what's the matter then?" General Kiljoy inquired tightly.

"Well," Tynee began, "unless I'm mistaken, he sounded like a drunken Hindi with the hiccups."

81

Among the many irritating inventions humans have devised stands the elevator. Its shafts enable us to scrape the sky (a disturbing concept, I might point out), to design a priapic skyline, to stack ourselves, and to kill ourselves in just one more dramatic way. Moreover, without elevators we might never have had the opportunity to stand in a box with complete strangers while we mutually wish for one another's absence, self-consciously counting the seconds and the floors until we can get the hell away from one another. They lift our bodies, though not our spirits, and according to Blip, you can feel your spirit being pulled from you as an elevator begins its ascent. Blip always takes the stairs, two at a time, and he's very self-righteous about it.

When in the company of a group of people you already despise, standing in a closet with them is an idea less appealing than fifty flights of stairs. Nevertheless, this was the situation that I realized was imminent when Tynee hit a button on his remote control that caused another portion of the bookcase to open. This revealed an elevator decorated in the same mahogany-walled, bearskin rug fashion as the observation lounge, as if one might want to relax in there and have a nightcap by a crackling fire.

"All aboard," Tynee quipped maladroitly as we entered single file. The doors slipped shut noiselessly, made all the more obvious by our own conspicuous lack of conversation. The close quarters concentrated Miss Mary's corrosive tobacconist's effluvium, making it all the more emphatic, and a meaty bouquet was rising out of General Kiljoy's duodenum, or perhaps slipping silently out the back door to mingle malevolently in an eloping liaison of fumes with Miss Mary's flagrant fragrances. I instinctively looked for the floor numbers as my soul was tugged through the balls of my feet, but there were none, nor were there any buttons on the wall. I could not help but state this observation.

"Not really necessary," Tynee answered. I wondered momentarily if the mahogany walls were really necessary. "There are only two stops in this elevator," he continued triumphantly. "The observation lounge and my office."

I nodded. General Kiljoy cleared his throat. Miss Mary fanned the air in front of her face. Tynee's words echoed silently off the hardwood walls, resounding in my head until the sounds had become nothing more than glossolalic gibberish. I began to feel some silly sense of anticipation, though I could not comprehend what for, and checked the time on my watch. It was 5:55, so I made a wish.

What did I wish for? Peace on Earth, of course.

82

The elevator hummed an unexciting tune, monotonous and dull, like a chorus of monks meditating upon a hissing teakettle. Their consciousness lifted as far as it was going to get, the monks simultaneously ceased their toning as the doors to the elevator opened to Tynee's office-apartment. Directly across the enormous room before us, five windows stretched from the floor to the ceiling, providing a panorama of the Green. There was, however, no Green to be seen. It looked as if some mad mosaicist had flung thousands of variously colored tessera across a heretofore grassy canvas, sneezed, and inadvertently breathed life into them. The pixels danced, the pixels swayed, the pixels chanted. The unseen teapot continued to shriek like a kamikaze pterodactyl, and the monks sounded as if they'd tired of their somber ruminations, thrown off their robes, and gotten a pickup game of coed naked Red Rover going with the nuns next door. Random yippees and squeals and hollers and wahoos slipped through Tynee's double-thick windows, and outside, a party that would have miffed the morals of Dionysus was in full swing, leaning back, pulling hard on the chains, pumping its legs till it was playing footsie with the sky (much nicer than scraping the sky), mocking gravity, sassing the centrifuge, tempting inertia, going for it, going all the way around this time.

General Kiljoy roared like one of the grizzly bear rugs in the observation lounge and elevator might have done in their more animate days. "What the devil is happening here?"

"Fuck off!" Tynee hollered back with equal intensity if not greater ferocity as he strode toward his desk. His pulmonary capacity could have blown a brick pighouse down. Astonishingly, this silenced General Kiljoy. Tynee, apparently, took no abuse in his own territory, even though his body weight was less than what General Kiljoy could lift above his head (as he would do later that evening). As if to emphasize his domain further, Tynee pulled out his remote control, and with some nimble fingerwork, had both the elevator hidden behind a bookcase and his secretary summoned over the intercom. He also set the Jacuzzi to bubbling, although it never became apparent to what end.

His secretary informed him over the intercom that his assistants were awaiting his arrival in the boardroom. "Have they taken any action yet?" he demanded.

"No sir," came a practiced and pleasant voice. "They're just waiting."

"What in God's name are they waiting for?" Tynee barked back. "Can't they wipe their own ass without my say-so?"

The secretary laughed obsequiously. "I guess not, sir."

"Well, inform them I'm on my way in." He clicked off the intercom and turned to us. "General, I'd like you to accompany me to the meeting. I'm going to recommend that the National

Guard be brought in." Before General Kiljoy had time to nod, a full beer can ricocheted off one of the windows. "Back in the seventies, before we paved over the brick roads, that would have been a brick," he informed General Kiljoy as they exited to an adjoining room.

Tynee was correct about the bricks. Blip and Sophia claimed to have a half brick whose other half was pitched through one of the administration's windows during an antiwar protest in the early '70s. Sophia painted it black and placed it on their mantel. "It's in mourning," Blip explained soberly. "Its other half went down in a blaze of glory."

"Yes," added Sophia, "but it was for a good cause."

83

Somewhere, a teakettle wailed away in creative agony, screaming as the steamy fruit of its womb burst forth. As the sound continued, I began to notice that the noise was cleaner, not as wet, and more constant. It sounded like a crystal wineglass singing or, more precisely, vibrating. Blip was fond of encouraging his wineglasses to sing at academic dinner parties, much to the chagrin of most others present. "Listen to that!" he would shout. "Do you know why the crystal sings? It's because the friction created is vibrating throughout the crystal's structure, creating this frequency of sound. This glass is literally shuddering with music. Come on, join in!" Inevitably, one of the more severe intellectuals would ask him to cease and desist, and he would politely comply, adding that he was "just trying to get us all on the same wavelength."

This recollection occurred to me as I gazed out a window at the lawless jamboree occurring below. In one section, a group of people were undulating like hurricane-happy driftwood as they were manhandled across the top of the bronze and amber waves of hands. The hands were connected to bodies costumed in attire ranging from furry cartoon characters to topless belly dancers, and floating through the currents of the crowd were the usual fare of vampires and devils and aliens and robots and gypsies and transvestites, along with tap dancers, jugglers, and a marijuana leaf, to name but a few. On the fringe of the crowd nearest to us, a circle of about twenty drummers, faces and bodies painted like psychedelic aborigines, sat beating out an impossible combination of cadence and chaos while another thirty or so danced around and between them. Bottle rockets shot into the air from time to time, eliciting cheers of approval from the masses. A band had set up stacks of amplifiers in front of the library at one end of the Green and was feeding the frenzy and freedom with a spirited jam of a dozen musicians doing their own thing together.

At one point I leaned forward a little and happened to touch the glass. I abruptly pulled my hand away. I was startled to feel the glass vibrating, buzzing my fingertips like a tuning fork on my front teeth. Evidently, the ruckus outside was causing the windows to vibrate and emit the high-frequency whine. I proceeded to touch all the windows, interrupting the feedback loop that caused them to reverberate. It worked, but only for a few moments, and soon they had tuned in to the frequency of the festivities once again.

I tuned in to the festivities again myself just in time to see, about fifty feet from the edge of the gathering, a void suddenly emerge like a dry spot of pavement from a swiftly evaporating puddle. Into the clearing stepped two Jesuses, one complete with stigmata on his hands and a crown of thorns around his bloody head, the other wrapped in a bedsheet toga-tunic and wearing a simple halo above his jesuschrist hair. The crowd immediately around them began chanting, "Fight! Fight! Fight!" It was all very good-natured, however, and both Jesuses were grinning like they'd recently turned a bottle of water into a six-pack. They obliged their audience and clasped their hands together, attempting to arm-wrestle while still standing. A brief tussle ensued until one of them was thrown off balance, and lo and behold, it was the halo-wearing Jesus that was left standing.

84 Miss Mary is a forgery without an original, which is to say, she is fake, although it is not really clear what she is faking. She is simply the essence of synthetic phoniness, like a woodgrain shower curtain, and yet a counterfeit likely to fool the art world's best auction houses. Miss Mary claims to have highly refined tastes, such as wanting two-fifths cream and three-fifths milk in her Colombian coffee instead of half-and-half—an unlikely gustatory sensitivity given her two-pack-a-day cigarette habit. The garish tobacco heiress, underneath the impressive facsimile created by her clothing, cosmetics, and pretensions, is less real than a middle-aged mannequin, and her head is emptier than puffed rice. She is a sycophant in charge, and she acts as if she draws her behavioral cues from daytime television.

Behind me, I heard her draw in a breath as if to speak, and I cringed at the plastic genialities she was preparing to hurl at me like sugarcoated water balloons. "Enjoying yourself today, Doctor?" she asked, as if I had been sliding down waterslides naked all afternoon.

I paused as long as I could, free of ignoring her question completely, then muttered, rolling my eyes along with my voice, "I guess," without turning around. I touched the window to stop its high-pitched buzz.

"Doctor, Doctor," she henpecked. "'I guess' rhymes with 'yes' but it sounds like 'no.'"

"What?" I spat, emphasizing the *t* and allowing a sharp edge to creep into my voice, hoping to puncture her swollen self-confidence. It mattered not if I succeeded in puncturing anything, for as I've said, she was as empty and contrived as a shopping mall after hours. I must have pierced something, however, because a malignant cloud of foul smog spewed out of her mouth like industrial waste and billowed around my head, swirling about in a particulate haze.

"You heard me, dear Doctor. Your well-being is a top priority with us." As she said this, Tynee and General Kiljoy returned, munching slices of pizza, and I was never so happy to see the other two people I had grown to loathe so completely. If nothing else, they could quibble among themselves. That was my hope, but it was not the case. Like passengers in the back of a Greyhound bound for Chatsville, they were forever intent upon including me in any conversation they were having.

"Hey Fountain," General Kiljoy called loudly across the room, his mouth full of masticated mozzarella. "Want some pizza? Better hurry before it's all gone."

I sulked a few moments before realizing that I was famished. I hadn't ingested anything since breakfast except three shots of Wild Turkey. I felt like a child whose parents had just scolded him at a picnic, saying, "Are you going to stand there and pout, or do you want to eat?" Thus humbled, I had to admit that, yes, I wanted to eat. My physical needs swiftly shoved my moping, melodramatic antics aside, and I found myself trotting to the boardroom to fetch some pizza, salivating in anticipation, damn near wagging my tailbone.

Along the way, my attention was momentarily distracted by Tynee's small bottle of urushiol, the extract of poison ivy, sitting unobstructed on a bookcase. I paused, looked around, and, without premeditation or precedent, swiped it.

85

The entire area of the boardroom was filled by an immense ovular table, the surface of which was cut out of a single piece of giant sequoia. The grain was impossibly straight, and the color so rich and deep that the surface seemed three-dimensional. It had a width of about ten feet at its widest point, and was nearly twice as long. The room had the same tall, vibrating windows as Tynee's office, and along the walls were pictures of frightfully nondescript white males. They all looked dreadfully serious, and were framed in the same rusty magenta wood as the conference table. Chairs were every which way, coffee cups and empty cans of soda interrupted the crumbs scattered evenly across the table, and four pizza boxes lay open in the middle of the priceless table. There was one piece of pie left, but it was not in any of the boxes. It was in the delicate and slender hands of a young man with blow-dried, blond hair. It was in the hands of Blip's original jailer, Captain Porton Down.

There is nothing like hunger to remind us that we are still animals. When hungry, I get pissy, testy, irate, and if anything goes wrong, if anything is out of place, I'm liable to throw a temper tantrum that would make the howl of the worst two-year-old hellchild sound positively numinous. I'm hypoglycemic, but I'm certain I'm not the only person who turns desperado when calorically deprived. From an evolutionary standpoint, it is adaptive for us to become aggressive when we're hungry, so that in the absence of supermarkets and agriculture, we might hunt up some chow. Modern humans don't generally hunt out of necessity, but we still get hungry, and the aggression is translated into crankiness.

Here, my entire life was going wrong, and, more immediately, the pizza was out of place. It was not wonderfully stuck to the greasy cardboard. Instead, it was in the manicured hands of a man who had expedited the deliverance of my best friend into the respectively beefy and bony hands of General Kiljoy and Tynee. I was crazy hungry, I was furious, and I imagined the buzzing windows were again a steaming teapot, and I imagined my head was that teapot, and I imagined taking my stubby hands and using them to throttle Captain Down's clean-shaven neck.

But I didn't. Instead I said to him, as if he owed me an explanation, "Got the last piece, eh?"

"Oh I'm sorry, Professor, were you going for this?" he said, taking a bite that pulled the cheese off half the slice. I shrugged nonchalantly. "Well, it's like my father used to say," he continued talking as he chewed. "The first one to reach across the table gets the most."

86

Captain Down is the kind of man who, like most politicians, has never in his life let more than two days go by without shaving. He is meticulous about his appearance, and he has perfected the ingratiating personality. He aspires to flatter his way into the Hotel Humbug of high political office, and is only now, in his present occupation, laying the solid groundwork for an unequivocal tough-on-crime platform to be preached from later. He's sharp enough to comprehend the underlying rules of the game, but not wise enough to realize that he's playing a game.

"Sorry to hear about your friend," he said between bites, but I scarcely heard him. I was obsessively wishing I'd had a second bagel this morning, for then, I reasoned, I would be that much less hungry. "Kiljoy drives a hard bargain, you know?" He took the last bite with any cheese or sauce on it, and I had a starvation-induced vision of myself standing on a cliff in the desert, arms outstretched to the heavens, bellowing, "Nooo!" into the night sky. "You want the crust, Professor?" came the voice of Captain Down on the tail of a shooting star. He held it out to me, like an angel bearing manna. Mercy me, for a moment I didn't know whether to be insulted or eternally grateful, but such higher mental questions were quickly overridden by physiology as I devoured the pizza rind like a gorilla eating contraband popcorn at a zoo. I grunted with satisfaction and looked to him hungrily for more.

"Your friend, Professor Korterly. He's a real nice guy."

"Yeah?" I answered, clearing my throat. "Do you know if there's a soda machine or snack machine around?" I fingered through the change in my trouser pocket, reminding myself of General Kiljoy.

He shook his head, and with a nervous glance toward Tynee's office, replied in a subdued tone, "The General, Professor, he won't let us leave this area. There are guards in the halls."

Us? I thought. Who did this stooge think he was kidding?

Was I to confide in my fellow comrade now? "Can't we send someone else?"

He shrugged. "I suppose we could send the bodyguards when they get here. Anyway, I have an extra soda." He picked up an unopened can off the chair in front of him and handed it to me like so much pork barrel to a constituency. Make no mistake, this man was slicker than oily dishwater on an icy sidewalk. Like any politician worth his weight in campaign contributions, he had a disarming knack for telling you exactly what you wanted to hear. Why, I almost cheered when he pulled that can of soda out. If there had been a flag with his name on it handy, I would have been waving it like it was the Fourth of July, 1776.

"Professor Korterly, you know, he taught a course I took in college."

"Mm?"

"He graded tough, but he knew what he was talking about, most of the time. Cynical, but charming, you know?"

"How do you mean?"

"I'm sure you know how he is. Always insisting that nothing is as it should be, and that he'd studied modern society enough to know that he didn't want to have a thing to do with it." Captain Down laughed. "It sounded good, and he was entertaining, but I'm not sure the world is all that bad, you know?"

"Hmm."

"He delighted in ironies like that. The first day of class, when he was introducing himself, he said society paid him to teach people what was wrong with society."

"May I ask what your role is here?" I cut him off.

"My role? At this time, I'm in charge of supervising the experimental environment and other miscellaneous tasks. It's fully automated, but I review records to be sure everything is operating smoothly, which it always is. I also manipulate paperwork on the subjects, hiding our tracks, dealing with the families, public relations sorts of things. You probably also heard me on the intercom, speaking to prisoners." He held his fist up to his mouth in imitation of a microphone and spoke in the flat but pleasant hospital ward tone. "Inmate 104, return to the primary observation area, Inmate 104." He flashed a masterful grin. "I do that, too."

87

We returned to Tynee's office in time to see another beer can bounce off the window General Kiljoy was standing in front of. He didn't even flinch, and he announced his fortitude to all present. He was watching the revelry from the window farthest to the right, while Tynee was farthest to the left, and Miss Mary was at the window next to him. Captain Down took the window next to General Kiljoy, and I (the pickle?) took up residence in the middle. The windows were no longer buzzing, apparently having fallen out of sync with the party.

There we stood, in accidental rank order by height, conspirators gazing upon the rebellious masses. When a can of beer glanced off my window, it caused me to involuntarily jump back and shield my face. General Kiljoy guffawed. "Like a stone wall, Fountain."

"What's the estimated time of arrival for the National Guard?" Tynee asked, a bit apprehensively. "This is beginning to become a real security issue."

"They were already on alert from the local police," Captain Down spoke up. "Shouldn't be more than a couple of minutes."

Conversation sagged, for there were far too many curiosities to view below. The flood of people was doing the wave, and those trusting souls who had been crowd surfing were now having the ride of their lives as surge after surge of collective motion tossed them about like drunken swell-junkies at high tide. Quite suddenly, a different sort of ripple began building toward the front, expanding rapidly and resisting the waves like a concrete breakwater as people's attention was drawn from one another and toward the sky. A whine that sounded like a swarm of militant mosquitoes announced the appearance of two helicopters. The National Guard had arrived.

They descended swiftly upon the crowd, tracing broad figure eight patterns above their heads. This served as a massive buzz kill for most, replacing the buzz in their heads with a buzz above their heads, and soon the majority of revelers were, hands in pockets and shoulders hunched, slowly milling apart, with occasional indignant glances toward the dark heavens. One defiant youth fired a series of bottle rockets at the choppers, which caused the helicopters to throw on their spotlights and illuminate the twilit and melancholy faces below. Simultaneously, at various points along the periphery of the Green, armored personnel carriers were pulling up, and National Guardsmen were storming out in full riot gear.

"We should get to where it's safe," Tynee suggested.

Captain Down chided him. "Relax and enjoy the show, Tibor."

"I don't want some sort of Kent State fiasco," Tynee insisted.

"Rubber bullets and tear gas, President Tynee," Captain Down reassured him. "Humane weaponry."

"Where are the bodyguards, anyway?" Miss Mary complained. "I'm getting hungry." She pulled out a cigarette, perhaps to suppress her appetite. I considered bumming one from her for that reason, but I just didn't want that sort of camaraderie with her.

"DISPERSE IMMEDIATELY." The voice of technocracy spoke at last, with all the spiritless authority of a hungover lifeguard. "DISPERSE IMMEDIATELY OR YOU WILL BE GASSED." Some insurgents responded to the threat with another volley of bottle rockets, which merely popped like Rice Krispies far below the helicopters. It was, nevertheless, a symbolic gesture, and its meaning was not lost on the authoritarian humans operating these particular tentacles of the state. They responded by dropping little turds of tear gas canisters directly along the center line of the crowd, attempting to bisect the throngs below, to divide and conquer, as it were. It worked. The masses of humans parted like the Red Sea, and the crush of people trying to get away from the noxious gas propelled a massive shove whose shock wave was still elbowing and jostling people two hundred feet away. "DISPERSE IMMEDIATELY." They need not have repeated themselves, for thousands of drunk and stoned and who-knows-what-else college students were suddenly very frightened, and pockets of panic were popping up like pimples during puberty. People were freaking out like cats running from a vacuum cleaner, and would have stampeded if there had been anywhere to go.

"I'll be damned," Tynee spoke up. "Those boys really know how to handle a crowd."

"Beautiful," General Kiljoy answered in reverent wonder, diddling with his piddler all the while.

"Like a machine," Captain Down contributed. "Now watch this."

The helicopters made another pass along the median of the frenzied crowd, scattering another round of gassy droppings.

"More?" I asked incredulously.

"Antidote, Professor," Captain Down answered. "Recently developed. It reacts with the tear gas and renders it inert."

"Wow," Miss Mary exhaled. I wondered if there was an antidote to her toxic fumes.

"REMAIN CALM AND DISPERSE PEACEFULLY." The helicopters broke formation and began larger loops, repeating their statement over and over. People calmed from their paroxysms of panic to a mere agitated anxiety, nervously bumping into one another like cattle at a slaughterhouse, but having no other choice than to obey the steely voice of technological hardware hovering above them. Despite their indignant cooperation, outward movement was slower than an injured turtle in line at the post office during December.

"See that, Fountain?" General Kiljoy reproached. "A swift kick in the ass is all most people need to get their attention."

"Who's gonna give that man a swift kick?" Miss Mary asked, pointing. She was referring to a man, a naked man, actually, with long white hair billowing behind him like a banner as he streaked through the opening in the center of the crowd. His grinning teeth could be seen from across the Green, as confident as the emperor in his new clothes. As he sprinted through the crowd he pulled a wave of laughing faces and cheers with him. We stared at the display in amusement, but as he drew closer, the details of his face came into sharper focus. It was Tynee who first recognized him.

"Jee-zus Chrrist!" thundered Tynee.

"Holy Moses!" echoed Miss Mary, falling into a mephitic fit of coughing.

"Oop," I managed, for it was not Jesus Christ or even Holy Moses streaking through the parted sea before us. It was none other than Dr. Blip Korterly.

88

If, upon discovering that a virus you have helped to create has somehow been released upon a crowd of one hundred thousand college students, if the proper reaction to this scenario is meditative contemplation, then we underreacted. We underreacted like a man who continues to hum the last random song he heard while a baseball bat is being swung at his head. We underreacted like a woman who giggles in amused confusion after stubbing her big toe. In short, we didn't know what had hit us, where it had come from, or what it implied. We continued to stand in front of the windows as the sky darkened, watching the fidgety crowd twiddle its thumbs impatiently and the helicopters buzz around the sky like belligerent fireflies. There was no moon, except for Blip's, and we watched as he reached the end of his route and disappeared into the crowd. We continued to stand dumbfounded.

"Was that," Captain Down hesitated, as if he were about to ask us all out on some sick date, "was that Subject 104?"

"We should get to where it's safe," Tynee suggested again. Miss Mary was pulling out her cigarettes, and he gestured to her that he would like one as well.

General Kiljoy, who all this time had been standing with his hands in his pockets, motionless for once, vaguely grinning like a shell-shocked Mona Lisa, suddenly snapped to attention like a vampire at sundown. "We have a situation." He began pacing, hands now flirting with his fiddle like the devil down in Georgia. "We must take steps. Question one: Is each one of us positive that was," he paused, "one of our subjects?" We all nodded, and he continued. "Our first priority is a massive quarantine of this area and evacuation of surrounding areas. Captain Down, radio your men and instruct them that no one is to leave this campus."

"You want to contain over a hundred thousand people?"

"Do it!"

"Yes sir." Captain Down pulled out his cellular phone and moved to the sofa to make his calls.

"What good is that going to do?" Tynee protested, allowing Miss Mary to light his cigarette. "You know this virus. This entire crowd has been exposed already, including the National Guardsmen. In less than an hour, nothing will contain these people. Jesus, it's probably already made its way out of this area. That's how it was designed." This pronouncement gave General Kiljoy and his frenetic fingers pause once again. He stood considering, delicately cradling his cojónes. Another stray beer can ricocheted off one of the windows, this time giving him a start. Tynee continued: "We should get to where it's safe. These windows are thick, and it's airtight in here, but in less than an hour . . ."

"What the hell are our options, then?" General Kiljoy raised his voice. "Down! Get over here!" Captain Down obeyed, clicked off his phone, and trotted over to where we were standing, near the still-bubbling hot tub. "Okay, let's think. Would you turn this goddamn tub off?" Tynee flicked it off with his remote. "Our priority, it seems, is getting ourselves to a safe place."

"Can't we just go back underground?" Miss Mary asked.

"Negative," Captain Down answered. "Professor Korterly has obviously been outside of the observation tank, and thereby contaminated unknown areas of the compound."

"Shit," Miss Mary cussed and took a deep drag, holding it as if it were a hit off a joint. "Where are those bodyguards with the limo anyway?" she asked. Smoke drifted out of her mouth and nose as she spoke, which, combined with her raspy voice, made her positively dragonlike.

"That's not an option," General Kiljoy answered. "The limousine may already be contaminated." He turned to Tynee. "Get Volt on the phone and find out where he is. Captain Down, do we have any access at all to our underground facilities?"

He hesitated. "We could terminate the experiment."

A few moments of silence ensued, as if his statement had been an unexpected twig snapping in the wilderness at night. Bold Miss Mary was the first to address the darkness beyond the light of the campfire. "No one is terminating this experiment." She spoke with the finality of the Supreme Court on Judgment Day.

"This is an extreme situation," Captain Down countered like some brash young Harvard Law School hothead. "Have we prepared for this contingency?"

"Not as such," General Kiljoy responded, wearing a face of pensive jurisprudence. "This actual situation has never been contemplated. But we're not wholly unprepared."

"We have to convene the committee," Miss Mary asserted, as have countless other worshippers of the demon god Bureaucracy, for whom "convene the committee" is as holy a phrase as the *Sh'ma.* (If you listen carefully, you can hear it chanted over the cubicle walls.)

"There's no time for that," came General Kiljoy, dictatorial tendencies emerging as they will in times of crisis. "Captain Down is right, we have to terminate, and the sooner the better. It'll be nearly two hours after we disinfect before we can return to the compound."

"May I remind you, Veechy," Miss Mary addressed General Kiljoy by his first name, "that I am the greatest benefactor on the committee? I've contributed far too much money to this project to stand by as it's terminated."

I snorted at this remark, startling everyone, for I had been silent ever since Blip was sighted. "Money is a symbol," I explained my outburst. "What good is money if people have no symbolic capacity?"

The Book o' Billets-doux

rosehips: We really must hand it to ourselves. We quibble and we quoth, and quack as much as quick, but quiver do we niver a cold and lonesome shiver.

sweetlick: Fe fi fo fum, enough of this enterprising ho hum. Yo ho ho and a bottle of pennies. Money is our shortage, loans, bills, and mortgage.

rosehips: Oh me oh my oh my oh me, will you ever see you're free? Won't you come and dance and sing, say the hell with everything? Won't you come and laugh and play, in the trees and grass all day? You think we need some dough, a deer, a female deer? Then hunt her like you do, tame her like a shrew. Mother Earth is docile, it's really quite facile.

sweetlick: Ray, a drop of golden sun may fill your life with fun, but a wad of greenish bills will give you all the frills. Ask anyone but me, a name I call myself, for the end is not fa, a long, long place to run it is not.

ROSEHIPS: So, a needle pulling thread is lost in the haystack, like trying to find air in a smokestack. Hopelessness abounds, but 'tis the season to be jolly fa la la la la. . . . A note which follows so sad a threnody will fall on ears deaf to most anybody but the maddest of the hatters whose words will never flatter.

SWEETLICK: Yes, and a wanderer looking for wonder will find only plunder. But please sit for tea, a drink with jam and bread, before we're six feet under and the heavens split asunder. Oh what a terrible blunder! We need some coinage to take our last voyage, which will bring us back to dough, dough, dough, dough.

89

Disinfection, it turned out, involved the same process that occurred before General Kiljoy and I entered holy hell: ultraviolet radiation, combined with electrocution and ozonization of the atmosphere, and a dose of cryogenic helium for good measure. It would take roughly two hours to completely sterilize and ventilate the entire compound. When the air was clear and it had warmed up, they said, there would not be a single biologically active presence down there, not a human subject, not a dust mite in the carpet, not a stray strand of DNA.

Miss Mary, more concerned about her financial outlays than the lives of the human subjects, asked if there was any way to maintain the subjects' quarters. Captain Down shook his head. "Complete disinfection. From here, we have no way of knowing what areas have been compromised. And Professor Korterly may well have had external assistance."

Apparently, this had not yet occurred to Tynee. He began to stare at me with the suspicious eyes of a bitter late-night convenience store clerk. I smiled weakly, feeling guilty though I had done nothing, as if I had just walked out of his fat, salt, caffeine, sugar, nicotine, and alcohol store without purchasing something. Tynee disconnected his phone. "There's no answer on Volt's cellular."

"We're terminating," General Kiljoy responded starkly, his words as bare as Blip had been, but more pornographic. "It is decided."

"I agree," Tynee nodded. General Kiljoy and Captain Down pulled out their remote controls.

"Enter your codes. It terminates with three simultaneous signals," General Kiljoy reminded them. "On three?" They nodded, and Miss Mary stalked to the windows in a huff, sulking as if her favorite soap had just been canceled. "Three, two," he paused just long enough for a kitten to sneeze on a dust mite. "One." At that, they each pressed the big red button on their respective remote controls, and in the space of a second, an impulse that had begun as an idea in their heads traveled through their nervous systems and out their fingers, transformed from an electrical impulse to an infrared signal in their remote controls, converged and converted back into a single electrical impulse at the infrared receiver on the wall, and, fifty feet underground, hell froze over.

90 A feeling of surreality crept over me like a sand-filled gust of cool wind, making my skin prickle and tingle and causing me to squint my eyes. Watching the three men in front of me engage one another in an utterly serious conversation about how to stave off the end of civilization was like watching bad actors congratulating one another on their talent. The real seemed unreal, and the severity of the situation commanded about as much of my attention as the understudy of an ingenue. I slipped away from their frantic planning, their frenzied disagreement, discussion, and debate, and returned to the windows. Miss Mary now had the middle window, and so I took the one farthest to the right. Like men at a wall of urinals, I avoided getting too close.

As General Kiljoy, Tynee, and Captain Down busied themselves making phone calls to appropriate heads of government agencies, planning a blockade and an emergency quarantine of the city along the freeway outerbelt, the oblivious masses below were still just drunk and having a generally bad time. The helicopters continued to slap at the atmosphere above their heads, beating out a staccato rhythm accompanied by an unreflecting voice tossing out imperatives with the frequency of department store Santas throwing "Merry Christmas" around. This technocratic symphony apparently passed for music in some circles, and scattered individuals were still trying to find their groove.

But even they ceased their jerky dancing when the helicopters suddenly flew away in opposite directions, taking their industrial celebration of dissonance, the perfect frontispiece for a society as ridiculously inharmonious as our own, with them. They were headed for the perimeter blockade.

A rustle passed through the crowd as people began chattering like autumn leaves before an Indian summer thunderstorm. After a few experimental notes, the musicians again began to play, at first quite dissonant themselves, but gradually evolving into a spirited rhythm of wild drumming augmented by an unlikely harmony of instruments. This had the immediate effect of healing the wound the choppers had cut in the crowd. The sea rushed together once again, drowning any would-be oppressors, and those who had been divided embraced one another like teeth in a zipper, with hugs of a sort only known among survivors of air raids.

And what of Blip, my best friend, the brave naked man who alone had crossed the parted sea? Well, that's a matter I cannot discuss right now, but suffice it to say that he transcended the allegory.

91 If I am to describe this crowd as a sea, then I feel compelled to say that a volcano was brewing beneath the depths of its collective unconscious. But why talk of such grand events when a flame beneath a mere pot of water, a simple teakettle, would do the trick? Thus, the heating coils on the electric stove were glowing red-hot and swirling inward toward infinity. Or on the gas range, if you prefer, the flames were licking high and curling around the edge of the kettle of consciousness, scorching the finish, the enamel of language. The shared embarrassment of being busted, the civil inattention paid each other for being stuck at a lame party, for failing in their attempt to make merry, was forgotten like a misunderstanding between true lovers. The party that had been placed on the back burner, nay, off the stove altogether, was back up front and turned on full blast. The temperature was rising, the molecules were getting excited, vibrating, releasing energy, rising momentum feeding the band and being channeled right back, pushing it further, further, ever further.

The musicians, who had been only mediocre previously, had now found a groove fifty feet deep and were flowing through it like spring melt through a mountain gorge. Loud, dangerous, and beautiful, they tore past the point of no return and plummeted over a cliff, a moment of pandemonium at the edge of understanding, then splashed down, reemerging in a pool of trickling notes that immediately rushed still further downstream. The drummer tapped his cymbals enticingly while the others laid aside their guitars and keyboards and took out their brass. Within moments the insistent rhythms of swing took over, and wild children swung effortlessly around and through one another in impeccable chaos as they roared their approval and hopped in their socks at the Glenn Miller score that ensued.

As any child with spunk can attest, when you are punished by being made to spend half an hour standing in the corner, you don't think about what you did wrong. You mope, pick at the wallpaper, or daydream that your parents will have a change of heart and release you. Such reveries are rarely realized. Even if you are fortunate enough to have parents with the vision to fathom the value of half an hour of childhood and they grant you an early probationary release, you're certainly not let go without a stern warning. This is the same for all those paying a debt to society, from the brat who throws a temper tantrum to the child who eats his boogers, from the shoplifter to the murderer. We're never *really* convinced that what we did was wrong, not as a result of punishment anyway.

But here, the in loco parentis role of the university had flown off without so much as a slap on the butt or an emphatic "I mean it!" Here, the fantasy had been fulfilled, Ma and Pa Kettle had ruffled their child's hair and all but given their blessing, and it was playtime again. Happy Halloween! A party that had been a kick simply because it was illegal became a party with a real purpose, a whimsical frolic of freedom regained. Things were back in full swing, I say, legs pumping hard, hands pulling back on the chains once again, one childhood fantasy fulfilled, going for another. They danced to the brass and scoffed at the physicists who claimed that it's impossible to go all the way around, that they would inevitably reach a point of free fall at the apex of the swing's rotation, at least in the absence of a push from Frankenstein's monster. Here, it was happening, higher and higher, the world spinning and racing past. Frankenstein's benevolent beast didn't know his own strength, pushing them harder, still harder, until all potential energy became kinetic, and instead of going all the way around, their chains snapped at the apogee, and they rocketed toward the heavens.

The Book o' Billets-doux

rosehips: Good eve and good night, may your peeves all be light, may you leave every fight, and cleave to the light. I boast with my toast, like a host at a roast, salubrious statements serving to send sincerest salutes to selfish myselfless. (P.S. I am discovering that this is a growing pastime of mine, a knowing pastiche of rhyme.)

sweetlick: Such an outcry of whiskey and rye heralds immediacy absent leniency. Stop this nonsense lest I'm driven to recompense and given to answer hence: I haven't the time to play with a rhyme, I haven't the space to give a good chase.

rosehips: Are there no rules for riddlers and fools and fiddlers and ghouls? A posthumous pattern emergent from chatter, a titter, a tatter, and we're all a bit fatter?

sweetlick: Must we participate? Must we pontificate? Is it ever our fate to perpetually obfuscate? Here lies an answer, there fibs a question, a fabrication of exaggeration, a mastication of our own creation.

Rosehips: Chew the fat and write a rhyme! Hurl the cud and compose the chyme! What the hell, oh bardic belle, the farma' in the dell, the dharma in the tell!

sweetlick: Oh my. Have we defeated our find and cheated our mind? Are we conceited or are we kind? Are our incantations prideful, our invocations invidious? Are our words really hideous, our intentions so piteous? Can we communicate in competitive elucidate, in pompous parades of toplofty tirades?

Rosehips: It does not matter, a me or a we, a he or a she, a to or a fro, a dart or a bow. It is comparative, a cooperative narrative, a take and a give dare for to live.

sweetlick: Perhaps. But does not categorization hide us from realization, from seeking sensation and peaking perception? It may be so simple, a frown or a dimple, but must we divide to trust and confide?

92 The bubbles that form when water is boiled are, of course, steam—water that has been liberated from its liquid state of existence into its gaseous form. In the crowd below, which itself was fast approaching the boiling point, bodies in various stages of undress were beginning to pop up like the first tiny bubbles in a teakettle. And despite aphorisms to the contrary, I tell you, I stood there and watched the frigging pot boil.

It is difficult to say for certain what role the Pied Piper virus was playing. After all, scarcely half an hour had passed since Blip's unabashed gallop. Nevertheless, it seemed that the general state of intoxication was contributing to the pace of the progression of symptoms. Every few minutes a new wave of intensity broke from the center and rippled outward, as if an enormous boulder had just kerplunked into a churning sea. This ripple lost no energy as it expanded. It only rushed outward, and people whirled faster and danced more untamedly in its wake, never slowing down.

Any way you look at it, from the kettle to the caldera, from the stove to the sea, great forces were building. The pot was boiling, the volcano was erupting, the indefatigable crowd was overflowing its boundaries. The National Guardsmen, cut off from any chain of command and nervous as inbred puppies, had retreated into their armored vehicles to await orders that would never come.

Then came the laughter, unmistakable in its source, for no frivolity was as ferocious and unfettered, and never was merriment quite so contagious as this infectious epidemic of uninhibited hilarity. The decibel level rose so quickly as this next swell swept the crowd that the conspirators' conversation was drowned before whomever was speaking could finish their sentence. General Kiljoy, Tynee, and Captain Down thus joined Miss Mary and me at the windows to see what all the ruckus was about. And so there we stood, five of us peering timidly at the mob. I couldn't help but feel rather dim-witted, instinctively wondering what was so funny. I'm sure my miserable companions shared this sensation. When one hundred thousand members of your species are seized with mirth of such absurd proportions, who wants to be left out of the joke, scratching their head and muttering, "I don't get it"?

Tynee, pretending he didn't care what was so funny, I initially surmised, busied himself examining the windows. Upon inspecting them myself, however, I discovered the glass in front of me vibrating like an imbalanced washing machine in an earthquake. The sound of the crowd was relentlessly throbbing against the thick glass, pushing it to such a high pitch that it numbed my fingertips to touch its surface.

Tynee appeared quite concerned, and General Kiljoy was shouting unheard at someone or everyone. In spite of the overwhelming volume he was competing with, his voice gradually began to become audible at predictable intervals. A most uncanny thing was occurring. Every other fraction of a second, the crowd became ridiculously silent, like an auditory strobe. It seemed that their mad glee had fallen into synchronicity with itself, such that every individual's rate of ha-ha eventually became identical. General Kiljoy continued his attempt to communicate, but, just as a strobe light makes movements appear jerky and unconnected, so were his words hopelessly garbled.

And stranger things were yet afoot.

93

Consider Crater Lake, on top of Mount Mazama in the Cascades of Oregon. Mount Mazama is actually a volcano that experienced a series of violent eruptions about seven thousand years ago. The explosions darkened the sky for weeks, throwing volcanic ash for thousands of miles across the continent and the ocean. But even these geological upheavals paled in comparison with what was to come. Mount Mazama soon spent itself, and the magma chamber underneath the mountain was left empty. Deprived of any underground support, the entire mountain collapsed upon itself, creating a caldera four thousand feet deep and five miles across, which eventually filled with water over the course of six hundred years and became a scene of overwhelming beauty and tranquillity.

Perhaps the most amazing aspect of this particular event in geological history is that it was observed, that is to say, there were humans around, specifically, the Makalak Indians. Their take on this topographical twitch was that there was a great battle between Llao, chief of the underworld, and Skell, chief of the world above. Skell ultimately drove Llao back underground, collapsing the mountain upon him, and the heavens were victorious. Now understand, this was no tree falling noiselessly in the woods. It made a *sound,* a sound impossible to ignore, a thunderous and resounding . . . boom. If you've ever stood under a railroad bridge while a freight train passes at full speed fifteen feet over your head, you still have no conception of how it sounds when the Earth quivers.

Nor do I, of course. I'm only pointing it out. I do, however, have an idea of what it sounds like when humanity kicks in its sleep, when history sneezes. I dare not suggest an exaggerated comparison between the two, but I do go so far as to suggest that the murmur of a hundred thousand people being tickled well past the point of abuse certainly lies far beyond that of the freight train. And in any case, I reckon it's considerably more hair-raising than either the mountain or the train, seeing as how it's emanating from your brothers and sisters. To put it simply and understatedly, it was as unnerving as hearing a thief in the night.

Mountains collapsing, trees falling, books toppling over, these are all examples of a phenomenon called *punctuated equilibrium.* When I first learned about this in graduate school, the professor likened it to a kaleidoscope. When you look through a kaleidoscope and turn it, the pattern very slowly unfolds and changes. This is continuous change. But every so often, the beads tumble over and the pattern collapses into an entirely new one. When this happens, discontinuous change has occurred. Punctuated equilibrium is the norm in nature, from genetic evolution to tectonic tantrums. Periods of continuous change are peppered with periods of discontinuous change. Stability and instability exist together, and both should be expected.

And so, watching the crowd below begin to explode outward, chaos spilling off campus and into the streets, it was apparent that the kaleidoscope of human history was in the process of shifting. Indeed, I felt I was witnessing the beginning of a rather jarring tumble into instability. Pondering all of this, I touched the feverishly vibrating glass and, discontinuous change be damned, a fracture appeared in the window, growing by perceptible millimeters and tracing a crooked path in front of me like a tributary off a lightning bolt.

94

The Pied Piper, it seemed, had traded his pipe for a flute, a Pan flute, to be precise, and there was no mistaking the Earthly roar of his primal music. Inevitably, panic was stinging my perception like a jellyfish congratulating a tourist. It riveted my attention to the cracking window and stapled it to all the fuss outside. But let me be clear, yonder maniacs weren't panicking. Rather, they were the embodiment of Pan-ia, the vibration of the reeds in the old devil's hands, the presence that produces panic, the cerebral stampede of divine madness, the skull-shattering orgasm of raw existence. Possessed of the Pied Piper's charm, horrified or overjoyed, they were riding the shock wave of Blip's ground zero like nuclear surfers. They skipped and danced and clicked their heels, flawlessly out of control.

Entranced by the novelty of the entire experience, my terror was akin to a goat staring down a pair of headlights. I didn't quite know what was going on or how to react toward it, so my mind retreated to the oft-omitted freeze reaction. In a desperate situation, it's actually fight or flight or freeze. I froze, and if the Pied Piper virus wasn't drunkenly driving my kind collectively mad, he would have had time to say, "Tickle tickle hee haw, whenever we get bored," before colliding with me.

As it turned out, it was the Piper's former caretaker who blindsided me. Before I realized what was happening, General Kiljoy had me behind his head and across his shoulders in a fireman's carry. The flight reaction. In five steps he had me at the elevator, where he hurled me down like Paul Bunyan swinging an ax. Next I saw Captain Down help him with Tynee and Miss Mary, both of whom had fainted upon seeing the windows crack. As the two of them dragged the three of us into the elevator, garbled franticities were whistling about my head like starving vultures. Somehow I was kicked in the face by Tynee, who, along with Miss Mary, was coming around and greatly agitated, ready to kill or be killed. The fight reaction. See what I mean?

Once we had all been assembled in the luxurious elevator and the doors had closed behind us, we began our descent. Once the decibel level decreased, General Kiljoy hit a button on his remote and halted the elevator. From a shoulder holster under his jacket, he pulled out a handgun.

"Get down!" Tynee covered Miss Mary's head along with his own. I instinctively shielded my head as well. But he wasn't directing the gun at us. He was pointing it, along with the remote control, at Captain Down. No one moved or spoke for a long moment, and the crowd, now sounding like a raging thunderstorm in the next county, drowned out the sound of thumping arteries.

"Captain Porton Down," General Kiljoy spoke at last, hitting a button on his remote with all the malice of pulling a trigger as the elevator began to ascend. "Time to pay the Piper."

95

The votes were in, counted and recounted, and no filibuster could delay this legislation. There was no disputing that the disarming voice and savoir-faire sensibilities of Captain Down had just been voted out of office. Throw the bum out! His lame-duck linguistic capacity had nothing to say or do but wait. He might have tried to let people know what he really thought of them, push last-minute legislation through, pay political debts, but he was so used to telling people what they wanted to hear that he had no idea what he really thought.

"General, what are you doing?" Captain Down managed feebly. "The windows may have broken by now."

"We would have heard a sudden increase in volume." General Kiljoy raised the gun to Captain Down's face.

"What the hell is going on, General?" Tynee yelled, regaining confidence as we got closer to his office.

"Quiet!" General Kiljoy bellowed above the increasing noise. "Captain Down is the only one with any access whose actions I can't account for 100 percent. This is a crisis situation, and the ship is sinking fast. I'm plugging a security leak."

The volume, rising with the elevator, prevented further comment on anyone's part. Captain Down stood, his face filled with passive fear as if he were watching a suspenseful movie, as the elevator came to a halt. One second later, the doors opened patiently, once again revealing Tynee's office, and although the middle window across from the elevator was now a nearly opaque cobweb of fractures, it was still intact.

When General Kiljoy fired, it sounded like a penny dropping on a tile floor. Had it not been for the sudden explosion of Captain Down's knee and his subsequent collapse sideways into Tynee's office, I may not have noticed at all, such was the volume of the Piper's call of the wild. Tynee noticed, too, and scrambled to push the lame leg of Captain Down past the threshold. Once accomplished, the doors closed, at their leisure and completely heedless of the desperation of the situation.

96

Sophia once told me about a psychological phenomenon medical doctors sometimes experience when they are required to inform a patient of a terminal illness or a family about an unsuccessful surgery. What sometimes happens is that when they are giving the grim news, they are suddenly seized with an irresistible urge to grin or even burst out laughing. This mortifying reaction is called grim-grin in some circles. Psychologists think it may be a defensive reaction against excessive emotional trauma, but Sophia always insisted that Western doctors are fundamentally sadistic and sometimes can't hide their pleasure. For reasons that will become clear, I prefer the psychological explanation for myself.

As bad as it is, many things are worse than standing in an elevator with people you loathe. Among these many things, however, exists a related situation, in particular, being *stuck* in an elevator with people you loathe, and on top of that, witnessing one commit an act of egregious violence upon another, whom you loathed, remember, only not enough to . . . shoot him. Worse than this, even, is finding oneself smiling like a jackass at the whole goddamn mess. In fact, all four of us were a goofy group of simpering simians in a box, a regular barrel of monkeys, and General Kiljoy was chuckling. Perhaps Sophia is correct about them, but certainly not me.

To be precise, we were not in fact stuck in the elevator, at least not in the sense of the elevator being broken. We were, however, stuck between insanity and a cold place, for the compound below would take at least another hour to ventilate and warm up. It could have been worse in some ways. At least the elevator was elegantly decorated. Bearskin rugs, while gruesome, are really quite comfortable.

For now, our immediate concern was the seeming possibility that, despite our efforts, we had somehow been exposed to the Pied Piper virus. This only added to the routine awkwardness of just being in an elevator, and made everyone extremely paranoid. We were all fighting the urge to smile like it was the devil himself. It seemed a ridiculous struggle.

At one point, General Kiljoy attempted to break our icy

smiles with some conversation. I'm not certain if I heard this exactly right, for it made absolutely no sense when he said it and there was no context at all to place it in, but his peculiar turn of phrase was something to the effect of "I don't know which is better—a juicy, ripe cherry or a firm tart."

Again, I can't be certain that's exactly what he said, but Tynee and Miss Mary seemed to think his assertion rather odd as well. No one commented on it. It just echoed around, and everyone was surely thinking that General Kiljoy was exhibiting signs of being intoxicated by the Pied Piper's music. After all, while the remark may still have seemed somewhat absurd, it would have made more sense if he had said, "I don't know which is better—a juicy, ripe cherry or a firm, tart *cherry*," but he didn't. He said "a firm tart." No cherry. Of this I am certain. So, for all we knew, he was beginning to become linguistically incapacitated.

Lest you be kept in suspense, this was not at all the case. After a couple of hours of sitting around waiting, all perception having turned inward, scanning, scanning, looking for any irregularities in our psyches like compulsive bookkeepers, we felt confident that we had not been exposed. As for General Kiljoy's peculiar utterance, none of us ever spoke of it again.

Nor should you.

97 Inane. Inane was General Kiljoy's comment. I looked *inane* up this morning in the dictionary that was on one of the bookcases in the observation lounge. It refers to "that which is void or empty," and is thus a good descriptive in this case. It also refers to "the infinite void of space," and can thus be a considerable invective. "Your head, sir, is like the infinite void of space."

While General Kiljoy's remark was certainly empty, it would be unnecessarily caustic of me to liken it to the infinite void of space. It has occurred to me, however, that the Pied Piper virus was turning people's minds into something resembling the infinite void of space. Is this an insult? Well, that remains to be seen.

98

It was a cold day in hell. While the climate in the observation lounge was still a bit chilly, akin to a cool autumn evening with no breeze, it was preferable to staying in the elevator. In more ways than one, actually, for there was still a relatively high helium concentration in the atmosphere. While I was explaining to my cellmates the psychological explanation of the grim-grin phenomenon, my voice began to sound as if I had just sucked down a helium balloon. It seemed appropriate. I've always thought a good deal of psychology is quack medicine anyway.

Our squeaky voices naturally limited conversation. The only words to be spoken were serious, and it didn't do for General Kiljoy to quack his orders. Instead, he pointed his remote control at the observation window, and an enormous talking head from the local news appeared, filling the space previously occupied by the conspicuous absence of Blip, Brother Zebediah, and Manny. The newscaster was telling whoever happened to be on the viewing end of the camera about Roundtown's annual pumpkin festival. It was the 78th Annual Roundtown Pumpkin

Jamboree, when all the urban professionals come down to spend their professional money.

After watching Dick Maalox, the reporter for the road camera crew, shout the rules of the jack-o'-lantern contest into the camera, I excused myself (by politely nodding, not speaking) to go to the bathroom. Normally, this activity warrants no discussion in a story because it is uneventful, as I've already indicated. This, however, was an eventful day for me, and, propriety shmo-priety, there can be no exceptions.

Thanks to the cultural echoes of all those dead Puritans, I can't help but feel some reserve about sharing this segment. However, it is essential to the unfolding, and fear not, scatology is not my intent. But the fact of the matter is that there I was, in the bathroom, on the potty, pants around my ankles and toilet paper in hand, when an event no less startling than some nincompoop barging in on me occurred. It was an event whose occurrence was nothing more than a moment of perception, although it occurs to me that all events are nothing more than a moment of perception. Nevertheless, in this case it was somehow especially so.

What happened is this. My eyes, previously preoccupied with wrestling more than one square of tissue at a time off the recalcitrant roll, were momentarily idle and happened to fall upon a phrase written in soap on the jade green tile wall before me.

It read: "For a good time, call Blip. 555-2012."

99

After finishing my business as quickly as possible, I grappled with the obstinate roll to get an ample amount of toilet paper to wipe the message from the wall before anyone else could see it. It would have been easier with paper towels, but to my chagrin, there were none, only an old electric hand dryer, one of the original models. While drying my hands, I discovered that it had the nearly ubiquitous electric hand dryer graffiti scratched into its metal surface. For posterity's sake, the directions, which had read:

1. Push button
2. Rub hands gently under warm air
3. Stops automatically

had been changed by someone into:

1. Push butt
2. Rub hands gently under arm
3. Stops automatically
4. Wipe hands on pants.

I couldn't help but wonder how on Earth this bathroom, in a top-secret military compound fifty feet underground, had failed to escape this clichéd piece of vandalism. As it happened, Manny Malarkey confessed to the crime by jaggedly scratching M. M. into the white enamel finish near the bottom of the dryer. It was easy to imagine him demonstrating his modified directions, pushing his posterior with his index finger and rubbing his palms gently under his arms like a timid giant.

100 Feeling guilty, and thus self-conscious, and thus awkward, I wasn't sure how one is generally expected to act upon returning from the bathroom. But my paranoid anxiety was moot, as no one even looked away from the TV screen. It seemed the immediate future held nothing more for me than watching more footage of the Roundtown Pumpkin Jamboree. When I returned, a man was being carried away on a stretcher, having dislocated a vertebra competing in the pumpkin toss. This was followed by a short interview with a farmer who had grown a six-hundred-pound hybrid pumpkin. At the end of the interview, he sat his baby granddaughter (whom he called "li'l pumpkin") next to the stem at the top of the enormous gourd. But she was no Cinderella, and that pumpkin was no magical carriage. She cried like he had set her on top of a firecracker. Grandaddy just patted his big pumpkin and smiled at the camera.

Every few minutes, General Kiljoy would mute the sound and say aloud, tentatively, "Testing, testing." He sounded like a pubescent emcee about to announce the limbo contest at some party hall wedding. Each time this occurred, he would clear his throat loudly and one of his hands would retreat to his pocket. Then he would hit the sound on the television again, and we'd be back to the Roundtown Pumpkin Jamboree.

Considering that it was the evening news, I was struck curious by the length of this segment. With everything happening topside, the station had been going on about this charming but frivolous tourist event south of the city for fifteen minutes. After watching a jack-o'-clown juggle four mid-sized pumpkins, I could bear my intrigue no longer, and ventured to inquire why this story had garnered the media attention of a presidential assassination. To mine and everyone else's delight, my voice was perfectly normal.

"Media blackout is routine in containment situations," General Kiljoy boomed, pleased with the return of his baritone. "The situation is completely under control. Every law enforcement agency and reserve unit in the tristate area has been mobilized by now to handle this situation."

"So we're safe?" Tynee asked, and Miss Mary gestured to second this concern.

"Affirmative. We'll be here a while, but this compound is equipped to survive a nuclear attack."

"How long?" Miss Mary demanded. "And where's Tippy?" Her voice still had a shrill helium edge at first, but a phlegmatic pop returned it to its tobacco rasp.

"As long as it takes the boys upstairs to take necessary steps."

"Necessary steps?" I inquired.

"Where's my Tippy?" Miss Mary demanded once again.

"Whatever steps are necessary to contain this outbreak." General Kiljoy chose to answer me, and for whatever infantile reason, I felt pleased that he had graced my question over Miss Mary's with a response. Then I remembered Meeko, and realized that I too was concerned about my dog's condition. Before I could voice this perhaps trifling matter, Tynee preempted me, albeit indirectly, by pulling out his mobile phone and attempting to reach the dog-sitting bodyguards.

"I'll see if I can get ahold of Volt and Agent Orange," Tynee announced, much louder than necessary. The results of Tynee's endeavor apparently interested General Kiljoy immensely. He leaned forward, elbows on his knees, awaiting the outcome. His action reminded me of Meeko, when I would sometimes make him sit politely with a stale dog biscuit perched on his nose for a full minute before allowing him to snap it into his mouth. I now wish I hadn't done that.

Presently, it seemed Tynee was playing that same game with General Kiljoy, letting the phone ring a ridiculous number of times before finally hanging up. To make matters more tortuous, he went through the whole song and dance twice, once trying to reach Volt and once trying to reach Agent Orange. When the resolution came at last, it brought General Kiljoy immense satisfaction, and since he didn't have a tail to wag, he settled for wagging his whippersnapper.

"What about Tippy?" Miss Mary pressed her issue.

General Kiljoy finally acknowledged her question. "Your dog's whereabouts are not a priority." He was cold and short in his reply.

Taken aback, Miss Mary pulled her own remote control out of her handbag. After punching several buttons with great delicacy and deliberation, she hunkered down and examined a small LCD on the unit. For a moment the lines that had been chiseled in her face by two hundred thousand cigarette drags—erosion ditches that began with her pucker and arced around her jaundiced cheeks to ultimately pull her eyes into an incessant squint—seemed to have vanished, and for just a moment her nauseated face relaxed and a visage of childhood purity fell across her countenance, flooding it with innocent curiosity concerning the gadget in her palm. It was a swift sparkle, briefer than the ephemeral flash of a shooting star. It pushed the lower limits of a moment, stretched the definition of fleeting. It was quicker than the wink of a cheetah running full speed down a moving walkway at an airport, and after it had gone, it left not a breeze to hint at its passing. The decaying fibers in her facial musculature snapped back into shape, and her face was once again musclebound into a sultry and sickly veneer.

"This is strange," Miss Mary announced.

"What?" Tynee sat down next to her and peered at her LCD.

"I had one of those locator chips surgically implanted under Tippy's skin two years ago, just in case she ever got lost."

"Let me see that." Tynee took over her remote control and examined the display. "General, look at this."

"What is it?" General Kiljoy asked impatiently. "What do you see?"

"According to this, Tippy is on the same horizontal plane as us. Miss Mary's dog is still in this compound."

"Then Tippy is dead. This entire compound was sterilized. Other than the four of us, there's nothing alive down here." General Kiljoy snatched Miss Mary's remote control out of Tynee's hands and switched the LCD off. "Now drop it. We have more important issues to resolve, such as where the food stores are located."

This did not fly well with Miss Mary. She insisted on locating Tippy, alive or dead, before she did anything else. General Kiljoy ignored her and barked orders at Tynee, who yelped protests back. Miss Mary threatened to make a motion to remove General Kiljoy from his position as chairman of the CPC, and on and on it went.

As they bickered about who was going to do what, my attention was drawn toward the TV's muted telecast of the Pumpkin Olympics (try to say that three times fast). Would-be gladiators were attempting to carry basketball-sized pumpkins up the down side of a sliding board and then throw them off the top onto a giant trampoline, to be caught by the next runner in the relay, who would repeat the action. One runner was roaring drunk and missed catching the pumpkin entirely, which collided with his chest and knocked him flat. Before I could see if he was injured, General Kiljoy clicked the screen off like an angry parent when there are chores to be done, which, as I discovered, there were.

It had been determined during my mass mediated daydream that Miss Mary would go pay her last respects to Tippy. Since I too had a dog, I was ordered to accompany her on this mission. That I should be trusted out of General Kiljoy's proximity initially surprised me, but then, given the situation, there really did not seem to be any possibility of me causing any trouble.

Tynee and General Kiljoy, for their part, were going to locate the emergency food rations. This was a bit of a problem, since they would first have to discover where these foodstuffs were actually stored. Captain Down *was* the administrator of this mostly automated compound, but naturally he could not be reached for comment.

So, ignoring the lessons of *Scooby-Doo,* we split up. But contrary to what might be expected, nothing bad happened. Nothing, that is, unless you count having to accompany Miss Mary on a bizarre funeral procession. She spoke not a word to me for most of our curt excursion. Of course, I was not terribly forthcoming in the dance of dialogue either, but I was only following her lead in this chitchat cha-cha. At least this way I could avoid stepping on her toes, not to mention having to twirl or dip her. Besides, she was the de facto leader of this expedition, and I was perfectly willing to defer to her direction. That was established when I crawled into the golf cart with her in the driver's seat. I didn't even know where we were going. She had the remote control. Still, as we approached the bank vault door that led to the garage after barely two minutes in the cart, I felt a little idiotic for not having suggested that we walk.

As I said, our short trip passed without talking but with much clearing of throats. As we neared the vault door, she interrupted the hum of the golf cart to inquire about this one thing we had in common.

"What pedigree is your dog, Doctor?" she asked, as if she were inquiring about his family, which I suppose she was.

"He's a mutt," I answered simply and truthfully. "His mother was a tramp and his father was a drifter." At least that's what I hoped. I had stopped in Roundtown, as a matter of fact, seven years ago to get some gas. A local hound whimpered at me just before I tossed the soggy remnants of a prepackaged submarine sandwich into the garbage, so I gave it to him. He was so grateful that he ran after my car when I left, and I watched him keep up with me through the rearview mirror for a few blocks before I decided to give him a lift. It didn't appear that he had an owner, and I liked him so much that I adopted him. Being a geneticist, I was especially pleased that he was a mutt. Mutts tend to be healthier and more energetic, like that big pumpkin at the Jamboree, a phenomenon called hybrid vitality, or, as I prefer, mutt gusto.

Miss Mary was not at all impressed with Meeko's lineage. It appeared that we had nothing in common after all. She let this be known with a barely audible "hmm," and complete silence prevailed thereafter.

It is my opinion that in situations where conversation is strained, it's better not to say anything than to make one remark and then fall back into silence. That's like giving a waitress a nickel tip; it makes you look like a cheapskate. Better to give nothing than to be minimal. Talk is not cheap; it's the most valuable thing there is, but only when you share it. So go forth, be generous in your conversation, and your tips, or others will spit on your words, and your food.

Food critics are fond of advising that a midafternoon visit to a restaurant gives a poor first impression, one that may have been much better during peak hours. The same may be true of people, such that meeting someone for the first time during the after-lunch slump doesn't bode well for favorable assessments. Having first met Miss Mary in like circumstances, I had remained open to the possibility that she was not so loathsome as I thought her to be. But she was. No more so than General Kiljoy or Tynee, I hasten to add, but aside from her *eau de smokestack,* it was somehow much more difficult for me to define the reason for my odium.

As I've tried to explain, she is fantastically fake, and on many levels. She is so fake that it seems like she is pretending to be an actress rehearsing for a role as an impostor. Under all her fabrications, however, there seems to be nothing but routine self-absorption driving her. And if the self is an illusion, which according to Blip is a matter of incontrovertible fact, then selfishness is a preoccupation with absolutely nothing. I don't mean to say here that she is fascinated with the concept of nothingness and the unmanifest potentiality it implies. Rather, she is obsessed with filling it with her own presence, which is quite like trying to fill a balloon that does not exist. Nothing stands in the path of the selfish, one might say.

Miss Mary is an empty character in this adventure, yes, for she is an empty person. Of course, everyone is ultimately empty, but not everyone is so dreadfully insistent in denying it. The best among us delight in the paradox and do their best to soften the foolish phantasm of the ego. The worst among us are so terrified by such emptiness that they invite spooks from other dimensions to take up residence within them. They then go to work proving to all of us nobodies that they are somebody after all, suppressing the heavenly hecklers who hurl cream pies of sweet Truth their way. This is a fair characterization of General Kiljoy and Tynee, who surely have demons in their cockpits, but I'm confident that there is only a foolhardy nothing in Miss Mary's driver's seat. That nothing, however, has a fake ID that says otherwise.

101 The day being Halloween, Christmas was right around the corner for Miss Mary, and she hummed a few bars of "Silent Night" as she coasted the golf cart to a halt and studied the homing beacon on her remote control. We were in the passage in which we had first entered the compound, with the vault door in front of us.

"Tippy should be just ahead," she said. "In the parking garage." It did not appear, however, that we could go any farther, for the vault door was closed. As we stepped out of the airtight bubble, I was struck by the utter noiselessness of the hallway, which only earlier that day had wafted with wails of the Pied Piper's presence. Now it was so quiet I could hear my own circulatory system roaring in my ears. Having forgotten about the rebounding acoustics in those halls, I gawkily asked about the door, and as I spoke, the air all around mimicked my words and shouted them back at me almost before the utterance had left my mouth.

"SSHHH!" The air, prompted by Miss Mary, responded. She was fiddling with her remote in an effort to open the vault door, but with no success. Frustrated, she approached the door and found it ajar, which explained why it was not opening electronically. That seemed odd to me, and I began to voice a reservation against proceeding but the air again shushed me so hard I felt a shower of reverberating spittle all around my head. Apathetic anyway, I acquiesced and trailed Miss Mary through the door of the vault portal. She had scarcely crossed the threshold, however, when some rogue pulled the fire alarm in hell, and a resounding shriek that would make a veteran firefighter turn tail and run with his hose between his legs filled the mouth of the garage. The source of this howl from Hades was Miss Mary herself, wailing like it was the latest trend out of Paris. Her scream so rattled me that even after I realized she was behind all the racket, it still didn't seem entirely out of the range of possibilities that we were in fact standing in the orifice of a gigantic, screaming orangutan.

After Miss Mary retreated to the golf cart and began smoking like she was trying to fumigate a hornet's nest, I peered into the garage myself. Miss Mary's super-loudmouthed screak was triggered by the sight of the body formerly occupied by Volt the Waiter, Chef, Chauffeur, and Dog Sitter. He was now Volt the Nothing. Volt was dead, as dead as Charles Dickens. More specifically, Volt was shattered. The multitalented and multilingual gopher agent was now multipieced, and as naked as a statue of antiquity. He had a physique to match, complete with limbs and other extremities that had broken or chipped off through the centuries. It also appeared that he had been bound with his own removed clothes, such that when he was caught unawares by the termination of the experiment and subsequent disinfection of the compound, his cryogenically frozen body toppled like large pieces of ice will when suddenly deprived of any animation and consequent center of gravity.

This took me quite by surprise. Reacting to the potential emotional trauma, I'm certain, grim-grin promptly grabbed my jawbone and had every intention of flinging rude guffaws out of my grinning gullet if I hadn't acted quickly and pretended for Miss Mary's, as well as my own, benefit that I was seized with the dry heaves. Retching was a reasonable reaction, to be sure, but the scene really wasn't as gruesome as it sounds. True enough, Volt the Nothing was in pieces (Agent Orange and the dogs, incidentally, were nowhere to be seen), but it wasn't a bloody mess. He was still frozen solid, so there was very little actual blood. Besides, it just didn't seem real, since, like most things that day, I had no category in which to place any of it. The sight was so ludicrous that I could only imagine he was a wax dummy that had toppled over.

Since I was not as offended at the situation, and because I was eager to hang out with someone I didn't despise, namely Meeko, it was agreed that I would check around and inside the limousine. If they were inside the hermetically sealed limo, she pointed out, they may have been protected from disinfection. Miss Mary was relieved when I agreed to investigate after she ordered me to. In retrospect, it was exceedingly foolish of both of us, as General Kiljoy would holler at us later. The door to the garage should not have been open, and was evidence of foul play. Even though the garage and Volt the Nothing were thereby disinfected as well, a viable virus might have existed inside the armored limousine. Admittedly brainless, but the ownership of a dog encourages a certain whimsy of mind.

Besides, Miss Mary was in charge. I was just following orders.

102 In any modern family or secret military compound, a sure sign of who holds the power is who holds the remote control. I was the only one without a remote control in this compound. General Kiljoy, Tynee, and Miss Mary were forever pushing buttons and altering the immediate environment this way and that, but I was not permitted to take part in these antics. Hence, I was particularly pleased when Miss Mary gave me her remote control and showed me which buttons to press to open the door of the limousine.

I did as she said. To my tremendous delight, Meeko, followed by Ratdog, came bounding over to the door as it opened. I quickly crawled inside and closed the door behind me. The dogs, blissfully oblivious as usual to the human crises that were occurring around them, bounded gaily around my feet as if I were juggling milk bones.

After calming them down and noting with some degree of surprise that Agent Orange was not inside the cabin nor up front nor outside, I realized that I was not only in possession of a remote control, but also privacy. Privacy means not being seen through someone else's eyes, and thus not being subject to their judgment or censure. While Meeko and Ratdog certainly had eyes, I wouldn't feel embarrassed undressing in front of them. I might feel silly, but that wouldn't be due to any action on their part. I'd feel silly or embarrassed because I'd imagine them to care what my state of attire is. But if their uninhibited and sometimes licentious behavior around fire hydrants and each other is any indication, they wouldn't look twice even if I performed a striptease, unless perhaps the performance included some wet rawhide I might fling them to chew on.

But my mind wanders down bizarre alleys, as it's been apt to do these past few months. Privacy was relevant to me here not on account of any sudden desire to buff my birthday suit, but rather because I was in possession of a remote control, a spiffy remote control with a built-in cellular phone. So, I did what any high school clod looking for a good time would do. I called Blip.

For whatever reason, I feel compelled to distance myself from any sexual connotations in the previous statement. Obviously, I wasn't looking for a good time. I was trying to find out how the holy hell he and his chums managed to escape. Let the record show that I have never been one to get (or give) dating tips on bathroom walls. *That's* bizarre.

The number, as I expected, reached Blip's voice mail. Because the greeting was precisely what it usually was, I was left rather puzzled.

"Hi, this is Blip. Please leave a message and I'll get back to you. Until then, be advised that all polar bears are left-handed, so if you ever find yourself in the Arctic or in the wrong place at the zoo, watch your right side."

Puzzling indeed. He'd had this same message for three years now, though he'd never been able to answer my question if there was a similar rule for grizzlies, a curiosity that had recently reemerged in my mind due to the pelts covering the floor in the observation lounge and elevator. I left a message, rather disconcerted that I had gotten my hopes up for naught.

“This is Flake.” I spoke into the phone, suddenly on the spot and not knowing what to say. “Just calling to see what’s going on.”

103 After tugging Meeko and Ratdog away from sniffing at Volt the Nothing, we exited the garage to find Miss Mary suffocating contentedly in a bubble of her own smoke. Seeing Ratdog trotting through the vault door, she popped the bubble by opening the door of the golf cart and met her precious in a reunion embrace that would put a lump in the throat of a macho giraffe. As a dog owner, I was especially moved, and I scratched Meeko behind his ears. He thumped his tail, barked once, growled, whined, then fell silent, bewildered by the acoustics. The aural situation was better once inside the golf cart, and Meeko scrambled and whined with excitement while Ratdog yipped, and we humans and dogs merrily made our way back to the observation lounge like old friends on a New England sleigh ride. Miss Mary was so overjoyed, in fact, that not only did she forget to smoke, but she also never asked for her remote control back.

Upon our return, we found General Kiljoy and Tynee standing by the bar, surrounded by several boxes that had been cut open. They were in the midst of cussing each other out, and so neither thought to immediately inquire how our dogs were still alive.

“Just figure out where the goddamn food stores are located,” General Kiljoy commanded Tynee.

“Figure it out yourself!” Tynee hollered back. “You’re the hothead who eliminated Captain Down. This wouldn’t even be an issue—” Before he could finish, General Kiljoy collared him and lifted him clear over his head. This act of aggression set Meeko and Ratdog to barking, but General Kiljoy ignored them as he strode across the room and heaved Tynee onto one of the sofas. Tynee landed as gracelessly as a hissing cat scrambling out of a tub of water.

"Search the schematics, find out how to access prisoner rations for all I give a shit. I don't care what kind of clearance you have with what agencies. Here, I'm in charge, and you will follow my orders. There will be a chain of command. Are we clear?"

Tynee stood up, stupefied, and nodded.

That satisfied General Kiljoy momentarily, and he turned to Miss Mary and me. "Shut your goddamn dogs up!" We did not hesitate to obey his order and soothed our respective canines, who continued to whine nervously.

After Miss Mary had calmed Ratdog, she stood and addressed General Kiljoy by his first name. "This may not be the best time to mention this, Veechy, but my Tippy needs to take a . . ." She cleared her throat properly.

"Shit?"

"Walk." Miss Mary voiced her preferred euphemism.

"Christ." He paced about. "Take her into the observation room." He pointed to the glass wall Tynee was staring at, which now served as an enormous computer screen while he searched through the mainframe files. "That'll be the 'walk' room for now." He pointed his remote control at a portion of the bookcase, causing it to open. His action had the effect of kicking the jump rope of my heart and causing it to trip as I realized that it could very easily become public knowledge that I was in possession of Miss Mary's personal remote control. I resolved to return it to her as soon as possible.

Miss Mary exited the room, carrying Ratdog. Although I could tell that nature was whistling for Meeko as well, I decided to wait my turn, or his turn. I did not wish to have any additional adventures with Miss Mary.

Shortly after she left the room, Tynee announced that he thought he knew where the emergency rations might be and shut down the computer screen. The image was replaced, of course, by the room formerly occupied by Blip, Brother Zebediah, and Manny. It was now occupied by Miss Mary, who sat at the table admiring her antique teapot that had served the Pied Piper virus to them, and Ratdog, who was squatting shamelessly, looking as if she were reading a Russian novel.

Once Ratdog finished her novel and Miss Mary primmed her disheveled self to no avail before the mirror, they exited the room. I, meanwhile, wandered over to the bar to look inside the open boxes. They were filled with hundreds of aerosol cans. I pulled one out and saw that it was a consumer product called Wrinkle-B-Gon. Wrinkle-B-Gon was a "fabric relaxant," possessing the remarkable ability to spray away wrinkles, and, as the manufacturers claimed, "all without ironing!" My immediate question was why there were cases and cases of something so perfectly useless as Wrinkle-B-Gon fabric relaxant in a survival compound. No one answered me, but Miss Mary was intrigued by the claims, dressed as she was in a linen day suit that had endured sitting two hours on the floor of an elevator. Flaunting more wrinkles than a used piece of aluminum foil, she emptied half a can on herself. It worked. The wrinkles-were-gon.

Her clothing now unwinding poolside with a cold beer, Miss Mary joined her garments. She plopped herself drunkenly onto one of the sofas, giggling stupidly, having discovered that Wrinkle-B-Gon relaxed much more than just fabric. Slackened as she was, however, the narrow nicotine ditches of disgust that webbed her face remained, erosion ruts of rudeness disinclined to loosen up, obstinate and aloof like a jackass on a high horse.

Wanting to escape the rapidly expanding cloud of Wrinkle-B-Gon, I excused Meeko and myself to take him for a . . . walk. Once in the walk room, I took a seat at the table where Blip had been sitting while Meeko marked his new territory. Knowing that I was being watched, I pretended to examine the teapot, doing my best to imitate Miss Mary's admiration. Nevertheless, I'm certain I gave a visible start when I happened to see what was scratched into the table's surface below the teapot. Blip, presumably, had marked this territory as well, for the present proclamation from Graffiti Bridge was carved into the shellac, much smaller in scale but a great deal more emphatic.

NOW!

104 Thus it became inevitable that I would risk calling Blip once again before returning the remote control to Miss Mary. Cunning as a duck in a kiddie pool, I hatched a scheme that turned out to be as flawless as a broken egg. After trotting Meeko back to the observation room, I excused myself to use the lavatory once again. Once I relieved myself of a triflingly small amount of urine, a wee amount of pee (tee-hee), I used the relative privacy to telephone Blip once again, running the water in the sink to camouflage the beeping of the phone. Clever, I thought.

Blip's voice-mail service answered again, and to my great surprise and relief, the recording had been changed. He now spoke with a great absence of effort, disregarding any impulse to hide his profound amusement, and I could hear Sophia's hysterical laughter snorting occasionally in the background.

"Ho there, O wanderer of the wasteland," Blip spoke loud and brazen, as if he were a medieval wisenheimer guarding the portal to some magical forest. "Do you want your questions answered or your answers questioned? What's going on is the question. What's going on is the answer. An answerable question yields a questionable answer. Such is the state of things, good friend. Feel no distress for my condition; forgiveness is as assured as sunrise. Your only penance is this: Write down what has happened. Leave a record of the past. It is no more, and deserves a last hurrah. And don't break up the festivities, man. History is spent. Peace and absurdity, old friend. If I don't see you soon, I'll see you soon after that."

Puzzled by his apparent glee, I didn't leave a message, but instead called back immediately to listen again, this time jotting down what he said on some toilet paper. Just as I finished, a sharp rap came at the door, followed by the sharper voice of General Kiljoy.

"Hey Fountain! Shit or get off the pot, you know?"

Startled but not panicked, I coughed loudly, simultaneously disconnecting the phone and shutting off the water in the sink. "Just a minute," I answered delicately, echoing the standard alibi of toilet tête-à-tête.

"Did you fall in?" General Kiljoy tossed another bathroom banality at me.

"No," I called out needlessly, pocketing the phone, pen, and paper, and scanning around for any other evidence. Satisfied, I boldly opened the door to greet him.

"False alarm?" he asked, a demented grin on his face.

"Excuse me?"

"This bathroom affords little privacy, I'm afraid. The pipes run past the lounge, and they carry sound very well, so we can hear toilet sounds through them. Miss Mary refuses to even use the bathroom, and was going to have the plumbing rerouted next week, but who knows now, right?"

I nodded noncommittally, and he continued: "You've been to the bathroom twice since we got back down here."

"Alcohol," I reminded him, feeling my eyelid twitch in panicky guilt.

"Doubtful." His hands strayed to his pockets. "And you don't have any prostrate problems. I've read your file."

"I don't understand," I replied, surprised that one of my glands had turned up in conversation.

"That was a powerfully pathetic excuse for a piss just now, wasn't it? We all heard it. Who do you think you're kidding?"

"I didn't realize I had an audience."

"The Armed Forces Code of Conduct requires that you begin planning an escape the moment you are captured." Deranged dimples collapsed into his cheeks like sinkholes over a landfill. "This situation is not interested in the sound of your urination." He drew close to me, his breath smelling like a recent shot of whiskey. "This situation is only concerned about your safety. This situation can't take any chances with you." He paused and leaned in closer. "You've got the look, Fountain. I've seen it before."

"You think I'm trying to escape in the bathroom?"

"Suicide." He stood upright and cracked his knuckles. "I told you I read faces. If you try it, I guarantee I'll save your life, just so I can cut off every one of your fingers and toes."

"I'm not suicidal," I assured him and my digits.

"Maybe not, but something's suspicious." He eyed me and winked, then slapped me on the shoulder. "You jackin' off in there?"

"What?" I recoiled, then thought better of it and pushed past him.

He laughed loudly from the bathroom behind me. "I'd rather you jack yourself off than off yourself, Jack!"

105

In my absence, Tynee had located emergency food rations consisting of peanut butter that tasted like sawdust paste and cheese product that looked like frozen phlegm. The provisions were several years old, I was informed after I'd tasted some peanut butter. Hungry as I was, I declined a sample of the cheese.

"Doctor, do you have any cigarettes?" Miss Mary addressed me from the sofa, where she sat rummaging through her handbag.

"Sorry," I replied. This agitated her greatly, and she dumped the contents of her bag on the cushions next to her.

"Tibor, are there cigarettes in the emergency supplies?" she asked as she picked through her possessions.

"Not likely," he responded. Before Miss Mary could react, the crash of General Kiljoy flinging open the bathroom door echoed from the side hallway.

"Fountain!" he snarled as he stormed into the room. "The hand dryer!"

I faced him in silence, figuring it was best to keep my mouth shut until I knew what was happening. Tynee, Miss Mary, and the dogs looked back and forth from him to me in bewilderment.

General Kiljoy forced my hand. "Tell me about the hand dryer."

"I didn't vandalize it," I answered, feeling like I was bluffing.

"That's not the issue." General Kiljoy poured himself another shot.

"What's happened to the hand dryer?" Tynee asked.

"Not the point," he croaked after taking his shot. "You never used the hand dryer. I never heard it. I heard the faucet running, I heard it running a long time, but no hand dryer. Don't you think that's a little curious?" He put his hands in his pockets, satisfied with his detective work, and began twirling his tamale.

"I wiped my hands on my pants," I attempted.

"Maybe." He crossed the room in one stride and before I knew what was happening he was manhandling the front of my trousers, giving me monkey bites all over my thighs and causing Meeko to bark at him. "Doesn't feel like it, though." He spoke over Meeko's show of ferocity, standing square in front of me. "Why were you running the faucet so long?"

I backed away and massaged my smarting quadriceps. I felt Miss Mary's remote control in my pocket, and could not believe General Kiljoy hadn't noticed it.

"What the hell is going on, General?" Tynee demanded.

"Our good doctor was whackin' off in the bathroom, isn't that right?"

"No," I responded instinctively as I tried to calm Meeko.

"I didn't think so." General Kiljoy paused, eyeing me malevolently as he wandered over to the sofa where the contents of Miss Mary's handbag were strewn about. "Where's your remote control?" he asked her offhandedly while flipping his flounder.

Miss Mary looked over her belongings. She let loose a belligerent cry like the cork off a bottle of cheap champagne, unsealing my secret and flinging it about the room like a tipsy bridesmaid at a rowdy wedding, splashing it all over the ears of everyone present. "My remote is gone!" A drunken best man hijacked my destiny for a beer run, and was now swerving across the double yellow line on a mountain highway. Anything bad became possible, anything bad and nothing good. Further forks in my fate could only be choices between rancid and rotten.

"Say, Fountain." General Kiljoy turned to me, plucking his pecker all the while. "Is that a remote control in your pocket or are you just happy to see me?"

106 Thus it came to pass that I became known as a threat to national security. General Kiljoy pronounced me this as soon as he reached into my hip pocket and pulled out Miss Mary's remote control.

"Congratulations." He pulled his handgun out of his shoulder holster and leveled it at my head. "You're now a threat to national security. That means I have the authority to kill you."

Since this was a considerable threat to *my* security, I was quite upset with the matter. I was somewhat comforted by the fact that I was not the only one. Tynee hollered at General Kiljoy in my defense, but only insofar as I existed as "an asset to the situation."

General Kiljoy lowered his pistol, then clicked on the phone. "Let's see who our threat was calling, shall we?" He hit the redial button, dialing Blip's voice mail.

"Who is it?" Tynee and Miss Mary asked in unison.

General Kiljoy frowned, raising his gun to my head once again. He clicked off the phone. "Error message. 'The number you have dialed cannot be reached.' Who were you calling?"

"I didn't call anyone," I lied without hesitation.

Tynee interrupted. "I'm getting the same response on my phone." He dialed another number and put the receiver to his ear. "Same thing."

General Kiljoy set Miss Mary's remote control on the bar and pulled his own out of his pocket. He dialed a number, and apparently got the error message again. "The electronic communication system is breaking down, just as expected with a Pied Piper outbreak," he said with a certain satisfaction. "Soon we won't even get a dial tone. If this were a field test, we could pronounce it a tentative success."

Miss Mary picked her phone up off the bar and tried a few of her own numbers, with the same result. Tynee watched her anxiously. "We're cut off from any lines of communication?" he asked.

"Cellular towers have probably lost power, as they would in the absence of human coordination and communication. But we also have a direct satellite link between this compound and the Pentagon, designed to withstand nuclear attack." He raised his gun to me once again. "Quite a situation, eh?"

"I didn't call anyone," I lied again.

"Maybe not, but I have no way of knowing how long the cell tower has been out of commission. Either way, there's still criminal intent. What were you doing with Miss Mary's remote control?"

"She gave it to me," I said, gushing with honesty. "She was afraid to check the limousine."

This information rendered General Kiljoy silent, for it was the first he had heard of it. Miss Mary filled in the explanation with, "The chauffeur was frozen."

"What are you talking about?" General Kiljoy demanded.

Hence followed a lengthy explanation of the vault door being open and the consequent disinfection of the garage and Volt as well, from which the limousine was apparently protected. This information infuriated General Kiljoy, for the vault door was not supposed to open in the first place. He declared us fools for risking exposure to the virus, which could have been inside the limousine. I blamed Miss Mary. She shrugged and sneered that we obviously weren't exposed in any case, for it had been over an hour and a half already. Then she searched her handbag again for a cigarette.

Meanwhile, perpetually oblivious to the desperate human drama unfolding around him, Meeko strolled over and sat at General Kiljoy's feet, panting. "What about Agent Orange?" General Kiljoy continued to interrogate me. "Did you see her body anywhere?"

"No."

This information made General Kiljoy pause. "I don't understand," he muttered, rubbing the panicky spasms bouncing around his brow. He looked down at Meeko. "Hey boy!" he said, suddenly enthusiastic, bringing Meeko to his feet and setting a wag to his tail. He patted Meeko and glared at me. "Enough bullshit, Fountain. You still haven't answered my question." He lowered his gun from me and pointed it at Meeko. "Bang!" he shouted, and Meeko joyously threw himself down on the floor as if shot. "Bang! Bang!" Meeko yelped and convulsed happily. "Bang! Who did you call?" He spoke over Meeko's gleeful yips and yelps. "Bang!"

"I called Dr. Korterly," I blurted, choosing, you see, between rancid and rotten.

General Kiljoy nodded, then, as suddenly as I say it, shot my dog. It was an explosion of sound, much, much more than a bang, and everyone jumped except Meeko, who whimpered feebly and ceased all movement. Stunned beyond horror, I could only scratch him behind his ears as my dog exhaled that which had animated his form.

107 Accomplishments are wastes of time. Dogs accomplish nothing. They have no ambition, for ambition only makes a virtue out of perpetual dissatisfaction. Dogs may chase their tail, but they give it up quickly enough and move on to other curiosities. Perhaps they recognize its futility and inherent limitations, or maybe they become bored with focusing all their energy on just one thing when there is so much else to do and see. They may be on to something. We modern humans live impatient lives chasing our dreams instead of living them, chasing the tail end of our lives, chasing the end of our tragic tale, ever eager for the future and our own demise.

Dogs are happier than humans. Hence, just as we strove to

imitate birds for their ability to soar through heaven, so should we imitate dogs for their easygoing vibe, their ticklish personalities of whimsical caprice. Is this not desirable? Is this not heavenly? Dogs live life wagging their tails and getting excited about every little thing. The life of a hound is a runner's high, panting and goofy but rhythmic as a heartbeat. They run high and free, unaware of any race, uncaring of any leash, running for the run, running because it's fun, our canine counterparts, our kinder better parts, helpers in the hunt, protectors of the plate, living and accomplishing nothing but infinite frolic and limitless levity, no lines on a résumé, no citations on a curriculum vitae.

How to eulogize a dog? What accomplishments can I list, what achievements can I enumerate? He learned to do dumb tricks at my command. He learned to hold it until I walked him, or should I say, until he walked me. I would have never taken walks if it were not for him. But to list such accomplishments is akin to saying he was as constipated and unintelligent as a modern human, which he was not. He learned to live within human parameters, to be sure, like any child who learns to go to bed before they're tired so they can get up before they're awake. But unlike children, dogs learn our rules, sit pretty, deal with our crap, and go on wagging their tails. The playful puppy is always present in a dog, but the innocent child has run away from the adult. Dogs are trained; only people are brainwashed.

Children grow up, become boring and bored, responsible and rational, as loath to play as Meeko was to orange peels. Dogs, on the other hand, will cavort as long as their bones allow, sprinting after sticks, performing all their tricks, and delighting in every scent from pumpkin pies to cow pies. Every scent, once again, except orange peels, as I established one dismal day watching Meeko sniff at an orange rind in my hand. Out of great nastiness or lethargy, I squeezed the peel, causing a mist of orange peel spritz to coat his sensitive nose and sending him into a fit of sneezing as intense as any hilarity, but without the fun. I possessed the amusement, and for as long as he sneezed, I did nothing but laugh. He existed in a world of sneeze, and I existed in a world of laughter. After that day, he avoided every form of citrus.

Meeko did not like it when I did that to him, but he had forgiven me within minutes. Dogs aren't man's best friend, what a diminutive statement! Dogs are our guardians. They comfort our loneliness and put up with the accomplishments of our egos. Meeko taught me that I enjoy taking care of beings other than myself, and though he howled at fire engines rather than the full moon, his mournful, piteous cries echo through the black hills of my imagination. My dog accomplished nothing, I'm proud to say. He was a mutt, a bastard son of a bitch in the finest sense of the words.

part Three:

prance of the pied piper

108 Every day is a day of reckoning, as any accountant worth his business card will tell you. If you're going to stay on top of your life, you have to be aware of what's coming in and what's going out. Come tax time at the end of time, some say, all accounts must be settled, and unaccountable actions tarnish your credit record. On your audit bed, it is said that your entire life flashes before your eyes, a comprehensive snapshot of your existence, every moment contained in an instant briefer than the moment of conception. All actions are examined, all decisions dissected, and ultimately you are alone, left to find your way out of the labyrinthine lies you have constructed to convince yourself that you exist separate from everything else.

The day I have been describing, the most eventful day of my life, a day that began with Agent Orange waking me before dawn at the country retreat of Valhalla Acres and ended with the murder of my dog, with the outbreak of the Pied Piper virus somewhere in the middle, was just another day of reckoning. As

I pen my penance, I cannot be certain how my actions will be evaluated, but please keep in mind that I am but a pawn. It's a lame excuse, I know. Even pawns can decide a game. Act or be acted upon? Patience, please. That's like saying kill or be killed. As Sophia once told me, "There are always other options. Tickling, for instance."

This is my penance, my act of contrition, my day of atonement. You are eavesdropping on a confessional. This is, however, different from my childhood experiences with Catholic confessions, where, because I couldn't think of any decent sins, I often made up some impressive mischief and misbehavior on the spot, and then proceeded to confess that I had lied a few times as well. Unlike those occasions, I have striven to be honest here, although slight exaggeration is to be expected in any story worth ten Hail Marys.

The most eventful day of my life concluded with my confinement in the small adjoining room where I had earlier talked with Blip. It was a symbolic gesture. After all, I was already imprisoned, though there seems to be no boundaries to the amount of freedom society can force you to sacrifice, no limit to the levies on life.

109 Animals sustain themselves by consuming other forms of life. While plants draw their energy from the sun, animals consume plants and each other. Life feeds off itself down through the levels of predator and prey. Hungry? Have some life. Rocks won't do, nor plastic, though shoe leather may keep you going in a toe jam. The best sustenance is the freshest, that which was most recently alive, still a source of life and not yet decaying. Sadly, the food stored as emergency rations was all but rotten, leftover government surplus forever preserved in a suspended state of decomposition, providing just enough flabby nourishment to keep us breathing. It was never actually intended to be eaten.

Despite my accommodations, I slept as soundly as a baby sloth for over ten hours, and only awoke when General Kiljoy roused me the next morning for a breakfast of canned chicken. He and Tynee spent the morning disposing of the remains of Meeko and Volt, then went searching for Agent Orange and any clues as to what exactly had happened the day before. I spent the afternoon in my makeshift holding cell while nicotine weanling Miss Mary huffed Wrinkle-B-Gon fabric relaxant and watched satellite television. Local stations were no longer broadcasting, the situation being what it was.

I was lucky to be separated by a steel door from her. She hadn't smoked a cigarette in over fifteen hours, and like a klismaphiliac without a rubber hose, there was just no way she could be satisfied. Despite her efforts, neither television nor Wrinkle-B-Gon sufficed to ease her craving. By the looks of her at breakfast, she had not slept all night, and she spoke to us as if we were squirting water pistols at her. Fortunately, having located some instant coffee, everyone else's addiction was appeased.

I thought I might watch some television through the small window in the door, but Miss Mary switched the channels enragingly often, like a chimp perusing endless varieties of pornographic bananas. Having nothing else to do but sit in the chair and stare at where Blip was yesterday, I examined the contents of my pockets and found the toilet paper transcription I had made of Blip's voice-mail greeting. Racing on three cups of powdered coffee, I resolved right there to pay my debt and honor Blip's request. Not quite knowing what to think of the second part of my penance, I focused on the first part and began to write a record of these events, and now here I am.

110 A host of unsatisfactory first paragraphs later, I got up to stretch and happened to glance out the window at Miss Mary. Apparently confident that nobody was looking, she held a half-eaten apple in her hand, a desirable commodity given our current food situation. She was chewing furiously, perhaps satisfying her oral fixation, taking bites without pausing to swallow. In so doing, a bead of apple juice lingered on her lower lip, glistening in the piped-down late afternoon sun like an orb of paradise. As she licked the nectar away with her tobacco-stained tongue, she looked around and made dead eye contact with me, startling us both. She froze, transfixed with a grimace of horrific self-consciousness, a sick look of frantic guilt, as if she were not in a bomb shelter but a garden, a plentiful, perfectly balanced garden of Earthly delights, and she had just devoured the forbidden fruit, the fruit of knowledge, self-awareness, self-consciousness, and was now facing an eternity of alienated existence filled with all manifestations of egoism.

Compared to the potential excesses of pride or anger, hiding and then hogging the only fresh food in the compound is a minor misdeed. It is gluttony, however, and all such behavior is motivated by the same fundamental selfishness, though now is not the time for such mealy mysticism. Miss Mary had concealed her possession of an apple and was as far from any Garden of Eden as could be imagined. She asserted herself by turning back to the television screen and finishing her apple, effectively pretending my perspective out of her reality.

As it happened, that particular apple was the probable vector for a disarmingly virulent strain of intestinal influenza in our otherwise disinfected compound. I suppose we were fortunate that the outdated food supply was not spoiled. This was established because Miss Mary had not touched any of the food rations when she fell ill later that evening. Tynee and General Kiljoy assumed she must have picked up the virus earlier in the day.

The rest of us had joined her in fever by the following morning. After having vague, nondescript nightmares of terrifying helicopters all night long, I awoke to a frenzied hallucination of the entire universe being sucked through a swirling vortex centered around my stomach. The vision returned with a profound nausea whenever I flushed the toilet. Gardyloo.

For the next three days, the four of us alternated between lying flat on our backs or stumbling to the bathroom. The fever dumped me into a torturous state of insane introspection, and guilt welled up within me along with the bile. "Serves me right" throbbed relentlessly through my head like a schizophrenic mantra. Perhaps that's why I didn't squeal on Miss Mary.

Big General Kiljoy, built like a brick shithouse, as they say, was pulverized by this tiny strand of RNA worse than anyone, and was too sick to care about anything except having priority in our own little brick shithouse.

111 How I wished for Sophia and Blip to stop by with one of their herbal remedies, which, they assured me, worked precisely because they were not prescribed by Western medicine. When I had the stomach flu once before, they came over an hour after they found out and set up a juicing machine in my kitchen to squeeze the juice out of some wheatgrass they grew in the garden behind their dome. It smelled like lawn clippings, but good gracious to grasshoppers, a couple of hours later I was sitting upright. My stomach remained sensitive, and I wasn't reaching for the jalapeños, but I was definitely recovering, as sure as a blade of grass regrows after meeting the blade of a lawn mower. I don't want to dispense landscaping advice without a license here, but it worked, and as I lay there retching and reeling in agony, I would have traded my John Deere for a single shot of that grass juice.

112 I once spent an autumn Saturday chatting with Blip as he encouraged his garden, harvesting wheatgrass and transplanting tulip bulbs. He never asked for assistance, but in retrospect, I'm not sure why I didn't offer to help. Maybe it was my suburban childhood, maybe it was my irritation at being invited over for a brunch that was not immediately forthcoming. Blip made no sign of ceasing his gardening, and I churlishly inquired when food would be available soon after I arrived.

"Haven't a clue," he grunted with horticultural satisfaction. "Sophia cooks on weekends."

"Where's she?"

Blip ignored me and held up a flower bulb. "Tulips. I can't

figure out where these keep coming from. This is the third year I've found them in my dandelion patch."

"What's wrong with tulips?"

"Nothing, I guess. They're pretty enough. I just prefer dandelions. They're sturdy, sunny, and they can take care of themselves. Why tiptoe through the tulips when you can dance through the dandelions?" He rose, strode a few feet to his left, and began digging a small hole to transplant the bulb into. "Did you know that in the 1600s, the Dutch used to think these were worth fortunes? Better than money. During the *Tulpenwoede,* the tulip mania, an entire brewery was bought and sold for one tulip bulb. People mortgaged homes, you name it, just to invest in tulip bulbs."

"Where did you say Sophia was?" I interrupted him, hungry and hypoglycemic.

"Probably up a tree somewhere," he replied offhandedly. "Don't misunderstand me. Tulips are nice, but just because some people agreed these runty little roots were worth something, they were." He patted the soil down, tucking the bulb to bed for the winter. "Ah well," he shrugged. "They're certainly worth a tidy sum more than paper."

113 Later, as Blip carried his garden tools back to the shed, Sophia's voice munched through the crunching of an apple overhead. "Why do you suppose Eve was doubly condemned for *sharing* her apple?" We looked up to where she sat, barefoot and perched on a comfortable branch, her long cotton skirt pregnant with a peck of apples. She may well have been asking the tree, for she never looked our way.

"It wasn't sharing, it was misery loves company," I answered, pleased with my rude wit and my view of the inside of her thighs, which were as smooth as a pebble in a swift-water streambed.

"Quick." Sophia smiled, commending me, delighted with any sort of wit. She took a final bite out of her apple and tossed the core toward some nearby brush. In so doing, she lost her balance just long enough to let go of her skirt and grab a branch. The cargo less important than the transport, it was an easy decision to make. I survived the consequent avalanche of apples much less hurt than you'd think I would be. I even caught one.

Sophia fluttered down from the tree, unencumbered, unhurt, and pleased as a peach in fourth grade, or a plum in fifth. "I was wondering how I was going to get all those apples out of the tree," she marveled.

"Gravity," said Blip, intended more as a Newtonian observation than an answer.

"I'm okay," I assured them, taking a bite out of the apple I had caught.

"Don't ruin your appetite," Sophia counseled.

"Why?" I asked covetously. "What's for lunch?"

Sophia looked up from gathering the fallen fruit, looking as miserable as a child practicing cartwheels. "Apples, of course."

114 Strictly speaking, we did not have apples for brunch, but Sophia was never very disciplined in her use of language. She could often be heard uttering phrases that made no intrinsic sense. Nevertheless, because she spoke with such absolute conviction, her nonsense made others stop and think. Blip and Dandy never hesitated to reply with something equally meaningless, leaving anyone else present all the more mystified. That said, we had apples for brunch, yes, organic apples, but more specifically we had apple pancakes with applesauce, ringed with apple wedges and washed down with freshly squeezed apple juice for Dandy and aged applejack cider for the grownups. It was an autumnal adoration of apples.

Blip and I were recruited to cut apples in the preparation of the meal, a tedious task made easier by their broken kitchen knives. I held one up and asked why a rivet was gone from the handles of all their knives, causing the blade to come off the grip at an angle rather than straight.

"Unnecessary linearity," Blip replied. "Nature isn't that tidy. Your hand comes off your forearm at an angle. See? Now look at the way these blades line up with your forearm. That's where the straight line belongs. Ergonomically, all tools should be angled like that. Not only does it make hammering or cutting easier, it reduces the stress on your joints. It's true. I overheard it in a coffeehouse."

"So you broke all your knives?"

"I didn't break them, I fixed them. They were broken to begin with, that's what I'm trying to tell you. Nothing is as it should be in this society. The handles of all tools *should* be at a 23.5-degree angle to the head of the tool. Why on Earth would anyone think it would be a straight line, or a ninety-degree angle, which never occurs in nature? That's just asinine. If you drew an angle of the human grasp relative to the straight line of their forearm, it would be 23.5 degrees, or its supplement, depending on your point of view, of course." He made a show of effortlessly slicing an apple. "Mother Nature is messy by our standards, as messy as birth, but she's also sly that way."

"As sly as a dime," Sophia asserted.

"And no straight lines," Blip continued, "but perfect parallels all over creation." He flipped his knife in the air, catching it again by the handle like some hotshot delicatessen cook. "Twenty-three point five degrees." He held up the knife for inspection. "See? The angle of the human grip is the same as the tilt of the Earth."

115 In the opinion of Dr. Blip Korterly, I try too hard. That he points this out to me when I am impatient or angry is unfortunate. Offering advice to an angry person is like congratulating a sleeping insomniac with a slap on the back. It is not only ineffective but also bothersome and entirely counterproductive. Nevertheless, he persisted in his self-righteous gestures of goodwill, and I continued to roll my eyes, until one day his point came through at last. As required, I was in high spirits already from the six-pack of fine Irish stout the two of us had shared that evening.

"Did you know that Sophia taught me how to rock climb?" His foot began to twitch like a hesitant sewing machine. "She scrambles right up the side of a rock like a gazelle sprinting across a prairie. I had a difficult time with it at first. She drove me crazy telling me to 'Let go, let go,' like she was my Jedi master or something. I wasn't about to let go. I clung to the rock face with all my might, and for two seasons I couldn't get past the bottom of this one crack three-quarters of the way up the rock we usually climbed. My arms would start shaking, trying to maintain equilibrium, and I couldn't move a limb without losing my balance. Eventually, I had to let go and let the harness take me, but that isn't what she meant. She wanted me to stop trying so hard and to just do what felt right.

"And you know what? She was absolutely correct. I finally understood what she meant one afternoon when she yelled, 'Move your ass!' instead of 'Let go.' I moved my ass, automatically I guess, and tucked my waist close to the rock face. All of a sudden, I was able to pull my body up the remaining portion of the crevice. It was unbelievably easy. Exhilarating. I whooped and hollered at my stubborn realization, and Sophia wouldn't let me down until I apologized for not listening to her earlier.

"The point, Flake, is I learned that day that I had a bad habit." Blip's leg was now tapping so furiously it could have outstitched an underpaid overseas garment worker. "My technique wasn't working, but I kept trying to make it work through brute force. That's like using toenail clippers to trim hedges. If you're trying too hard, then you're *trying too hard.* When I changed my technique, things became practically effortless. An unbalanced body can't be strong or graceful or effective at anything, because it doesn't know which direction to focus its energies.

"So, whenever you find yourself putting forth great effort without success, you're trying to force something that will not fit under the circumstances. That's a destructive waste of time. And if that isn't enough to keep in mind, your techniques must always be allowed to evolve and change, in relationships, in life, in science, in society. Otherwise you stagnate, and you won't get anywhere in the long run." He sat down and swallowed the swill at the bottom of his glass. "You know what the philosopher

Aldous Huxley said? He said, 'Consistency is contrary to nature, contrary to life. The only completely consistent people are the dead.' Well-spoken, you'd surely agree, since he considered the manipulation of genetic structures one of the three major scientific breakthroughs of the twentieth century." He sat back and relaxed, his feet as motionless as a forgotten thimble in an old sewing trunk in an attic.

"What were the other two?"

Blip yawned. "The splitting of the atom and the rediscovery of psychedelics."

116 Habit, habit, habit, habit, habit, habit, habit, habit, habit. Say *habit* until you forget what it means, and you've broken a habit (a habit, if you've forgotten, is an involuntary tendency to act constantly in a certain manner). Habit, habit, habit. There are good habits, such as smiling at strangers, and bad habits, such as picking your nose and wiping the boogers under the couch. Habits are addictions. You can be addicted to love, which is generally a good habit, or you can be addicted to heroin, which, terminal patients aside, is not the most desirable of habits. The angle of our tools is a habit, as is everything from the design of our automobiles to the design of our teacups. It is not an exaggeration to say that society is an immense conglomeration of obsessive-compulsive habits.

Scalded tongues could be vanquished. I say this because I paused to sip my instant coffee here, and am reminded that in addition to turning his ordinary, straight and narrow kitchen knives into a pack of freewheeling culinary cutups, Blip also chipped the handles off all the teacups in their house, no doubt with an angled hammer. He did this after he learned that the Zen tea ceremony is performed using cups with no handles to prevent one from drinking the tea while it is too hot. If the cup is too hot to pick up, it's too hot to drink, a simple logic that eludes our fast-food culture. And while a cup of coffee at a fast-food dump has no handle, the clowns put it in Styrofoam, which is even worse since it doesn't conduct heat at all. Ergonomics, patience, and ceremony are homeless in the land of opportunity. Habit, habit, habit. We don't have to do things the way we do them, it's just habit.

Habit, habit, habit. Western society, in the condition it's been for the last few centuries, has been shamelessly picking its nose, flicking and wiping gooey debris every which way. Society, presently conceived, is a disgusting habit, and just because everyone pretends not to notice doesn't make it okay.

117 "What exactly does that mean?" Sophia asked me after an extended period of silence at our apple luncheon. I raised my eyebrows and resisted asking her to what she was referring, for she frequently left her demonstratives undefined. It was a long wait, and I nearly gave in, but she finally elaborated. "Misery loves company. Is that supposed to mean that miserable people strive to make others miserable just for some company, or does it mean that miserable people love to have company, because it cheers them up?"

"We're not miserable." Dandy, perhaps five at the time, happily popped a piece of pancake into her mouth.

"Not at all," Sophia assured her.

"I think it's the first meaning," I replied. "Miserable people want to make others miserable for the company."

"But says who? The structure of the words can be taken either way. The second way is much more positive. Miserable people just want to have some company to cheer them up. There's nothing wrong with that."

"I like company," Dandy added.

"Well, that's not what I meant when I said it," I replied, defending my earlier witticism like a grammarian who insists that *ain't* ain't a word. If it works, use it, and let us evolve already. Habit, habit, habit.

Sophia paused, the look of nonsense twinkling in her eye like an octopus dancing with a pair of polyester slacks in front of a fun house mirror. "Do you mean to say that you say what you mean?"

Blip directly rejoined. "Did you dream today what tomorrow you'll seem?"

Sophia was unflappable. "Can a rhetorician retort?"

"Is a magician a wart?" Dandy snickered hysterically.

The matter settled, we fell silent once again and returned to our fruit.

118 Much to the delight of Blip and Sophia, Dandy was in the habit of playing with her food. She amused herself that afternoon by carving a smiley face out of her second pancake. Before the grin was complete, she set her fork down and made as if to speak, but paused, as if hesitant to blow the bugle that would bring the walls of Jericho tumbling down. At last, she delivered her doomsday query and demanded to know why aren't apples called reds, since oranges are called oranges, and also why aren't lemons called yellows.

Despite her misgivings, the walls of civilization were quite sound, and society chuckled through its adults. Ah, children! If they only knew how trite this question and others of its ilk really are. When it inevitably dawns on a child, they ask it as if they'd just caught grown-ups in a lie. In fact, the less socialized have just discovered one of their first of far too many inconsistencies and contradictions in our culture. This is not the explanation given, of course. If it were, *Why aren't apples called reds?* would not have become the self-important bachelorette borne of centuries of involuntary virginity. Instead, we sigh and pat their heads, smoothing any rebellious wisps of hair back into place. How could they know, after all, that this is a question that, in one form or another, has struck everyone weaned on the wonderful but decidedly unparallel English language?

Still, the presence of this question serves as a troublesome reminder that there remains a loose end out there, tickling our curiosity like unwelcome gropes from an ex-lover. This matter of the color of oranges, the riddle of the citrus, continues to elude us despite our technological fantasticry. The question is common, but the answer is as rare as an orange apple. Is it really possible that a question every child with any sparkle has considered has never been answered? Could it be that through centuries of linguistic evolution no one has answered it adequately, or if they have they've kept it to themselves? And if so, why?

Why aren't apples called reds? She had certainly made her rounds across the generations, yet invariably her presence was insulted with various answers of the ignoramus persuasion presuming to present themselves as potential suitors. Finding its other half is all any question wants out of its utterance and contemplation, searching for union like everything else. Sadly, most of her contemporaries had long since graduated into the realm of fact and trivia, dancing around their other half and hooking up with other couples, a swinging nexus of questions and answers realizing ever further connections in the gigantic jigsaw of cogitation. Newer questions, such as *Why are our children using drugs?*, provided her no companionship, for they were much too academic and urbane for her country-girl sensibilities. So, *Why aren't apples called reds?* pined for her answer in shining armor, occasionally gossiping with the enigmas and quacking with the quandaries, and forever heckled by the raving paradoxes, that breed of boastful loners who have gone quite mad thinking that they're better than the masses of romantics. "You're a stupid question, and you deserve a stupid answer!" The paradoxes taunted our heroine heartlessly.

To be perfectly honest, *Why aren't apples called reds?* was quite attracted to another question, the ponderous hallelujah known as *Why are we here?* They never had a future, of course. That would be homoquestionality. (All literal parallels to human sexuality must necessarily cease at this point, if only for the sake of rhythm, which is, after all, what sex and love are all about anyway, no matter your politico-sexual persuasion. The important distinction is not so much male and female as it is compatible opposites, that is, questions and answers.) *Why aren't apples called reds?* sighed and meekly bore her share of the consequences of the Adam and Eve fiasco, dreaming unmentionable dreams.

"Why aren't apples called reds?" Dandy's singsong voice interrupted the homoquestional fantasizing of *Why aren't apples called reds?* Though she would have liked to ignore it and begin her masturbatory daydream anew, she had no more control over when she was spoken than we do over when we are born. But as soon as she saw the humans gathered around the latest incarnation of her vocalization, she quickly straightened herself and thrust her chest forward, hoping to attract her long-lost answer, daring to believe that these strange people might be the ones to introduce her to her soul mate. These people were different, full of nonsense and kindness. Instead of hurling some cop-out about not all apples being red back at their daughter (and she was so weary of finding excuses not to go out with that buffoon), they paused, pondering her as if she really deserved contemplation.

"It's about time you asked that," Sophia smiled at Dandy, reassuring her that the walls of society were quite sound. *Why aren't apples called reds?* held her breath and checked her reflection, and for a moment thought she saw her other half gazing back through the looking glass, serpentine eyes gleaming like the Hope Diamond. It appeared he was a Victorian prude turned dreadlocked Rastafarian, wild but uneasy, a know-it-all, for after all, he was the answer to *Why aren't apples called reds?* If nothing else, he was what everyone was curious about. At least he had that, and he clung to it, protecting his virginity (he did everything but) even though he was spoken often, though never in the right manner. He guarded his secret, and he wasn't about to give it up just because every five-year-old thinks they've thought of something that's never occurred to anyone else and every forty-year-old is too lazy to give them a straight answer. But come the right people, asking the right question, at just the right time, and reunion will occur, an orgasmic act of originality borne on the stale winds of interrogative banality. Such is Creation, sticky, slick, slimy, and wonderful, birthing contentment, answering all questions, for a little while.

But wait. Maybe he should think about this. Perhaps she wears too much makeup. Perhaps *Why aren't apples called reds?* is misrepresenting her own true question. Perhaps she does not know her true nature, her true question. Perhaps she feels a homoquestional attraction to the ponderous *Why are we here?* because it is the real question, the only question, the Source of all questions. Perhaps *Why aren't apples called reds?* only exists because of what we are afraid to ask ourselves. Perhaps we shall soon see.

119 "Why aren't apples called reds?" Dandy repeated, patiently awaiting the mastications and ruminations of her parents. I couldn't help but chew on this dilemma as well as I munched my apple wedges and sipped my cider.

"What are you really asking?" Sophia calmly asked her daughter. *Why aren't apples called reds?* hesitated, wanting to flee, afraid of what lay ahead. Destiny, however, had its own ideas, and she was but one of them. The time for resolve had come. Dandy's mind was already racing with possibilities, peering into secrets *Why aren't apples called reds?* wasn't even aware she held. For a moment, *Why aren't apples called reds?* took exception to this penetration. This was not at all how she had fancied it would be, but moments that matter seldom are. Regardless, exception turns to acceptance in the hands of innocence, and *Why aren't apples called reds?* felt herself deepening, her perspective widening, her true question tossing off illusion and confusion like an anonymous lover the morning after a masquerade ball. *Why aren't apples called reds?* blushed.

"Good question," Blip complimented Sophia. After countless centuries, it appeared that all that was needed was a little encouragement, nudging *Why aren't apples called reds?* in the right direction, and allowing ourselves to be nudged in turn. Such simpletons we seem.

Dandy irrigated a canal through her applesauce. She fortified it with apple wedges before opening the levee and dripping her apple juice down the slopes of her smiley face pancakes. The sweet liquid must have turned the wheels of her mind, cranking out a smile as if she were creating the land flowing with milk and honey right there on her plate. With a lick of her finger she pronounced the true question of *Why aren't apples called reds?*

"Why don't we call things what they are?"

120 "Why indeed," Sophia mused. "Why do we call *red* red?"

"What else would we call it?" Dandy was again concerned about the structural integrity of the walls, which shuddered from the force of the calmness beyond. Declawed and housebroken cats are we, terrified of the enormous space beyond the doors, aware of it, even curious, but wary nonetheless.

"How about *rojo*?" I answered, always pleased with myself when I could contribute. "That's how they say red in Spanish." *Why aren't apples called reds?* was swollen, tumescent, but each step closer to union seemed shorter than the last, slowing, slowing down, yet still advancing toward the inevitable incredible.

In truth, everything was moving much faster, vibrating to another level, leaving time behind like a never-before-noticed blindfold, astonished at how nice things could have been but now are and always were. We know this much: The faster we go, the slower time becomes, courtesy of one called Einstein (though it's said his ex-wife had a hand in it as well). Reality is relative. It sounds very interesting, it even makes sense somehow, but we never really accept such a perception of everyday experience, unwilling, perhaps, to venture where really necessary. *Why aren't apples called reds?,* if she could say anything other than "Why aren't apples called reds?" might have advised us to just go with what feels right and let things happen for themselves. Enjoy the tranquillity, relax, leave everything behind, and drift into the fourth dimension. But she could care less about us timid apes. The deepest parts of us are already there anyway. Who are they? Who am I? I am I, and that goes for you, too.

"*Rojo?*" Dandy asked, perplexed. *Rojo.* Latin lover or not, *Why aren't apples called reds?* did not think she could endure much more of this teasing foreplay.

"Sure," said Blip. "And it's called a hundred other things in a hundred other places."

Dandy looked to her mother for confirmation. "It's true," Sophia nodded. "If you want to come up with something else to call apples or oranges or reds or whatever, let us know. Or, if you can think of a better way to organize things," she pointed haphazardly around her, "that would be wonderful."

"This," Blip gestured every which way, "is just the best we've come up with so far. Grown-ups are just children, too, remember, though most of us try to convince ourselves otherwise. The major difference between children and adults is that adults have forgotten that they're just pretending." He paused to sip some warm applejack from his handleless teacup. "There's an old Zen proverb that tells us not to mistake a tree for a tree. 'Tree' is just what we call it, but words don't begin to capture what the tree actually is. Forgetting that is like forgetting that the map is not the road."

"Does that answer your question?" Sophia asked. Dandy nodded happily. Her belly was full, her questions were answered.

"So why aren't apples called reds?" Blip quizzed her.

Dandy, grinning like an apple wedge, replied honestly and not at all sarcastically. "Because you say so."

121 *Why aren't apples called reds?* and her answer were cavorting in the next room, paradoxes peeking in, making fun of the way they looked, blind to themselves. She could not believe what had happened. It seemed far too simple, yet undeniably right. *Because we say so.* Tough, sexy, a gentle truth hidden beneath an arrogant exterior. Her answer wasn't what she thought it would be, but then she wasn't who she thought she was. Embarrassingly simple, yet she had no cause to be flustered. I quote Blip: "Do you want your questions answered or your answers questioned?"

Amor becomes agape, ad infinitum. The embrace of Love knows nothing of individuality. Love is the commonality, the community. *Why aren't apples called reds?* and her answer were never separate from each other in the first place. Come to think of it, their union was not separate from any other. A ménage à trois had formed here, a trinity of divinity, between a question, her answer, and the ambidextrous *Why are we here?*, who was, it turned out, present at every act of creation, linking the body and the mind with the soul. The homoquestional urges of *Why aren't apples called reds?* were not so deviant after all.

Why aren't apples called reds? Because we say so.

Why are we here? Well, we're peeking up the skirt of the ineffable now, and the answer is hidden by the poetic panties of language. We can't formulate an answer because the question is its own answer. What's going on? What's going on. She doesn't need us for anything. She is us. We are us. Existence exists. Division is a false dichotomy. Why does the universe exist? Because that's what it does. It exists. It's like asking why words mean anything. Because that's what they are, what they do. Because we say so. Why is the universe here? Because it is, because it says so. It is what is. I am who am.

Why are we here? Look now, what are we doing, wailing our dirge of needless despair? She pauses, patient as the hundred trillionth person utters her as if no one else has ever considered it, arrogant morons every one. She wants to shout, "You're closer to the answer before you ever ask it!" but instead she smiles. "I can only ignore the question posed," she thinks with parental compassion, "for in truth, it neither tickles my nickels nor twists at my nipples. Content is secondary to presentation. Tell me about nothing, good human, but do it in style, and style is what it is, my friend, how it's done, where it's at. It's what's properly occurring between the perceiver and the perceived, the subject and the object, the giver and the taker, to get it in tune, to get it in sync, to get it going on. What can I say but to live for today? Play as you pray, and gather together one another as lovers, sisters and brothers, miscellaneous others. Style is a smile, a four-minute mile, a jump rope of awareness presuming to dare us, spinning and grinning, faster and deeper and further and longer, till we break through and sing of ridiculous things, for who's left to question the laughter of children, the hilarity of love, the rhythm of coincidence, the happenstance of circumstance? If you can speak you can sing, if you can sing you can dance, if you can dance you can prance, and if you can prance you can ponder. 'Cause if you've got style you've got rhythm, and if you've got rhythm, you've got it all . . . all or nothing, and all together."

The Book o' Billets-doux

Rosehips: Here's a point to consider. If the shortest distance between two points is a line, then what is the point of this line?

sweetlick: From my vantage point, the line itself looks like a point.

Rosehips: See now, here we have written at least two points, yet there is no conceptual distance at all between them. So, how can we distinguish between points in time and points in space, and, most important, points to make? I have a point, and I still wish to make a point, and yet I can't see the point of it all.

sweetlick: The point of existentialism is that there is no point, but the point of Zen is both pointness and nonpointness.

Rosehips: Perhaps this points the way to an entirely new ethic, wherein the sage advice is not that it's impolite to point, but rather that it's simply an impolite point.

sweetlick: I think I see your point, but I'd like to point out to you that in pointing out your point, the point has become lost in the pointing.

122 Still breathless with the climax of her colloquy and flushed redder than any apple had ever been before, *Why aren't apples called reds?* hung a DO NOT DISTURB sign on the door and closed it, but not before mooning the paradoxes with her scarlet derriere. I too must turn away from my voyeurism of their verbal intercourse and allow them the privacy of a postcoital embrace. May God bless them.

Back in the realm from which I have retreated and to which I am reluctant to return, General Kiljoy, Tynee, Miss Mary, and I were down with stomach flu for three days. Combined with her nicotine withdrawal, Miss Mary may well have shaken herself to death. Luckily for her, Ratdog sniffed out a few cases of stale cigarettes stashed in a cabinet behind the bar. I watched from across the room as she blissfully blew the by-products of her addiction into our atmosphere. Only a few moments passed before the stench clenched up my nostrils. She smiled insipidly, then malevolently. I sighed a shallow sigh, rolled over, and considered that as quickly as her exhaust had reached me, so could have the Pied Piper virus.

The Pied Piper virus. What's that renegade ribbon of ribonucleic acid up to? Whistling for the children to follow him toward what lay beyond the city walls? Not quite, for the walls had been thrown up farther outside the city. Just as planned, a massive blockade was in effect along the city's outerbelt. General Kiljoy informed us of this soon after he established a communication link with the authorities up above. Eventually, we even had some video footage on the monitor, though no audio.

Quarantine was enforced on the city, laying siege to the sprawling metropolitan area. The three lanes of the outerbelt (five with the shoulders) were a no-man's-land. Razor wire and heat-sensing automatic weapons greeted any source of infrared radiation, so that even with the freeway shut down, groundhogs and rabbits continued to be killed right on schedule. They were soon joined by stray humans. At first, only separatist militia types living in the hinterlands of the city attempted to make a break for it, but eventually this dwindled down to the occasional stray suburbanite wandering about confused and unable to understand the warnings from the loudspeakers or even what the commotion ahead implied. Lacking these social faculties, curious people would amble ahead, typically skipping and snickering, and quickly become so much goopy roadkill. TV has become more violent lately.

Nothing much else could be done about this stalemate since the Pied Piper virus was never supposed to leave the compound. In the meantime, every scientist in the world with any relevant expertise at all was recruited to work on developing a vaccine. This included me, of course, and General Kiljoy arranged a read-only computer network connection so that I would be informed of any significant new developments. He expected me to work twelve hours a day in the compound's laboratory facilities developing a cure. I welcomed the isolation from the company of my odious employers, but I was not about to do any work.

Thanksgiving came and went, and we dined on a feast of canned turkey and cream-style corn. I joined everyone for the meal, but excused myself when Miss Mary began stringing some Christmas lights that she'd dug up somewhere on the antlers of the once noble and now gaudy elk's head mounted on the wall. It was the first meal I had shared with them since Halloween night. I join the others only when I must, and spend the rest of my time in my workspace. That's where I have been writing this account for the past month. I type it on the computer. General Kiljoy thinks I'm working on his problem. He pokes his head in from time to time and asks if there's been any progress. Since he doesn't specify to what he is referring, I can always somewhat truthfully reply yes. He caught me smiling at the screen once. Shortly thereafter he demanded a progress report, which was easy enough to fake for a group whose understanding of genetics went no further than how it could serve their ends, like any common killer whose knowledge of pistol mechanics is limited to how to pull the trigger.

Here he is now, sticking his head in and barking, "Do good work!" like some fast-food manager trying to motivate team spirit at a shit job. What a prick. A general deserves respect, certainly, but only to the extent that he defends the lives of those he represents without causing undue harm to others. By these standards, he's the worst general I've ever seen. He oversees the creation of the neutron bomb of biological warfare, infects some of his own countrymen, and kills my dog. Hooray for the hero!

As for searching for a cure for the Pied Piper virus, I didn't really feel like it. I'd sooner flip hamburgers. In fact, I'd sooner kill myself, as I attempted two weeks after Thanksgiving by swallowing a teaspoon of the urushiol I had stolen from Tynee's office. It should have been enough to give a hundred million people a scorching case of poison ivy, so I reasoned it should have been enough to kill just one. I suppose I was trying to escape. There was just too much cognitive dissonance in being expected to save human civilization while working for these jerks. They're not the caretakers of the Earth. They're the bad guys, the destroyers. As far as I was concerned, the mad flutist was free to prance the children away. We deserve it. We broke our promise.

123 I found myself standing under a tree, a tree identifiable only by the flaming mop of crimson foliage it was shamelessly shedding, liberating each leaf to a slow and seductive pirouette of ecstasy. This was neither vanity nor pride, understand, only delight in its form and colors, thanksgiving through actualization, a realization of potential.

"This sucks," I groused, then watched from a point neither near nor far as I transmogrified into General Kiljoy. General Kiljoy was in no mood for beauty. General Kiljoy was grumpy, and the perky autumn breeze did nothing to improve his dismal disposition. It only made his digits cold, and he muttered further vexations as he stuffed his thick hands into his tight pockets, grateful at least and at last for the opportunity to adjust himself.

Adjusted, he trudged up a formerly verdant hillside where Mother Nature was now enraptured in a seasonal celebration of self, an autumnal burlesque of Gaian proportions, a liberation of libido, leaves blushing as they swayed enticingly in the lusty breeze. The trees are stripping, the world whispered and whistled, and soon will be naked!

A good woman, Sophia by name, had earlier that morning imagined that it was a fine day to be a leaf. The temperature was lukewarm, the texture silken, and the wind was blustery though not boastful. A sultry, sexy day, she thought, perhaps I will join the nymphs of my deciduous kinfolk in dancing the day away.

This she did, and was so doing when she spied old General Kiljoy grumbling up the hill whose top she graced with her presence.

He moves in a way inappropriate to the day, she observed, while twirling slowly in the gusts of the zephyr, arms outstretched, gauzy layers of gratuitous and flamboyant fabric billowing around her form, making a visual display of the air currents, imitating the alluring frolic of foliage around her. The colors of her raiments were many and rich, and she had made it a point in dressing that morning to complement, not compete with, her environment, of which she was only a part, after all. Her mood was as gossamer as her garments, and her awareness of General Kiljoy was as fleeting as brushing a fly away, a momentary disruption of rhythm, an ebb in the flow.

"Hello," she greeted General Kiljoy when he reached the summit. His hands were still in his pockets, tickling his Twinkie. "Beautiful, isn't it?" she continued, her cheeks as red as a leaf on its last lark as she fluttered by. Windblown locks of hair danced across her face.

"Beautiful?" This gave General Kiljoy pause, as if she had just suggested how peaceful a traffic jam was. "Real beautiful, you fool. All the leaves are dying, and winter's coming." He harrumphed and resumed fooling with his flinger.

"And then spring comes again." Sophia's skirt relaxed upon the Earth as she bent to pick up a leaf, not the most attractive, certainly, but ravishing nonetheless. She tucked the leaf behind her ear and resumed dancing.

"What are you doing?" General Kiljoy snarled at Sophia as he rustled his ricky. She was again lost in the gyrations of the season.

Turning to him only when the wind permitted, Sophia smiled, her locks dancing crazily behind her, chiffon pressed close against her skin, emphasizing her seductive aerodynamics. "I'm doing what we must, of course!" she shouted since she was speaking into the wind.

"What?"

Sophia eased herself through the currents until she was dancing beguilingly around him. "It's autumn, silly man. Doesn't that make you happy?"

"Happy? It's slippery, slimy, and wet, and all these leaves will turn into more muck. Don't you see? This sucks!"

Sophia sniggled at the face of discipline before her. "Life is slippery, slimy, and wet. Don't you know anything about sex?"

General Kiljoy reddened, and Sophia giggled some more. "Now you match the season," she said as a gust of wind encouraged leaves to leap in increasing numbers, hastening the pace of the striptease and compelling her to twirl away. The wind blew harder, and Sophia fluttered obligingly down the hillside. A stray breeze carried her final phrase to within earshot of General Kiljoy. "This is a dream!" she yelled radiantly. "This is a *dream*!"

At that, General Kiljoy drew his pistol and shot her dead.

124

"This is a nightmare!" I heard myself scream. "This is a nightmare!" Someone slapped my face. "This is a nightmare!" I wailed insanely, and my face was slapped again.

"This is reality!" It was the bellow of General Kiljoy, and it was his heavy hand that struck my face yet again. "This is reality!" he roared. "This is reality! Wake up!"

I came around at last, bruised, beaten, heaving, and itchy. To my dismay, I recovered from my urushiol ordeal within a few days, and was placed under General Kiljoy's close supervision. Though his threat concerning the removal of my fingers and toes went unfulfilled, I was made to sleep in his bed with him for over a week. This ceased when he awoke one morning spooning me. The urushiol, clearly, did not work, though it did put me in a delusional coma for thirty-six hours. The bottle of toxin was found near me, and Tynee knew enough to inject me with a massive dose of vitamin C, which neutralized much of the poison. The urushiol was years old anyway, Tynee informed me in condescension, and most of it had broken down into simpler molecular forms.

Everyone suspects I'm still suicidal, which as a matter of fact, I am. I'm depressed. I'm in a recession of consciousness. My life has been a speculative economy, counting on tomorrow, but it has finally crashed. The bulls were only running because a bear was on their heels. Writing no longer offers me any solace, for not much has happened lately. Life in a fallout bunker becomes routine very quickly. This dullness has spilled over into my consciousness like an overflowing toilet with no plunger in sight, and so the shit riseth, and life is crappy.

I have not slept well since Tynee and Miss Mary first consummated their inexplicable attraction toward each other. My nights have since been colored by the sound of their moaning slapsex right next door. Tynee's cheeks are invariably rosy in the mornings. On top of my sleeplessness, General Kiljoy wakes me before dawn, gives me coffee and some unidentified hot chunkiness for breakfast, and gets me to work. He makes me take breaks in the observation lounge, where we all hang around watching the boring crisis aboveground. If nothing else, I enjoy the natural light piped into the room, but my circadian cycles have lost their cadence nonetheless. I no longer possess any circadian rhythm. I stumble to the slosh of circadian Muzak.

Earlier this morning, I found myself pacing around the laboratory, clenching my hands, daydreaming about dancing and drumming around a fire until I had stomped my self-awareness into dust that blows to where the wild things are. Freedom to scream, freedom to roar, freedom to swim naked on a moonlit shore. A childish fantasy, to be sure, and not at all characteristic of me. I considered the possibility that I might be going stir-crazy. This worried me, and I tried to reassure myself aloud. But I sounded anxious and apprehensive, and thus only succeeded in making myself paranoid as well.

As I said, the monotony has dulled my motivation to write. My pace has slowed to a few sentences a day, if at all, and upon review amounts to little more than the rambling refuse of an academic recluse. This is also worrisome, since it occurs to me that I write to prevent myself from going mad. Yesterday, in desperation, I even tried doing what I was supposed to be doing just to do *something*, but that just depressed me all the more. Suicide presents itself again and again at every turn of thought.

Escape is demanding that I pay him heed. The sounds of his desperate cries reverberate through my head, spasmodic screams and primal anxiety bouncing the echoes of pathological frustration around the inside of my skull, kicking the life out of my survival instinct. As a rule, when a situation becomes intolerable, an egress is desired. Thwarted, frustration builds, the spirit expands, driving you to remove yourself from the situation in any way possible, for the spirit will not be confined. Not here, not anywhere.

Polite at first, the voice of freedom becomes increasingly fierce and unforgiving, fighting as it is for the love of life itself. We ignore it at our own peril. It either forces change or it forces death. The spirit must be free, I've discovered. It will not be shackled by the concerns and worries of the material world. It will be heard, it will get its way, and it will make us die before it will give up.

125 Things change, we constantly need to be reminded. Today is the winter solstice, the darkest day of the year. On this unlikely day my mood suddenly soared, and I realized how fantastically selfish suicide is. Seeing as how life kicks everyone in the shins from time to time, what passing despair could possibly convince one to return the most spectacular gift in the universe? How do our dinky difficulties drive us to dicker with death? What belligerent buffoonery in the face of such benevolence! Suicide? Good heavens, I must have gone silly in the head. I almost deleted the previous passages out of existential embarrassment, but it's not likely that anyone will ever read this anyway after what occurred today. I write nevertheless.

(General Kiljoy is looking in on me now. He looks afraid, and I strive to look the same. Nothing going on here, just diligent fear and work. I pause to rub the stress out of my temples.)

Why the sudden change of outlook, this sudden gaiety and glee? Aside from the glad fact of existence, I'm specifically pleased that I existed in time to witness what I'm about to relate.

Around ten o'clock this morning, as I sat at my desk trying to think of something to doodle (such were the depths of my crushing boredom), General Kiljoy summoned me to the observation lounge. Once I had joined Tynee and Miss Mary on the sofas, General Kiljoy commenced pacing, nay, marching, to and fro before us, stern and erect, clutching his military discipline with all his authoritarian might. "I have good news and bad news," he began without a break in his step. "First, the good news. The situation upstairs will not continue. I was informed this morning that the entire quarantined area is to be sterilized."

"The whole city?" Tynee spoke.

"The entire quarantined area," General Kiljoy corrected, clinging to his euphemisms like an infant clinging to his mother's silicone breasts. "The sterilization is scheduled tomorrow night at midnight. A warhead of undisclosed size will accomplish this objective. Everything within a sixty-mile radius of ground zero will be incinerated. The Pied Piper virus will then exist only in the laboratory once again."

"What happens to us?" Miss Mary demanded, forgetting, for once, her monetary investment in the Pied Piper virus.

"We are irrelevant to national security," General Kiljoy stated flatly. "We're safe in this compound, in any case. This is, after all, a bomb shelter."

"They're going to drop a bomb, *the* bomb, on the greater metropolitan area?" Tynee asked, more confused than thunderstruck. "And right before Christmas? How the hell do they plan to get away with that?"

"I'm amazed it took them this long. It is a theoretical possibility that a bird could carry the virus out of the quarantined area. Confronted with the risk of a plague, there has been little resistance to this plan of action. It is generally regarded as unfortunate but necessary by the public."

"Come on," Tynee snorted. "The government can't just nuke a small city and its few hundred thousand inhabitants and expect to maintain legitimacy. What's going on?"

General Kiljoy paused, hands in pockets, nudging his nubbin. "The release of the virus is being called a terrorist attack."

"Wow." Tynee chuckled. "That's a whopper."

"Negative. The automation routines of this compound have been thoroughly examined and reexamined. There was no malfunction. Someone is responsible."

"Terrorists? Did they find something on the videotapes?"

"Nothing that we don't already know. Whoever is behind this was thorough."

"So what's the bad news?" Tynee asked.

"We will be taken in for questioning after sterilization."

"What? I helped to conceive the goddamn idea!"

"Did you think they'd just give us a hug and say they're glad we're okay? This is the worst breach of national security in world history. We may not be publicly responsible, but each one of us is guilty until it is established exactly what happened. For all they know, one of us is the terrorist."

"Us?" Tynee blurted and sputtered, flabbergasted at the notion. "I've been with this project longer than anyone!"

"I've already explained that Agent Orange is unaccounted for. She is currently suspect. They're looking into it. She may be a double agent. She couldn't have accomplished such an objective without massive assistance."

"Did you tell them your theory about Captain Down as well?" Miss Mary's haughtiness was returning with the news of her imminent release and subsequent limitless supply of fresh smokes. She spat a cloud in General Kiljoy's direction. He deflected the insult with a roll of his eyes and a toss of his twerp.

"Why now?" I asked. "Why not earlier?"

"Things are occurring," General Kiljoy answered without turning to me. He pointed his remote control at the observation window and turned on the video screen. "The release of the Pied Piper virus on such a massive scale has had consequences unanticipated by our limited observations of individuals and small groups."

"Meaning what?" Miss Mary demanded, again concerned about the status of her investment.

"Meaning there is more bad news." General Kiljoy directed our attention to the screen. "This is an aerial view of the city recorded earlier this morning by a remote-operation surveillance plane. Notice anything peculiar?"

From such a distant perspective the city looked like a massive scab, a clumsily grid-lined, malignant scar on the natural landscape. Aside from that, there was nothing particularly unusual about it. Tynee, however, strode to the screen and immediately pointed to a barely visible line that encircled the entire city. It appeared to be a nearly perfect circle.

"What's that?" he demanded.

"Isn't that the outerbelt?" Miss Mary suggested. It would have been my first guess as well.

Tynee pointed to a thicker line, outside the original circle, which meandered its way around the city, connecting to other easily visible traffic arteries. "This is the outerbelt."

"Good eye, Tibor." General Kiljoy congratulated him.

"So what is it?" Tynee demanded once again.

"Watch." General Kiljoy hit fast-forward, and the view of the city became gradually closer as the aircraft descended. Once we could distinguish windows on buildings, he resumed normal playback speed. The view presented by the camera revealed streets deserted exactly like a fresh ghost town. Newspapers and other artifacts of an abandoned civilization lay scattered about like tumbleweed. The stillness was interrupted only once by a pack of five dogs trotting down the middle of the street, utterly mindless of the extreme strangeness around them. "Reports estimate that approximately one-tenth of the city's residents have perished," General Kiljoy informed us as if he were relaying baseball statistics. "Widespread panic, random rioting, a lot of suicide. Interestingly, not many died of starvation or exposure. Apparently, finding food and shelter are drives independent of the ability to communicate."

"One-tenth of the population? Where are all the corpses?" Tynee asked.

"Buried."

"Buried?"

"Some were burned."

"How is that possible?"

General Kiljoy cleared his throat in hesitation. "It seems that the sanitary disposal of corpses can be accomplished independently of the ability to communicate."

"What?" Tynee was incredulous. "That doesn't make sense."

"What about everyone else?" I interrupted. "Where are they?"

"Just watch," he said, gesturing to the screen, where the camera was now moving out from the center of the city and over progressively wealthier neighborhoods. Miss Mary pointed out a country club at which she had attended a splendid wedding and twaddled on about the hand-painted set of dinner plates she'd commissioned for her gift to the couple and wondering who got to keep them after they got divorced.

Eventually, we reached the fringe of development, camera panning over as yet undeveloped woods and farms. It was then, just before it came, that I began to suspect what was coming. I was astounded nonetheless. It was a simple thing, a line of people holding hands, yet it could not have violated my expectations more completely. There it was, like some Red Rover revelation daring us to come over, a line of people so long that they formed a circle around the entire city.

126 In grade school, standing in line created its own particular form of play. Rules existed, yes, but they only provided the conditions of the game. Standing in line naturally preceded giving the person in front of you the knee wobblies, or even better, set the stage for a rousing round of human dominoes or some such horseplay. Absent such diversions, we'd chatter and whisper and snicker and generally enjoy ourselves despite the rules. Do you remember? Little did we realize how things would change, how our fellow linemates would change, how we would change. Unruly no more, we wait in line, shut down our awareness of everything but the progress of the line, despising all whose existence made the line possible. We dare not knock the hat off the person in front of us, or even make idle chatter. Shh! Be quiet, you! Stand in line!

If I romanticize the queues of childhood, it is only to indicate that the line of humans before me now made them seem totalitarian in comparison. Chaos springs to mind as an initial description, yet this was a line. There was an unmistakable order, a perfect order, a perfect circle of collaborative chaos. Panning down the line revealed human after human of various colors, sizes, and ages engaged in games we never dreamed of as children. There were those occupying their time spinning, arms outstretched, slapping hands with each other at every half rotation. This activity gradually faded into the most blatant line jumping I've ever seen, though since this line was ultimately a circle such prohibitions become moot. A person would jump out of line and almost immediately back into a space left empty only a moment before by another, jockeying for position like birds on a wire, a high wire, precariously balanced on the tightrope of thrilling existence. This went on and on down the line, but it too eventually melted into a game I shall call the whip. The whip was like a narrower version of the sports arena wave, but unlike the wave, there was not just one wave of motion. Movement in the whip was more properly understood as a wavelength, in that a discernible frequency of motion emerged, with an estimated wavelength of seven persons. This was the game of the day, it seemed, for it went on and on, and I suspected it would eventually overtake the spinners and the jumpers and whatever else preceded them.

Despite the ostensibly grim reality of the situation, it was great fun to watch, and actually left me feeling elated. These were not the gaunt survivors of an experiment in germ warfare gone horribly wrong. These were thousands of strangers and neighbors doing some thing, some fantastic dancing thing I could scarcely comprehend. Watching this hosanna hoopla of hoi polloi, this hula-hoop hullabaloo, this hocus-pocus hokeypokey dance, I felt like I was witnessing a circus, an enchanting circus of consciousness performing stunts clearly possible but nonetheless unbelievable. What the hell? How on Earth? Such thoughts sprinted through my mind leaving wild fascination and mad anticipation in their wake. What was I anticipating? Something else, I suppose, something more, something improbable, something I could not imagine; something wonderful, something delightful, something unfathomable. Throw it at me, that's what I wanted. Untame the lions, copulate on the tightrope, make that baby elephant fly! I was ringside at the greatest show on Earth, an unparalleled congregation of hilarity and verity where audience and performer became worthless distinctions. It was real and it wasn't stopping, and though my body was buried under tons of granite, and my oohs and aahs and wows were strangled in my throat, my spirit had jumped aboard at the first sign of mutiny. Here was freedom at last! They weren't incapacitated, but liberated. Yes, the Pied Piper virus had unforeseen consequences all right. As a weapon, it was about as useful as a squirt gun. The victim only sniggled and went after its attacker with the garden hose. If the goal was to conquer by removing the building blocks of language, it was an unmistakable failure. Something else had emerged in its place, something unforeseen indeed, something better, something true, something coordinating human action like language never could. Joy to the world!

127 Of course, this is mere inference, my own on-the-spot theorizing. But watching these events unfold, an unspeakable calm hugged me like a five hundred-pound grandmother. I was comforted, I was reassured, and I knew that everything was going to be all right.

In the face of celebration, however, it's hard to believe anything but that everything is okay. So perhaps it was the inevitable laughter that characterized the Pied Piper syndrome that put me so at ease. It made me chuckle inside; I honestly couldn't help it. But I pause to consider: Is this feeling of glorious well-being false, or are we experiencing what is so? That is to say, are we simply blind to contentment and peace when not laughing? Do we fail to notice the cartwheels and jumping jacks in front of our faces? Smile. A stranger, though unrecognized, exists nonetheless, and has only to be introduced properly for us to remember that they are a long-lost friend. We mustn't be timid apes. Shyness is self-consciousness, remember. Refocus your consciousness toward others and everything will become clear, the jesters will appear and tickle your fear. They've been there all the time. You'll see what I mean.

Giddy as I was at these turns of events, General Kiljoy, Tynee, and Miss Mary were not noticeably laughing. Nor was I, of course, but I don't think they were suppressing any glee. In fact, they seemed rather miffy, not sharing in the amusements perhaps because they were the joke, they were the numskulls, the dimwits, the dolts. In this, the ultimate round of Ring around the Rosy, they were the pickle in the middle.

It was when the wavelength shortened to six persons that the laughter began. Further, this dance of disarming foolishness only begat more perfect reproductions of itself with each passing moment, a frolicking fugue of infinite faith. Fellow vibrations, they bobbed along the wavelength, facing the center, the city, technocracy incarnate, the clueless monster, the grand ramification of human selfishness, the tactless boast of false progress. They looked at the slapdash and slipshod handiwork of humankind, our alibi for the sin of sloth and our evidence for the sin of vanity, and they roared in kindly fury, unleashing their collective torment and frustration in an uncontrite catharsis of conscience. They laughed heartily at the modern city and everything it implied: the abuse, the anxiety, the devastation and ruination, the loneliness, the sorrow, the pride, the anger. Seeing these monkeyshines roused a mighty chuckle of a ruckus. The modern city, or what it represented, had become the most scoffworthy notion since the flat Earth hypothesis. They laughed at the folly, the pettiness, and the self-absorption. "Who do you think you're fooling?" they guffawed at the authoritarian fabrication before them. "What pretentious nonsense!"

At least that's the snicker I thought I was sharing. I have lately realized that I've been living in a bushel of rot my entire life and been fed a lot of cosmopolitan claptrap about excitement and variety to make up for urban misery. What does it say about our society if the centers of our civilization are destructive to social cohesion? Diversity is wonderful, to be sure, and something akin to a city is probably necessary for it to exist, but surely we can do better than this. Are we honestly expected to take such flubdubbery seriously? Must we spend our days wandering such noisy pits of idiocy? Bullshit and baloney! Sell that applesauce to Cousin Tomfoolery. The follies of the past are not ours to inhabit. We are alive, and the shortsighted shenanigans of our ancestors are destroying us.

128 Speculation and conjecture abound here, I am aware, but I make no apologies. This is a firsthand account, and these events demand explanation, so you will just have to take it as it is. Verification and validation are impossible under these circumstances, and anyway, all memoirs of events are intrinsically filtered through someone's perception. So yes, you should know it is possible that I am misrepresenting the facts, or misleading you in some way. You should also know this about any account of events at which you are not present. This is an unfortunate characteristic of language. I wish to take what's in my head and put it in yours, but I cannot do so directly, and you cannot see what's in my head. Thus we are left with the indirect route of language, arbitrary symbols, random designations that we trust are agreed upon. The eminent Professor Blip Korterly taught me that.

Once, I was in first grade. I had bright eyes, a full head of hair, smooth skin, and mittens. After snacktime, we sometimes played a game called Telephone. Sister Lolita, our kind teacher, would whisper a phrase, something to the effect of, "Billy wants a black-and-white kitten for his birthday," to the first student, who would whisper it to the next, and so on around the room until the last student stated aloud what the phrase had evolved into, something like, "Willy got a black puppy for Christmas." One day, however, someone got the smart idea to change the phrase on purpose, to make up a completely different phrase, such as, "You can see the teacher's bra," and pass it on. Whatever the original or made-up phrase might have been, the last student got to say, "You can smell the teacher's underwear." This changed the nature of the game, and made Sister Lolita very upset. We never played Telephone again.

Words are both clumsy and easy to manipulate. Communication is indirect and covert, and true intentions and meanings are invisible. This is what makes deceit possible. If communication were direct and overt, that is to say empathic, we would exchange one another's perspectives immediately and without dispute. Intentions would never be misconstrued. Mistrust, deception, or disintegration of meaning would be impossible. Hence, I assert that the Pied Piper virus does not destroy the ability to communicate, for humans can scarcely communicate in the first place. If we could, there would never be a disagreement, misunderstanding, or war. Such asininity is an expression of mutual dementia, a recondite stupidity, an inability to empathize with each other's experiences. Language only makes matters worse by allowing us to manipulate our own and one another's perceptions of the world. In my estimation, the Pied Piper virus removes this blindfold. Absent such illusions, bare naked minds each to the other cannot disagree. Flawless communication can only result in immaculate perception.

129 Nutshell. Picture a nutshell.

I'll bet you pictured a peanut, which is not, in fact, a nut. It is a legume. If you did not picture a peanut, good for you! That's the point I am trying to make. I pictured a peanut shell (which is not, I know, a nut), and that is what I hoped to trigger in your mind with the symbol *nutshell.*

So let me be more precise. Picture a peanut shell. More

specifically, picture a roasted, uncracked peanut shell. Are you seeing what I'm seeing? I am visualizing a mutant peanut shell I once picked out of a bag at the zoo. It actually had three peanuts inside, which is not remarkably uncommon, except that in this one, each peanut had its own apartment connected at the center like a clover. What is more, two of these segments were pushed very close together, giving the larger peanut shell a provocatively feminine shape. Mr. Peanut would have tripped over his own cane and popped his monocle out at the sight of this voluptuous she-nut.

Now do you see what I see? Close enough, I'm sure. Close enough that I can proceed to talk about it anyway. However, I did not draw a picture of this leggy legume in your head to discuss Mr. Peanut's sexuality. My point, in a nutshell, is that despite my best efforts, you will not know exactly what this she-nut looked like. I can go on and on explaining more and more minute details, while you go on and on visualizing those details as you see fit, but we will *never* achieve a perfect transfer of information. Not through language. The best we can hope for is an analog bootleg.

Thus, it is my theory that the Pied Piper virus, in dissolving the human habit of communicating through shared symbols, has only allowed a deeper and more perfect form of empathic communication to blossom in its place. Based on my limited observations, the resulting consciousness is not a prelingual, but rather a supralingual state of mind, a perfectly social sentience that experiences no communication breakdown, distortion, or disintegration. I have no other explanation for the flawless coordination that I witnessed. How this has occurred I cannot say. I can only observe, with an incalculable degree of astonishment, that the social instincts of our species are not so easily suppressed.

130 I was beginning to grow accustomed to experiencing the profoundly improbable. Despite this, I was nonetheless amazed when the line of people on the screen suddenly ceased all movement whatsoever. It was as if they were participating in an unfathomably immense game of Freeze Tag and had just been tagged en masse by an omnipresent It. I was doubly surprised, and a little disappointed, when I realized that General Kiljoy was It. He had paused the playback. I was so thrilled by what was happening upstairs that I had forgotten we were watching a tape from earlier that morning. Given recent events, after all, a simultaneous standstill didn't seem so preposterous.

But it was preposterous, and as soon as I had sorted out my confusion, I inquired about the state of affairs at the present time. I was joined in this behest by Tynee and Miss Mary. General Kiljoy took his self-abusing hand out of his pocket to wave us off as he fooled with his remote in the other. After a few impatient moments, he succeeded in giving us real-time video on the screen.

I silently rejoiced as the line of dancing people flickered back on the monitor. It was immediately apparent that their shindig had become a great deal more rambunctious since this morning. Like any good party, things had gotten completely out of control, or out of conscious control anyway. As I've said, *something* was guiding this wingding; this was demonstrated by the spellbinding synchronicity of movement. The whip was still chasing its own vibrations through the circle, but the wavelength had decreased to three persons, demanding a staggering pace of all participants. No one, however, seemed to be weary in the least. Indeed, the whip's frequency was only the background upon which each individual was stomping out their own interpretive boogie. Judging from the fact that everyone looked as ecstatic as a belly dancer's navel, this was the greatest party ever thrown.

This busting blasting blowout was anything but some faceless mob of maniacs. Mobs are dangerous because everyone acts only for themselves. A mob is a mass of clods mindlessly trampling one another. Here, something was clearly weaving these people together in coexistent parallelism, uniting them in spite of, or because of, the Pied Piper virus. The virus was like a mad and hypnotic choreographer, a charismatic visionary encouraging his troupes that the show must not only go on, but that it must achieve a transcendent perfection. It seemed to be at once the relentless gusts of a fierce tempest and the gentle strokes of a silken comb. On the one hand, it was whipping the crowd into a windblown frenzy, while on the other, it was smoothing any tangles and snags out of the mane of the masses. Such complementary high jinks were creating a wild and merry frolic, a peaceful prance of drenching happiness, a gleeful spree of serendipity. But this hoedown of eloquent revelry had not yet peaked in intensity. Poetic and boisterous, tranquil and flabbergasting, giddy and serene, the hierophantic antics were accelerating. Within minutes, the wavelength had decreased to every other person flawlessly alternating between stepping forward and backward, and all the while matching this breakneck pace in their own personal grooves.

If you were to stumble on a pebble and find yourself on the ground with both legs suddenly behind your head, you would experience an incredulity of preternatural proportions. Such amazement at your own breathtaking clumsiness would be equivalent in degree to my own astonishment at the graceful chaos unfurling like Eleusinian fractals before me this morning. It was just too unlikely, yet it was more magnificent than seeing the aurora borealis during a solar eclipse. It was more enthralling than seeing a birdsong and hearing a rainbow. It was an extraordinary sight to behold.

General Kiljoy did not share this view. To be frank, he was freaked out, though in an appropriately disciplined manner. He stood as he watched these events unfold, arms akimbo like a bossy parent, clutching his remote control like a hastily removed belt, trying to decide how many lashes to mete out to his insubordinate children. "What the hell is this?" he snarled, turning to face the rest of us. His eyes were wild, perhaps panicked, and though his brow was furrowed in fury there was a peculiar tranquillity about him. He looked funny, and for the first time I noticed that the crease between his eyebrows formed the inside of a peace symbol.

God only knows how he managed to go so far in the military hierarchy with the footprint of the American chicken stamped on his forehead.

131 According to General Kiljoy's physiognomy book that I found on the bookshelf in the observation lounge, it takes approximately two hundred thousand frowns to etch a permanent crease in your brow. To accomplish this, you would have to scowl at least nine times a day for sixty years. General Kiljoy had no problem achieving this goal; he probably frowns nine times an hour. But his resulting peace crease must have vexed him considerably. He is certainly aware of this feature. As a self-proclaimed amateur face-reader, he surely must have trained his physiognomy to reveal as little as possible and to mislead as much as possible. After all, he could hardly go parading around the Pentagon with a peace sign chiseled between his eyes and expect to get any respect. That's why he looked so unusual. Current events were wearing on him, and he was losing control of his well-trained facial muscles in the process. He was becoming unbuttoned, expressions long hidden were suddenly flashing their privates to anyone who would look, tossing off their ridiculous cloaks in pathetic exhibitionism.

Yes, I am convinced he is aware of his stigmata. The peace crease flashed only briefly, and was quickly replaced by his conventional furrow as he regained some composure. He disguises his accidental groove with an intentional trench, an inverted peace symbol superimposed upon the original. To illustrate, the drawing on the left is his unadulterated brow pucker. On the right side is General Kiljoy's efforts to camouflage his pacifistic countenance. It is his war paint, so to speak.

Admittedly, I am recently suicidal, and thus not entirely of sound mind, and I do not claim to be a face-reader. Nevertheless,

I contend that General Kiljoy has calculated to carve his peace symbol into a stick figure of the Great Seal of the United States, a much less distressing symbol for him to display on his brow.

To see what I mean, look on the back of a dollar bill. The right-hand side of the seal displays a bald eagle with a fistful of arrows in one claw and an olive branch in the other. It is appropriately symbolic, with thirteen leaves and thirteen arrows and thirteen stars and thirteen stripes, and most important for General Kiljoy's purposes, it is rousingly patriotic. And yet, upon closer examination, it is just as exhibitionist as the flower children prancing around his forehead in secret, long-haired and topless, singing "Give Peace a Chance." The legs of the eagle, after all, are spread-eagle. Indeed, this is the origin of that phrase. Believe it, the legs of our nation are splayed out in both directions like some tasteless but true sexual provocateur. To be fair, the intimate details are discreetly loinclothed by some sort of shield or coat-of-arms negligee, but this only demonstrates an awareness of the innuendo. In any case, whether it is offensive in its gross carnality or admirable for slipping past the censors of a nation first settled by Puritans, whether it represents prudishness or licentiousness, zealous modesty or fucking fanfaronades, no matter its meaning, it is an appropriate third eye for General Kiljoy.

I say this because it is aggressive in either event, and aggression in any form and for any cause was more attractive to him than peace. So, he continued the struggle to keep his sentiments suitably attired, and was partially successful in his insistent tailoring. He at least prevented them from completely dropping their underpants once again. Though he was standing in front of a sidesplitting sideshow of unconsciousness unleashed, he managed to hold his countenance clad with a bumbling sermon appropriate to the Normandy invasion.

"We," he grunted after a few spontaneous sputters and miscellaneous mutters. His brow twitched as if it had just been snagged with a fishhook. "We are being threatened," he continued. "A sinister force has attacked. Our way of life is at stake. Enemies have conspired to destroy our society." He pointed to the thousands of dancing merries behind him on the screen and smiled like a conceited maggot. "The few must be sacrificed to save the many."

His platitudinous oration aroused nothing but stirring disgust in me. I was about to mouth off and say as much, and remind him that the few actually numbered in the hundreds of thousands (at least I prefer to think that I was), but Miss Mary preempted my retort with a croaky imperative.

"Look!" she practically puked, sounding like she was speaking through a mouthful of beer-soaked cigarette butts. She pointed at the screen with her cancer stick, looking like she just realized she had shown up for school naked.

The smoldering tip of her cigarette directed me toward the screen. Again, it displayed an unnerving scene of absolute stillness. This time, however, it was not to be dismissed as preposterous. The formerly frenzied hominids had fallen suddenly dormant, but a breeze was clearly visible. This was a real-time video feed, and nothing had paused but the people themselves. It was as if the whip was now vibrating so fast that they appeared to be standing still. They stood with their feet anchored to the ground, hands joined, chests heaving in collective hyperventilation. They stood like this a good long while, until everyone had caught their breath. At least four observers underground were equally motionless. The crucial difference, however, is that we didn't know what was next. Christ, we didn't even know what was currently happening. They, on the other hand, most certainly did.

Simultaneously, and I mean absolutely simultaneously, no false starts or dillydallies, but at the *exact* same moment, everyone let go of one another's hands and spun completely around. Once, twice, they stopped at two and a half turns, nine hundred degrees, and faced away from the center. By the time the remote-controlled aircraft had swung around to shift the camera's perspective, the masses had their hands in the air and their mouths open, screaming in ecstatic agony what could only have been the last gasps of ennui, the hysterical funeral cry for a culture whose technology had extended its demise to the point of frothing impatience.

132

Solstices used to puzzle me. Why, I wondered, if the shortest day of the year is on December 22 (give or take a day), why does it continue to get colder even though the days become longer and the sun's rays grow more direct by the day? Conversely, the longest day of the year is around June 22, yet the dog days of summer are in July and August. What accounts for this? Like the penny that I kept forgetting was in my coat pocket all through graduate school, I carried this question around with me for years. I came across it occasionally, but I never got around to putting forth the effort to toss it on the sidewalk or visualize the astrophysics of the solar system. Astronomy was not my specialization, after all, and my academic training had discouraged me from straying outside my discipline. Instead, I posed it to others when it occurred to me during conversations about the weather. Invariably, they were as mystified as myself. Most had never before considered this climatological contradiction.

I was disappointed when I finally received the answer. It was during a cold snap in February, and it came from a clerk at a fast-food restaurant. After being charged $1.01 for a cheeseburger (94 cents plus tax—couldn't they have made it an even dollar, for chrissakes?) and remembering at last that I had a penny in my coat, I was unable to find it and had to break a twenty instead. I was bummed. What purpose did that persistent penny serve if I never succeeded in using it? Such anticlimax was doubly experienced when I commented on the cold and proceeded to complain absentmindedly about the aforementioned contradiction. He had the answer, and it had little to do with astronomy and much to do with meteorology. "Thermal lag," he said. "Air and water currents warm and cool at a pace slower than the phases of the sun. Air and water temperatures determine immediate climate patterns, not the sun's position in the sky. It's like the noonday sun; it's not yet the heat of the day."

Oh.

Today anyway, December 21, the winter solstice, when the angle of the sun is at its southernmost point, when the sun gives the northern half of our planet the cold shoulder, on this particularly beautiful, warm, and sunny darkest day of the year, on this watershed day something supremely more celestial occurred among the animated descendants of stardust assembled around our lifeless city.

They ran for it.

133 "Remember, man, dust you are and to dust you shall return." Father Whippet, no doubt hungover from his own private Fat Tuesday party at the rectory, used to mumble these words to me just before smudging soot on my grade-school forehead on Ash Wednesday. He was only partially correct with his blessing, for he left out the stars. We are *star*dust, not just dust. The entire solar system, from its life to its rocks, ultimately formed from different molecular patterns of stardust. When we die, we bite the stardust.

Blip said it well one sunny vernal equinox just after he focused a prism's rainbow on my forehead. "When you're born, you pass through the prism. Life is a rainbow, an infinite spectrum of radiant souls. But remember, man, light you are and to light you shall return."

134 I once read about a weirdo who maintained a soap bubble for over a year. Looking closely at a bubble, you can see the swirling rainbows flowing downward. Gravity. In the absence of a collision, the soap will drip off the bubble until it can no longer maintain its surface tension, and it will pop. So, in order for this bubblehead to keep his precious sphere of suds alive, he had to keep feeding it soap. How he managed to do this I cannot recall; only the memory of his ineffable waste of time continues to loiter about the corners of my mind.

Point being, society is like a bubble, kept alive by continually feeding it language—hence the strategy behind the Pied Piper virus. Stop feeding the bubble, and it will explode. No conflagration, no destruction, just an inaudible pop, and no trace of its existence remains. But why are we so hung up on feeding the bubble in the first place? Why participate in such a thankless task? Perhaps because it provides a very convincing illusion of meaning, security, purpose, and order, and is therefore an excellent place to hide from reality. Those who labor the most diligently on maintaining and defending the bubble are merely the most gutless among us. Cowardice makes for a good citizen, it seems.

In any case, when the circle around the city broke huddle and people ran in their own radial directions, it was not clear whether the bubble had popped or if it was expanding to encompass all that it had heretofore neglected. Perhaps it was a little of both. The bubble burst, to be sure, yet all available evidence indicated that the Pied Piper virus had somehow backfired. It was like a trick gun that not only blew up in its user's face, but also invigorated its intended victim. What of this order, this coordination, this choreography? This was not mass anomie, pandemonium, and normlessness, but its perfect opposite. The biggest, wildest, most mind-blowing game of Ring around the Rosy ever held had come to an extraordinary finale, and instead of falling down dead the players had exploded outward into God-knows-what.

Ring around the Rosy, as you should know, is another one of our blind habits that has persisted brainlessly for generations, since the days of the Black Death, according to some.

Ring around the rosy,
Pockets full of posy,
Ashes, ashes,
We all fall down.

Reportedly, the nursery rhyme is describing the rings of dried blood those afflicted with the plague got under their skin, herbs hoped to treat it, and the burning corpses of more than half the humans on the Eurasian continent. A playful memoir to the largest catastrophe in Western human history, but now some brash upstart plague had rewritten the words.

Ring around our city,
Laughing off our pity,
Dancing, dancing,
We all get down.

Or something to that effect.

Just two months ago, this city had a little over a million inhabitants. If, as is claimed, a tenth of the residents perished as an indirect result of the outbreak, some nine hundred thousand children of stardust made their mother proud today and went supernova. To attain supernova status is the highest ambition of a star (and is, incidentally, something our good sun will never itself achieve—it's not big enough). In exploding, a star achieves a luminescence up to one hundred million times brighter, and then begins the long process of coalescing into something entirely new. An alternative is to collapse into a miserable black hole, a mass of matter so dense that not even light can escape. How pleased our sun must have been to witness its naughtiest children escape their own vortex of avarice and outshine even her.

135 I was not the only one who recognized that the Pied Piper virus had double-crossed its designers. Whereas I was amazed and amused, however, General Kiljoy was flabbergasted and furious. "What the hell is this?" He kept snapping and growling at no one in particular like a rabid crocodile as he paced hither and thither in a dither, all the while flashing peace, love, freedom, and happiness from his forehead.

"What does it matter?" Miss Mary said with an icky grin as she mashed out a cigarette butt. "They can't leave the city anyway, and soon it will be sterilized."

"What the hell is this?"

"General, she's right." Tynee stood to address him. "The situation is under control." Tynee had to gallop alongside General Kiljoy to match the pace of his strides. He looked like the cartoon Chihuahua trying to keep up with the bulldog. True to the image, General Kiljoy shoved Tynee away from him. He pushed him so hard that Tynee toppled over the back side of the sofa and landed spread-eagle on the cushions, sprawling all over the place like an overdeveloped city.

"Goddamnit!" Tynee roared after he'd regained his balance and stood back up. "Touch me again," he threatened, but was so flustered he could muster no menace with which to complete his warning.

General Kiljoy wasn't listening anyway. "It doesn't work, can't you see? This field test is an absolute failure. The Pied Piper virus is useless. I've spent the last thirteen years of my life directing a project whose grand achievement just blew up in my face." His lower lip trembled. "This was supposed to be the ultimate weapon, my enduring contribution to ensure the security of our way of life." He turned and stumbled to the bathroom, from which he did not emerge for some time.

Good riddance. In his absence, no energy was expended

concerning ourselves over his little occupational crisis. His whiny panic attack had been an irritating distraction from the curiosities on the viewscreen. And anyway, perhaps it was for the best that he did not witness the further adventures of this rowdy band of city folk.

Followed by the spy plane's camera, the dancers bolted away from the city at an all-out sprint, not a lope or a jaunt, but a barreling getaway, a split-beating hasty retreat. What is more, their get-the-hell-out-of-Dodge dash was sustained long enough to trip an Olympian's ticker. They tore along at the edge of control, feet scarcely touching the ground, limbs barely keeping up with the spirit. If you've ever flown down a hill on twenty-foot strides and accelerating, perhaps you can imagine the wings on their heels.

Haste makes waste? This mad rush of human expansion seemed to be heading toward a grisly end, tangled among the rows of razor wire and slaughtered by the heat-sensing automatic firing squad. If this was the case, they didn't seem the least bit concerned. Their rip-roaring race was punctuated by cartwheels and handsprings and other such scampering feats of acrobatic grace. Apparently, the Pied Piper virus gives one hell of a pep talk. Two months of ebbing and flowing dancing manias had licked the lot of them into supernatural shape. They looked like sprites on speed, and their double-espresso eyes, dilated pupils swelling with vim and vigor, shone so radiantly I could almost see myself reflected in them.

This, along with the collective effervescence they were currently experiencing, must account for the boundless energy coursing through them. A few sips from the seltzer of fizzing exultation and suddenly people are off their asses and running together like wolves on the howl. Pied Piper virus or not, partaking of such a sparkling nectar makes for a divine hiccup, a cosmic catharsis of gushing goodwill, a resonant belch of peace. The supreme spiritual quest is really nothing more than the search for a volcanic and barbaric burp to share with our fellows, relieving us at last from the gassy bubble of a sour society, the heartburn of desperate loneliness that so cramps our metaphysical style.

I did not witness such a Brahmanic brap. Such a thing cannot be seen anyway; it can only be experienced. I did, however, hear General Kiljoy blowing his breakfast of aged pork and beans into the toilet through the pipes that ran past the lounge. Since the spy plane provided only a video feed, no audio, the sound of him barfing provided the sound track. He was coughing and gagging, off and on, for over fifteen minutes, and he doubtless would do so for much longer after Tynee ordered me back to my lab and informed him of what came to pass in his absence.

This is what happened. After we watched the running of the humans to the point where their antics were becoming tiresome, they ran across the freeway outerbelt and beyond, completely unencumbered by razor wire or bullets. It occurred without any fanfare on their part, but to us troglodytes, the realization of it was as sudden as a smack in the face from a passing stranger. Momentarily, the viewfinder panned down the outerbelt and the source of this breach was revealed.

There, a mile or so down the freeway (and elsewhere around the city as well, it was determined later), and occurring with very little resistance by the automated military hardware, a posse of renegade eighteen-wheelers was systematically and successfully demolishing the blockade.

The Book o' Billets-doux

rosehips: So what's it like, being somebody else?
sweetlick: Same deal. Learn, grow, love, laugh, cry, work, play, die.

136 Tynee sent me to my room as if he were a puritanical patriarch and there had just been a swearword on TV. I trotted off to my lab without dispute, inspired and eager to record these events in my journal. I wrote furiously for the rest of the day and into the night, not pausing until I had recorded the full history of the day's breakout. Excited and exhausted, I fell asleep at my desk, only to be awakened around three A.M. by a forceful shove.

Roused but not startled, I blinked my eyes at the dark figure before me, a figure who had interrupted my slumber once before, months ago on Halloween morning, on my last day at Valhalla Acres. It was my long-lost bodyguard, Agent Mella Orange, and she was in no kind mood.

She clapped her hand around my mouth, rather dramatically I thought, as if I might cry out or scream. Although that is the cinematic reaction to being awakened by a stranger, all I experienced was an irritated and perplexed speechlessness.

"Shh," she warned as she slowly removed her hand. She

needn't have, for as I've said, I was stunned into silence anyway. "Do you know who I am?" she whispered.

Still speechless, I squinted at her. She was certainly a bit more unkempt, and her eyes were so heavy it looked like she had dreadlocks for eyelashes, but her daunting beauty was unmistakable. I nodded.

"Listen very carefully. The release of the virus was intentional. General Kiljoy orchestrated it. I acted under his orders, but I didn't know what it was that I was doing. He gave me a device a month before we ever came down here. He ordered me to arm it and to activate it on his command. He gave the order on Halloween, apparently just before the four of you went up to Tynee's office. The device created a fifteen-minute deviation from this compound's automation routines. It darkened this entire compound except for a network of passages leading from the observation lounge to the garage exit, and ordered the subjects out. As far as I can tell, the deviation is completely invisible, both in the data records and video recordings. I think that's why Kiljoy eliminated Captain Down. As the administrator of this compound, he was a loose end. He knew too much about how the system worked, and Kiljoy had to be certain his tracks were covered. As for me, I was just supposed to be killed in the sterilization of this compound."

"How did you manage to avoid that?" In my grog, I failed to comprehend the enormity of the conspiratorial information just relayed to me, preoccupied instead with irrelevant tangents.

She clapped her hand over my mouth again, just as I was yawning. "Shut up and listen. I was suspicious, so I crawled up the elevator shaft to investigate. I was on top of the elevator during the sterilization."

I pushed her hand away from me in defiant drowsiness. "Why are you telling me this?"

She slapped her hand over my yap once more. With her other hand she held up a disk. "Your journal, Doctor. I've read it."

Astounded, I forcefully pulled her paw off my chops. "What did you think?" I asked eagerly, blind to any ulterior motives. I had written these memoirs, after all, in a literary desert, and had developed a powerful thirst for feedback.

She shrugged and dumped her pail of water at my sand-burned feet. "A little self-indulgent." She waved the disk in front of me. "The point, Doctor, is that I am in possession of a copy of your little diary. I could very easily make it so the others happen across this if you don't do exactly as I say. Do you understand? This is blackmail."

I was insulted by her review of my masterpiece, so I snapped at her. "If you've read it then you know I've already attempted suicide. Why should I care?"

"I also read what you wrote yesterday. You're not suicidal. You're 'enthralled,' Doctor." She paused, nymphs and imps frolicking about the corners of her mouth. "By the way," she allowed a cagey smirk. "That passage wasn't half bad."

If her half compliment was intended to soften my defenses, it worked. After all, a parched man will chew another's dirty toenails for less than a drop of contaminated water. "How do I know you're telling the truth?"

"About that passage?"

"About anything!"

"You don't." She shrugged. "And keep your voice down."

"Oh. But didn't you dislike following orders from General

Kiljoy without knowing what you were doing? Are we to perpetuate this pattern of abuse? Is this to be some kind of hazing?"

She placed her hand over my mouth yet again, though this time very softly. "Save the diatribes for your opus and listen. I'm not motivating you solely through the threat of punishment, I'm offering you the promise of a reward as well." She put the diskette inside her jacket pocket and pulled out a remote control in its place. "This replicates some of the codes on General Kiljoy's remote." I blinked stupidly, and she continued impatiently. "Do you understand? If you do as I say, this is the key to—what did you call it? 'The escape demanding that you pay him heed.' "

"Escape?" I snorted in dismissal. "Escape to what? The virus is loose, don't *you* understand? It's no longer contained. It'll take over this entire continent before the new year. It's a weapon of mass incapacitation."

Agent Orange flicked the tip of my nose with her middle finger and leaned toward me. "You despise these people around you, and the weapon backfired. You're delighted with this turn of events. You think the virus liberated the human spirit, that it freed those people from what was shackling them all along, and I think you're right. I've read your book, Doctor. What I'm offering you is what you've been pining for." She stepped back and held me in skeptical regard. "But you're all talk, aren't you? You're weak. You're a coward. You'd like to get on the bus, but you hide at the bus stop. You want to join the party, you want to dance, but when your chance comes you duck out. Maybe you'd like to think you want to dance, but given the opportunity you'd rather stay constipated, living off the rotten food in these caves because that's secure. Or you'd kill yourself before trying for a better life."

I cringed at her evaluation of my character and remained silent a long while, defenseless against her coercive compassion. She was right, of course, but I had my own fears of the Pied Piper virus. The original subjects, the death row inmates, went unmistakably insane, and in a hellish bad way. That was also the apparent fate of the one-tenth of the city's population that didn't survive the initial outbreak. Yes, the majority of the city not only survived but blossomed into something better, into boundlessly confident telepaths or some divinely foolish thing. But where would I fit in? I was a bootlicker of bureaucracy, a tool of technological stupidity, and a minion to my own self-importance. I was an ethical flunky. I knew my weaknesses and sins, and I was well-acquainted with my demons. I was afraid that I wouldn't make the Pied Piper's cut. I was afraid I'd end up on the losing team.

Agent Orange knelt down before me, wearing a shrewd smile. Her eyes glowed like a comfortable and confident campfire, crackling with a fierce warmth. She palmed the crown of my bald head to stop me from shaking it to and fro. "Doctor," she whispered, her eyes flaming with intimidating sexuality. "Would you care to dance?"

137

Agent Orange's calculated coquetry was entirely effective at mowing down my resistance. In fact, it was probably overkill, for I didn't have much of a center from which to resist in the first place. In any case, her sly flirtations overrode my typical timid aloofness. It was her style, I think. She made me feel pleasantly combative. She didn't cast sheep eyes, she flashed coyote eyes. She didn't play footsie, she played shove-sie. It was all deliberate and measured, but I didn't care. Let her play the svelte Svengalette and I'll play the pathetic patsy. I enjoyed the attention. She knew I knew she was vamping, but it didn't matter to her either. It was a fair trade, and much more effective than threats or blackmail. It was a comfortable dynamic, and we both knew that it worked.

"Why haven't you left?" I asked, pointing to the remote. "You have the means. What do you need me for?"

"Escape is not my present objective." She pursed her lips in determination. "I followed my orders in good faith, and that bastard Kiljoy sent me in to die and made me into a scapegoat. I'm not expendable in anyone's equation but my own."

"Revenge?"

"I'll turn the other cheek until someone tries to kill me, Doctor. Then all bets are off, and I take karma into my own hands. I have to be sure he gets what's coming to him."

"He's already a wreck. The Pied Piper virus is loose. His weapon failed its field test, which, incidentally, I see no reason to believe he was behind. Why would he test it on Americans?"

"I don't know why you doubt it. That's standard operating procedure in weapons development. We've tested thousands of chemical weapons and mind-control agents on our own soldiers and citizens. We've injected them with radioactive isotopes just to see what would happen. When the Manhattan Project achieved its objective, the planners went ahead and tested the first atomic bomb over the Nevada desert, even though the physicists weren't certain that it wouldn't ignite the planet's atmosphere. Then they field-tested it over the civilian populations of Hiroshima and Nagasaki."

"But there's no vaccine. Why test a biological weapon on domestic soil when there's no cure?"

"Impatience. He's dying."

"And how do you know that?"

"I've seen his medical record. His heart is on its last few pumps. He's had two heart attacks already, and he was scheduled for open-heart surgery in mid-November. I don't think he expected to survive to see the completion of the project."

I looked at her dubiously.

"I'm a spy," she said. "I don't just spy on who they tell me to. I cover my ass. I'm telling you, he orchestrated the release of the virus so he could see a field test of Operation Small Change before he died." She drew close to me. "Think about it, Doctor. He's been directing this project for the last thirteen years. Testing the virus on prisoners was only the beginning of the human trials, and as you've seen, they weren't terribly predictive about its field utility. He's dying, and he needed to know that he did something meaningful. He figured it would work, and he'd get his satisfaction."

"At the cost of thousands of lives?"

"I was expendable," she shrugged. "So were the subjects, including your best friend. It doesn't matter if it's one, two, or thousands. You give the authoritarian mind far too much credit, Doctor."

"What about you?" I challenged her. "Volt was apparently expendable for your purposes."

Agent Orange pointed her finger at me. It was threatening and not at all playful. "Understand one thing, Doctor. Kiljoy murdered Volt. I didn't even know what was happening at the time. After Kiljoy gave me the order to activate the deviation device, I drugged Volt. That's why he had the hiccups when Tynee called to tell him to pick up the four of you at his office, and that's when I started to feel suspicious. I left Volt tied up outside the limousine and went to investigate what the hell was going on. I did not know the compound was going to be sterilized."

I apologized for my implication, and she nodded severely.

"If you wish to escape, leave a pencil on your desk pointed toward the door. I'll contact you. Otherwise, stay the hell out of my way, and I advise against any dumb ideas you may have of thwarting me." She turned and walked toward the door. "You had a good dog, Doctor. Kiljoy slaughtered him, too. What more proof do you need?"

She slipped silently behind the door, exactly as a spy should, and left me profoundly stupefied. I sat motionless, paralyzed by implications and possibilities. I only snapped out of my daze when my gaze happened to focus on my right hand lying listlessly on my lap. I looked at it a good long while before I was flabbergasted by the sudden recognition that I was inexplicably clutching the very disk with which Agent Orange had threatened to blackmail me five minutes ago.

138

Despite my rude awakening and subsequent confrontation with my own cowardice, sleep returned quickly to me and offered me peace in its gentle embrace. I must have dreamed madly the rest of the night. I remember none of it, but I awoke feeling fully refreshed and possessed of a clarity of thought I had not experienced since before I ever noticed its absence. The first thing I did was walk over to my desk and clear its surface of everything but a pencil pointed directly toward the door. I was busting the hell out, come what may. *Que será, será,* as my father used to bellow as he made me Italian toast.

My upbeat and confident mood was at considerable odds with that of everyone else that morning in the observation lounge. I mirrored their grim faces well, I thought. Their faces were so unsmiling that it would not have been hard to convince me that they had never grinned in their entire life. I, on the other hand, quite enjoyed myself, parodying their behavior for no one's amusement but my own.

To be certain, they had more than ample cause to be upset. All contact with the world outside of the cozy dungeon had been lost. According to the trembling General Kiljoy, who seemed to have turned into a feeble old man overnight, this in all likelihood implied that the Pied Piper virus was running rampant across the country and the continent.

"Wasn't there any contingency planning for this?" Tynee asked. "I mean, they had to have realized that escape was at least a remote possibility."

"What about internationally?" Miss Mary added. "Is the rest of the world going to declare North America a no-man's-land?"

"Negative." General Kiljoy shook his head. "They weren't blind to the possibility of escape, but their primary response was offensive. A permanently incapacitating biological agent was released on domestic soil. For all they know, for all *we* know, the virus was released as a terrorist attack against our nation."

"What kind of a counterattack could they possibly launch if they don't even know who the perpetrator is?"

"The only counterattack possible when playing with ultimate weapons."

Tynee paused. "MAD? Mutually assured destruction? Are you kidding me? Did they let other nations know this?"

"Other nations would assume it. The United States of America is not about to just vanish from global geopolitics without a fight. If we go down, the enemy goes with us, whoever the hell and wherever the hell they may be. That's the way the game is played. As far as the Pentagon is concerned, the release of this virus constituted the first shot of World War III. Agents were immediately dispatched to every nation on Earth with copies of the virus to be released in the event of containment failure. Containment failed. It's unmistakable."

"What are you saying?" Miss Mary coughed to cover up a hoarse giggle. The grim-grin phenomenon reared its goofy face. I saw Tynee smirk as well. I let an honest snicker escape my own lips.

General Kiljoy's mouth bounced into an enormous grin, then back to a bulldog frown, and back into a grin again, snapping up and down like a flexible yardstick. "Well," he shrugged limply, choking back a chuckle and swallowing some tears. "It's the end of the world as we know it."

139 There we were, talking about the day's news, the end of the world as we know it, the collapse of civilization, Armageddon or what you will. General Kiljoy hobbled to the bathroom to retch some more as soon as he spoke the words. Tynee couldn't accept it, scratching his head and counting his fingers. Miss Mary pillaged the cabinets, counting her remaining stash of cigarettes. Ratdog yawned and lay down. I poured myself a drink, rum, thick and rich. It was the first thing in the morning, but what the hell, it seemed appropriate to the occasion. I tried to think of a toast to share with me and myself, but all I could think of was Blip's favorite cheerio, "To excellence in human communication."

And how, old friend. Bottoms up.

140

I poured myself another and, wanting to check on the status of my pencil, excused myself to my laboratory. I was immensely pleased to see that she had received the message. This was apparent because she left the pencil balanced on its eraser, pointing straight up. This clandestine communication gave me immeasurable satisfaction. Topic aside, the process gratified some part of me that fashioned secret agent fantasies and then presented them to my consciousness in daydreams. There had certainly been plenty of this sort of activity around me lately, but that was exactly the problem. It was *around* me, poking at me like a cattle prod while I cowered and jumped and rubbed my smarting ass. This time, with this pencil, I knew the code. I understood the subtext. I was in on the secret. The bus was coming, and I knew the driver.

I was sipping my rum in a euphoric haze of self-congratulation when the door was flung open. In marched Tynee, and he wasted no time getting to the point.

"Have you made any progress at all in your assignment?" His demeanor suggested that he thought we were back in his office, and I was his underling.

"Nope." I drained the rest of my glass and paused as the alcohol washed over my brain like the first warm breeze of an ersatz springtime. "It's impossible. It took years to create it, and it would take at least as long to develop a vaccine, and that's with an entire research team."

He ignored me and changed the subject. "General Kiljoy's lost it," he said, pointing to the door. "What are we going to do?"

"We?"

"This could be the end of the world, Fountain! We need to pull together."

"It *is* the end of the world, *Tynee.* And they *have* pulled together."

This gave him brief pause, but he quickly pushed reality out of the way. "I have to see things with my own eyes. I've suggested to General Kiljoy that we take a little field trip upstairs. The limousine is practically indestructible, and it's hermetically sealed. We'd be perfectly safe inside."

"General Kiljoy agreed to this?"

"As much as he was able."

"And Miss Mary?"

He nodded.

"Why are you inviting me to come along?"

"The four of us need to stick together. This situation is," he paused, "unprecedented."

I didn't know what Tynee expected to find upstairs, but I was more than willing to get out of this dungeon. I shrugged. Perhaps this would be my chance to escape.

"Are you ready then?"

"Right now?"

"Do you have something else to do?"

"Well, can you give me a few minutes?" I asked, thinking about my journal. It only existed on disk, and I would need to print out a hard copy.

"For what?"

"I don't know. What's the rush anyway? Just give me a few minutes. I'll meet you in the lounge."

Tynee left without replying, and I assumed it was agreeable. No sooner had he left than Agent Orange landed directly in front of me. I might have been startled if I wasn't intoxicated. As it was, it merely flumbled me.

"I pointed the pencil up for a reason," she said.

I looked up at the ceiling and saw two small eyebolts from which she must have been suspending herself. "Sorry," I answered, chastising myself for missing the secret clue.

"Listen, I have to get to the limousine before the rest of your party. If you're cooperating with me, stall as long as you can. I can't give you the remote control because I'll need it. But you'll still have a chance to escape if you can get Kiljoy's remote once the limo leaves the compound. Just do it as soon as possible, because that limo isn't going to get very far. Press the big red button, remember?"

As soon as I nodded she was gone, out the door without a word or a sound. What a marvelous woman. She moved with a remarkable lack of noise. She could have done a backflip wearing a cowbell and not made a sound. Some people learn to tinker with nucleotides, some people learn to walk quietly, I suppose.

141 The printer tossed out page after page of my manuscript as if they were no different from any academic paper I had tapped out in my years. Perhaps it was correct. I wasn't even sure why I was printing it out in the first place. It would be utterly useless where I was going. After all, who would read it?

What the hell am I doing, anyway? When I began writing this, the situation was not quite so out of hand. It was still possible that someone else would read it someday. Now, I'm writing what would appear to anyone else on the planet as utterly unintelligible hieroglyphics. Nevertheless, I was and still am clinging to my words, like a child clinging to the side of a bridge over a swimming hole, trembling, knowing I'll do it eventually but still afraid to jump and join my friends frolicking below.

If all of your friends jumped off a bridge, would you? What of this pestiferous piece of folk wisdom? It implies that the decision of one's friends was foolish, possibly lethal, as in another version of the same question, *If all your friends jumped off the Empire State Building, would you?* Consider, however, if that actually came to pass. Putting teenage peer pressure aside, as a settled and mature adult, what if every friend you had in the world decided to jump for it? Would you join them?

More to the point, what if every human on the planet except a few cavemen had contracted a virus that destroyed their linguistic abilities and thereby altered their fundamental experience of consciousness? Would you join them? There is absolutely no possibility of potentially making friends with your cellmates or anyone else. You are condemned to spend the rest of your life hanging out with three ogres underground. Do you jump? Do I?

If all your friends jumped off a bridge, would you? This poor question has been browbeaten into thinking she's a rhetorical question, a question never intended to have an answer, in fact, a statement in disguise. It is my intent to put an end to that linguistic legerdemain. The answer may be unsettling, but it is also thrilling and perfectly obvious, at least with the above qualifications. I do my matchmaking as much for their sake as for my own. And so, may they live happily ever after.

If all your friends jumped off a bridge, would you?

If you had any sense at all, of course you would.

142 The others were already waiting impatiently in the golf cart by the time I got to the observation lounge. Tynee occupied the driver's seat this time; I joined General Kiljoy in the back. His eyes were unfocused, and his hands were not in his pockets but in his lap, halfheartedly prodding and jostling his boytoys.

Tynee and Miss Mary chattered about how eager they were to see the outside, if only through the windshield of the limousine. They talked about the weather, and how unusually warm the December had been. This eventually led them into a conversation about how all the people infected with the Pied Piper virus would fare the coming Ohio winter. The depth of Miss Mary's insight was that it had to get cold sometime. Tynee went so far as to remind her that they could still make fire.

"They'll do just fine," General Kiljoy croaked, interrupting their remarkably mundane speculations. "Didn't you idiots see that footage? Things are not at all as they should seem."

Tynee ordered him quiet, and General Kiljoy complied, lapsing back into his catatonic onanism. Tynee and Miss Mary returned to their pointless dialogue, talking for the sake of talking, talking because they could, talking because they were afraid not to. Mostly they talked at each other in mutual monologue, communicating nothing in a comfortable rut of oblivious stagnation.

This state of affairs continued in the limousine. General Kiljoy and I had the entire back of the limo to ourselves. Once we'd seated ourselves in the same seats we had occupied two months prior, General Kiljoy caused the opacity of the polycarbonate windows on either side of us to fade away with his remote control. When he was finished, he let it hang loosely from his hand and looked out his window. He never spoke a word to me.

I watched with some degree of interest as we exited the air locks of the compound, ascending a very long helical ramp until we came out in a parking garage near campus, next to the jail. It felt incredible just knowing I was once again on the surface of the planet, and my thoughts turned immediately to escape. The big red button on General Kiljoy's remote was dangling a foot and a half to my right, daring me, teasing me. Glancing at the doors, I saw that Ratdog was in my way, sitting in front of the doors, blocking my escape path. That little she-devil stared me down, and I could swear she knew what I was thinking. She even growled.

That's what did it. I wasn't going to be intimidated by some inbred, mutant hound from hell. I was a geneticist, for chrissakes. With a swift snatch I grabbed General Kiljoy's remote and pressed the big red button before Ratdog could even stop growling. She immediately barked and ran at me, while simultaneously the doors behind her flew open. Glaring and radiant sunshine dazzled my eyes shut instantly, and I scrambled blindly toward the light like an enraptured mosquito into a flame. I think I must have kicked Ratdog in my dash to the door, but I made it out and was off and stumble-running before anyone could react.

My lope quickly turned into a sprint as my eyes squinted open. I tossed the remote control away, for no other reason than that I certainly did not need it anymore. That mindless act of efficiency saved my life, as General Kiljoy apparently had the ability to cause his remote control to self-destruct. It exploded seconds after I flung it aside. After that, and once I was sure I had lost them, I stopped and collapsed on the wet ground. It wasn't out of exhaustion; I felt like I could run around the planet. I had never had such an adrenaline rush in my life. Rather, I collapsed from an overwhelming emancipation of emotion. The shackles of years of pent-up aggressions and repressions simply vanished with my bold and easy act of escape.

I was free at last, and the energy surging through me was not content to sit on the ground and weep for long. Before my atrophied and gelatinous legs could relax or begin to protest, my spirit yanked them off the ground and raced them through the familiar campus, bounding and leaping in athletic perfection. I ran like prey from a predator. I ran like a schoolchild with a ten-minute recess. I ran like a white rabbit late for a very important date. I ran like a gust of wind to a tornado party. I ran like my dog did the first time I took him to an open field. I ran like a poet through a rainstorm. I ran like a bliss ninny to a happy house.

I ran like nothing so much as a bat out of fucking hell.

143 My heaving exhilaration eventually petered out, and I found myself standing in the middle of the Green, hearing absolutely nothing but the sound of my own panting. As I caught my breath, a seething solitude gradually began to pour into me, flooding a growing pit in my stomach with a dreadful and eternal loneliness. It was so quiet I could hear my tinnitus resounding in my ears, the reverberating shrieks of a bus screeching its brakes in my face long ago. Dense silence screamed at me from all directions. My ears begged to hear something, a car horn, an angry yell, any sort of noise pollution to assure me that I was not alone. Where was the hustle, the bustle, the clamor, the din? Where was the life? A squirrel scampered up a tree. I was grateful. A chilly wind blew past me. I shivered. I cleared my throat. It echoed. Walking along the sidewalk sounded like I was skating across sandpaper.

I was around to hear it, but no tree fell. I was offered instead the barren sound of one hand clapping. I felt compelled to sound my voice, but was inexplicably self-conscious. I uttered a tentative "Hello?" into the atmosphere. Satisfied with the result, I spoke it much louder. Nothing but my own faint echo replied. Finally, I summoned as much breath as I could hold and roared "HELLO!" with all my might into the morning air. My resounding salutation sounded disturbingly more like "Hell!" than "Hello!" and I counted four overlapping waves of my own desolate cries before an angelic shiver bearing a fierce truth trembled throughout my body.

I misspoke myself earlier. I do not know the sound of one hand clapping.

I do know the sound of one voice speaking, and it is horrifying.

144 I like dogs. I do not like cats. When I was a child, my family had a snobby Siamese cat named Ming. Ming detested me. Ming detested all men, except when she went into heat.

Then she would yowl and growl and thrust her posterior at any male of any species in her presence. Her apparently bestial invitations greatly aggravated my father, who always kept a squirt gun on his nightstand to chase her out of the bed. After being thus spurned one Saturday night, Ming crawled into a heating duct in the basement and wailed all night long. Nobody could reach her or get her to come out, so she kept the entire house awake till sunrise, her torturous cries of sexual ardor resounding through all the vents in the house. This infuriated my father, and he vowed again and again that night to "get that moth-eatin', flea-bitten cat!" Come morning, my mother still insisted that he get up and go to Sunday Mass. He acquiesced after an extended argument, but he tossed the cat outside as we were leaving. Ming had been an indoor cat since she was born, and so was overwhelmed by the sudden immensity of her surroundings. She was plastered to the front door in terror as we drove off. We went to Mass, then to brunch, then the obligatory and incredibly dull visit to a friend of the family. When we came home late that afternoon, Ming was exactly as we had left her. She had herself pushed up so close to the door that she might as well have been two-dimensional.

I spent the remainder of my first afternoon of freedom in just such a petrified state. I huddled up against the locked doors of the main library, shivering less from the cool air than from raw fear. I was scared stupid, incapable of rational thought. I was in the middle of a metropolis, and it seemed I was the only one alive. My city, my own daily familiarities, had become a ghost town. Intellectually, of course, I had known this would be the case. I had seen it on the monitor. But here I was in the middle of it, not just watching it through closed-circuit television. There was no retreating. There was the entire world, it appeared, and there was me. There was no one else, no one with whom to talk. I felt like a castaway of Eden, an exile of happiness, adrift in a cold universe and marooned in a deserted civilization. The emotional experience of this awesome abandonment frightened the skin off my skeleton and made me chatter from my teeth to my tibias.

By and by, I shuddered myself into a dreamless sleep. It was a comatose nap, but judging from the sun's relative position it could not have lasted for more than thirty or forty minutes. I awoke with a cotton plantation in full bloom in my mouth, and the beginnings of a headache from the rum I'd had for breakfast. A nauseated hunger was poking me in the ribs. Despite this crusty awakening, I smiled. There was a very young puppy in my arms, and it was licking my face.

145 My new canine companion was a very small pup, no more than a month old, if that. His mishmash markings bore an uncanny similarity to those of Meeko. A note was attached to a solid black bandanna around his neck, along with what looked like the key to my car. This is what the message said:

> Salutations!
>
> Your escape was impressive. "Ratdog" had a litter of three. I helped her to hide them wisely. This is the pick, and it's the only pup that survived. Meeko is the father, I presume. The cowards fled back down below, hiding in hell. I decided to leave them to their miserable doom. Karma can take care of its own business after all.
>
> Hello! I heard you hollering. Have you forgotten? You are not alone. Get up and dance! Head for the hills!

Meeko's pup will keep you company until you are ready to leave the past where it belongs. May we meet again.

Namaste,

Mella Orange

146 *Namaste?* I was mystified by her chosen valediction. I thought it might be an anagram, but I could come up with nothing more meaningful than *tan seam, mean sat, man eats,* or *same ant.* I didn't spend much time on it though. A few days later, I thought to look it up in an encyclopedia of religion and mythology I found lying on Blip and Sophia's living room floor. It turns out that *namaste* is a Nepalese expression, and it roughly translates as "I honor the divinity within you."

What a nice thing to say.

147 I continued to thumb through their encyclopedia of religion, and the entry for Loki caught my eye. Loki is a Norse deity, and his character intrigued me. After reading the entry, I found several more articles concerning his mythological significance in Blip and Sophia's extensive library. Here's my ten-cent report.

In Norse mythology, Loki is the god of mischief, the swift-witted trickster, the merry prankster. Brazen, irreverent, and heterodox, he is the recalcitrant force of change in humanity, the troublemaking and monkey-wrenching antidote to stagnation. Loki revels in every child suppressing giggles in class or in church, and flickers as the spark of naughtiness in everyone's eye. He beguiles every quietly desperate soul and gnaws at our sanity as the suppressed scofflaw of bureaucratic authority.

Religion represents a comfortable though counterfeit ordering of chaos. Therefore, most deities are answers. But Loki is a mockery of all answers, a braying heretic. He raises hell, so to speak. He encourages the sacred subversion of the social order, for this demonstrates its plasticity and guarantees eternal innovation. In this way, he is humanity's greatest benefactor, granting us a universe of perpetually vivid novelty.

Hilarious, cruel, goofy, immoral, disgusting, and charming. At his discretion, Loki may tickle us tenderly or fling the wickedest of insults, but he promises to leave a greater approximation of Truth in his wake. He may ignite forest fires with the lightning bolts of his impish delight, but the forest survives and grows back stronger than ever. Suppressing periodic forest fires only creates a denser tinderbox, such that when the fire does eventually erupt, it is total in its devastation. Similarly, suppressing social change creates social discontent. Suppressing social discontent creates the conditions for revolution.

Similar to Prometheus of the Greek pantheon, Loki gave humanity fire and culture, and was consequently imprisoned by the rest of the Norse deities, tied underground with his son's bowels while a serpent dripped venom on his face. But Loki's fires are inextinguishable; the drive toward social change that he represents is what makes us human, what sets us apart from our animal brethren. Over the past few centuries, our species has warmed to the boiling point, to a turning point in our existence, and yet we permitted our reactionary fears to direct our actions. Instead of allowing our water to boil and ourselves to evaporate, to evolve, into an entirely new state, we continued to listen to the curmudgeons of the old pantheon, hoisting a brick atop our own lid. This was unwise. Loki's inevitable destiny thus became the catalyst of apocalyptic convulsions.

Loki topped his own greatest stunt of all time with his Pied Piper job. First he gave us communication, now it appears he has given us perfect communication, tuned us in and eliminated the static. He overthrew the old guard with their own mal-intentions. He pulled off a numinous coup d'état. He had the last laugh.

I named Meeko's son Loki that day, a few days after I found him in my arms. It seemed appropriate.

The Book o' Billets-doux

rosehips: Goddamnit.

sweetlick: Excuse me?

rosehips: Goddamnit.

sweetlick: Why do you say such things?

rosehips: Why not? It's a satisfying cuss. God is in me as much as anything else, and sometimes God stubs her toe. In saying "Goddamnit," I'm merely disapproving of the location of that book you left lying on the living room floor last night.

sweetlick: Isn't there a commandment somewhere that says, "Thou shalt not take the name of the Lord thy God in vain?"[9]

rosehips: Yes, but there are no forbidden words. I know you're a little funnier in the head than I am, but what do you think that commandment means? The name of the Judeo-Christian Ultimate Source is *Yahweh.* It is a form of the Hebrew verb *to be*. God is, and thou shalt not take the Is-ness in vain.

sweetlick: The Is-ness? Is you is or is you ain't my baby?

rosehips: I is, oh flamma-lamma-ding-damn. But listen, the commandment is reverence. Do not take being in vain. Do not profane existence.

sweetlick: Goddamn right.

148 Loki was a fine pup. Playful, energetic, and eager to please, he was already almost as big as Ratdog. This is not to say that he weighed anything. I've held bags of popcorn that were heavier. Nevertheless, every tendon in my legs groaned out my throat as I got up from huddling against the door of the main library. I had done an excellent job of shredding my muscle fibers in my goofy gallop around campus. Loki licked my face encouragingly. "Okay, okay, boy," I said.

I was hungry. I seem to remember resolving that my body could use a fast, as I had become chronically constipated from our survival fare's almost complete lack of dietary fiber. Whenever I could muster a movement, pardon me, it was like shitting shards of shrapnel. Sophia, beamingly proud of her colon, was forever lecturing me on the importance of periodically denying yourself food. According to her, fasting provides a physical and spiritual cleanse, and gives you a visceral experience of your own connection to the Earth and the cycle of life. She's probably correct. She's even shown me research that demonstrates the greater longevity of animals fed low-calorie diets relative to animals fed high-calorie diets. That may be so, but I've always been an American, and I like to keep my belly full. I was famished, and any notions of a healthy asceticism now struck me as ludicrous. I wanted some food. Besides, I had a puppy to feed.

Where to get food in the middle of a deserted city? Most supermarkets have no more than a six-day supply of food on hand, and I was certain they had already been emptied by the quarantined population. Although emergency food had been air-dropped around the city, my chances of locating any of this fare seemed equally unlikely, at least in the short term. I thought about catching a squirrel, but the fastest human alive would starve before they'd succeed in that small task. No, as a human, my survival depended on others, or the food others had left behind. My best bet, I decided, was Blip and Sophia's 50 percent self-sufficient dome on the outskirts of town. They had a solar-powered refrigerator and a pantry outfitted for survivalist health nuts. I figured I would either encounter them and have to be okay with the consequences, or raid their well-stocked pantry and refrigerator like an insolent raccoon. With any luck, I could live well for a couple of seasons.

So I headed for my car. As I approached it, I saw what appeared to be a weathered parking ticket stuck under the windshield wiper. This, of course, was ridiculous. I was not parked illegally, and such laws were now meaningless anyway. As it turned out, it was indeed a parking ticket, though it was written for Blip's car, not mine. Along with a gigantic smiley face, Blip had scrawled a note on the back. It was short and simple.

"The dervish spoke the truth."

149 After a few moments of deliberation with the seat belt buckle in my hand, I decided not to put it on. I would be the only car on the road, after all, and I was no longer intoxicated, although the overflow of adrenaline was still giving me the shakes. I was confident I could avoid hitting any stationary objects, even though I was about to do every forbidden thing I had always wanted to do with an automobile. I pulled out of my parking space, revved the engine, and laid rubber on my way out of the parking lot. I careened wildly around corners, tires squealing, the whole deal. It was much easier than running, and satisfied nicely the demands of the leftover epinephrine still tickling my nervous system. Despite being tossed about by the forces of inertia, Loki enjoyed himself as well and yipped along with my yowls and yee-haws.

I headed for the freeway, with every intention of finding out if my car could actually move at 125 miles per hour, as the speedometer claimed. On my way, however, racing down a straightaway, I suddenly caught sight of a lone pedestrian on the side of the road. He didn't even look toward me as I roared by. He was gazing instead at a stop sign, as if perhaps he was waiting for it to turn green.

His unexpected presence unnerved me, and after I was a good way past him, I slowed to the speed limit, locked my doors, pulled my seat belt on, and thanked the American dream that I had been driving with my windows closed and the heater on. I hadn't really anticipated encountering anyone. This complicated matters. I did not feel at all prepared to meet my fate. This was my luxury. I knew the larger circumstances, but with a little ingenuity I felt I could delay the inevitable until I decided it was the proper time.

When is the proper time? According to Blip's comrade-in-spray-paint, NOW! is the proper time. As I approached Graffiti Bridge, however, I realized that NOW! had already happened, NOW! was old news. The message, which had broadcast NOW!

the last I was aware, had been changed, presumably by Blip. He hadn't changed much, simply and neatly shifting the meaning by adding a single letter K.

It would be the final proclamation of Graffiti Bridge.

KNOW!

150 And so I took up domicile at Blip and Sophia's dome, where, as I said, I found the encyclopedia of religion lying on the floor. Clearly, they were no longer in residence. I considered myself a house sitter. I kept the place neat, and paid myself in food—mostly beans, rice, nuts, sprouts, potatoes, and vitamins. It was an excellent place to take shelter for the region's mild winter. I've lost weight and become much more regular. Thanks to their paranoid self-sufficiency, I even have a limited amount of electricity. Between their solar panels, windmill, and a backup propane-powered generator, I have a stove, refrigerator, and a computer, although I can't reasonably use more than one of them at the same time. I have a television and radio as well, but there is never anything on. It's just as well. I spend most of my time reading their books and editing, writing, and rewriting my manuscript. It's coming along.

Other than Loki, I haven't seen another soul since I arrived here months ago. I have, however, heard one. Blip and Sophia told me their dome was haunted, and by my reckoning, I'd have to agree. Every few nights I jolt awake to what sounds like a Sunday paper being thrown across the room. Sophia dubbed it "the paper poltergeist." While I have no training in parapsychology, I have exhaustively investigated the phenomenon and have been unable to discover a physical cause, or even propose an alternative hypothesis. Other than repeatedly startling the living nightlights out of me, the paper poltergeist seems harmless enough. Hence, the most I can do is echo Blip's glib reasoning on the matter whenever the paper goes bump in the night.

"What you do not fear cannot hurt you."

151 Alone. Sometime around the beginning of February, it dawned on me that there was no reason to get dressed. Although it was crisp outside, domes are known for their excellent resistance to drafts. I was quite comfortable inside, and Loki didn't seem to give one lick of a vegan milk bone whether I clothed myself or not.

Shortly after I decided to go naked (or half naked, anyway, as I could not resist wearing at least a towel or a robe most of the time), I came across a curious book in Blip and Sophia's bookcase. It was bound in rainbow tie-dyed fabric, and it was handwritten in deliberate, perfect penmanship. The title was written on the first page, *The Book o' Billets-doux.*

Its hundred pages were filled with dialogues between two characters named Rosehips and Sweetlick, ostensible aliases for Sophia and Blip. I picked my favorite passages and inserted them into this manuscript, both for posterity's sake and for a reason that is about to become clear. Here follows the final passage from *The Book o' Billets-doux.*

The Book o' Billets-doux

sweetlick: It is finished.

rosehips: Eh?

sweetlick: It's over. The quest. We have found the promised Word, the Word whose existence was whispered to us by the whirling dervish all those years ago.

rosehips: You've found the grail?

sweetlick: We've found the grail.

rosehips: Well what is it?

sweetlick: You'll see.

rosehips: Please tell me.

sweetlick: I tell thee you'll see.

rosehips: Pretty please tell me.

sweetlick: Listen very carefully, for I cannot talk for long. You will see.

rosehips: What am I to make of this teasing?

sweetlick: Oh my suckle-doodle-doobie! I cannot tell thee. Language is what hides it. Language limits us to approximations. How can I communicate the ineffable except by trusting that you know what I mean? Don't you see? The fall of humanity was the fall from the actual to the symbolic. Language abstracts us from the real world, keeping us from direct, intuitive perception. Words, like the ego, are merely guides. Don't mistake them for the real thing. Pull aside the filthy curtains of the social. Language makes an enigma of simple existence, it obscures the true nature of reality, and of your Self.

rosehips: Oh dear. What am I to do?

sweetlick: Just be your Self. Don't put your ego where it doesn't belong. Your ego is just a tool to assist you in life. Don't mistake it for who you are. The ego is a distracting backseat driver who thinks it knows everything. Keep it in its proper place. Tape its mouth shut, so you can better enjoy the ride instead of trying to control it.

rosehips: Leggo your ego?

sweetlick: Hoo-wee absolutely! Judgment day is simply whether or not you can let go. The less self-absorbed you are, the easier it is to let go.

rosehips: I feel funny.

sweetlick: It's going to get funnier than you can possibly imagine.

rosehips: But what is it that's so funny?

sweetlick: The stupidity of your social self. You will laugh, as everyone, at the foolishness of your self-presentations, and at the idiocy and inadequacy of language.

rosehips:	Very well. But first I must tell you something. Remember Graffiti Bridge?
sweetlick:	Certainly.
rosehips:	I know that you started it.
sweetlick:	You're quite the detective. Guilty as charged.
rosehips:	There's something else.
sweetlick:	Pray tell me.
rosehips:	I couldn't let you have all the fun.
sweetlick:	Come again?
rosehips:	I am the other vandal.
sweetlick:	You are joking.
rosehips:	I am laughing, but I am not joking.
sweetlick:	How perfectly marvelous! But my my my, who are you and who am I? Who are we to have performed such courageous exploits?
rosehips:	We're nobody in particular. We're just a couple of days.
sweetlick:	You said it, baby-waby! Just a couple of days, you and I.
rosehips:	Saturday and Sunday.

152 A single strand of DNA is two-billionths of a meter thin. This is approximately one forty-four-thousandth the diameter of a medium-sized human hair. So, is life nothing more than a skinny molecule containing all the information most organisms require for their pointless survival and reproduction?

Not at all. DNA is only the beginning of life, at least as far as we can see. DNA is life's furious librarian, forever organizing and reorganizing information in the form of genetic traits necessary for a given organism to adapt to and thus survive in its environment. Among mammals, however, something else emerged, a novel manner of adapting to the environment. Learned behavior, information acquired during the lifetime of an organism, is what mammals, especially humans, depend upon for survival. It is an *extragenetic* source of information. Thus, while species may adapt to environmental conditions over the course of eons at the genetic level, humans can adapt much more efficiently within one lifetime, at the cultural level, in the information we share between one another.

At the strictly genetic level of information, humanity is laughably ill-equipped to deal with its environment: Our claws are thin, our senses are dull, our teeth aren't terribly dangerous, we're not very strong, we're not very fast, and we hardly have any hair. And yet we survive and thrive due to our immense capacity for learning and communicating information. DNA is much too crude a mechanism for the transmission of this information. It was enough for it to provide the materials and workmanship for the neocortex, the outermost layer of our brains, to emerge. Here, the organism stores and transmits extragenetic information. To put our place in nature in the proper perspective: Reptiles have no neocortex to speak of in their tiny heads, while the neocortex accounts for 85 percent of the human brain.

Obviously, the neocortex confers a tremendous evolutionary advantage. It makes the organism, as well as the species, more resilient, able to learn and share new survival information fairly quickly, rather than wait centuries or millennia for the genes of great-grand-progeny to adapt. But despite the immense potential granted by the almost complete dominance of the neocortex over the genes, we have continued to allow ourselves to be driven by our selfish genes for most of human history. Perhaps we've behaved like such brilliant barbarians because we have been deficient in some vital aspect of ourselves. Let us take a closer look.

Is there not something unique about humans that sets them a class apart from all other species? An animal that can teleport its physical form does not exist, but if it did, it would be unique in a more particular way than the mere fact of it being a separate species. That is, no other animal would possess the ability of teleportation. In the same way, humans can develop an elaborate cultural universe of their own, live within it, abide by it, and die for it, all without recognizing that it is ultimately only an estimation of the world. This degree of sociability is a trait not shared with any other species. Not even remotely.

So, to be social is to be directed toward others, to ultimately function as a larger group organism. This trait emerged, like everything, because it enabled survival. Its presence, however, introduced a contradiction in our genetic program. Like any other organism, we are selfish at our genetic core, and yet these same genes gave rise to a capacity to transcend themselves and evolve into the realm of the purely social. My own predicament notwithstanding, we simply cannot survive as lone humans.

The primary self-interest is validation from others, assurance that we are not alone. Our sociability is not optional, and we only survive at all because of each other. Yet our cooperation, in this era anyway, has been decidedly selfish. This has gotten us into our climactic fix, increasingly threatening our individual and collective survival. None can survive if everyone tries to be the fittest individual, but all can benefit if together we try to build the fittest society. Thus is our evolutionary conflict. Which is ultimately more adaptive to survival: selfishness or sociability? To act social is to trust that each will act in one another's mutual interest. Obviously, such a thing cannot be achieved alone. To minimize our individual pain, we must come together. Anything less is no longer adaptive for individual or species survival, let alone happiness. And this requires a leap of nothing so simple as faith.

And faith? What is this nonsense? To whom are you being faithful in a leap of faith? If you wish to vault the chasm of eternal emptiness, you can only trust in yourself to carry you across in safety. It would be arrogant and foolish of you to race toward such an abyss without a studied concentration of effort, a perfect understanding of the steps necessary to accomplish such a feat. Faith is not blind optimism, it is honest determination. And yet faith is not the proof required by reason. Faith is the genuine trust of intuition.

Think of it this way: The classic way to throw a billiard partner off his game is to ask him what he does with his right arm when he shoots his cue. Preoccupied with pointless analysis, he is thrown off balance, and the cue stick feels awkward in his hand. Similarly, athletes achieve their greatest potential when they cease thinking about what they are doing, when their actions become so perfect that their movements flow through them rather than from them. In the same way, making the leap to trust requires opening your door, shedding your pretensions, your self-consciousness, and presenting your soul unabashed to the world. This is a leap of faith. Faith is not belief in God. Faith is the awareness that you *are* God. *Namaste.*

The problem, oh Invisible Risibility, is that we are not human enough. We are the only species that can laugh, yet far too much of our modern lives were spent actively not laughing—griping, complaining, stressing, arguing, despairing. We spent our time in the false comforts of primitive consciousness and all the jealousy, anger, and hate it implied. Though we remained boastfully ignorant, we are in truth far more intelligent than we led ourselves to believe. We are humans, the clever monkeys, and we possess the tremendous potential to shape not only our selves, but our entire world. Why settle with the hand-me-downs of the past when we can do so much better?

I am nothing but what you think I am. You are nothing but what I think you are. Thus are we linked, for better or for worse. We are nothing but each other. Before the Pied Piper came prancing along, it did not require paranormal abilities to predict the future of our species. A horrifying apocalypse was not our destiny. It would have become apparent that the planet did not fear our vanity, and the universe did not care one speck of stardust whether we lived or died. We would have learned that our future, and the lives we lead, were wholly up to us. We would have recognized our potential and directed our own destiny, or we would have perished.

The future, as our best prophets have always said, is love (or that which the overuse of the word fails to express). This is a certainty. Regardless of everything, our species will eventually go where it must. There is no other conceivable future for the simple reason that if we do not learn to love, we will surely die away, individual agonies in a collective nightmare. That could be the climax of the human story, and that is why the future is so certain. There is no future in death and destruction. If we cease to exist, then the future ceases to exist as far as we are concerned, and all speculation necessarily becomes moot.

Things are not as complicated as we think. Which would you rather do, hoot and howl or harrumph and growl? Which would you rather do, twist and shout or maim and kill? The choice is as clear and easy as that. Everything else is just static. Tune your Self in.

Humanity is a wild species, daring and reckless, playing the highest stakes, risking extinction. We are the nuts dangling from the tips of the petioles in danger of falling off the Tree of Life altogether. But not to worry in any case. Perhaps a tumble is necessary for us to leave the bad habits of the past behind.

After all, it may be only after we fall that we can flower.

153

This chapter is purely academic. I include it only because I sense a logical incongruity in my own reasoning. Feel free to skip it and get back to the action, but if you're up for it, try to follow me on this.

Evolution is dependent upon error; mutations drive evolutionary change. If, as I have argued, culture represents the next layer of evolution, then miscommunication is the equivalent of mutation. In other words, miscommunication drives evolutionary change at the cultural level. If this is correct, then it is precisely our *mis*communicative powers that have allowed our species to adapt so efficiently and so quickly to our environment. Consequently, if the Pied Piper virus perfects human communication, as it indeed appears to, then it seems to follow that the human species has in fact lost its greatest evolutionary advantage. What is worse, and despite all the happy dancing, we are apparently left to rot in paralytic stasis and stagnation.

This is a delightful contradiction. How can I, a molecular biologist, cheer for the end of evolution? My answer, which satisfies me completely, is simply that evolution has not, in fact, ceased. Rather, evolution has merely reached a new level. In the same way that the evolutionary shift from the genetic to the cultural carried with it a tremendous leap in the rate of change, the shift from the cultural to the God-knows-what must carry with it a similarly exponential leap, a million-trillion titters and teehees coalescing into one gigantic guffaw. I am talking about a transcendental quickening, an eschatological escape into a higher state of being where we evolve all but instantaneously. Beyond language, there are no cultural habits of thinking to slow us down. We evolve in immediate response to all new stimuli, asymptotically attaining a fractal Truth where we see that all is one and we can do no greater good than to observe the universe and ourselves at play.

But it is not quite so simple as this. Coming from such a prudish culture, I have overlooked one crucial component of evolution: sex. Miscommunication may be equivalent to mutation, but communication is equivalent to sexual reproduction. Sexual reproduction mixes new patterns of genetic traits together, increasing the likelihood of a species remaining well adapted to its environment. In the same way, communication mixes new concepts and ideas together.

Sadly, however, most communication is akin to bad sex. Do you know what sex feels like? Admittedly, I myself have but a vague recollection, but I nevertheless remind you that sex, good sex, is, as they say, orgasmic. That is what evolution feels like. Do you know what communication feels like? Nothing like sex, I don't have to assure you. Impotent and dry, flaccid and frigid, brief and unsatisfying, our linguistic intercourse leaves much to be desired. But then along pranced the Pied Piper, mooning and shining and flashing the world, and communication suddenly became perfect. Empathic communion, then, must feel heavenly.

Hmm. It occurs to me that if my analogy is correct, then we are having sex right now. How awkward. I apologize if our encounter has been less than fantastic. It is a limitation of language. Talk to me on the far side of the Pied Piper virus and I'll show you a good time. But perhaps I stretch this allegory too far. Or perhaps I've been celibate for far too long. *Caveat lector.*

I'm bored. I wonder what everyone else is doing. The Pied Piper virus has surely touched all but a few handfuls of humans on this planet by now, and in time it will tickle every last one of us. I wonder how the experience of life has changed. Do they just dance forever in postapocalyptic merriment, eternally marveling at the miraculous devastation of it all? Not likely, but this is a question that I cannot answer. I can no more answer it than I can answer what happens after death. I can say that I have witnessed no mourning over the culture and civilization that has been lost. Quite the contrary, I have seen nothing but unconditional and unrestrained joy at what has been gained. Like death, it is only those who are still alive who would mourn. For the dead, this world surely fades as quickly as a dream.

Think about this: Etymologically, apocalypse comes from the Greek word *apokalyptein,* meaning "to uncover." If this outbreak is really it, then what has such a merry-hearted apocalypse uncovered? Listen up. Hell comes from the Old English word *helan,* meaning "to cover." Do you understand what I'm saying? The Pied Piper virus is it! It has blown the lid off hell, freed us from prison, demolished the delusion of separateness, and put our species where we properly belong. Humans are back, and our destiny holds nothing you or I can possibly imagine, not in our wildest, most far-out reveries, for our destiny lies further than the imagination itself.

Well, this is all chuckles and cheers, but what of our drama, our excitement, our intrigue, mystery, and espionage? What of it? Are our lies really worthy of such lamentation? Must we romanticize deception and glorify war? We've had a few cliff-hangers, sure, and maybe they're fun, but life is too often lack-luster and lonely. To pule, pine, whimper, and whine over the loss of a perverse fascination with our own pitfalls is the worst kind of self-obsessed navel-gazing.

Of course, what else can I do? There is no sense in grieving over my lack of hyperawareness and empathy. I am what I am, with nothing better to do but what I do. If I'm in prison, why should I grieve over the open fields I believe to exist just past the concrete wall topped with razor wire? I should revel in the glory of the sunshine I have, perhaps marvel at the nest an enterprising and daring cardinal built suspended in the barbs. And yet, simply because I can enjoy watching an anthill in the prison yard doesn't imply that I wouldn't enjoy traipsing naked through rolling hills of wildflowers more. But remember, in prison, I only imagine these wildflowers to exist—sort of a nostalgic premonition. Who knows what experiences actually lie on the other side? How can I hope to compare them to what I know on this side? On the one hand, there may exist a whole new level of experience just beyond that wall, with pleasures and aesthetics that humanity's greatest artistic, linguistic, and musical manipulations only hinted at, mere signposts along the path to the garden of the gods and goddesses. On the other hand, there may be some mean bumblebees among those wildflowers, and I may be wishing I was back in prison, predictable and safe, playing with ants in the dust.

154 In the olden days, back when language was all the rage, when people mistook words for the world, people used to argue whether life was the result of creation or evolution. It was an utterly meaningless debate, arrogant individuals (myself included) bickering over the semantics of their comfortable metaphors instead of pushing them further. I suppose my grandfather belonged to the creationist camp. As he explained to me when I was a child sitting on his knee one afternoon, evolution is wrong for the apparently self-evident reason that there are still apes. "Hey," he said. "If man evolved from apes, then why are there still apes?"

Despite his supreme confidence in making this assertion, I was unconvinced that his logic was ironclad. Perhaps that's why I became a geneticist, to find some answers that would satisfy me. I studied and I studied, and pounded my simian chest with the standard arguments of evolutionary theory. Because I could describe it, I believed I knew what life was.

In the end, however, it was Dandelion, barely five years old at the time, who proved my explanations incomplete. It could have been any child, mocking me with the automatic gamesaying of "Why?" to every answer I put forth. No matter how deeply I delved, this question was left unanswered.

"Why evolve?"

"Because of an accident of matter."

"Why matter?"

"Because of the nature of energy."

"Why energy?"

"Umm . . ."

"Not umm," Blip corrected me, stroking his daughter's hair. "*Aum,* as in *aum mani padme hum.* Buddhist monks meditate on that phrase. It means 'the jewel in the heart of the lotus,' which basically means 'God is within,' or something like that."

"You should listen to Dandelion." Sophia counseled me. "A mystic named Jesus once remarked, 'Lest you become as little children, you shall not enter the kingdom of heaven.'"[10]

"Take the Holy Middle Path," Blip advised.

"Evolution is the process of Creation," Sophia quipped, as smart as a smack in the face from a Zen master. "Create. Evolve. Crevolve."

155 If a man hollers "Hello!" in a city and no one's around to hear it, does it make a sound? Most certainly, but it is the soundscape of nightmarish loneliness. Loneliness is emptiness. It is the space between the stars. It is nothing. Creation is God's defense against loneliness.

And who is God? According to Sister Lolita, my first-grade teacher with the purportedly smelly underwear, God is an old, old man who was never born and who will never ever die. As a six-year-old, I took her word for it. I accepted her description with innocent faith, though I was utterly mystified by it. I could swallow that he would never die, but *never be born*? Come on!

This paradox consumed my young imagination for some time, but I eventually resolved it. My juvenile explanation does not make a lot of sense to me now, and indeed, my recollection of it is so vague I can't even be certain that I'm not making it up. Nevertheless, what I came up with is this: God is some old man who walked over the hill one day. That's it. That's how I comprehended eternity. God walked over the hill one day.

And now as I ponder this koan of my childhood, it occurs to me that I may merely have been making a random association. God, as far as anyone had yet explained to me, was an old man. And to be "over the hill" is a colloquialism for old age. Definitionally, then, God is over the hill.

In any event, I was reminded of my youthful reasoning this morning while taking Loki for a walk. We had just crested the peak of the hill upon which Blip and Sophia's dome was built, and Loki ran a bit down the other side to pee on a tree, as is his custom. I followed him over the hill, but stopped short when I saw what looked to be a child, far below. She waved up at me and sang out a series of beautiful and meaningless sounds.

I waved back. God may be some fool who walked over a hill one day, but she's also some child who scampered through a ravine one day.

156 Waving is an instinctual gesture, a innate form of communication intended to display friendliness as surely as a smile. It must be. Otherwise the child, presumably prancing on the heels of the Pied Piper, would have been unable to manage it as a learned symbol. Whatever the case, I continued waving like a perfect doofus long after she skipped out of sight. The vision of another had bedazzled me into a silly and peaceful contemplation, a wonderful state of clarity and idiocy, grace and befuddlement. I whistled for Loki to follow me, immensely pleased to contribute to my surroundings with such a bucolic gesture.

A lone dandelion enhanced my cheerful amble toward the dome. It was small but brilliantly yellow, almost orange, like the yolk of a cosmic Easter egg. An impudent early bloomer, bold and beautiful, it was the first flower I had seen in over six months. A breeze whiffed past me, licking my face. A warm front. Spring was casting its worldspell, perfuming the air with a subtle sexuality and flooding me with an unspeakable *joie de vivre.* Entranced, I stood absolutely still, a racing velocity of perception surrounding me like a flurry of faeries.

I was admiring the dandelion as if it were the entire universe when a honeybee bumbled along and settled upon it. After collecting its pollen with all due busyness, it buzzed itself aloft and danced among the brush, searching for a flower, a flash of color, a perfumed scent. It came to me, to my hands, the hands I had recently washed with Blip and Sophia's homemade dandelion soap, and it landed on my thumb. Undaunted, I lifted my hand to peer at it. The honeybee froze, peering back at me for a long moment, and then, with a very precise insertion of its stinger, it let me know that I was unmistakably alive.

157 Spring has arrived, and every day there is a greater funk of sex in the air. Yesterday I saw a pack of six humans racing each other down the hill. They were entirely naked but for the fantastically colored rainbow cloaks fastened around their necks, fluttering like a gang of butterflies in their wake. I myself was almost naked (I had a towel around my waist), and washing dishes in the kitchen at the time, but when I saw that vision, I got dressed and locked the house up tight. I can make no excuse for my actions. I am pathetic. I'd like to race naked down a hillside with my brothers and sisters, but instead I hide inside and monkey around with my little collection of words. I am alone, and I write because it gives me the illusion of social contact. But this time is swiftly passing, and the end of my story waits only for me. I am a social creature. Tomorrow I resolve to join the rest of my species in our destiny. Better to go crazy with others than by myself. Better to die together than to live alone.

But first, these past months in my hermitage I've figured out a few things concerning matters metaphysical. As I began to explain earlier, loneliness is nothingness. And as already mentioned, the Hebrew word for God, *Yahweh,* is simply a form of that most fundamental verb, *to be.* God is what is, understand, but God cannot be without being perceived. God is all that is, and yet God is nothing unless God can look upon God. God is one, but God is not lonely. Loneliness is a contradiction of Creation. Creation must be, but God did not create the universe. God is the universe. God is not the Creator. God is Creation. There is no difference. There was never anything but Creation, and there will never be anything but Creation. Creation requires nothing but itself for its own existence.

If you ever find yourself lonely, you are only undermining your Self. You are God, for chrissakes! Is the Truth really so tremendous? Look around and see what else you've created! Do you think you were born for nothing? Dreadfully sorry, but that just ain't so. You asked for it and you got it. You have a will. Have you forgotten what you wanted to do with it? Or worse, have you surrendered it and become a tool of some other blind facet of your Self?

Humans take about twenty-two thousand breaths a day. Take just one deep breath and experience it. Live your life, for the Spirit that resides within you is only on vacation. Your soul is but a lungful of air, giving individual life while it resides within you but dissipating when it is ultimately released back into the infinite sea of the divine atmosphere. Trying to hold on to your breath will get you nowhere, and it will make you purple and ugly in the process. Enjoy your Self while you still can.

Do you really think there is no purpose to existence? You magnificent mop. You profound poop. You who make a brooding puzzle out of the simple experience of life, you make yourself worthy of severe ridicule with such sentiments. Unclench your ass. Don't be so freaking constipated. You deserve a smack upside your goofy, beautiful head. Do I have to spell it out for you? Very well. Hear ye, hear ye! *You* are the purpose of existence, as surely as I am, and as surely as are the birds and the bees and the flowers and the trees. Chirping, chattering, whistling, buzzing, and rustling. Moaning, groaning, writhing, wriggling, clawing, sucking, and fucking. The secrets of ceaseless peace and uncontainable joy are being whispered all around you. A squawking crow, a hissing cat, a howling wolf. A dripping faucet, a slamming door, a clanking pot. A falling tree, a clapping hand, a stomp, a slap, a kick, a kiss. A gently shifting shadow, a swiftly shooting star. Bees are bumbling, stomachs are grumbling, humans are mumbling, fumbling, and crumbling. Smell it. Taste it. Hear it. See it. Touch it. Love it.

You who are reading these words, this story is for you. Fear not the Piper. Fear not your Self. Paradise is yours to regain.

Ride the gales of divine laughter, the maelstroms of sacred mirth. It is your right, it is your purpose, and it is so easy. It is child's play. It is one small step for a human, one giant glide for humankind.

Godspeed.

158 Good morning, people! I don't know what's happening, but scores of the most majestic, noble creatures I have ever seen are ambling, skipping, and gallivanting down the hill outside, apparently on their way into town. I have spent almost four months completely alone, and I can assure you with a certain measure of hermitic authority that *nothing* between sunshine and clear water is more wonderfully necessary than other people. We are not born to be alone, nor are we born to act like we are alone, which is really what selfishness is all about. We are each of us fish, and we are water to one another. Without each other, we struggle, we flounder, we suffocate. But together, living for our sisters and our brothers, what is there to want? As one, what is there to fear? Yes, yes indeed. This is my day of reckoning. This is my prelude to spontaneity, my so long to solemnity. Woop woop woop!

Ahem. Yes then. Dearly beloved, we are gathered here today to witness the realization of human potential. Behold our marriage of madness and mirth, our matrimony of lunacy and piety. Mark the moment, for today we walk down the aisle of laughter and love, we run the gauntlet of tickles and wisdom. These are the nuptials of the nonesuch of nonsense, when nothing short of everything has changed.

Who did we think we were anyway? We who whispered lies about our lives. We who wanted what others held, and held what others needed. We were the desperate and lonely of life. We were the weary, the wicked, the wrong. We were our own whip. We were the cranky monkeys, the cantankerous pipsqueaks whose deeds of disgrace sullied our own race. But as I look out the window—hold on—as I *open* the window, I see nothing of this past in the humans before me. Edenic smiles define every face. Indeed, smiles engulf the entirety of every person. Posture literalizes perfection, movement describes grace, bodies radiate health, and there is no ugliness anywhere. Poetry is personified. These are prelapsarian people, and every individual shines with a supreme and indefatigable confidence of being, an attitude of beatitude.

I've been noticed, it seems. A woman is sprinting toward my window. Her tight braids lash out fiercely behind her, a toga of sorts is flattened against her steel-belted physique. She seems to recognize me, and she's smiling like we're old friends. Loki is yipping in apparent delight, and so I pause my scribbling to greet my eager visitor. . . .

She came up to the window, a resonant laugh tearing forth from her with all the force of a rowdy goddess. I scarcely recognized her at first, but when I saw her sharp, foxy eyes it was unmistakable. This glowing woman before me was Mella Orange, and when her sonorant snickers subsided, she looked me over and sighed as if relaxing from an orgasm, then sneezed through my open window. I held my breath for just a moment before filling my lungs. She winked, I think, and began to sing a song with no words. Her voice had an unfathomable intensity of tenor that set geese and ganders mating all over my skin. I saluted her and she cocked her head like Loki was apt to do when I was training him. She's still singing her song of redemption now, waiting for me to join her, I believe. I mustn't delay.

What's left to say? So near and so clear, the everlasting epiphany, my friend, lies in bumping your head, scratching your ear, blowing your nose. Savor every random event in the perpetually poignant present. Pat your head, rub your belly, and beat on your chest and roar! Pitch a fit for love. Toss a tantrum for life. It's the least you can do. Get back to the beginning, before you ate the apple, and life was a joyous, jolly jubilee. Go for broke and let it ride! Make our mamas and our papas proud!

What can I offer thee, what sort of a guarantee? Gloves and mittens, cubs and kittens, jujys and jubas, trumpets and tubas, elves and faeries, mountains and prairies, a jingling jangling jazzy jug of jiggling wiggling jelly. Why jelly? Because you have everything else you could possibly want. You have life, and you have each other, and if it'll make the crucial difference between life and death, between happiness and sadness, well then the hell with it, you can have jelly too. Feel better now? God, you can be such a baby.

Am I making sense? Not likely, for how can one facet make sense of the entire jewel? Creation is a beautiful fact, take it or leave it. Take your next breath, and you have accepted it. Creation is, after all, and there's really nothing more to say. And so I cease this tale of nothingness, these tirades of irrelevance, these grandiloquent sermons of homiletic hogwash. Hearken however! Consciousness before me, we must keep our wits about us, never forgetting that whatever else this and everything may be and become, it still is. The realization of the ultimate equation, merrily indifferent in its glorious simplicity, it is. It just jolly well is.

It's never been any different. It ends as it begins, with just a couple of days in between.

Welcome home.

epilogue: supralingual sex

Why aren't apples called reds? giggled at her extraordinary light-headedness. She sensed her meaning dissipating, her very conceptualization losing its identity. And yet, there she was, naked and supralingual, and soon she couldn't remember ever being otherwise. *Because we say so* drifted by, licked her apostrophe, tickled her question mark, and their words evaporated into pure and unabashed poetry . . .

What's to say,
with words so wimpy,
words so skimpy
they scarcely cover
my private parts?

I lay bare
my soul
in communication,

in communion.
Come,
you and one called I.
Our'n eyes have seen the glory,
and it's a wonderful story.

Once upon a time,
when time stood still.
A man and a woman.
A lingam and a yoni.
An ape and an ape.
A soul and a soul.
One soul.
One beautiful soul
yodels the dirge of death,
an indication of Creation,
a fractal ejaculation.

What cry does drive this elegy?
What voice can sing such melody?
It is not you,
it is not I.
It is the one and only

Sigh . . .

Notes

1. Matthew 7:1
2. *Variation on* 1 Corinthians 6:9–10
3. Isaiah 5:20
4. Psalms 5:5
5. Matthew 12:37
6. 1 Corinthians 6:20
7. Matthew 5:8
8. Matthew 7:23
9. Exodus 20:7
10. Mark 10:15

Acknowledgments

Without the inestimable assistance of Jessica Maguire—my partner in percolating this project—without her my soul lay dormant. It is a discredit to the muses of the world that their names are not known, and it is laughable besides to think what this might have been without the amaranthine advantage of Jessica's attentive eyes and ears. May I help her as much as she has helped me.

Eternal gratitude goes out to my mother and my father and my sisters, Mel and Jay, my family and my unceasing source of encouragement and support. Everywhere we go, people want to know, who we are, so we tell them . . .

Thanks also to the original crew who encouraged me in the first phase of this project: Todd Albert, Trevor Blackann, Tina Burger, Tim Curry, Brian Green, Richard Heinberg, Ryan Higgins, Matthew Moffitt, Michelle Pinkman, Tom Robbins, Michael Regallis, Amanda Sledz, Larry Stahr, and Kristen Talley. Thanks also to Old Man's Cave.

And as this project has developed beyond any of my expectations, numerous personalities have emerged and assisted me with the synchronicity of their presence. Special thanks to Vaughn Andrews, Matt Bialer, Patty Berg, Michelle Blankenship, Sara Branch, Jennifer Brehl, Laurie Brown, Jennifer Gilmore, Jennifer Glaser, Hannah Harlow, Mike Harrigan, Jenna Johnson, Sarah Melnyk, Christopher Moore, Hannah Pfeifle, Tina Pohlman, Ashley Rabin, Cathy Riggs, Lauren Rille, Larissa Rogers, Kris Saknussemm, Becky Saletan, Andrea Serbonich, Debi Taylor, Teri Tobias, Paul Von Drasek, Lindsey Weidhorn, Kent Wolf, and anyone else whose name I have inadvertently left off this list. Thanks also to the wonderful community of Athens, Ohio, who could only be reincarnated from a glorious pirate ship.

Lastly, I am forever indebted to the anonymous ninja vandal who first painted the phrase JUST A COUPLE OF DAYS on the bridge outside of Athens. I borrowed your phrase, my bold friend, but only to immortalize it. And incidentally, "Just a Couple of Days" happens to be an anagram for "caused a joyful spot." I hope that it succeeded for you.

In 1936, during the depths of the Great Depression, forty young women arrived at the Cooper Pants Factory near Gainesville, Florida, sat down at their sewing machines, and set about stitching hems and seams, another dreary day in the land of opportunity. Shortly after they began their busywork, and as if this debasement of their imagination were not tragic enough, a tornado came along and bumped into the factory. Thirty-nine of the forty women ran panicking and screaming to the stairwell; a Mrs. Boyd Shaw remained at her station. She had inadvertently sewn her own dress into the seam she was stitching, and so was unable to beat the hasty retreat. As she struggled to free herself, the tornado ripped the roof from the building, ultimately causing it to collapse, but not before it tore Mrs. Boyd Shaw clean out of her clothes and tossed her a block away, stark naked and bruised, but otherwise fine. All thirty-nine of her coworkers died in the ensuing inferno that consumed the factory.

There are hundreds of substantiated oddities like this surrounding tornadoes. A tornado once opened a barn door, pulled a wagon out, turned it around, wheeled it back inside, and closed the door. A phonograph recording of the song "Stormy Weather" was once found wedged into a utility pole after a tornado had swept through the area. A butter churn once dropped out of the sky and landed on a cow's head, half an hour after a tornado had hit twenty miles away. Chickens are routinely stripped of their feathers, and the feathers are sometimes found speared into planks of wood. In 1974, a farmer reclaimed a mirror, a carton of eggs, and a box of Christmas ornaments—all undamaged—from the otherwise total wreckage of his house. A tornado in 1996 even had the audacity to hit a drive-in movie theatre in Canada while it was screening the movie *Twister.*

Then there are those who claim that tornadoes can blow a jug inside out, or a cellar upside down, or a rooster into a bottle, or even that a tornado can change the day of the week and knock the wind out of a politician. Although these assertions are ludicrous, the essential point should not be lost. Tornadoes introduce chaos, and chaos makes anything—short of changing the day of the week—possible. To describe the situation in terms of probability theory: Tornadoes provide a high probability that several of millions of low-probability events will occur. Of course, which of these millions of low-probability events actually occurs is pure chance.

Probably.

Diablo was still inside Billy Pronto's truck when he regained consciousness. The truck was about seventy feet from the road, and neither his severed middle finger nor Billy Pronto were anywhere to be seen. Frustration descended, and, like a paper clip in idle hands, Diablo was bound to get bent out of shape. His finger, or the lack thereof, hurt like hell. His hand and head were bleeding, and he wanted to get himself to a hospital, preferably with a finger for some surgeon to heroically reattach. Never mind that he had no insurance.

To make matters worse, Diablo's simulacra of satori had split, evaporating like a two-minute sprinkle in the desert. This was no longer the perpetually flaring present, the big day of everyday; this was the worst day of his life. Jesus Christ, Diablo thought, did I *swallow* my goddamn finger? Maybe the heroic surgeon can retrieve it? Decisions. Final scan for finger and Billy Pronto. Nothing. Keys? Still in ignition. Does it start? Yes it does. Go? Go.

Diablo floored it, tore up the fallow field, crashed over a ditch, and bounced back onto the road. He had accelerated to sixty miles an hour before his zeal began to sag. Though the sky above him was as azure as he had ever seen it, the sky above Normal—still four miles away across the Illinois flatland—was a sickeningly greenish black, clouds tumbling and boiling, thrashing and roiling like the underbelly of a rabid dragon in a pit of petroleum. Then he saw it, a wound-up towel snap from the bottom of the enormous cloudmass and slap the ground, the finger of God tickling Mother Earth, causing her to convulse with hilarity. She bucked and threw a swarm of debris back at the roguish overtures of the sky, where it circled like vultures all along the dancing windpipe, writhing like a stripper's whip, squirming like the trunk of an elephant about to sneeze.

Dumbfounded once again, Diablo continued racing toward Normal for another few seconds. He might have continued farther if a curtain of hailstones the size of golf balls hadn't suddenly collapsed all around him. He braked hard but only succeeded in marbling across the abruptly hail-covered road, spinning a dozen times easily, each rotation marked by a barrage of hailstones pelting him through the open driver's-side window. At some point he let out a cry, shielding his face from the punctuated bombardment of ice and his eyes from the relentless madness of the world. He managed to roll up the window once he realized he had stopped, and there he sat, shivering from shock, realizing he could no longer cross the fingers on his left hand as thousands of berserking devils stampeded over the outside of the truck, hooves whammering, clamoring, riding jackhammers for pogo sticks. After a few minutes, the swarm had mostly passed, with only an occasional straggler pinging like the last few kernels of corn to pop.

Relieved, Diablo picked up one of the smaller hailstones littering the inside of the truck and tossed it in his mouth. It gave way to a satisfying and refreshing crunch. He smirked, rolled his window back down, stuck his left arm out, and defiantly extended what remained of his middle finger to the sky.

No sooner had Diablo proffered his profanity to the heavens than a new peril presented itself. Squinting down the highway, he saw a surge of cars emerging from the dusty mist and charging his way, taking up both sides of the road and then some.

The tornado had attacked the highway through Normal, peeling slabs of pavement and tossing them here and there like so much citrus rind. This had triggered a universal reaction of internally combusted flight as hundreds of drivers shrieked their automobiles in the opposite direction and toward Diablo. Several cars were tapped out as the tornado chased the retreating pack down the highway, adding still greater imperative to the evacuation. It was later estimated that the tornado was moving across the ground at speeds approaching seventy miles an hour.

Of course, Diablo was unaware of those affairs. The funnel cloud was no longer visible amid the dust and debris it was producing, and he could only see the ripsnorting onslaught of automobiles bearing down on him. Alarmed, he turned the ignition, fully expecting it to cough and sputter, but it defied the cliché and roared to life. Diablo gunned the engine, turned the truck with a gratifying fishtail, and just as he shifted into third looked in his rearview mirror and saw the leaders of the pack less than a hundred feet behind and an enormous tornado suddenly in full view a mile or so back. Within seconds the first wave of cars tore past him, honking and squealing, and before Diablo knew what was happening he was in the middle of a high-speed traffic jam. He shifted into fourth at sixty-five, and made it to fifth by eighty miles an hour. He was still being passed on all sides. On the median to the right an SUV was bouncing across the grass, taking the beating it'd been waiting for since its manufacture. Farther behind an ambulance was wailing its siren and flashing its headlights, trying to bully its way forward, but no one was having any of that shit. The emergency, after all, was perfectly apparent.

Diablo pushed harder on the gas pedal, hoping to open the throttle another micrometer, anything to accelerate, anything to get the holy fuck away from that windy monstrosity. When he next glanced at his speedometer the needle was bouncing back and forth across the gauge, maxed out and indicating that he and everyone around him were barreling down the highway at well over a hundred miles per hour. Soon afterwards the tornado veered off the road and dissipated over some trees. Traffic gradually slowed, people pulled over and got out of their cars, and within ten minutes the road was mostly empty again. Diablo kept on driving. It was all he had going for him, the way he figured it. The accidents of the day had conspired to trade the middle finger of his left hand for a pickup truck with three-quarters of a tank of gas and half a bag of corn chips. It was a start, and it seemed like it would lead him somewhere.

No sooner had he reasoned this out than the truck was rocked by an unseen collision. Diablo probably yelled "Jee-zus Christ!" in the ensuing melee of braking, screeching, and the window shattering, but such a synchronicity would border on the preposterous. After all, an eight-foot crucifix had just dropped out of the sky and into his flatbed, managing to shatter his rear window in the process. Once he had the truck pulled over, Diablo jumped out to investigate, still thinking he'd hit a deer or vice versa, and was for the third time that day dumbfounded, finding instead a bronzed, life-sized, crucified Christ gazing placidly up at him from the flatbed as if it were a loyal pet.

Growing accustomed to the profoundly improbable, Diablo set about arranging the crucifix securely. Most pickups are designed to hold the standard cut of plywood, a 4 × 8 sheet, in their bed, and so the crucifix, four feet wide and eight feet tall, was a perfectly snug fit. After regarding the curiosity, Diablo got back in the cab, pausing to inspect both of his hands. He would not have been surprised if his missing finger had mysteriously shifted to his right hand, or even, given recent events, if it had miraculously regenerated itself. The situation seemed stable, though, and the bleeding had even stopped. He sighed, and after accelerating back up to fifth gear, Diablo tucked his left hand under his thigh to soothe its throbbing, shook his head at the bizarre events of the day, and drove away from Normal, confident that God was with him.